THE ZONE

#7

KILLING GROUND

Books by James Rouch

The Zone Series
#1: Hard Target
#2: Blind Fire
#3: Hunter Killer
#4: Sky Strike
#5: Overkill
#6: Plague Bomb
#7: Killing Ground
#8: Civilian Slaughter
#9: Body Count
#10: Death March

World War II Collection
#1: The War Machines
#2: Tiger
#3: Gateway to Hell

THE ZONE

#7

KILLING GROUND

James Rouch

SPEAKING VOLUMES, LLC
NAPLES, FLORIDA
2013

THE ZONE
KILLING GROUND #7

ISBN 978-1-61232-915-4

I cried when I saw so many good things. The whole regiment went on an orgy of eating and drinking. Even the officers. When a detachment of the Commandants Service tried to stop us we turned our machine guns on them.

> Private Ivan Yesualkov, the only survivor of Motor Rifle regiment 191, nuked while looting an abandoned NATO warehouse.

All the fuss about you guys in the infantry makes me sick. Where'd you be without me and my boys? I'll tell you, chucking stones and sharpening sticks for spears, that's where.

> Quartermaster Sergeant Gary Ball, 66th Infantry Division.

Some of our most important storage facilities inside the Zone are extremely vulnerable, following the latest Warpac advances. If a vital dump, such as the one at (censored) were to fall into their hands when their offensive operations had slackened due to materiel losses, it would be like a transfusion to them. We must make better provision for their defense now.

> Lieutenant Colonel Daniel Taylor, in a submission to the Joint Chiefs (Allocation of Army Manpower sub-committee, sitting 127. Decision deferred.)

CHAPTER ONE

The flamethrower's roar echoed back from the buildings around the square. For a moment it died away, and then the squirting yellow flame arced above the cobbles again. Its savage glare was reflected by the wet stones and illuminated the facades of the shattered stores and houses.

"That should do it." Thorne slipped the wide straps from his shoulders and lowered the tanks to the ground. They were empty and rang hollow as he dropped the projector and hoses on top of them. "You know, that's the first time I haven't enjoyed using the bloody thing." Thirty meters away a growing fire crackled and lit his face with a ruddy glow.

In other corners of the square two more of the huge bonfires were already well alight and beginning to push the night back into the surrounding windowless ruins.

Retreating from the growing waves of heat, Burke looked critically at the stack of civilian corpses topping the untidy pile of timber. "Might not. The skinny ones are always difficult to burn, and there're no fat civies left in the Zone now."

But even as he said it several of the mutilated corpses began to add their dripping body fats to the pyre's rough fuel. As their blotched and bruised flesh roast and split further, the drops became streams that burned a vivid yellow, sharp contrast to the dark red flame curling from beneath.

Grouped around their patched and battle-scarred armored personnel carriers, the rest of the company displayed no interest in so common a scene. Hunched beneath helmets and raincapes, their gruesome work complete, they awaited the order to reboard.

As the area became lighter it illuminated the exhausted, stress-lined faces of the men, and revealed that some who leaned against the shell-gouged hulls had their heads bowed and eyes closed in fitful sleep.

Major Revell and Sergeant Hyde stood a little distance away, beside a mud-spattered Volvo bus. They flanked a fussily dressed elderly German official who was making notes.

A young woman, haggard and disheveled and clutching an ill-wrapped coughing baby, stammered names and addresses as she waited, last in the queue to board. She hesitated in her nervous recital as the administrator imperiously raised his hand to signal a halt while his painstaking writing tried to keep pace.

His slim silver pen was the only metallic object to catch the light in that tableau. The bus had long since lost the glamor and colorful livery of its earlier days. Evidence of its widely traveled pre-war past showed in the ghosts of old signwriting beneath a thin and heavily scratched layer of drab olive paint.

A row of faces pressed against the dirty windows of its interior. Tears made streaks down the panes but were lost against the beads of rain washing mud from their exterior.

"Hold it, lady."

Too surprised to resist immediately, the young mother hesitated as she made to climb aboard and just looked blankly at the tall black medic who had stopped her. Only when he reached into the bundle she held to

8

expose a child's arm, painfully thin and almost translucently white, did she try to recoil.

In a single well-practiced movement, Sampson wiped a swab over the tiny limb, pressed firmly but gently home the tip of a hypodermic, cleansed the area a second time and stepped back.

Numbed, frightened and confused, the woman made to board again. It was Revell who put out his hand to steady her when she threatened to slip from the worn step, after she'd shied from the sergeant's offer of help.

Hyde moved away, averting his face. What would have been a face if the grafts and reconstructions had left him with more than mere openings for mouth, nose and eyes.

Above the sound of the rain and the flames came a new sound. Revell recognized the thunder of a Russian rocket barrage, 240mm judging by the powerful concussion of the distant overlapping detonations. They were getting uncomfortably close if they were able to employ such comparatively short-range weapons. It was doubtless such an onslaught that had devastated this hamlet. Now the enemy had switched their attention to some other modest collection of homes and businesses, again where the only claim to legitimacy as a target was that they were grouped about a crossroads.

"You'd best get moving, Herr Klingenberg. It's bad enough you've kept these civies here to watch what we've been doing, without keeping them hanging about to wait for the Russkies' artillery to sweep back this way." It was difficult to check a tight smile as Revell noticed the official abandon his slow, almost pompous manner and replace it with a twittering burst of nervous activity.

"Ya, ya. I am going now." Klingenberg shouted to the bus driver, "Schnell, schnell."

After several ineffectual stabs at a control, the driver had to haul himself, with obvious irritation, from his seat and kick the doors closed. As he resumed his place, started and gunned the engine, the clattering growl of the big diesel was almost drowned by the growing roar and crackle of the fires. That in its turn was smothered by a grief-stricken wail coming from within the bus.

It soared above all other sounds, going on and on, louder and higher than it should have been humanly possible to sustain. The distinctively dressed body of a child, a little blond girl, had rolled from the top of a stack and flopped untidily to rest on the steaming cobblestones.

An arm and part of the torso had been burned away; what remained gave off clouds of foul vapors. Sparks scudded, wind whipped from the smoldering frayed edges of clothing. They made tiny spiral points of light that were quickly lost against the more dramatic outpourings from the main pyre.

Heavy drops of rain began to fall.

Impatiently Revell watched the haughty German as he, with meticulous care, stowed pen and notebook in the proper compartments within his document case. A perceptible shade faster than was strictly in keeping with his earlier demeanor, he made for his own transport. He forced himself to slow when a glance back revealed that the big medic was grinning broadly. Then a stray round blasted the edge of the village and Klingenberg threw away all pretense at dignity and scuttled the last few steps.

Throwing the case onto the back seat of the Mercedes Estate, Klingenberg wrenched at the door when his first attempt to slam it shut was prevented by the buckle of his raincoat becoming jammed in it. His pinched face reddened as it took several tries before he managed to release his clothing and secure the door.

10

The amusement Revell experienced, though, was not directed at that but at the vehicle itself. Whoever had executed the complex disruptive camouflage paint job on the vehicle had failed to extend their painstaking handiwork to the chromed fenders or full-length roof rack.

Its heavy-duty tires crunching over broken brick and shards of glass, the Mercedes led the bus out of the square. Spectral faces were indistinctly visible inside the big vehicle. None remained pressed to the windows. They were leaving hell and daren't turn back for a last look.

"I hope he goes over a mine." Sergeant Hyde watched the shrouded taillights of the little convoy disappear from sight.

"No chance, Sarge." Sampson shied the hypodermic into an anonymous ruin. "Infantry and marines die, civies just get slaughtered, but German civil servants, they're immortal. Man, when I buy my farm, if I'm reincarnated then all I want to come back as is some poor-paid boring little filing clerk in some piddling hick town hall."

"Get them on board, Sergeant." Revell turned his back on the noxious pillars of flame and black smoke rising into the predawn sky of another ugly day inside the Zone. Now that the job was done and the surviving civies were on their way to safety he felt the return of the sapping exhaustion that had been dragging at his mind for days. Or perhaps it had been weeks. Time had almost ceased to have meaning. There were times when it took conscious effort to recall what month, or even what year it was. It was with only half his attention he watched his men lethargically climbing into the APCs, and the others, who had been watching approach roads, return. He should have injected a note of briskness into the proceedings, but it was no more in

11

him than it was in his company, or what was left of it.

Since the Russians had launched their offensive . . . how long ago was it, four days, five? . . . they had been steadily falling back before the relentless pressure of mass attacks. The Warpac forces had been using ammunition as though they had a limitless supply, and every thrust had been preceeded by devastating barrages, like the one that had virtually wiped this inoffensive little place from the map.

Revell could only be thankful that his Special Combat Company had been operating on the flanks. In the center, whole NATO divisions had been obliterated. And even so, in the course of less than a week's fighting they had sustained losses of nearly seventy percent. Of a reinforced company he now had thirty-five men left. Of the sixteen APCs he had begun with he now had four, and one of those was being towed.

But he knew in his heart it was wrong to say they had been fighting. Almost from the start they had been denied that opportunity. Time after time they had prepared positions, road blocks, ambushes, and every time they had been ordered to withdraw before enemy attacks had developed.

It was the massive Soviet air superiority that had caused their losses. Now it had reached the stage when any movement by daylight was inviting destruction. Fighter bombers and helicopter gunships were roaming at will, and to be seen on the open road was an invitation to a series of attacks. The onset of the bad weather twenty-four hours earlier had bought some slight respite, but neither low cloud nor night could completely halt the attacks. With the wealth of sophisticated targeting devices carried by the gunships and bombers it was most likely only a shortage of experienced pilots that had brought about the slight respite.

It was bitterly frustrating to take such punishment and not be able to strike back. What Revell and his men wanted was something real to fight for, not some anonymous ridge or railway cutting from which they were ordered to withdraw without even sighting the enemy.

Sharply, above the more distant rumble of the barrage, came the punching crack of cannon fire.

"Let's get moving, sergeant. That's the Reds taking out the barricades on the edge of town. Their tanks won't take long to smash through. Are we still being jammed?"

"On all frequencies. They're pumping out that mush at tremendous power. If any of our fliers were in the air the transmitter would be standing out on their screens in 3-D." Hyde stepped onto the rear ramp of the M113. "So we're still pulling back?"

"That was the last word we had, as soon as we finished here." Revell scanned the hellish scene in the square, now filled with the stench of the burning bodies. "Why they wanted this done though, God only knows. Is this any more decent than decomposing under a pile of rubble?"

Shrugging, Hyde ducked into the tracked carrier. "Probably the home village of some German politician who pulled a few strings . . ."

"Don't fucking wait for us, will you." Running and shouting, Dooley charged from an alleyway. He put on a spurt as he saw the last of the company boarding, was overtaken by Scully who had followed him but now reached sanctuary first.

"Move over, you shits." Scully scrambled inside, shouting down the complaints from others who objected to being sprayed with the muddy water escaping from the cloudy plastic sack he carried. He sneered answers to his noisy and rude greeting. "Piss

13

off. This is important stuff. You want to fuck up your guts on army rations, then that's your bloody lookout. It took me an hour to grub up this lot. I'm not chucking them out now. I volunteered to cook when you lot wouldn't do it, and if I'm going to do it then I want some decent vege in the pot."

"You reckon they're decent?" Ripper watched the little man contort himself to push the soil-blotched turnips and carrots into an underseat locker.

"Of course they bloody are." Rearranging various bottles of soy sauce and ketchup and scooping back handfuls of stock cubes, Scully succeeded at his second attempt to fasten the improvised catch. "It's the stuff grown above ground that glows in the dark."

Seated by the rear door of the APC, Ripper suddenly stuck his leg across the opening to prevent Dooley entering. "Now you ain't bringing them in here, boy."

"Don't fuck about. It took me bloody ages to catch this lot." Supported in both arms Dooley carried a highly ornate gilt cage filled with a mass of twittering bright blurs.

Shrill cheepings and showers of multi-colored feather and millet husks accompanied his attempts to push it inside ahead of him.

Other voices joined Ripper's drawl in protest and Dooley reluctantly backed off.

"You miserable load of cruds. Don't you ever tell me I haven't got no soul again. Shit, I've got more feeling in my head than you've got in your little fingers." For a moment, at the back of Dooley's mind there lurked the doubt that he'd got that a bit wrong, or at least not quite right. "Oh sod the lot of you. Someone sling me an empty kit bag then."

Catching a bundle of frayed and stained canvas, Dooley crammed the cage into it. In the process he almost disappeared within a screeching cloud of flying

14

plumage. With elaborate care he fastened the bundle to a broken tool rack on the hull's exterior.

Sluggishly the tired hydraulics closed the ramp and sealed the troops within their armored cocoon. With a bellow from holed exhausts and some misfiring, the old battle-worn APCs pulled out of the square, the last in the line starting off with a jerk as its towline tautened.

As they clanked and crunched over the rubble their passengers fell into an exhausted sleep. Only Dooley stayed awake. He stared at the spot where only a thin slab of aluminum armor separated him from his prize. For a moment the hell that was the Zone could be forgotten, and he smiled, to fall asleep with a look of smug satisfaction on his face.

CHAPTER TWO

They were too late, by just a matter of seconds. The bridge was blown even as they came in sight of it.

At first, for a few tantalizing moments, it had seemed as if the charges had failed in their work. Revell had urged their driver on, but even as Burke had floored the pedal without consideration for the surge of fuel consumption by the straining motor, the long precast concrete structure had twisted, sagged and fallen to ruin in the broad churning river far below.

There was no time for the luxury of self-recrimination. With dawn only an our away Revell knew they had to find a crossing, to find shelter beneath the protecting umbrella of the main forces anti-aircraft defenses. This side of the river they had no chance. Once light they would be unable to move by road, and on foot it would only be a matter of time before they were mopped up by Warpac reconn units.

Even as the last massive chunks of steel-reinforced debris were plunging beneath the turbid waters, Revell was turning the column in a fresh direction.

The heavy overcast was holding back the morning, but it was growing perceptibly brighter when they topped a hill overlooking the river once more.

"It hasn't been blown, yet." Scanning the lattice steel structure, Hyde first used binoculars and then an image intensifier.

"So? It is still of no use to us." Andrea sat beside the sergeant on the edge of the roof hatch. She leaned an arm·on the barrel of the TOW launch tube and rested her cheek against the cold wet metal. "That is not a bridge. It is a long slaughterhouse."

Revell hardly heard her. Barely a kilometer away, the bridge might as well have been a hundred. Its full length and the approach roads were choked with an unmoving jam of military and civilian transport. Tanks, APCs and armored cars were inextricably mixed with every nationality and type of soft-skin transport, and between every one of them were locked masses of refugee carts. There were even one or two civilian motor vehicles, doubtless their gas tanks holding the last few dregs of carefully hoarded and precious fuel. But nothing was moving.

As he watched, Revell saw a pair of Hind gunships sweep the length of the stalled traffic with cannon and rocket fire. They took no evasive action during the run, not even to the extent of releasing decoy flares against AA missiles. The degree of their complacency was illustrated by the second machine even displaying its navigation lights.

Fires leaped from a score of locations and added their jet smoke to those already rising into the pre-dawn light. A ruptured fuel tank flared a brief bubble of flame and a bursting tire made a small fountain of blazing rubber.

A single broken line of tracer curled toward the second gunship. Well-aimed, it was shrugged aside by the armored belly of the machine. Turning tightly, the pair swept back and saturated with a storm of fire and steel the location from which the weak resistance

17

had come.

Only a few hundred feet above the Russian helicopters a single Mig fighter flew top cover for them, sometimes lost to sight in the low cloud.

A gasoline tanker stalled in the center of the bridge exploded and liquid fire poured toward the river far below. Ammunition aboard trucks close by began to detonate and made sparkling fountains of white, red and green.

Spreading a map on the wet metal of the hull top, Revell screwed up his eyes in the half light to trace a path with a grimy finger. "We've fuel for maybe another thirty kilometers, if we go easy on it. We'll have to drop the cripple and pack everyone into the other three."

Hyde craned over the major's shoulder to look at the point he was indicating. "A railway bridge. What are the chances of it still being intact?"

"Wish I knew." Revell refolded the map. "But it's the only one we have a chance of reaching."

Stretching her arms above her head, Andrea watched without real interest as the Hinds soared to skim the bottom of the clouds and then dived to commence another strafing run. She turned away as the gunships tore into and pounded to scrap a dozen more vehicles. Fresh fires erupted. "We will be crossing the front of the Russian advance. It is likely we will run into their reconnaissance units."

"Maybe." There was nothing else Revell could add.

"We'll be traveling by side roads." It was Hyde who found a crumb of comfort. "That country is rough; unless the Reds are trying to sneak around the side it's not very likely we'll encounter a main axis of their advance."

"Only one way to find out." Patting the anti-tank missile launch tube, Revell took a last glance at the

18

bridge. "So let's be on our way before those commie fliers get cheesed off with hammering wrecks and start looking for stragglers, like us."

Bracing himself behind the major's seat, Sergeant Hyde took out the map and examined the route the officer had chosen. In the dim light of the APC's interior, and with it swaying and jolting over the poor back roads, it took him a while to orient himself. He studied it for several minutes before an indistinct nagging doubt crystalized into coherent thought.

"Doesn't seem to have been a lot going on around here, not up until now."

Revell almost let the point go as a chance remark, then had second thoughts and re-examined the area. He was surprised he hadn't noticed the fact himself. It was further indication of just how tired he was.

While all of the remainder of the eighty square kilometers displayed by the map were covered in a mass of additional symbols, denoting old battlefields, dumps, contaminated areas and minefields, the area they were traversing was entirely free of such information.

"Printing error?" It hardly rang true, but Revell had to consider it, even as he dismissed it from his mind.

With a shake of his head Hyde discounted the idea. "I've never been this way before, but I've always had a feeling that it's about where Paradise Valley should be."

"No such bloody place, Sarge." Driving gingerly to conserve fuel, Burke was for once able to take part in a conversation. His first in days, since the intercom had broken down. "That's a bleeding fairy story, put about by staff officers and base barnacles, so we'll live in hope and go on defending the bastards."

With supreme delicacy and skill Burke nursed the GM V-6 over a rise without having to change down, and saved another spoonful of diesel. "Hell, Sarge, you don't believe those stories do you? They've been going the rounds as long as the Zone has been in existence."

"Hey, can someone clue me in on this?" Ripper stepped on toes as he hauled himself forward and into the exchange. "What the heck is Paradise Valley?"

"It's a fiction." Clarence gave up trying to sleep, and flexed his fingers around the long slim barrel of the sniper rifle propped between his knees. "Like Burke says, it's a fairy story. But if you have to know, think of it as the Quartermaster's version of the elephants' graveyard. It's supposed to be a fabulous dump where they keep all the goodies and essentials that are permanently in short supply. The rumor of its existence probably sprang into being after the first Warpac attack, when some poor devil on the NATO side ran out of what he needed most. You know, little things, like ammo, or morphine."

"Or fuel," Thorne butted in. "Or maybe transport, for a fast retreat. We seem to have been doing that since the evening of the first day."

"Holy shit." Ripper was all toothy enthusiasm. "I don't give a damn if it's rumor or fairy story. Hey, if it's no more real than that, maybe we can still trade on it. My Daddy used to make money out of stills that weren't real. He used to tell the revenue about them, always collecting cash money up front. Then when they hit the site and there weren't nothing there he used to swear they must jist have moved on. By then he'd spent the reward so there weren't nothing they could do."

"I've seen everything traded in the Zone, but never fairy stories." Thorne leaned back against the bare condensation-streaked metal of the hull, and by closing his eyes took himself out of the conversation.

20

"There are plenty of refugees trapped in the Zone who've paid fortunes for bogus maps of safe routes to the west, or handed over all they've got to so-called guides who dump their customers as soon as they've been paid. In advance of course." Clarence too had tired of what he saw as pointless speculation. Settling back, he sought what comfort he could in the vehicle's hard shell, festooned as it was with sharp angles, projecting brackets and hanging equipment.

He flinched and his eyes flickered open as another body slumped against his. He relaxed his instantly tensed muscles when he saw that it was Andrea. With her alone he could bear any form of physical contact. Even that, by insinuating a pack between them, he kept to a minimum. Still he could not repress an involuntary shudder as the warmth of her breath on his shoulder permeated his layers of clothing.

Ripper was not so easily to be put down, and after a short pause made another attempt to draw one of the crew, anyone who could profess to some knowledge on the subject in which he'd taken such interest. "Well, if we do come across it we'd be sure to be able to take on extra gas, or maybe even swop these ancient wrecks for better transport." He looked around hopefully.

"It's a dream; forget it." As Revell hoisted himself into the command cupola he caught a glimpse of Andrea, where she snuggled against their sniper. Much as he loathed the sight of her with anybody else, it took an effort for him to pull his eyes away.

Through the mud-smeared thick prisms he viewed the road ahead. It twisted and turned constantly, sometimes flanked by shallow banks but fairly level, but then suddenly climbing with a broken rock wall to one side and a precipitous drop to the other. They passed through a tiny village, just fifteen half-timbered houses, a tiny combined store and gas station and a tall

21

spired church. It had been looted and abandoned long ago. Except for fading paint on doors and shutters there was no color about the scene, with even the defoliated trees adding to the impression that he was looking at a black-and-white photograph. The same drenching of chemicals that had killed shrubs and trees had also inhibited the growth of weeds that would otherwise have enveloped the road and paths, but though that facet of dereliction was missing, the drifts of dirt and other wind-blown debris more than compensated.

They slowed to negotiate a tangle of branches from an old elm that some storm had thrown down to partially block the road. The brittle timber snapped in a shower of water droplets, and then they were clear and picking up speed again when a hail of twenty-millimeter cannon fire lashed at the APC.

The tracer-towing high-velocity rounds smacked hard against and into the mass of spare track links, sandbags and scrap metal that crudely reinforced the front plates. They ricocheted wildly, leaving scraps of their phosphorous bases to smolder among the shattered remnants.

Burke threw the APC into a skid turn to take them off the road and out of the line of fire, but the tracks only scrabbled at the loose shale of the bank. As he hurled the machine into reverse for a second attempt, another burst of armor-piercing and incendiary shells lashed out.

There was an ear-punishing crash as a round found a gap among the remains of the protective litter on the hull, penetrated the splashboard and almost punched its way through the hull. A semi-molten scab of aluminum flashed the length of the crew compartment to smash a first-aid box beside the rear ramp.

"Make smoke." Revell wrenched at the door-control

lever. "Out, out, out."

As Burke scrambled from the driver's position a third and longer burst of enemy fire put a round clean through the smoke-wreathed armor, smashing the instrument panel and shattering against a control stick. Flames licked from destroyed wiring and the padding of the seat covering.

Jamming in the half-lowered position, the ramp tore weapons and equipment from the crew's grasp as they bailed out fast, with the fire already taking hold behind them.

CHAPTER THREE

Slewed at an angle across the narrow road, the boxlike bulk of the old APC gave the squad cover as they scattered among the flanking trees.

As he bailed out, Sergeant Hyde caught a glimpse of a four-wheeled Warpac armored car barely fifty meters away, parked close against the bank at a bend in the road. Stabs of flame from the snout of its cannon marked another score of shells unleashed against the now abandoned M113.

Masked by the wreck, the driver of the second vehicle in their little convoy wrenched his machine into reverse and brought it into clanging collision with the last in the file. Track links snapped and both slewed to a stop with their drives broken.

Hyde's swearing made him overlook the fact that the Russian gunners' preoccupation with the hulks of their armor had given the company time to scatter into cover. But it was only a momentary lapse. Those few precious fractions of time wasted by the enemy when he failed to switch his fire to the fleeing crews were quickly made up for when a torrent of co-axial heavy machine-gun fire was hosed into the woods.

There was a brief pause as a belt or magazine was changed, and then the rapid-firing weapon probed again among the trunks for human targets. But already the best chance had been missed. Only three of the grenade dischargers on the lead APC had been fired but now they added their swirling clouds to the output of the fiercer blaze inside the APC.

The steadily falling rain prevented the smoke from rising and caused it to swirl in confusing wisps into the woods. Hardly diminished by the downpour, it wreathed the intervening ground in a fitful screen.

Again the air was full of metal from the high-velocity Russian cannon as tungsten-tipped shells smacked great scabs of bark from the trees. Where some lodged, their incendiary content added to the artificial fog.

In nervously erratic ripples the streams of bullets stitched across the timber, betraying the gunner's lack of fire discipline, as he fired blindly, expending ammunition at a prodigious rate.

From inside the flame- and smoke-generating APC came the crackle of small-arms ammunition cooking-off. At the noise, the enemy turret-gunner reverted his attention back to the wreck.

"This is our chance." Having failed to find the major, Hyde grabbed Dooley, and then kicked out at Thorne to get his attention also.

Thorne gave up his elbow-armed conflict with Scully to get equal shares of the cover of a slim tree barely adequate for one, and joined the NCO behind an insubstantial holly bush. "I'll strangle the shitty flier who sprayed this lot with crap and stopped them growing to a useful width. If I live to get the chance to look for him."

"If we don't do something about that scout car you won't." Hyde hugged the ground as a random burst scythed through the shrub and showered them with fragments of dead leaves and wood. "The fucker's ammo won't last much longer at this rate, but I'm not prepared to sit on my arse in the hope I'll still be in one piece when he runs out."

They ran crouched low, ignoring the cuts and scratches inflicted by low branches and thorns as they made a wide detour around the ambush site.

They threw themselves down as another wild burst slashed slivers of bark from standing timber only inches overhead.

"What the fuck is that thing doing here?" Almost dropping his M16, Thorne hitched the three-pack of rocket-launchers more firmly onto his back after a series of jarring collisions with low-hanging branches and the tearing effect of the several dense thickets they had passed through.

"It's a fucking scout car. What would it be doing? It's fucking scouting, that's what." Carefully moving aside a tangle of undergrowth, Dooley still succeeded in drenching himself with the mass of droplets of water it discharged.

The trio's circuitous route had brought them to a point level with, and slightly above, the Russian armored car. Inching forward farther, into the heart of a long-dead briar patch, they made their preparations.

"There's a Hummer behind it." Whispering, although there was no chance of their being heard at fifty meters distance, and above the rattle of automatic fire now returned at the four-wheeler, Thorne pointed to the much-holed vehicle close by the scout car.

Along its doors and side panels showed the close-stitched holes of a burst of machine-gun fire, each dark center surrounded by the bare metal ring where impact had smacked away the paint. Against the starred windscreen lolled the head of its driver, his face barred with blood that streaked the shattered glass.

Reaching across, Hyde helped Thorne slip the heavy pack from his shoulders, and taking one launch tube for himself, withdrew a second for Dooley. His actions

26

being mirrored, the sergeant extended the firing tube, not bothering to raise the sights at so short a range.

"Why are the fuckers hanging about?" Shouldering the rocket-launcher, Dooley instinctively waited for the sergeant's fire order. "Those little shits haven't got any armor, so why's he hanging about when he got lucky and kicked our wheels from under us?" The four-wheeler filled his field of vision, and his finger took up the slack on the trigger. "It don't make any sense, those recce wagons of theirs usually avoid a scrap."

"Who cares . . . ?" Hyde took a moment longer over his aim, and then whipped his launcher sideways to clout Dooley's downward and prevent his firing. "There's one of our blokes down there."

For the first time Thorne noticed two men huddled against the embankment for its protection from the incoming small-arms fire skimming past the Warpac armored car.

One of them wore the distinctive latest pattern NATO camouflage jacket and helmet. An obviously Russian officer had him covered with a pistol.

Pinned there by the fire from the woods about the disabled armored personnel carriers, they could neither board nor scramble to the comparative safety of the trees.

The scout car began slowly to reverse, turning slightly to offer the Russian and his captive the protection of its flank, and set low in that side was a small hatch that swung open.

As the scout car began to move, the fire aimed at it increased dramatically. Hyde knew he could do nothing as the captive was propelled toward the opening. Everything told him he should fire, let the NATO man take his chances, but still he held back, willing the man to make a break for it, do something.

The intensity of small-arms fire from the woods was

such that external fittings on the scout car were being broken and wrenched away as streams of tracer swept back and forth across the angled steel plates.

A burst aimed low plowed sparks and fountains of mud from the road, ricochets passed under the belly of the vehicle and both men staggered as they were struck.

Slumping against the armor close to the hatch, eyes closed and teeth clenched against the agony of his smashed ankle, the NATO soldier did not resist when strong hands reached out and roughly hauled him inside.

The officer was not so lucky. Falling to the ground with both legs broken, he was hit again, in the face. Blood, teeth and tissue spurted from his mouth. He twisted around to make a desparate lunge for the closing door. Fingers locked on the edge of the opening, he was dragged as the scout car began to reverse. Twice the door was cracked hard against his hand, but his grip held. The third time it was opened fully and then slammed viciously. Fingers severed, the officer sprawled and had no chance to avoid the deep-treaded wheel that passed over his stomach. A last writhing contortion and he was finally still.

"Do I fire?" Dooley had reshouldered the launch tube and was tracking the retreating target. "Do I bloody fire?"

For a moment the scout was stalled as it became entangled with the Hummer. Watching, with his mind locked almost into a trance, Hyde couldn't give the order. He could picture the frightening scene inside the vehicle: the dim red light, blurred by swirling fumes and smoke that carried the sour stench of cordite, the non-stop hail of bullets striking the armor blending with the thunder and rattle of the cannon and co-axial machine gun.

And there'd be blood everywhere, some from the

crew where they'd been cut by flying scabs of metal punched from the hull where tungsten-tipped rounds had almost penetrated, and much more from the injured man on the floor.

That's just what it had been like when Hyde had lost his face to the furnace heat generated by a Soviet anti-tank round. A hollow-charge shell had struck the APC square in the side and jetted a plasma stream of molten metal and explosive across the crew compartment. Their East German prisoner, laid bound on the floor, had instantly become a demented, screaming blazing torch.

"A couple of seconds and it'll be gone . . ." Getting no response from Hyde, Dooley took aim. "Fuck it, I'm bloody firing." He bellowed his rage as the missile clipped a sapling, veered from course and pancaked onto the ground far short of its target.

Broken open by the impact, the solid fuel spilled and burned to form an instant smokescreen that masked the target, and when it cleared, it was gone. Seconds later the warhead self-destructed and sent a plume of steam and woodland debris above the treetops.

The three men exchanged no words as they trudged to rejoin the others, now emerging from cover.

Following a few paces behind, Hyde looked at his hands. They were shaking. He realized that deep within himself the months of combat were finally taking their toll. Circumstances, and his own stubborn refusal to see it, had driven him to and beyond his limit.

Passing the Hummer, Hyde checked the driver. Sometime during the brief action he had died. Alone, uncomforted, ignored in the skirmish going on about him, he had succumbed to the massive headwound that had blown a chunk from the front of his skull. Pulverized brain matter still dripped into his lap. Most likely he had known little about it after that single

29

smashing blow. He had probably even been beyond pain. It had been a mercy, of sorts.

"We lost Solly, Ferris and Lang. They caught a burst trying to get out over the top. Same as ours, the door jammed." Preoccupied with a dozen thoughts, Revell didn't register the British sergeant's detachment from the scene. "Apart from that just a few scratches." He took off his helmet and, in wiping sweat away, added more dirt.

The light rain was doing little to disperse the blood from the three corpses huddled by the interlocked APCs. Except in one place, where it mingled with a large puddle that was gradually reddening.

"They're both fucked, Major." Burke reported his examination of the collision-damaged transports.

It took that to snap Hyde back to reality. "Do you fancy being just a trifle more precise? Or would you like to be carrying the fifty-caliber for the rest of this trip?"

"Reporting, sir. Command carrier burned to a crisp, number two carrier has broken back, three links damaged, and jammed transmission. Number three has jammed transmisison, commander's cupola ripped away . . . Oh yes, and the electrics have been buggered by a bit of shit a penetrating shell sent flying about inside. They're both workshop jobs."

Ignoring his sergeant's glare, Burke looked back at the APCs. Fuck it, he was a combat driver, not a bloody infantryman. And all this bloody hassle caused by one sodding little stray Warpac scout car. He spat in annoyance.

"What's up, boy?" Ripper displayed his mass of little green teeth in a broad grin. "You reckon you're too ancient to learn how to use your feet again?"

"Salvage what you can, Sergeant. Ammunition and ration packs to take priority." Revell walked across to the Hummer. Something about it had been bothering

30

him. He walked around it twice. Somehow it jarred, but he couldn't figure why.

"It is new."

Revell started; it was as though Andrea had read his mind yet again. That was the thought he'd been forming. A glancing re-examination confirmed it.

Beneath a superficial coating of mud the Hummer was factory fresh; it didn't even have any unit or other markings.

"How long is it since we saw any new NATO transport in this sector of the Zone?" Stepping back, Revell took in the perfect paint work, new tires and complete complement of shovels, axes and gas cans.

"I cannot recall." Andrea looked to the blazing APC and the collision-damaged pair of M113s beyond it. "I thought that all replacement equipment was issued to headquarters staff and their like, for the vital movement of filing clerks and senior officers."

"You're all sick. You know that, don't you?" Pushing between the officer and Andrea, Sampson felt the driver's neck for a pulse. At the first brush of his fingers the cooling of the man's flesh told him there was no point. He wiped blood from his fingers, dragging them down the side of his jacket to rid them of the last adhering clots. "Half of West Germany is a blitzed and contaminated wasteland and all you've got to complain about is who's getting the new sets of wheels."

There was a loud shout and the three of them saw Dooley plunging into the billowing smoke shrouding the fiercely blazing APC.

He staggered out of the pall seconds later, clutching a bulging, smoke-stained kit-bag. There were two ragged-edged holes in the tight-stretched drab material. When Dooley pulled it aside, in contrast to the earlier noisy excitement there was just a single plaintive "cheep."

The bright-colored birds clung forlornly to their perches. A beak, a foot and a scatter of yellow and green feathers marked the only mortal remains of the Russian gunners' unwitting target. The victims' abrupt demise had for the moment at least tamed the excitability of the surviving birds.

Satisfied the loss was no worse, Dooley recovered the cage and slung it over his shoulder. "Well, what are we waiting for then?" He ducked as a large chunk of red-hot metal flew overhead, propelled from an explosion on the side of the APC's hull.

"That'll be my flame tanks." Struggling with the straps, Thorne attempted to shift a bulky pack to a more comfortable position. He didn't bother to turn and look. "There's always a spot of residue left in them."

Sergeant Hyde detailed men for the point and rearguard. Ammunition aboard the burning M113 was beginning to cook-off, making almost too much noise for him to make himself understood. He was relieved when the major signaled for them to move out.

Of the many dozens of actions he'd been in, it was the first occasion in which Hyde could recall having been bothered by the sounds of battle. He noted it as perhaps a further indication that his nerve was cracking.

As they filed past the flattened corpse of the Soviet officer, few of them gave it as much as a cursory glance. Only one man deliberately averted his eyes.

"Now don't you go on letting things like that upset you, boy." Ripper gave the man a hearty slap on the shoulder. "It's gonna come to all of us. And besides, he wouldn't have wanted to live no more. Not with his pecker flattened and the end shot off his tongue. His sex life wouldn't have been worth a pinch of chicken shit."

32

Boris made no reply. It was not the sight of a body that he avoided. He had seen more than most, and having suffered fates far more horrific than this lone example. What bothered him was that as a Russian deserter who had for more than a year been fighting on the NATO side, he was becoming less and less able to look upon the death of his fellow countrymen.

It had not always been like that. When he had first gone over he had exulted at every Warpac death he had witnessed. During his time in the Red Army, many men had attempted desertion from his unit. Most had been dragged back and brutally executed in front of their comrades as an example. And now, as he gradually learned more of the methods by which the communists were keeping their forces together in the field, the sight of the remains of an ordinary Russian soldier filled him with sadness.

In the Soviet army the penalty for failure, even if through no conceivable fault of his own, did not result only in a man's death at the hands of the sadists in the Commandants Service, the field police; it usually meant a similar sentence on some or even all of his family. It was to that they had sunk, to the methods of Stalin's time, and worse.

The junior officer whose blood he had walked through had been a victim of that system. His crew had jettisoned him to avoid putting their mission at risk. The system was run by fear.

For Boris it held a special terror. He had deserted during the confusion of a heavy air raid. If for an instant his disappearance was suspected of being anything other than total obliteration beneath a falling bomb, then already his family would have suffered.

As he trudged with the others through the rain, sometimes beneath the scant shelter of the dripping trees, he felt as though he no longer cared whether he

33

lived or died. All that was important was that he did not fall alive into the hands of the KGB, or their military equivalent, the GRU.

"I wonder who the poor sod was that they carted off." Burke didn't address the question to anyone in particular, but his gruff voice carried to others in the file. "They must have wanted him bad to take risks like they did. If we'd had any TOW rounds left or been keeping company with an Abrams they'd have been deep in the shit."

"I made a note of the driver's I.D." Sampson wiped water from his face. "He was with some piddling little supply company, Dutch I think. Whoever the guy was who was with him he couldn't have been that important."

"Perhaps." Clarence didn't raise his voice, but with its precise clipped tones it carried. "Perhaps the Reds have heard the stories and they're looking for Paradise Valley."

"Quiet back there." They had a long way to go, and Revell wanted to put an early stop to speculation like that. With Russian reconnaissance patrols already probing the area they could not afford to waste time on a wild-goose chase in search of some mythical end-of-the-rainbow-type supply dump.

He was about to order an increase in pace, to take their minds off the speculation, but against the continuous and virtually ignored thunder of artillery came the much louder, and closer, throbbing of a Soviet gunship. Their step quickened automatically.

CHAPTER FOUR

They were lost. Time after time Revell and Hyde had conferred at crossroads as to the right or best direction. Almost as often, within a kilometer their chosen route had veered to the wrong heading. In the rugged mountainous terrain they would have been slowed to a crawl if they had struck across country, and so their compasses were virtually useless. The instruments served for little more than to act as general indicators that now and again they were heading in the desired direction.

Their only map was no better. Many of the roads were not marked and in any event all signposts had been removed long ago. It was an action planned to confuse the enemy, but as now it often had the reverse effect. Also against them was the fact that even before the war this had been a sparsely populated area of West Germany. The few scattered houses and farms they glimpsed were all abandoned and anonymous.

A first halt had been called after a couple of hours, while officer and NCO scaled a wooded ridge in the hope of identifying some landmark. They tried hard to conceal their frustration when they returned exhausted after the fruitless effort.

"At this pace it's going to take a bloody week to get back to our lines." Scully felt no benefit from the forty-minute rest when they restarted. The straps of his pack and his rifle sling bit into his shoulders. Their weight felt doubled by the water that lay on them and dripped from every crease of his combat clothing. Save where a tear was letting in an occasional icy stream he was still dry, but the wind was cold and beginning to burrow its way through to him.

"Keep it moving." Revell looked back from the head of the main group and noticed a perceptible slackening of pace. "We must keep them moving, Sergeant, keep them on their toes. Another hour and then we'll fall out, look for somewhere sheltered where we can light a fire and prepare something hot. That's if we don't have any more Hinds buzzing around us then."

"I think we'll have to take that risk anyway. Put a hot meal and a drink inside them and this lot will work wonders. Another stop under the trees with just a sip of cold water and a nibble at an oatmeal block and we're going to have a hell of a job getting them on their feet again."

Revell had to agree. "Pass the word that's what we're going to do. In return I want to up the pace."

"Major, Major!" PFC Garrett came sprinting back from the point, shouting at the top of his voice.

Hyde's snarled warning got the young soldier to lower the volume but did nothing to abate his excitement. His words came tumbling out in a breathless rush that had nothing to do with his exertion.

"Dooley's seen something, Major. We've all seen it. It's incredible. You got to come and see."

There was little to be got out of the eighteen-year-old while he was so worked up. Revell had seen him in the same state before, when he was on the substitutes' bench at an inter-unit football game. A rush of emotion rendered him almost inarticulate and completely

36

incomprehensible, and it would be simpler to follow him than attempt an interrogation.

Taking Hyde with him, Revell moved cautiously to the apex of the sharp bend that had taken the point out of sight. Dooley and another man stood in the middle of the road, holding their rifles casually, just staring ahead.

"What's all the bloody fuss?" Hyde punched Dooley on the shoulder, raising a miniature cloud of spray.

"It's all green. Can't you see it, everything's green."

And it was. Ahead the road lay dead straight for several hundred meters. Trees made a canopy over its entire length and the weak light of an overcast day filtered down in a soft green light through the mass of fresh spring leaves that sprouted from each branch and twig.

Tired though he knew he was, Revell realized that his eyes were not mistaken. That gentle verdant light was the same as the others were seeing. And there was grass and other low plants growing at the roadside, making gentle avenues of soft waving color where they flourished between the moss-covered trunks.

But that wasn't all. Among the lush undergrowth were patches of yellow and, less obvious, swaths of delicate blue. Flowers, primroses and bluebells. And there were others, tiny delicate blooms, that had no right to be there.

"There's no flowers in the Zone." Dooley gawped in total disbelief. "I thought I'd seen everything in this fucking oversized no-man's land, but I didn't think I'd ever see flowers. It's, shit, it's beautiful."

They walked slowly forward along the gently climbing avenue, surrounded on all sides by the luxuriant carpet and canopy of fresh foliage. The rest of the company followed, all vigilance forgotten as they took in what they saw. Even Andrea, the hardest of them all, appeared unable to fully comprehend the sight that met them as they walked forward.

Retrieving the bird cage from the man he'd left it with, at a price, Dooley pulled down the canvas and lifted the miniature aviary high to swing it about. "Come on, you lot, this'll cheer you up. It's just like home."

Revived by the clean, natural scent of the woods, the birds began a chorus that within seconds had an answer. A lone thrush warbled a reply, and Dooley shook the cage to stimulate his choir to greater effort, but it had the reverse effect.

Below the overhanging trees they had a respite from the rain, the overhead cover reducing it to a fine mist. Not a single plant, stem or leaf had the tell-tale blotches of unhealthy color that would have betrayed the use of chemical weapons in the vicinity. Even the litter from the previous fall smelled wholesome and invigorating. The combined scents saturated their every breath and with revived memories washed away death and suffering and battle.

As Hyde deliberately slothered through the moulding debris, he noticed tire tracks, and called the major's attention to them. "Only the one set, fairly fresh." Kneeling, he spanned his hand across them to gauge the width. "Not a Russian pattern, and certainly not wide enough for that Warpac scout car. I should think it's likely they belong to that Hummer."

Nodding, Revell decided not to mention that he'd recognized the track pattern. Inhaling deeply, he enjoyed lungsful of the untainted air. Since long before, he'd thought he'd lost his sense of smell, in all but the most extreme of conditions. But now it seemed as if the months of breathing chemicals and the stench of partly consumed explosives and super-napalm had only been serving to prepare him for this experience.

Still audible, the echo of the Russian barrage reminded some of them of the danger of completely dropping their guard. Nearly all of them had seen friends killed in an unwary moment.

Gradually though, as they walked silently forward, experience reasserted itself through their awe, though they could savor what they saw. Ahead of them, a blackbird scavenged among the dead leaves, flicking them aside as it searched for insects. It held out until the last moment before flying off ahead of them.

"Everything I know tells me this place just shouldn't be here." Try as he could, Revell could see no evidence at all that this oasis of life and color had ever received any dose of the poisons that drenched every other part of this great swath of German territory.

"It's like finding the garden of Eden in the middle of the Utah salt flats." Garrett picked a flower and finally succeeded in entwining it among the sparse dead foliage adorning the netting on his helmet.

"More like the eye of a storm." Sampson shrugged his sixty-pound pack of medical supplies higher, but otherwise his gangling frame showed no discomfort under the crushing load. "Listen, man, the Zone is a killing ground that's been well turned over. The Reds push us, we dig in, then we push them and they dig in. The next time we just push and dig in different places. Result, everything gets turned over, blown up, killed off. Only we found a slice of real estate that they've all missed. You got one guess where all hell is going to break loose next."

Garrett looked at the radiation counter on his belt. It registered little more than background, as if it too was reluctant to admit what they'd found. His chemical-level indicator was reading an unflickering zero. He double-checked with Thorne's meter before he could bring himself to believe it.

"They wouldn't do anything to mess up this place, would they? Hell, they just couldn't, could they?"

It was as if being among the fresh greenery had revitalized them. Even Andrea caught something of the mood. She accepted a flower that Dooley half jokingly offered. To his ill-concealed surprise she picked another to go with it and threaded both through the pin of a phosphorus grenade at her belt.

Their luck changed also. They struck a road that with only minor and brief deviations kept them headed in the right direction. And it was just as well. The country through which they passed now became more rugged with each kilometer. Frequently the road was flanked by the precipitous walls of a gorge of steeply rising hillsides that were plentifully littered with outcrops of rock and scree slopes.

They emerged from a belt of dense woodland into a patch of open meadow and the sudden silence, without the patter of rain on leaves, was strange.

Before crossing, Revell made a careful sweep through his binoculars. The road was dead straight for a half kilometer, and almost level. Where there was a slight dip a shallow flood was creeping over the asphalt. On the far side of the open ground the way plunged between near-vertical slopes lightly grown with stunted firs.

"Shit, what was that!" Burke jumped and several rifles were leveled at a patch of tall grass. "Bloody hell, it's pigs."

A small herd of wild boar broke from cover and plunged into the concealment of the trees.

"There goes breakfast." Fast as his reaction had been, Sergeant Hyde saw only a glimpse of the rump of the last animal to disappear.

"Not to mention bacon butties for lunch and pork chops for dinner." Reluctantly, Burke lowered his M16 and set it to safe.

"Would have gone a treat with these vege." Scully slapped the plastic of the bulging bag slung over his shoulder.

"You are mad dragging those along." Sampson had taken advantage of the halt to seat himself on a rotting stump. "When you ever gon' to get the time to cook them?"

"You'll see. Anyway, why are you dragging about enough medicine and bandages for a battalion?"

"He sells them, I've . . ." Ripper stopped abruptly as he saw the anger in the black's face.

"You shut your mouth." Effortlessly, despite his load, Sampson got to his feet and advanced a step toward Ripper. "And you keep it shut when you don't know what it is you're talking about." With a last glare he turned and resumed his seat.

"I was only saying that's what I heard."

"Well, you heard wrong, so forget it, okay?"

"Yeah, fine." Moving away, Ripper passed their sergeant. "Shit, that must have been a real sore corn I stood on then. But if he's not putting them out in the black market, why bother carting them around?"

"He gives them away." Hyde noticed the PFC's look of blank incomprehension. "To refugees who need them. I've seen him stay up two nights in a row when we've been camped near one of their settlements. And he doesn't just do basics either; he'll tackle surgery, even an amputation on a couple of occasions."

Altering the focus a fraction, Revell again turned his attention to where the road left the far side of the open ground. There was something there, but he couldn't quite make it out . . . small white objects, of no uniform size or shape. Just scattered at random . . .

41

"We'll cross in extended file." Revell returned the glasses to their case. "I want thirty meters between each man."

"Any reason to expect trouble, major?" Hyde checked that he had a full clip, and unfastened a pouch that held two more.

"Not that's obvious. Let's go."

CHAPTER FIVE

The leading man was halfway across and the last of them leaving the cover of the trees when they heard a vehicle coming up from behind. It was motoring fast and there was only just time for them to throw themselves down in the wet grass beside the road.

Every weapon was aimed toward the gap in the trees, as the harsh note of a diesel engine being pushed to its limit came to them. Rounds were chambered, grenades clenched, and then in rapid sequence each of them held their fire as a Mercedes Estate flashed past at high speed. The station wagon's camouflage paint was topped by a chromed roof rack.

Only Garrett snapped off a single shot, that missed, before he recognized the Mercedes.

"Crazy shits." Scully jumped up and shied a stone at its rear window. It missed and bounced sadly along in the mist of spray to roll apologetically back to the fields. "I hope you fucking . . ."

Flame and smoke erupted beneath the rear of the Merc. Its sheer speed, so much faster than the target for which the anti-tank mine had been intended, almost defeated the device. Almost but not quite.

The powerful blast lifted the back of the Estate, rupturing and igniting its fuel tank. The flaming wreck turned a complete somersault to crash back down on its side. Echoes of its pounding impact rolled through the meadow.

"Don't move. Don't anyone fucking move." Hyde's drill-sergeant bellow checked Sampson as he stood to go forward.

A figure crawled from the wreckage. Hoops of flame rippled its length, then turned it to a pillar of flame as it lurched to its feet. It reeled forward a half pace, staggered sideways, and then there was a second, smaller explosion. The effect was no less horrific. A limb spun through the air, and the debris cloud of the anti-personnel mine detonation cleared to reveal the smoldering hulk of what had been a human being.

"Where the hell is the bus?" Using extreme caution, Burke retraced his footsteps to the road, as the company moved forward using the faintly visible wheel marks as safe paths.

When they came to the partially flooded section, those who walked in the nearside track had the nervewracking experience for several meters of being unsure whether or not they were still precisely on course.

Garrett stood retching for a minute after safely regaining the barely visible trail beyond the ankle-deep water. "Fuck the bus. I'm just thankful that old bastard Klingenberg showed us we were in a mine field."

"Yeah, it was very kind of him." Dooley was having to sweat more than the others as his large feet with each step came dangerously close to overlapping the safe lane. "I'll tell you something, though. I don't think the old guy meant to do it."

Revell paused a moment to wipe water from his eyes. As he did his fingers brushed the edge of the camouflage cloth covering his helmet, and the part of the brim that felt brittle, and broke into dark flakes at his touch. It was a reminder of how close a twenty-

44

millimeter cannon shell had come to scattering his brains. The cloth still held the pungent tang from its brush with the tracer base of the shell.

"If I was feeling charitable I'd say that Klingenberg got separated by accident from his wagon-load of civies." While he was speaking Revell did not for an instant take his eyes from the narrow path he followed. "But having had to deal with that old louse a few times, I'd say it's much more likely he ran out on them."

Speculation on the fate of the civilians, though, Revell knew to be pointless. What mattered now, all that mattered now, was getting the survivors of his company back to the new NATO defense line. Wherever that might be. But still he could regard it as some small mark in his favor, a sign that there remained a spark of humanity within him, that he could feel a fleeting moment of sadness at what might be the fate of those civilians.

Death, fast and painless if they were lucky. If they were not, then months of gradual starvation, disease and lingering death in a squalid refugee camp. And there were a thousand gradations of suffering and degradation between those two unsought options.

"So that's what they were!" Almost saying it to himself, Revell filed one more snippet of knowledge of the Zone into his mental survival kit. The white objects that had puzzled him were bones. Not with the readily recognizable outline of human shape, but the scavenger-scattered remains of several boar. The automatic killing devices that had slaughtered those lumbering wild hogs had not been triggered again by the foxes, rats and carrion feeders that had alighted on the feast.

"A little more speed and he might have got away with it." Thorne had reached the edge of the shallow crater that marked the end of the tire tracks.

"I don't think so." Clarence pointed to a dull-colored

tube supported on tripod legs.

The blast from the explosion had blown camouflage from it and now the off-road mine stood fully revealed.

Scanning the slopes on either side of the road, Revell identified ten more of the sophisticated self-activating weapons, and as many claymore mines. Several trip-wires criss-crossed the road and laced the trees on the lower slopes. Immediately beyond the crater, at random intervals, slim antennae marked the position of more buried mines. They waited only for the brush of a tank's bellyplates passing overhead to unleash their huge charges and the semi-molten slugs of super-hard steel into the weakly defended underside of the fifty-ton machines. Igniting ammunition and fuel, they worked with devastating effect.

"Get Carrington up here." For Revell it had not been a difficult selection to make. No other among them knew as much about mines, but Carrington had another, special talent. He appeared not to have a nerve in his body. Revell had seen others spring the most diabolical stunts on him, in an effort to make him jump, or lose his temper, or show some reaction, but they'd always failed. Even a thunderflash under his bunk had failed to elicit much of a response. According to Dooley, who'd been present, if not the actual instigator, Carrington had opened his eyes, watched the thick smoke drift to the ceiling, then turned over and gone back to sleep.

"Problem, Major?" With the tip of the barrel of his Colt Commando, Carrington scratched his tangled black beard.

"You might say that. We need to get past this lot, fast."

Borrowing the binoculars, Carrington examined the various evidence of the extensive minefield. "Very amateur. What we are faced with here is a massive

46

overkill situation. That makes it harder. A regular minefield would be more logical and so predictable, give or take the odd new wrinkle some genius manages to introduce."

"So?" Revell didn't find it easy to cope with Carrington's laid-back manner. "I said we want to keep moving."

"Quickest way would be to lay down a firestorm. But that depends on how much ammo we've got to waste, and even then there's always something that gets missed. Or maybe aimed fire. Clarence could take out everything we could see with single shots, but it'd take longer."

There was sense in both suggestions, but Revell was forced to take into account another factor. He shook his head.

"It's tempting, but the way that scout car was operating we've got to reckon the Reds are interested in coming this way. We can't take out what might be the only decent roadblock likely to slow them."

Lips pursed in thought, Carrington again examined the road, and the nature of the ground around it. "There's another option. That Merc bounced a good way. I'd say there is a fair chance that we'd be all right as far as that. Just past it there's about the only section I've seen that we've got a chance of scrambling up without resorting to rock-climbing techniques."

"That still leaves us in the middle of a minefield."

"Maybe not, Major. From the way it's laid I'd say this load of nastiness was emplaced in a hell of a hurry. If I'm right, then they wouldn't have had time to do the mountain goat bit and do the higher slopes. Once that climbable section is cleared we can scoot around the rest. That's the best I can offer."

"What do you need?" There was no decision to make. They had no choice.

That was underlined by a stray shell from the barrage constantly passing high overhead. Tumbling far offcourse, it plummeted down among the trees of a distant hillside. A mushroom of gray-streaked black smoke soared above the treetops. The reverberation carried clearly and its echo took seconds to die away.

"Just someone to follow and improve the route markings I make, as we haven't any tape."

"Take Taylor. And as we haven't got tape, get a few rolls of bandage off Sampson, to mark the worst places."

Glad to be lightened of his pack for a while, Taylor otherwise showed no emotion; not so Sampson. It took an order from Revell to get him to surrender four large rolls of cellophane-wrapped bandage.

As the medic handed them over he scowled at Taylor. "You get yourself blown up, you're going to be sorry you laid these in the dirt."

Scanning every inch of ground before taking a step, the pair started off. Through the crater and its litter, past a scorched door torn from the Estate, they edged forward. A slim silver pen lay among sodden scraps of paper. Carrington ignored it and knew his follower would do likewise.

Both had seen too many men killed or maimed in the course of mindless or even pointless looting. In the Zone the art of mine warfare and booby-trapping had reached new heights of ingenuity and calculated frightfulness. But never before had either of them seen such lavish use of the weapons. Well-sited and concealed, a dozen assorted mines spread out over a half kilometer of road could stall an armored column for hours, unless they were determined to press on regardless of the casualties. Here at a glance they could identify three times that number.

They were nearing the Mercedes. Waves of fierce heat and smoke swept over them with an eddy of wind trapped between the hills. They froze as the acrid cloud bit into their eyes and blinded them, not moving on until they had blinked them clear of tears.

Several of the automatic anti-tank launchers stared from among the lower heaps of boulders and from among sparse clumps of firs. Carrington knew that the little logic boxes bolted to each tube would be registering their progress, electronically gauging what they were by shape, size, infra-red signature or any one of a whole host of methods. Right this instant they would be crossing at least one beam, maybe sonic or laser. Or perhaps the careful impact of their steps was being compared with the memory bank of a seismically activated mine

The anti-tank mines would not be interested in them, but buried at the roadside or lodged on a rock shelf there might be a shotgun mine silently ticking off their progress. Many now were set to detonate only when several bodies had passed, calculated to knock out patrol commanders, who rarely took the point and could be caught farther down the line. Well, there was nothing he could do about them. That was down to luck.

That word played a big part in the so-called science of mine clearance, but Carrington had never had any time for it. He was a fatalist. He didn't court death, even took what steps he could to avoid it, but he saw no point in worrying at every turn, every time a shell passed by so close he felt the draft of its passage, or when a grenade fragment rapped hard against his helmet or flak jacket. No, when it was his turn it would happen, and until the instant it happened he could savor every pain-free breath he took.

Through the roar of the flames Carrington thought he heard another sound, but couldn't place it. As he took another step it came again, but once more just too indistinct to label.

He unslung his weapon and looked around. There was nothing. Just the rocks and trees and the blazing auto. The slopes held nothing he hadn't observed previously. Those mines in sight were exactly as he'd noted them only thirty seconds before.

There were the pair of launchers by the big rock with the prominent quartz seam, another propped in the lower branches of a gnarled pine, the claymore mine at the bottom of the scree slope just below that chunk of panel from the Merc . . .

"Down!"

It was pure instinct that made Carrington hurl himself full length, even then though with the presence of mind to turn and dive into his own footsteps.

A sheet of flame erupted from the concave cast face of the claymore. It unleashed thousands of fragments at a broad arc of the road, while its less powerful but still devastating backlash made multiple perforations in the sliding wreckage that had triggered its anti-handling device.

Carrington felt a numbingly heavy blow in his side, and an instant drenching in warm, pulsing blood.

CHAPTER SIX

The blood that soaked him was not his own. Carrington lifted his head to look at the savagely torn remains that had been thrown against him. A wisp of steam rose from ribbons of bowel that trailed from the legless torso.

He knew that Taylor had been only a few paces from him, and only fractions of a second slow in taking cover. There was a persistent tinny ringing in his ears, the aftermath of the masses of impacts against the hulk of the Estate. It had been that which had saved him.

Inches from where he'd lain the road was scored with a mass of tiny furrows that were quickly filling with water.

Revell had seen the burst of red mist that had marked Taylor's end. It was only a moment, but it seemed an age before Carrington got to his feet. Without any gesture to indicate he was all right, he took a roll of muddy bandage from the grasp of the dismembered hand beside him and started up the hillside.

"There's something wrong with that bloke." Burke watched a tripwire being carefully marked. "No wonder he didn't bother to check if he was hurt. If he loses any of the ice he's got in his veins he can always top up with a glass of water."

"Well, at least he hasn't got the worry of that Red artillery." Garrett cocked his head to listen. "They're putting down a heck of a plastering to either side and ahead of us but we seem to be in the clear so far. Gives him a chance to concentrate on what he's doing."

"What sort of a nerd are you, boy?" Ripper, after rummaging through every pocket, produced a bullet-hard, fluff-impregnated wad of chewing gum. "Anybody with half an ounce of the sense they were born with would know why that is, and it sure ain't good news."

"It's not coming down on us." Garrett felt the color rising to his cheeks. "So that's got to be good, hasn't it?"

"Use your brain, boy. It ain't just for holding your eyes apart, although maybe in your case . . ."

"Why don't you just tell the kid." Hyde interposed to prevent friction.

"I was going to, in my own way." Giving the wad a cursory inspection and nothing else, Ripper popped it into his mouth. "As I was saying before the sarge butted in, what we've got here is a pail of crap held over our heads. That ordnance going down ahead of us ain't the sort of stuff that's heavy enough to break a railbridge but it kinda sounds like it's ample to stop traffic on it. And that works two ways—stops us getting out or help coming over. You with me, boy?"

"The rest of the barrage is still way off to the left and right. It's no bother to us."

"What do they teach you in basic? What we have here appears to be a classic case of a three-sided box barrage. Boxes do two things, keep people out or keep 'em in. This one is thrown by the Reds. It's meant to keep our boys out, but it's gonna keep us in as well."

Listening more attentively, Garrett could now make out the three directions where the deluge of explosive was crashing down. "So what's behind us?"

"Well, as the commies seem to want to keep this slice of territory for themselves, I'd say that what's coming up behind us is a touch more than an army of guys wearing red stars."

"Shit."

"Shit indeed, good buddy. That's what I'm gonna do when they arrive." Ripper spat out the recycled chewing gum. "What have I been doing in my pockets?"

"On your feet!" Hyde passed among the company, prodding awake those who had been able to rest despite the rain that now lashed the road where they waited. "Come on, pull yourselves together. We're about to take a hike through a minefield, not stroll to the PX or NAAFI. Anyone who does something stupid is making trouble for his mates as well as himself. If you cause your own problems you'll be left behind, and I'm not kidding. We can't carry you. Best we'll do is leave you a grenade so you can make the big decision for yourself. Move!"

"Where the hell can they all have come from?" Dooley had tried keeping a count of the anti-tank mines they had passed. He'd quickly given up when the difficulties of negotiating the slippery rocks and grass had made it more important to watch his footing than keep a tally.

"Who knows." Burke tried to pull together the torn edges of material on his sleeve, where he'd slid the last few meters to level ground once more. "I do know that I haven't seen gear used on that scale for eighteen months or more. Bloody hell, in the past we've been lucky to have ten to lay in front of a position, and we've had to lift those for re-use before pulling back."

53

Scully too had been thinking it over. "How come in the middle of nowhere we stumble on a mass of state-of-the-art nastiness, but when we're pulled out of the line for delousing and clean underwear we can't get our hands on so much as a decent T-bone?"

"Because everywhere out of the line is packed with all the guys who don't want to be in it, and they scoop all the goodies before we get there." Sampson opened his mouth to catch a drink, but turning his face to the sky sent rivulets of water down his neck and inside his raincape. "Since we're in a minority out there there's got to be a better than even chance we'll trip over any shit that's lying around."

They reached a crossroads, and halted as a set of tracks were examined.

"Four-wheel utility, quite recent." Even as he watched, Hyde saw the steep-walled ruts crumbling and becoming less distinct. "Could be that Hummer again."

"If it is, then they must have known about that minefield. The tracks run off down that little side road. The way we've come would certainly have been the quickest, the most obvious route to where they bumped into that reception committee."

"Knowing about it didn't do them any good. One dead and one in the cage, or worse." With the toe of his boot, Hyde idly made a dam of leaves where water was overflowing from a puddle into the tread-patterned rut. "They came from the direction we're heading."

"I hope our luck holds better than theirs." Burke muttered that under his breath. The novelty of the unspoiled scenery had worn off for him.

As they moved off, Scully cut a slice from the turnip he had washed in a shallow stream beside the road, while the others had refilled their bottles. He'd hacked the skin from it in a series of thick chunks, reducing its weight by nearly half. He bit into it, and grimaced. "It's fucking terrible."

"You're supposed to cook them." Sampson enjoyed their self-appointed cook's disappointment. "Why didn't you try a carrot? You can eat them raw."

"I know that. I was a chef in civy life . . ."

"Wouldn't have know that from the last meal you did." As he walked, Garrett broke tiny pieces from a chocolate bar in his pocket and surreptitiously slipped them into his mouth.

"What was wrong with it? That was borscht, and it came out all right, considering the conditions under which I was making it."

"What were those little bits of meat floating in it? They were tough as old boots." Finishing the last of the bar, Garrett balled the foil and wrapper together, and when he thought he wasn't being observed, flicked it away.

"Cat."

"Oh, you've got to be kidding." Garrett tried to recall the taste but could only remember the texture, or lack of it. "The only cat I've seen in the Zone in the last six months is that one the major's APC went over . . . Oh, sweet Jesus, you didn't, did you?"

"Why not? Think what it would have been like if it hadn't been tenderized that way. Made skinning a bit messy though." Scully crammed the remains of the turnip back into the bag. "Hey, Boris!"

Farther down the line the conversation had been hardly audible to the Russian. "Yes?" He was surprised to hear his name called.

"What did you think of my cabbage soup?"

Hesitating, Boris considered his answer. He could not be sure that Scully, who had never talked to him before, was not simply involving him so as to score some obscure point. He hedged. "I did not have very

55

much, but . . . it was quite good."

And it had been, too. Boris had been surprised. Of course it did not have the special touch that made the dish so distinctly Russian, but it had been close enough to bring back many memories . . .

"Pity I didn't have any sour cream." Scully sought to excuse Boris's slightly less than enthusiastic response, for the sake of appearances in front of the others. "Wouldn't you say?"

"Yes . . ." Sensing what Scully wanted, and pleased to be involved in any conversation, Boris sought the right answer.

"But then every cook in Russia has his own recipe, and your cabbage and beetroot were perfect." That was not the perfect truth, but Boris had been so glad to be taken off the permanent cooking detail he would now have said anything to maintain the current happy arrangement.

It had been hard for him, after he had settled down in the post of signaler for the company and had begun to gain the men's grudging respect, if not Andrea's, to be taken off such sensitive work because of orders from headquarters. There was still so much distrust toward those who had changed sides. Yet they were the ones who had most to fear from a Communist victory. A NATO soldier, if he was lucky, might survive as a prisoner; for him that was not an option.

The talk of food had reminded him of his hunger, and his mind drifted back to the last time he had enjoyed a steaming bowl of borscht at home, his last leave before . . . His mother must have saved coupons for several months to make the meal.

With the borscht had been a cheese pie as delicate as only she could make it, and there had been fresh black bread and from heaven-only-knew-where she had produced ice cream, and homemade kvass on which,

56

with several glasses of cognac, he had become quite drunk. He pushed the recollection from his mind. He no longer knew if she was alive or dead, or among the living dead in a labor camp.

They crossed a single-arch stone bridge. On the far side, partially overhanging the road and the water, was an old flour mill. Scaffolding and the rotting boards of working platforms surrounded it on three sides. The attractions of its beautiful setting among the rugged tree-covered hills had not been enough to tempt its owners back into the Zone to complete the restoration.

For several hundred meters beyond the lone building the road climbed steeply to a brow that gave a rare panoramic view. In the middle distance, perhaps two kilometers in a straight line, a great column of bare granite thrust high above the trees that masked its base. Topping it stood a Disneyland-style Gothic castle.

Its gray stone walls soared to intricate turrets, spires and battlements. Wisps of cloud threaded between its highest features.

Clarence unslung his rifle and used its powerful telescopic sight to examine the ancient fortress. The masonry seemed to grow directly out of the rock and in places it was hard to determine the point of transition.

"There sure is a lot of shit going down around us." Ripper listened, and recognized the thundering report of an artillery missile impacting. Ages after the heavy report of its one-ton warhead came the distinctive double "boom" of its recent supersonic passage.

There was no time to take cover when the scream of jet engines filled the air. A contour-hugging Mig fighter-bomber flashed past close overhead and the clouds were lit with the glare of its afterburners.

"He won't get very far." Clarence rejected the instinctive but futile urge to send a bullet after the aircraft. "At the rate he's burning fuel he is going to have to come down soon. One way or another. Something must have scared the hell out of him . . ."

Flares ejected as decoys drifted down. The last was barely brushing the treetops when a slim flame-tailed missile lashed under incredible acceleration from the vicinity of the castle and hurtled after the plane. Ignoring the flares, it screeched past and bored into the cloud in pursuit.

"Go on boy, go get him." Ripper cheered the Rapier. "It'll get him. It ain't even a contest. That's one Warpac pilot who won't be fretting himself over his fuel consumption for long."

"Did anyone pinpoint the launch site?" Even through the field glasses Revell could make out nothing that would betray the missile's lift-off point. Not for the first time he regretted his thermal imager had been lost with the APC. With it the location, bathed in the residue of the hot exhaust gasses, would have stood out like a neon sign.

"Pretty close to the castle, I think." Lowering the rifle, Clarence used his keen sight in an attempt to decide if a smudge he saw among distant high ground was a trick of light or the faint remains of rapidly dispersing smoke. He couldn't be certain. "I've got an idea it came from within that circle of hills. If you look, the road runs along the base of its plinth of rock, and the circle of hills is on the other side of it."

"That's close enough. So somewhere down there is one of our air-defense batteries, or at least part of one. Their transport allocation is usually generous; maybe we can hitch a lift."

Taking the point, Revell was disappointed when they lost sight of the castle the moment they started downhill. The trees prevented more than an occasional tantalizing glimpse. But at least each one showed them that little bit nearer.

Setting a fast pace, he maintained it even when he began to feel the strain himself. They had to make contact. Even if like themselves it was another bunch of strays, there had to be benefits from their falling in together. For an anti-aircraft unit the advantage would be increased infantry to protect it. For his men it was a lifeline. Transport meant a chance' to recover from their weariness, perhaps the opportunity to get sufficiently far ahead of the Russian advance to prepare some hot food. But most of all it offered the opportunity to move fast enough to escape being encircled by the enemy and killed or captured. And being captured by the Warpac forces was merely death postponed.

Looking back, the major saw that some of the company were straggling.

"Sergeant Hyde, have them close up, regular intervals. If anyone falls out they're to be stripped of ammunition and left behind."

It worked, as nothing else would have done. Those to whom each step was agony found the strength to withstand the pain; those who felt they were about to drop from sheer exhaustion found untapped reserves of energy.

Like walking zombies they kept moving. With almost mechanical strides and with labored breath whistling between gritted teeth they kept going. They knew they had to.

CHAPTER SEVEN

Rain dripped from great banks of razor-wire flanking a high spike-topped steel mesh gate. The massed coils of serrated metal strips had been added to at different times. Most strands were heavily rusted; others, though streaked or spotted with the same dull encrustments, could still show lengths that gleamed brightly. A moss-blotched reinforced concrete guard post flanking the gate was unmanned, and the gate itself hung open.

Above soared a towering cliff of dark granite. The walls of the castle extended it still higher. Tire marks showed a single light vehicle had been through that day.

"Do we knock and wait for the butler." Scully felt nervous, overpowered by the sheer scale of the rock face.

"There can't be anything special in here." Checking quickly for booby-traps, Carrington went forward a few meters, but could see the side road for only a short distance where it followed the base of the cliff. "They wouldn't leave the post unmanned and the gate open if there was."

"Maybe the two guys in the Hummer were the last to leave." Ripper also felt oppressed by the sheer scale of their surroundings. When he looked up he had to fight down the fear that the whole mountain was looming over him, falling to crush him.

"Wouldn't it be great if this was the entrance to that Paradise Valley?"

"You think they'd leave the gate open if it was?" Hyde snorted. "A place like that would be protected by a battalion at least."

"We're never going to find out by standing here." Revel checked he had a round chambered and with Andrea at his side led in through the gate. Carrington tagged close behind them.

Andrea loaded a smoke round into the grenade-launcher slung beneath the barrel of her M16. "When I was in the camps there were many stories about a special place that held vast stocks of everything we could ever want. All that we so desperately needed was supposed to be there. Food, clothing, medical supplies, arms, everything."

Though she talked as they walked, Andrea never for an instant relaxed her vigilance. Revell made no response, giving all his concentration to trying to anticipate what lay around the next bend.

"An old man came to one camp I was in. He was crippled and almost deaf and covered by many great scars. Always he spoke of a wonderful valley where anything could be had. If you could get in. Eventually he persuaded some men to go with him. He would not tell them the location in advance, only that it was in this general area. We never heard of any of them again."

Still between high frost-cracked walls of granite, the road curved around the base of the cliff. Beside the road there was room only for a shallow stream that crossed and recrossed the metaled surface, and where they had to wade through it the water lapped ice-cold to their ankles.

Throwing himself against the illusory cover of the

rock, Revell edged back a few paces. "No wonder they didn't bother with the guard post." His breath came in gulps and he could feel his heart hammering inside his ribs.

He had seen it for only a second, but it was locked vividly in his mind's eye. A massively strong bunker seemed to grow from the rock itself. Perhaps a meter of concrete faced with inches of steel, the snouts of machine guns protruded from step-sided embrasures. The weapons could sweep a hundred-meter straight stretch of road that offered no shred of cover. Even attempts to rush the position using smoke would have been doomed. Firing blind, the guns could not have failed to hit anyone attempting that suicidal run.

Armor would have been no protection. Niches cut in the rock held well-protected directional anti-tank mines. At point-blank range the hull sides of the toughest main battle tank would be penetrated effortlessly.

"Maybe the Russians are here before us." Carrington too had seen what lay in their path. "Anybody who strolls that way is going to get creamed. I'm impressed."

Revell was too, but someone was going to have to go out in the open and . . .

"You can come forward."

The bull-horn blared into life without crackling a pre-warning. "I promise you are quite safe." Each heavily accented word bounced back and forth in echoes that gradually diminished to a confused babble.

"It is no trick. We are on the same side. We have been watching your approach on remote cameras, but only in the last few moments have we picked you up on our microphones."

There was a pause, and Revell made no move. He laid a restraining hand on Carrington's arm. "We'll take no . . ."

"I see that you doubt me." The disembodied voice blasted out again. "That is understandable. I shall expose myself."

Dooley tittered. "That's supposed to set out minds at rest?" He had to shove fingers in his mouth to comply with Sergeant Hyde's order for silence.

There came an electronically amplified thud and then a resonant "click," as if the bull-horn had been put down while still switched to full power. There was a brief period of dead silence and then from behind the machine gun nest strolled an unarmed officer. Walking into the open, he turned to beckon behind him and was joined by three young soldiers. Their battledress was immaculately new, but long hair straggled from beneath their helmets.

The trio lounged against the blockhouse, masking the machine guns. Reassured, but still maintaining a degree of caution, Revell went forward with Andrea and Carrington. Advancing to meet them, the first man made a careless salute.

"Lieutenant Hans Voke, commander of Dutch Pioneer Company seven four nine." He grinned a broad grin that exposed a gold tooth. "I am welcoming you to NATO supply depot number twelve. You may have heard of it; the unofficial name is Paradise Valley."

"Doesn't look much like paradise to me." Keeping a tight grip on the side of the truck, Thorne was bumped by others as the eight-wheeled Foden wallowed through huge potholes.

The basin of land dominated by the castle was over two kilometers in diameter. They were nearing a small village set in its center, and dwarfed by the jagged ridges and precipitous slopes around it.

Apart from the straggling collection of about twenty houses and a small church, the only other sign of habitation in the valley was a picturesque farm on the slopes opposite the castle.

All of the buildings were from another and gentler age. Half-timbered for the most part, some with shutters and fenced gardens, the only sign that the twentieth century had created any impression on the place was the abandoned hulk of a farm tractor beside a rotting woodpile.

Pulling into the yard of a small sawmill that was little more than an open-sided shed beside a house with blue shutters, the truck came to a stop with a hiss of air brakes. When they'd all dismounted it drove forward beneath the shed.

"So where are all the goodies that are supposed to be stashed here?" Looking about him, all Dooley could see was a typical abandoned West German village, scruffy from long neglect.

"You are standing on them." Voke displayed his gold tooth again. "But perhaps it is improper of me to say that. You are standing over them, a small part of them." Beside him stood an electric saw bench. The drive belt had perished and fallen off. He pressed the start button.

There came the subdued hum of a well-maintained pump starting up and the sigh of powerful hydraulics. The Foden began to drop smoothly as the floor beneath it sank.

"What you tell me about the two men in the Hummer is a cause for worry." Voke led the major down a long well-lit corridor that smelled of gun oil and linseed. "They were two of my men; they deserted early in this morning, I think." He tapped the side of his head. "Here they have knowledge of this place. You can be certain one was taken as a prisoner?"

"My sergeant saw it happen. The man was wounded, but he thinks not fatally. But what can your man tell them—just what have you got here?"

"It would be more quick to show you while my men show yours where fresh clothes and boots are to be found. Of course they are not mine to give, but the provost sergeant and the last of the stores clerks were evacuated by helicopter last night, and you can see," he indicated his own impeccable turnout, "I am not in a position to tell on you."

They turned a corner and with a sweeping wave of his arms Voke announced the huge subterranean hangar they'd entered.

For a battle-weary commander like Revell, who for a long time now had almost given up hoping for, let alone trying to get hold of replacement equipment, it was an Aladdin's cave.

In the great cavern beneath the floor of the valley were row upon row of factory-fresh wheeled and tracked armored personnel carriers, armored cars and armored re-supply vehicles. In the distance was what looked like a small mountain of crated engines and other spares.

Voke tried to hide his amusement at the major's open-mouthed amazement. "There are seven more rooms like this."

"All filled like this?"

"Certainly all filled, but not all like this." Voke led the way out again and talked back over his shoulder. "Another holds pieces of light and medium artillery, another contains engineering equipment. Two are filled with soft-skin transport; I cannot recall what is in the others. But that is not all. There are other storage areas for elecronic equipment, radar spares and the like. And then yet more for clothing, small arms and ammunition. All on the same scale."

They were passing a series of large rooms whose fireproof doors had been strongly wedged open. Looking in as they passed, Revell could not identify all that the various crates and racks held, but he saw sufficient to be more impressed and more bitter with each he hurriedly scrutinized.

"Why the hell hasn't any of this stuff ever been issued? There's enough here for two or three battalions. We've been screaming for it for months."

"Actually, a clerk told me that here there is enough to equip at least a brigade, or even to refit a division. One of my men swears he has even seen several crated gunships. I do not disbelieve him." Voke's tone had an edge to it now, and he was no longer smiling.

He led into a large circular room. The center was dominated by a crescent of computer terminals and telex machines. Leaving only space for two or three doorways, the walls were lined with filing cabinets. Voke tugged at the handle of the nearest. It was locked. "You see, for a bureaucrat the turning of a key makes everything safe. We should have fitted the Free World with a lock, and kept communism out that way." He unleashed a massive kick at the cabinet, denting its front. "We give them the latest machinery, the best computers, and still they only feel happy when they are pushing pieces of paper from tray to tray."

"Doesn't any of this material ever get issued? The road in hasn't seen real traffic, maybe not all winter." Tapping at a keyboard, Revell was surprised when the screen glowed to life, displaying the gibberish he'd typed. Its green glow was eerie in the dimly lit room.

"I have not been here even that length of months. All

66

I have seen is perhaps five or six small loads being taken out by Chinook. High-value specialized equipment, radar, that sort of thing. Not enough to keep the cobwebs off the stacker trucks."

"Is that your task here, materials handling?"

"No, Major. I was sent here to prepare all this for destruction."

CHAPTER EIGHT

Tugging open the elevator gate, Voke led across the dusty interior of the shell of a house and out into the rain.

Looking back as he instinctively closed the street door behind him, Revell could see nothing about the property, even at this distance, that would betray its real purpose.

Voke noticed the inspection. "It is good, isn't it? As far as we know it has fooled all the Warpac sky-spies, surveillance satellites and reconnaissance aircraft. Certainly they have made no attempt to destroy this very tempting target."

"You think they still don't know it's here?"

"Well, perhaps by now they do. I understand their interrogation techniques are crude but effective." Voke shrugged. "I expect by this time our man has told them everything. We shall have to hope they do not arrive quite yet. It would spoil my preparations."

"What are your plans for getting out?"

"We were due to be picked up at about the time the jamming became so bad." Rain plastered to Voke's face the long blond hair that made a fringe below the brim of his helmet. "The chopper did not arrive, so we altered our plans."

"Reckon they forgot about you?" Revell noticed that

68

the road was not the soft asphalt it appeared, but concrete thick enough to take the biggest trucks. It had been washed over with tone-down paint, but a small patch that had been missed revealed its true color.

"Forgot? Yes, certainly it is possible. At this time a company of pioneers will not rank high in the list of transport priorities, especially as many of my men are too old for combat duties. Old William admits to fifty-six, but I think he could well be sixty, or even more. There are about five of us under the age of thirty, out of ninety-six. No, it is ninety-four now, isn't it?"

"So what are you going to do, gas up a few of the Bradleys and make a run for it?"

"Surely you are familiar with the ways of the Dutch army, Major." Voke laughed. "Even in battle they have to vote on everything. My men discussed the position this morning, when it became obvious the pick-up was not going to happen. I was not invited to the meeting. There I was kicking my heels expecting them to produce a demand for overtime pay, and instead they said that they wished to stay and defend this complex."

"With less than a hundred men?" Revell tried to keep the amazement out of his voice. "This place is vast. You'd be spread far too thin. Sure you've got limitless ammunition, and if it was just a case of holding that narrow pass we entered by I'd say you could hold out for some hours. But there's nothing to stop them pushing infantry through these hills at any one of a dozen points. The ground may be rough, but it'd only delay them, not stop them. Or they could come in low and fast and drop a few chopper loads before you could get Stingers on to them."

A smug look came over Voke's face. "For air-defense there is an RAF regiment battery dug in at that farm. They too were due to be air-lifted out this morning, so we are not alone in being overlooked."

Revell had forgotten the Rapier they'd seen chasing the Mig. He had to concede that point. "But you still haven't the manpower to defend the whole area. You're just wide open."

There was disappointment in the lieutenant's expression. "I had hoped we could persuade you and your men to stay, but we cannot force you to join us. Look, Major, I know that time is precious, but will you give me just thirty minutes, that is all I ask? Just thirty minutes to show why I believe we can defend this place against whatever the Russians throw at us." He could see he was not winning the argument. "Listen, it will take at least that time to bring some transport to the surface and fuel and load them with ammunition. Tell me what you need and I will have my men do it right away. When we get back, if you still wish to go, then no time will have been lost."

"I suppose I've nothing to lose."

"You just can't fucking do it."

"And why the bloody hell not?" Scully resented Garrett's objections. "What's so fucking wrong with it, that's what I want to know?"

"It's . . . it's wrong. It's not decent. You can't cook a meal in the oven of a mobile crematorium."

"You are picky, aren't you? Look, this place has a cold store the size of a house. It's packed full of food I had forgotten existed. The only kitchens I can find here are run off a ruddy great LPG tank that's bone-dry." Scully patted the steel flank of the trailer-mounted field crematorium. "This little beauty has its own bottle already connected. It's never been used to burn bodies, so where's the harm in me using it to womp up a meal?"

"Like I said, it's not proper."

"Well then, you don't have to eat what I cook, do

you?" Refusing further discussion, Scully finished levering apart great slabs of frozen steak. He threw the last frost-covered chunks inside. Partially closing the heavy semi-circular door, he played with the setting controls until he had a low steady flame.

He turned his attention to hammering the contents of the sacks of frozen vegetables into more manageable-sized lumps. "Same as usual." He grunted as he swung another overarm mallet blow. "All welded together. Those civilian contractors must make a fortune out of pushing the old stuff onto the army. It's probably from the bottom layer of one of the first E.E.C. food mountains."

"How long is it going to take?" Hyde tapped the metal tip of his toecap against a portion of meat that had fallen into the mud. It rang, as if it too was metallic. "Looks like they'll take a week to thaw."

"This is not what you'd call a standard catering kitchen." A slight touch on the flame control and Scully jumped as they instantly transformed to roaring blue jets. He made a hurried readjustment.

"I asked how long."

"Give me a chance, Sarge." Having finally satisfied himself that the flame was about right, Scully carefully closed the door and secured it. He had to go on tiptoe to see that all was well through a small thick glass porthole in the side of the oven.

"When the major went swanning off he said thirty minutes. I've still got twenty left." Filling two buckets with assorted lumps of glistening vegetables, Scully added a gallon of water to each and then they too went in. "This lot should be done just before he gets back. It won't be *cordon bleu,* but it'll be done. Salmonella special coming up," he muttered under his breath, and then out loud, "It was never like this at The Dorchester."

The rest of the company were asleep in an underground barracks. A couple of the hardiest had showered but the others had not bothered when they'd discovered there was no hot water. They'd been content with clean clothing.

Scully had left them down there as soon as he'd kitted himself out. Even in the lift going down he'd experienced the all-too-familiar sensation of claustrophobia. Volunteering to prepare a hot meal had got him out without having to explain. As much as any of them he needed rest, but not in that stark warren with its hollow sounds and the perpetual thumping of the air conditioning.

Satisfied he'd done all he could, he sat on a pile of boxes containing more of the ice-encased steak, shifting to an upturned pail when the cold struck through to him. In under an hour they'd be trying to fight their way out through a tightening ring of communist armor and artillery, groping almost blindly in closed-down APCs from one desperate situation to the next. And then there was still the river. At least the Bradleys' new water-propulsion system might give them a chance in the strong currents, if the bridge was down, as by now it most likely was. In the elderly M113s they wouldn't have had a hope. Pushed and spun by the currents, they would only have been target practice for Warpac gunners on the banks.

Shuddering at the thought, Scully tried to blank it from his mind, but failed. All he could see was the cramped inside of that horrid aluminum box as they were tossed and drenched and hurt and gradually sank. "God, don't let me die in one of those tin cans."

"I know exactly how you feel."

Scully hadn't realized that in his abstraction he'd been staring past the sergeant at the first of the Bradley APCs to be brought above ground, and had spoken out loud.

"I learned to hate them a long time ago." Tentatively, Hyde put his fingertips to his face. The scar tissue and layers of grafts meant that he sensed rather than actually felt the touch. It was unreal, not a part of him, feeling as it might have done after a local anesthetic. Only he lived with that sensation all the time. He gave a start as fat spat loudly in their improvised field kitchen. There was a slight tremor in his right eyelid. That always came on when he was exceptionally tired.

Hyde looked for a distraction. He walked down a pathway between the church and a house whose ground floor appeared once to have served as a small general store. From that side of the hamlet a narrow road ran between unkempt fields and pastures to the slopes beneath the castle. It then climbed steeply through a series of hairpin bends to the gate of the ancient fortification.

Looking that way, he could see the West German countryside as it used to be and could imagine himself back in time. Back to when you could drive all day and not see a single burned-out tank, a ruined town or masses of decaying bodies. A time when men were not astounded by green leaves on trees, a time before shells, nukes and chemicals had transformed almost every part of it into a land fit only for the warriors of hell, and him into one of them.

Revell wasn't in the least surprised when the lieutenant drove the unissued Range Rover staff car straight up to the castle. He'd been more than half expecting it.

The steep and twisting approach road was the only way to it. With a sheer drop of at least a hundred meters on every other side, combined with the building's massively thick walls and commanding situation, it certainly had an air of impregnability. But it had been constructed in another and far distant era. It was possible the architects might have envisaged future wars when ways might be discovered of delivering blows against the fabric from a greater distance off, but in their wildest dreams they could never have imagined the power of those new projectiles.

They drove through a narrow double gateway and into a small courtyard.

Voke was the first to alight. "If you will come with me, Major."

"You two stay with the transport." Revell made to follow the Dutchman. "And Dooley, don't go wandering off on one of your famous scavenger hunts."

"Who, me?" Dooley adopted his hurt look, but at the same time could not resist casting a speculative eye over the property.

Andrea didn't even bother to acknowledge the order. Pulling the hood of her raincape forward over her helmet like a monk's cowl, she cradled her rifle and, not bothering to take shelter, watched them enter the ground floor.

Checking his watch, Revell resisted the urge to hurry his guide. He was led through a series of spacious paneled rooms, through a magnificent oak-beamed banqueting hall and into what must once have been the kitchens.

"Nearly all of the furniture has been removed, quite legitimately, but I understand a few choice pieces did disappear between here and the West. I find it amusing that perhaps there is somewhere a refugee hovel furnished with priceless antiques." Voke took a large key from an inside jacket pocket. "More likely, though, it has already passed through the hands of several dealers in London and New York."

74

The door he unlocked was set in an angle of the wall at the back of the kitchen. Despite its obvious age and heavy construction it swung open smoothly and almost silently on well-lubricated hinges.

Reaching into a small recess just inside, the lieutenant flipped a switch, and from deep below them came the sputter of a generator coughing into life. A widely spaced row of lights glowed into life to illuminate a steep stone stairway.

Taking another quick look at the time, Revell then had to give his undivided attention to the worn and slightly damp steps.

"We're running out of time, Lieutenant."

"I know that, Major. For me and my men it is running out very fast."

CHAPTER NINE

There were at least thirty cellar rooms and vaults, ranging from little more than a cupboard-sized space to the three or four that would have garaged comfortably a brace of Challenger main battle tanks.

Most were lined with racks of small arms of every description, including mortars and anti-aircraft missile launchers. All were accompanied by stacks of the appropriate ammunition. The largest was filled with anti-tank weapons TOWs, already uncrated and assembled.

Several times Voke talked down the major's comments or criticisms. "Wait until I have shown you everything, then tell me what you think. I am being as quick as I can," he added to forestall that objection.

"There is ample fuel for the generator, and its standby. Water, rations, chemical toilets—even a well-equipped dispensary. See, you can enter the cellars from several places inside the castle, but this is the only entrance or exit outside the walls."

Drawing back three huge bolts on a studded door, Voke pulled it open with an effort and a gust of wind slapped rain into their faces.

For the first time Revell didn't mind; it was very cool and refreshing after the exhaust-filled fetid atmosphere of decay in those catacombs.

As they stepped out, behind and above them soared the castle wall. To their left a narrow path hewn from the rock started down across the cliff face. It was slippery, and overgrown in places. Between them and a long drop to the trees far below was a ruined wall that bore faint signs of once having been crenellated, to offer its defenders firing positions. Now it was mostly gone. Unlike the main body of the castle this small outwork had been allowed to deteriorate. As they cautiously worked their way lower they passed several small towers built around natural fissures and caves in the face. Covered with creeping weeds, walls sagging, their interiors were dark, forbidding caverns they did not investigate.

Once Revell fancied he heard something behind them, but though he paused to listen, the sound wasn't heard again and they restarted.

The path ended in a tower more substantial than the other, set with a gate made of timbers that could have been hewn only from whole trees. With some difficulty they scrambled up the inside of the tower until, by bracing their feet against the stubs of roof beams projecting from the stonework, they could look out over the parapet.

"Just one minute more, please, Major. Then we shall start back." Voke pointed down toward the pine-woods. "Look there."

Barely visible between the close-spaced trunks, Revell could make out shapeless bundles of cloth. Though the material had not yet begun to fade, already they were disappearing beneath the perpetual shower of needles and cones.

"A couple of dozen dead civies. So? It's hardly anything out of the ordinary in the Zone."

"At various other locations around the valley there are several hundreds more. And not just ordinary refugees. Many of them were members of deserters' gangs and other similar bandits."

"How come?"

Voke grabbed the opportunity offered by the major's curiosity. "Until yesterday this complex was under the command of a captain in the Royal Engineers. He had passed up promotion to stay here. He was too old for a field command and felt that this was the closest he could get. He was very reluctant to leave. He had been here since shortly after the outbreak of war. I had several long talks with him before he left, and of course he showed me over the whole site." Sensing Revell was about to look at his watch again, he went on faster, gesturing with wide sweeps of his arms so that Revell had to look up to see what he was indicating.

"During his time here a vast amount of ammunition and equipment had to be condemned. Either obsolete or at the end of its shelf-life, it could only be destroyed. There was in fact so much to be got rid of that an ordnance disposal section was stationed here permanently. I am not sure I remember all the figures correctly but in total I believe there to be about two thousand tons of shells, mines and bombs in the valley."

"I've seen waste on the sort of scale you're talking about." Revell's thoughts went back in time. "And not just in this war either. My uncle was in 'Nam during the last months. He said one of his regular duties was guard on a dock where they loaded ships to dump ammo in the gulf. There must have been thousands of tons shipped out."

"The waste here would have been in proportion."

"How does that explain those stiffs?"

"Very simple." Voke could not repress a chuckle. "He hated waste. There was a disposal site in the hills, but it was never used. Every unwanted mine, rocket, bomb, shell, and grenade has been used to construct a wide killing zone around the valley."

"We passed through a roadblock in a gorge about six, maybe seven kilometers from here. On the road out past the old mill. Was that some of his work? If it was, it may be formidable, but it wouldn't stall Soviet combat engineers for long."

"That?" Voke laughed outright this time. "My men laid that in a couple of hours. Think what it would have been like if we had been adding to it and refining it for two years."

"And it's all unofficial?" Revell tried to picture the ordnance experts using all their skill and ingenuity over the months and years to lay thousands, perhaps millions of mines and booby-traps.

"It is all very unofficial. The captain was very unhappy when he was ordered out. He wished to stay and see his plan put to the test. Of course, during his time here it was, on a fairly small scale."

"You mean refugee gangs like those down there." Revell found the whole concept fascinating but flawed, deeply. "Knocking off a few civies, even when they come at you mob-handed, is very different from trying to stop a Soviet Guards Army with all their resources."

"I am aware of that; so was the English captain. His theories were well tested. Gangs have tried to break in using vehicles and armor salvaged from the battle-fields. Once it was a single Challenger backed by several APCs. Another time a large group of deserters tried it with Leopards and T72s. All were stopped. And there is more than just explosive devices, machine-gun-rigged to sweep avenues of approach, gas shells, flame throwers . . ."

"What's that low concrete structure at the bottom of the cliff?"

"That was one of the captain's favorites; there are

two others positioned where they'd be appropriate. '
Although Voke knew exactly where to look and what
he was looking for, the camouflage of the bunker was
so good it took him a moment to pinpoint it.

"In there mounted on an old semi-trailer is a large
generator. There is a spring down there and the ground
is wet all the year 'round. Triggered by the approach of
infantry it will start up and push a very high voltage
through the ground."

Impressed, Revell tried not to sound it. "The instant
it starts up it'll stand out on the IR screen of every
Soviet tank and SP for miles, and be picked up
instantly by every Warpac electro-emissions detector
truck."

"So what, quite frankly?" Voke was not about to be
put down. "The concrete is two meters thick and the air
intake and exhaust pipe are well protected. It has fuel
for two-and-a-half days. Tell me, how would you walk
up and switch it off? It cost the captain his spirit ration
for two months to bribe helicopter pilots to lift in the
trailer and concrete, a load at a time."

Seeing the advantage he had gained, but sensing the
major was still not convinced, Voke pressed on. "You
must understand, that is just one tiny part, almost an
afterthought among the mass of defenses. And every
precaution has been taken against countermeasures. A
high proportion of the mines are resistant to the over-
pressures of fuel air explosives if the enemy uses that
method, and of course most of the ground is highly
unsuitable for the deployment of mechanical means of
clearance."

In the distance a gunship beat fast across country. It
trailed a tail of black smoke from its cabin. Too far
away to identify, Revell knew it had to be a Warpac
machine. No NATO helicopter in trouble would be
heading in that direction. The source of the smoke

suddenly showed a bright speck of flame and the chopper dipped from sight behind a ridge. Moments after, a puffball of dark smoke rose to be lost among the rainclouds.

"Look, Lieutenant, you've been trying to impress me and you've succeeded, but—and it's an insurmountable but—you're basing your defenses on the castle. That makes it a nonstarter. That great pile is a dream target for any gunner, and it wouldn't take long for some commie missile battery observer to pass the coordinates back to his commander, and then they'd bring the roof right down on our heads."

At the sound of a light footstep Revell swiveled around to level his combat shotgun. He checked himself in time. It was Andrea. He was frightened, relieved and angry all at the same time. "I told you to stay with the transport."

"It is as well I did not; there is something you should see."

Halfway back to the castle's postern door a body sprawled across a pile of rubble. Its legs made a partial dam to the water sluicing mud down the steps in a series of tinted cascades.

"Spetsnaz." Andrea made the word an obscenity and rolled the corpse onto its back with her heel.

The man's head lolled at an unnatural angle and blood still pulsed from a gaping neckwound so deep a sliver of spinal column showed between the parted tissue.

"I was following you down when I saw him. He came from one of the little towers. He was too intent on watching you to notice me. Come, there is something else."

They stepped over the body. Rain was washing spattered blood from its face, revealing Slavic features and eyes still open wide with the shock and terror of

81

sudden death.

Retracing their route, Andrea indicated the interior of a tower. "Look in there."

Jutting in a half-circle from the rock, the structure was in better condition than most. Clambering over the rotted remains of its broken door, Revell entered. It was dark inside and lightened only gradually as his eyes adjusted to the gloom. The two floors above had rotted through and their crumbling remnants littered the floor. By the sparse illumination shafting through an arrow slit he saw that the defensework had been built around a fissure in the cliff, which had been widened to form a small room.

Andrea pulled aside a debris-covered ground sheet. Beneath it lay a rolled sleeping bag, a stack of Russian ration packs, ammunition, and a radio. Quickly checking that it was not rigged with a booby trap, she flicked a switch. Turning the tuner, all that came through was a selection of oscillating whines.

"Those jammers of theirs are pumping out so much power it's even queering their own channels." A heap of dead branches in a dark corner caught Revell's attention and he pulled them aside. "I thought I might find one."

His actions revealed a small microwave dish complete with transcriber unit and headphones.

"What does this mean?" Voke examined the bowl of the satellite link.

"With this he could have kept in constant touch with his base. So long as he kept transmission time to a minimum there was virtually no chance of detecting him." Looking about, Revell went to a corner that appeared largely free of the rotten boards and joists. He dragged his boot back and forth, raking up the deep layer of compacted rubbish. At the second attempt he exposed the crushed remains of empty ration cartons and cans.

"There's a lot of them. So, Lieutenant, it would appear the Reds know all about Paradise Valley, and have done for a long time. That Special Forces man of theirs must have been hanging around to report on the movement of supplies and additions to the defense measures. If they've been taking that sort of interest, then I can tell you why that billion dollars' worth of gear hasn't been bombed. It's because they want to capture it intact, for themselves."

Voke almost had to run to keep up with the major. "Knowing about the minefields is not the same as clearing them." He got no response. "Wait, Major." He grabbed Revell and held him back at the postern door. "I know how vulnerable the castle is while still whole. The first task I had in the field was salvage work at Anholt castle, almost on the Dutch border. That Canadian battalion took shelter there during the second advance by the Soviet Second Guards Tank Army. We pulled out only two or three alive, out of six hundred."

"Then you see why this place is a death trap . . ."

"Yes, Major. That is why the top floors are already rigged with several thousand kilos of explosives. The ground and first floors have walls up to seven meters thick. On top of that our demolition will put a layer of rubble of not less than the same depth."

"Twenty feet of solid stone?" Even after years on the continent it still took Revell that moment of time to convert from metric.

For an instant Voke's hopes soared, then plummeted once more as the major's next question veered to a tack.

"How have you got the valley rigged for destruction?" Revell recalled the huge caverns filled with unfueled transport. "There's several acres of storage down there. Have you been as thorough with that?"

"We have had only six days. The fuel and ammunition dumps presented no problems but they are a long way from the transport and other less flammable equipment . . ."

"So if you tried to hold out and failed, the Reds are going to get a present of sufficient goodies to re-equip most of their front line in this sector."

"Not necesarily. Like the captain, I resorted to unconventional measures. I ran a pipe from the Av-gas tank at the landing ground to the air-conditioning inlets." Voke allowed himself a weak smile, even though he felt sure he had lost his argument over defending the valley. "Turning a valve wheel will flood every part of the complex with aviation fuel. We have wedged all the fire doors open; you may have seen that. Ignition will blast open the floor of the valley and turn it into a sea of fire."

CHAPTER TEN

"Have you a large-scale map of the area?"

With a reluctant sigh, taking a hand from the wheel, Voke reached into his jacket and handed one over. "Keep it. I shall not be needing it."

No one spoke as the Range Rover left the courtyard, negotiated the tight turn onto the road and started down. Voke because he had failed in what he'd hoped to do, Andrea because that was her way. Dooley's silence had yet another reason. When Andrea had gone off after the officers he'd spent some minutes in searching several of the castle's lower rooms, and found nothing worth looting.

Revell studied the map, making notes on the soiled margin, having to brace himself against the vehicle's roll on the steeply cambered corners in order to keep his writing legible.

For Dooley, even the sight of the three exhaust-pluming Bradleys in the village street, bringing with them the prospect of their being off soon, did not cheer him. He stayed sullen, head bowed. He'd thought the great castle would have held a fortune in valuables. Instead it had been stripped as bare as any refugee shanty town after an enforced move. Shit, how the hell was he supposed to build up funds for when he finally got out of the army? That creep Cohen* had been full of bright ideas, but he'd bought it before it could do him any good. So he'd lasted longer, big deal. His wealth at that moment amounted to maybe ten thousand in back pay and a handful of rings, gold teeth and assorted scrap gold jewelry worth perhaps another two thousand. Fuck it, if he was going to batten on some rich old dame in Miami then he'd need at least three times that for some smart threads, a flash car and the right sort of watch and accessories. He was jogged from his thoughts by their arrival back in the village, and the smell of cooked meat.

With a self-satisfied smirk, Scully was using an ash rake to drag the steak from the furnace. Each man in the company was given a part-burned slab weighing about a kilo, and a large ladleful of soft cooked vegetables. Nothing else would have roused them from sleep.

"All ready to move, Major." Hyde's report was rendered almost indistinct by the massive bite of sirloin he was chewing. "I've checked them over."

"Right. I'll want that one." He indicated an APC whose turret-mounted Bushmaster cannon had been supplemented by a pair of Stinger anti-aircraft missiles instead of the more usual twin TOW launch boxes.

"So you are going, then?" There was no pleading in Voke's voice but he could not keep his disappointment out of it.

"Not far. I want to meet the commander of that Rapier battery. If we're going to hold this valley then we'd better get our acts together."

Voke's wide grin exceeded by a considerable margin any he'd produced so far.

* * *

* Zone 2

"We need to buy time." Revell looked up. The cloud ceiling was down even lower. The topmost towers of the castle were now hidden for much of the time. "It's what they push up by road we have to worry about most, at present. If we can push that stone bridge down that should hold them for a while."

Voke looked at the map. The old mill was marked in also. "Of course when we blow the top off the castle much of the wreckage will fall onto the road, and of course the way into the valley will be blocked at the same time. It would take the heaviest earth-moving equipment some time to make them passable even for tanks."

"That's fine, but I'd like to hold them off a bit farther away than on our own doorstep. Have your men throw an assortment of mines and demolition gadgets aboard a truck. We'll try to get to the bridge before them and see if we can't blow it up in their faces."

"No problem, Major." Voke called in Dutch to one of his men, who immediately dashed for the church. "Before the order came to complete the setting of charges and evacuate we had prepared such a load. There was no point in unloading so we parked it under camouflage behind the church."

As he finished speaking there came the bellow of a powerful diesel engine starting, and out from between the buildings came the great slab front of a Scammel eight-wheeler.

Revell was relieved to see it was a version with an enlarged crew cab. "Perfect. Sergeant Hyde, pick two of our bunch and take two of the lieutenant's men as well . . ."

"I have two who are good with explosives, and can speak some English," Voke butted in.

"Okay." Revel cast an eye over the partially sheeted load on the Scammel's long cargo deck. "And grab a fifty-caliber for the ring mount and take a couple of Stingers if you can find the room. We'll blow the castle in . . ." He glanced quizzically at Voke.

"It is ready now. The detonator box is in the timber yard."

". . . one hour, so you'll have to shift. We daren't leave it longer."

"I'll take Burke as driver, and Ripper. I'd like Andrea, as well. She's got the best eyesight and her accuracy with a grenade thrower could make all the difference if we run into trouble." He watched the major's face at mention of the woman, but saw nothing to betray any emotion.

"Fine." The word did not come easily. Revell would have preferred her to stay with him. As he said it he saw her climb into the cab and struggle with the weight of the heavy machine gun Ripper handed up. "Remember, one hour. Once the fort comes down and blocks the road in, the only way back will be through the minefields. It's not really an option; I've seen them."

From a low growl as it idled, the motor sent its exhaust note rising in volume until with a last stab at the gas pedal Burke sent a spout of carbon-laced smoke high above the vehicle.

Not waiting to watch it go, Revell turned away. He pointed to the Bradley. "Thorne, driver. Clarence and Carrington in the turret." He paused, and held the map out toward Voke.

"I know you didn't have time to show me everything, but I made some notes in the margin of things we might need. If they're not already up there, can you move them inside an hour? If not, we'll have to manage without. Minutes after we press the button I want us tucked up inside."

Scanning the spidery writing, Voke nodded. "The grenades are there in large quantity, and terminal-guided rounds for the mortars." He pursed his lips. "I should have thought of thermal imagers, and I'll see if I can find some drum magazines for that ferocious shotgun of yours. Fire extinguishers and NBC suits and respirators I have not seen here, but with so many . . . I will put as many men as I can spare on to searching for them."

"Do your best. You seem to have everything under control." Revell added that, feeling the lieutenant deserved a pat on the back, but more especially because he had appeared so crestfallen at having those omissions brought to his attention. It must be hard for him too, to hand over when this might have been his first independent command in a combat situation.

It took the young Dutch officer only a moment to regain his spirits. As Revell boarded his transport he could already hear an indecipherable gabble of orders being yelled. As the door closed Scully risked a traumatic amputation and shoved a huge slab of steak into his hand. It was nearly cold, but his teeth were in it almost before he'd registered the fact.

Not taking the chance of bogging in the water-logged fields, Thorne stuck to the side road to the farm. Even so there were sections where the tracks slewed out of line when the loose surface failed to offer traction.

There was no conversation over the internal circuit, only the sounds of energetic chomping and swallowing. Revell welcomed the silence. It let him finish the food, and gave him a little time to think. He would rather have taken longer over his steak. How the hell Scully had done it he couldn't imagine; it tasted as good as the best he'd ever had. But then field rations made you feel that about any food eaten immediately after you'd been on them for a prolonged period.

For the short drive to the farm he'd almost relinquished responsibility. Thorne was a driver who could be trusted, though he was not a patch on that goldbricker Burke. And Clarence and Carrington in the turret were a duo he'd back against the best from any nation. So he could sit back, enjoy the aftertaste of the meat and relax. Relax—it was in truth a word whose meaning he'd virtually forgotten, and a practice he'd long gotten out of. Strangely apt that they were going to a farm. In just a few hours some, or most, or perhaps all of them would have bought one.

What they were doing was crazy, Revell knew that. Stark raving mad. Everything they knew, the type of barrage, the Spetsnaz infiltrator, the determination of the crew of that scout car to take a prisoner: they all pointed to a fixed determination on the part of the Warpac forces to capture the valley and all it held.

And to oppose them, what could he offer? A fifteenth-century castle, a hundred elderly pioneers, his own thirty or so battle-weary men, and one small RAF air-defense battery.

Why the hell was he bothering, why . . . He broke his train of thought as he sensed that both tracks had begun to slip, then heard water cascading against the steel-covered aluminum hull. For a moment the APC skidded bodily sideways, then the tracks found their grip again. It took him a few moments to regain his train of thought.

Yes, why should they hang on around here? They could have grabbed all the armor they needed, topped it off with a handful of combat engineer tractors and been fit to punch their way out of most anything the Reds would have had this far forward by now.

He couldn't even put it down to Voke's enthusiasm and persuasiveness. No, he'd stayed because he'd wanted to, because of his desire to dig his heels in, to turn around and face the Russians and show them they were going no farther. He and his men had taken enough, more than enough. If the politicians were content to fudge and compromise, he wasn't, not anymore. Europe was being nibbled away piece by painful piece. Well, not anymore, not any fucking more. They were going to be stopped, and they were going to be stopped right here.

Ripper stood with his upper body out of the roof hatch. He kept one hand on the traverse ring holding the Browning and the other he rested against the launch tube of the Stinger missile where it nestled between the back of the cab and the folded arm of the onboard loading crane. Often he had to duck to avoid low branches, and after each occasion had to clear foliage caught on the machine gun. All the time he kept watch for enemy gunships, working mostly by touch so as not to relax vigilance for a second.

Picking a shred of steak from between his teeth, Burke made appreciative lip-smacking sounds as he flicked it out through the side window. "Don't you tell him I said so, but considering it was done in a bloody crematorium, that meat were good." He shifted down through two gears as a sharp bend before an incline gave him no chance to take a run at it.

"Hey, Ripper." Burke shouted to make himself heard by their roof gunner. "You're always spinning stories. Tell me, how do I ever get people to believe me when I tell them I've had a dinner cooked in the oven of a crematorium?"

There was no answer, but Burke had hardly expected one. The Southerner was always touchy when anyone cast the slightest doubt on the veracity of his homespun stories.

"The bridge is just over this next rise. Take it slow."

All his training, all his experience, all his common sense told Hyde they should stop short of the crest and go forward on foot to reconnoiter the brow of the hill and what lay beyond, but their schedule was too tight to allow such caution.

At the back of the cab the two middle-aged Dutch pioneers were deep in whispered conversation. Hyde took no notice, until it appeared to become heated, and voices were raised. He turned in his seat.

"What's up?"

"We are having to argue, thank you."

"I can hear that. What about?"

Again there was a gabble of Dutch between the pair, then the other spoke up, scowling first at his compatriot. "I do not think we should blow the bridge. It is my thinking that we should instead drop the mill onto the road and bridge as the Russians pass."

In bottom gear Burke crawled the truck over the brow, and there below them the view was exactly as they'd last seen it.

"It's very tempting and I'd love to see it happen, but we haven't the time for fancywork like that. Okay, Burke, what are you hanging about for? Put your foot down."

The Scammel surged forward, and was doing sixty before the brakes were applied. For a moment it seemed the back end was going to break away, but Burke corrected before a skid could develop. "Where do you want it?"

"See if you can turn it around without any more bloody dramatics. Then park it out front of the mill." With the motor now warmed and running quietly, Hyde clearly heard a distinct new sound against the background thunder of the barrage.

Andrea heard it also. "Mines." She listened again. "And ammunition. The Russians have run onto the minefield where Taylor was killed."

They jumped from the truck, Hyde shouting to Burke before slamming the passenger door. "Get a bloody move-on, and don't ditch it."

"Fucking great." Burke took the precaution of speaking after the door had closed. "I've got a wagon longer than the road is wide and he wants me to try for the world's fastest three-point turn."

"If you reckon you ain't up to it, boy, I'll always have a go."

"Shit," Burke muttered under his breath. He'd forgotten Ripper still manning the anti-aircraft mount. "You just concentrate on what you're supposed to be doing. If we get jumped by a gunship we'll be in worse crap than if I drop a couple of wheels off the road."

Before the Scammel finally rocked to a halt facing back the way they'd come, boxes and cases were already being hauled from the back and broken open on the road.

The Dutchmen had made a hurried survey of the bridge and when they returned to Revell they were arguing again.

"So what is it now?"

Grudgingly they broke off their acrimonious exchange.

"It is stronger than we expected. With the charges we have they will need to be placed right underneath to be sure of bringing down the span. Anywhere else and . . ."

"How long will it take?" Even as he said it, Revell knew he'd made a mistake by addressing the question to both of them.

"One hour, not more . . ."

"At least two . . ."

"I say one . . ."

"So help me if you two start up again I'll leave both

of you here." Hyde's bellowed threat cut them short. He stabbed his finger into the chest of the older man. "We'll go for your idea. How do we drop the mill?"

He looked smug and was about to make a sarcastic aside to his companion when he saw the NCO's expression and decided against it. "That is a fuel-air bomb." Gesturing at a tarpaulin-shrouded hump aboard the Scammel, he began to unfasten a securing rope and then tugged at the heavy waterproof material.

It fell away to reveal a drab-painted cylinder about two meters long and half as wide. This was the first time Hyde had seen one close-up, though he'd witnessed their tremendous power from a distance.

"Get it emplaced as fast as you can. Time's running out on us." Taking up a heavy case of claymore mines, Hyde went to join Andrea and Burke, who were setting various anti-armor and anti-personnel devices to cover the approaches to the bridge.

They worked quickly, hardly needing the prompt provided by the distant reports of mine explosions. Cannon fire blended into the destructive chorus and told Hyde that the Russians were putting down a firestorm in order to blast their way through.

Hurried though the preparations were, they were thorough. Mines and launchers were set where they would be protected by the devastating sweep of shotgun mines and these in turn by smaller ones scattered among the undergrowth.

Those hidden most carefully were fed instructions to delay detonation until a certain number of armored vehicles had passed, in the slight hope of catching a command APC or even a bridgelayer. In any event their discharge over a period of time into the flanks of the enemy advance column would be bound to disrupt it, if not bring it to a halt while the area was cleared.

"Right. That'll have to do. Back to the truck."

The fat pressure tank was just being lowered behind a low wall beside the mill. In the shadow of the building, with the added embellishment of a few broken planks and sheets of corrugated iron, it blended in perfectly.

"About five minutes to make the connections, Sergeant."

"Six," muttered the other Dutchman.

"Seems a pity." Looking wistfully at the building, Burke gave a heavy sigh. "Whoever was doing that up must have been sick as a pig when they had to abandon it. A bit of sympathetic restoration and it would have made a lovely home. I could retire to a place like this. Look at the setting."

Andrea was arming small mines and throwing them to lodge among the crevices of rock below the bridge. "None of us will live long enough to retire."

That was virtually the first time she had ever spoken to him directly, and then it had to be that. Shit, Burke had been happy with his delusion. Why the hell did that hard-faced bitch have to bring him back to the reality of this nightmare?

CHAPTER ELEVEN

With his hands cold and wet it took Hyde a while to strip the insulation from the ends of wire. He handed them to the Dutchmen fussing about the still sentient bomb and clambered over the wall to the road, unreeling the small cable drum as he went. "In theory this should stop those commies dead, for a while anyway."

"I had an uncle who was big on theories." From his lookout post on the cab roof, Ripper watched the sergeant carefully conceal the first few meters of twin wire along the base of the wall, weighting it with chunks of rock and other litter.

"You want to hear about him?"

"We're going to anyway, aren't we?" Burke realized as soon as he'd said it that he'd made a mistake by drawing Hyde's attention to him.

"Since you're not doing anything,"—Hyde thrust the reel into their driver's hands—"you can run this up the hill to the crest and connect it to this." He placed a small but heavy matt-black box on top of the drum.

"Me? Run? All the way up there?"

"Don't piss about, move. And you can stay up there. I'll bring the transport."

Watching the ace goldbricker of the Special Combat Company break into an ungainly trot, Ripper tried hard not to giggle and almost succeeded. He failed completely to hide a laugh when a snag in the wire almost jerked Burke off his feet.

"You boys can listen if you're not too busy," Ripper called out to the pioneers. "Like I was saying,"—he shook his head and a bead curtain of raindrops flew from the brim of his helmet—"this uncle of mine, he used to screw with a crazy dame from the county funny farm. His theory was, if she ever upped and told on him, who was going to believe a crazy lady. And it worked a treat, for a couple of years. That is until the old shrink who ran the place got himself run over and squashed flatter than Scully's tenderized cat."

That he didn't appear to have anybody's attention didn't bother Ripper. He plowed on.

"The new boy they brought in was fresh out of medical school, full of new ideas and fancy notions. First thing he did was to halve the number of pills being swallowed. The old boy had kept all the crazies doped so he could have a quiet life. So just after that my uncle comes sneaking around, looking for his weekly blow-job. First he knows that everything ain't all it was is when his crazy lady throws a fit and bites the end of his pecker. I heard tell that his yell carried clear across to the next state."

"How did he explain that?" Despite himself, Hyde had to ask, though he knew he'd regret it.

"He kinda tied a bandage on it, only needed a little one, and goes staggering home. The fool tried telling my aunty that he lost it to a snapping turtle while crossing the creek. He must have been in shock because that was a mighty foolish story to come up with, seeing as how it had been dry for the best part of a month."

Andrea looked over the parapet of the bridge. The water was churned white as it butted the piers. A coping stone she dislodged disappeared with a noticeable splash in the turbulence.

'"Destructive." Despite what they were about to unleash on this idyllic spot, Hyde resented the act of minor vandalism.

"I have become used to destroying things. Perhaps it has become a habit." Shouldering her rifle, she sent a spray of tracer-laced bullets into a dovecote built in beneath the mill's eves.

The flaking cream-painted woodwork burst apart in a welter of blood and feathers and tumbling bodies as the rotten structure disintegrated under the impacts.

"You're bloody mad." It was a moment before Hyde could bring himself to comment on the senseless action.

"Of course. We all are, as insane in our decision to stay in the Zone as others are in their determination to get out. While we stay we kill. They would kill to leave. For me there is no distinction."

There was no inflection in her tone, and Hyde saw no change in her expression either as she clipped in a fresh magazine. To her it was a simple statement of what she saw as fact. But he couldn't debate it with her. Inside himself he could detect some of the same ingrained sense of combined resignation and determination to keep hurtling from one danger to another. As yet though, the urge had not stifled his instinct for self-preservation.

That he couldn't argue with what she said made him angry.

"I don't give a fuck about your dangerous urges to destroy everything about you, but don't do bloody stupid things that can drop the rest of the squad right in it, including me. If the commies have managed to push elements past that minefield they could be close enough to have heard that demonstration of mindless venom."

His words were undercut by a ripple of blended

cannon fire and secondary explosions. Though on that point his mind was put at rest, he still felt the rage burning inside him.

"Get in the truck." If he couldn't take it out on her, perhaps he could take it out on the enemy.

They needed a backup in case the fuel-air bomb didn't function. He'd already fused several bar mines, and now he laid them on the bridge, just over the brow where an approaching vehicle wouldn't see them until it was too late. Especially if they were closed down and racing to make up lost time.

But it wasn't very likely they'd charge onto so obvious an ambush site without checking it first. There were times, though, when the obvious could be the hardest to deal with. The Reds wouldn't be able to dispose fo the bar mines by gunfire for fear of damage to the bridge, and removal by hand meant more delay. Even then he'd chosen mines with a variety of anti-handling mechanisms whose assorted difficulties would tax the ingenuity of the most experienced assault engineers.

The last in place, he ushered the pioneers on board and climbed into the high-set driver's seat. "Right. We're ready to start killing again."

Looking straight ahead, Andrea's lips hardly moved. "I did not know we had ever stopped."

As the Scammel moved off, its tailboard clipped the brickwork and sent another of the coping stones end over end into the water.

With the truck parked just beyond the crest of the hill, they gathered about Hyde as he lifted the safety cover over the firing switch. His thumb was actually brushing the short slim stick of bright metal when they heard the approaching motor.

99

"Say, someone has their foot hard down." Ripper screwed up his eyes to be first to see the lead element of the Russian column. "Hell, that ain't no . . ."

"Oh God. No, no!" Hyde screamed at the top of his voice, but the effort was wasted. They were too far away.

The luck that had brought the bus around the minefield on its wildly circuitous journey had finally run out, and brought it to the bridge. There was no attempt to check its speed as it started across.

A massive explosion erupted beneath the driver's position. The front of the vehicle burst apart, propelled outward by a huge bubble of flame. Aluminum panels, seats and showers of glass fountained high in the air. A legless body soared in a slow cartwheeling arc to be lost in the river.

Its impetus carried the shattered bus onward and a second bar mine was triggered by the impact of the tangled metal. This blast hurled the vehicle sideways, to slew in a mass of sparks into and almost through the parapet.

Through his fieldglasses Hyde could see that half the length of the interior was piled with bodies, some moving feebly. The rear window had been forced out by the blast and lay in the road unbroken, complete even to its rubber and chrome strip surround.

Survivors began to climb from the wreck, some handing out blood-covered children to those who had been first to exit.

"Someone get the dressing pack from the cab." Hyde put down the control box. "Come on, we can't leave the poor buggers."

"No, we haven't the time. They will slow us."

"Piss off." Hyde tore Andrea's fingers from their grip on his arm. "They're your bloody people. Now get that first-aid kit . . ."

As she grudgingly obeyed, he looked again at the distant scene. Panic appeared to have set in among the injured civilians; some tried to claw their way back into the bus, others ran in frantic circles. One of them collapsed and lay still, and then another and another.

"What . . . ?" Panning the ground with binoculars he saw the cause. "The Reds are through the minefield; they're shooting the poor bastards."

From the partial concealment of a bend in the road, where it emerged from the woods, a lavishly camouflaged, squat-hulled tracked APC was hosing long bursts of machine-gun fire at the refugees.

Trapped on the bridge, their escape blocked by the hulk of their earlier transport, the women and children flopped to the ground. Even when the last was down the firing continued, sending hundreds of rounds into the heaped bodies until there was no more movement.

"No! They haven't seen us." Barking at Ripper, who was traversing the Browning, Hyde choked down his own urge to retaliate, but not his revulsion at what they'd witnessed. He checked his watch. They had still a few minutes to spare before they'd have to start back. So they'd be cutting it fine, so be it. He wanted to pay those shits back tenfold.

The reconnaissance vehicle edged cautiously forward. Very slowly and hesitantly the turret roof hatch opened and its commander appeared. He seemed unwilling to expose himself to danger and stayed so low that his nose appeared to rest on the turret top. The hatch made an angled roof over his head.

Traversing slightly, the turret brought its main armorment to bear on the bridge, but it was not with its 73mm gun that it opened fire, but with the anti-tank missile mounted above it. The commander ducked back hurriedly only a second before the launch.

Riding a bright tail of flame, a threshing coil of fine

wire unreeling behind it, the chunky broad-finned rocket soared along the road. Twice it veered abruptly to correct its trajectory.

Powerless to interfere, Hyde watched and recognized the lack of training or experience of the operator controlling the flight. A good man would have kept the transit time shorter by manipulating the controls more smoothly. The fact that he was going for a stationary target at short range should have made it a textbook exercise. He was not surprised when at the end of the missile's erratic course its impact was several meters short of the bus.

Lashed by the hail of fragments, the grotesquely stacked bodies leaped into macabre animation as the powerful warhead pounded a hole through the road deck.

Reappearing, the commander surveyed the damage. As the smoke drifted to give him a clear view, the vehicle's co-axial weapon again sent ripples of tracer at the bridge. A crew member climbed from the loader's hatch and began to reload the launch rail.

"A perfect target." Andrea sighted for her grenade thrower, then turned and snarled at the sergeant as he punched the weapon toward the earth. "Why?"

"Because, you stupid cow, the major may love you but I don't. With me you get away with nothing. You try something like that again and I promise I'll see that you go in the cage with all the other rubbish, the other East German border guards. Understand?"

His fist stinging from the hard contact with the barrel, Hyde was forcing himself to bide his time. From what he had seen of the overcautious, even timid, performance by the Russian advance guard he concluded they were either from a freshly formed unit, or an old one so leavened by replacement drafts as to be little better. And if he was right in that, then the losses

102

they'd sustained in their recent encounter with Voke's minefield would also be having a marked restraining effect on them.

But still it took an effort to hold back. He again had the control box in his hand. He longed to throw the switch, but after what they'd done simply blocking their route was not enough. Not by a long way.

That the bus had driven onto mines he'd laid he would have to live with for the rest of his life, but he'd never intended that as the outcome. The communists' act of shooting down those wounded women and children had been cold-bloodedly deliberate. It was not something he would shrug aside as a fortune of war.

"Better keep our heads down. They'll start a bit of probing in a minute."

"I'm already underground, Sarge. I'll send you a postcard with a kangaroo on it." Using an entrenching tool with more energy than was usual for him, Burke had hollowed a scrap at the roadside. Sparks flew from the tip of the entrenching tool as it struck flint below the topsoil. "I hope they don't use mortars. A couple of tree bursts and we're all fucked."

Ripper had to duck as heavy machine-gun fire stitched a path across the crest of the road. A ricochet zipped past, clipping the ring mount and sending splinters of fine lead particles into his hand. Blood welled instantly from the multiple flesh wounds.

"Aw shit." Wiping the back of his hand on his jacket, Ripper examined the mass of almost invisible punctures. "I'm real cheesed off with using eyebrow pluckers. Last one like this was in my face and I was shaving out bits of metal for a week."

He lowered himself into the cab and released the brakes, waiting for the Scammel to roll a little way before reapplying them. "Now the only thing they're gonna see of me is the lead I'm throwing."

Its tracks fanning spray and mud, a T84 rocked to a halt beside the APC. Hyde could make out the slab features of an officer who appeared immediately to start shouting at the APC's reluctant commander. The tankman unholstered a pistol and waved it wildly.

"He's giving the poor bugger hell, and I bet it's not for killing civies either."

Perhaps it was his imagination, but Hyde thought he saw the commander's face pale as he reluctantly climbed out and was clearly ordered to stand in full view on the tank's engine deck.

"Wouldn't Clarence enjoy a target like that." Hyde could imagine the quick precision with which their sniper would have eliminated both men. He would hardly have needed to move to shift the graticle from his first victim to his second.

"If he could be patient he would only have needed to fire once." With her sharp eyes Andrea could see almost as clearly what was happening as the NCO with his aided vision. "Watch for a moment and you will see what I mean."

The tankman appeared to be working himself to a frenzy, making extravagant gestures with the pistol. Suddenly the APC's commander crumpled onto the deck of his machine.

"Oh jeez, will you look at that." Ripper heard the faint report of the shot. "What the hell can we expect from them if they do that to their own?"

CHAPTER TWELVE

"The Reds can jam us for all they're worth, use any electronic countermeasures that take their fancy. It won't make the slightest difference. We'll still hack them down as fast as they appear."

Revell tried not to appear so, but he was skeptical of the claims made by the lieutenant in charge of the Rapier battery.

"Come on, I'll show you." From a corner of the main barn, Lieutenant Sutton pointed out the dispositions of his men and equipment. "I hate to disappoint you but I should tell you we don't have a battery here, nothing like it, just part of two detachments.

"Actually just two launchers, but God knows how many reloads. But we also scrounged a towed Vulcan system from that marvelous Aladdin's cave down there. That's over by those old hayricks. One of the launchers is by the tractor shed and the other at the edge of that little copse higher up the hill."

"Wouldn't you be better throwing in your lot with us?"

"Very kind of you, Major, but no thanks." Sutton waved to one of his men who was leaving his sandbagged post. "I say, where are you . . ."

The man waved a shovel.

"Oh, yes, all right. Well, have a good one." Again

Sutton turned his attention back to Revell. "As you can see, we're very well dispersed and the component parts of a towed Rapier system really do make a jolly small target when they're spread about. Plus of course we've dug in the generators and roofed their little houses over with turf to reduce their IR signature to almost zero. Would have been nice of course to have had some of those lovely armored mobile versions instead. Then we could have flitted about and confused the commies even more, but what we've got will do."

"How will you manage with our radar blinded, though?" Revell was surprised by, could even admire the skill with which the launchers and their ancillary equipment had been blended into the countryside, but for days his men had been hit by Soviet air strikes when jamming had rendered useless the most sophisticated air-defense systems.

"You infantry chaps are all the same—got this sort of blind faith in technology, and when you find out it's not working for some reason you dash about like chickens with your heads off. No offense, of course."

The slightly sheepish grin on Revell's face was sufficient unarticulated evidence of the truth of that.

"If they persist in jamming, then we'll simply wait until we can actually see them. Jets right down on the deck or choppers actually touching down, it's all the same. Boom, instant wreckage. Mind you, if they come at us mob-handed it might present the odd problem."

"What do you call mob-handed?" He didn't want to, but Revell had to ask the question.

Lieutenant Sutton considered for a moment. "Well," —he paused again—"when we were up near Hanover, with the same number of launchers, we did take out five of those damned noisy helicopters inside three minutes. We can certainly engage and make problems for that number. But I tell you what, I have an absolute maniac

106

of a gun-layer on the Vulcan who'd make sure that if a chopper did touch down nothing would get out of it alive. Does that set your mind at rest in any way?"

Overwhelmed by the RAF officer's aura of self-confidence, Revel could think of no answer. "Have you got land lines to the castle?"

"No, but then they'd hardly survive your dropping a few thousand tons of brickwork on them, would they? If you get lonely you'll just have to wave."

The lieutenant's sense of humor was beginning to wear somewhat thin on Revell, but he realized the young officer might be using it as cover for nerves. "You can take care of your own close-in defense?"

"I've forty men altogether. Working the launchers with minimal crews I can put most of them into my perimeter defenses, and of course I've got the Vulcan. My problem has been persuading my chaps that not all of them can have GP machine guns. They all came back from that dump toting M60s and draped with more ammo belts than an army of Mexican bandits."

Across the valley the castle still stood intact. It looked as though it had been there forever and as if it would continue to be, as if the very landscape had been designed around it. But there was nothing in the Zone that could be regarded as permanent, not even the landscape itself.

"I have to get back. Good luck." Revell held out his hand.

Sutton hesitated a second, then accepted it. "You too, but it's the Russians I feel sorry for. You wouldn't believe the number of rounds we've got for the Vulcan."

The top of the hill had been raked by cannon and machine-gun fire that had pulverized the road and slashed the pines to ribbons. There had been no need for Sergeant Hyde to insist on fire discipline. It would have been instant death for any of them to raise their heads and attempt a puny retaliation.

The probing fire slackened, and then ceased. Cautiously Hyde looked out, the act made less dangerous by the masses of piled bark and cones. "Here they come."

A dismounted squad of infantry were moving toward the bridge. They crouched low, automatics leveled. Behind them came a pair of tracked infantry carriers. Half out of the open rear-deck hatches stood more soldiers, tightly clasping rifles and grenade launchers.

"I should think it will be . . ." Hyde gauged distances, "right about now."

The second armored personnel carrier was suddenly hidden by a shower of white sparks. Fire belched from the open hatches and its passengers were enveloped by scorching pillars of vivid flame. Hidden from sight within the pall of gray smoke, the APC shuddered off the road into the trees, and then simply dissolved in a tremendous explosion as its ammunition ignited.

Surging forward, the T84 opened up on the mill. A billowing mass of white dust marked the violence of the first impact. Slowly, a section of the building's roof sagged and tiles slid from their place to shatter on the road and bounce from the roof of the bus. A second shell followed but passed clean through the structure without exploding.

Machine guns and light cannon lashed out at the mistaken target. Bullets raked the walls and the few windows. Glass shattered and lengths of scaffolding were wrenched away and thrown down to land in a wild tangle.

Another mine was triggered, and this time it was the squad of infantry who took the force of it, every man being mown down by the inescapable blast from a claymore.

Trying to press on, the Russians brought on their own destruction. A fragmented steel scythe swept away another squad.

The T84 stopped and its commander waved on more APCs. The mines concealed among the trees silently ticked off the numbers, and then the verges were lit with a series of yellow stabs of flame.

Pierced by a jet of molten metal, another tracked carrier began to burn, its fuel tank's contents boiled by the stream of plasma. Hatches flew open, but by the pressure of furnace-hot gasses, not by human hand.

With a track blown off and its turret torn away, an APC swerved into another alongside, crushing its hull and riding onto it.

Surviving crew leaped clear and made for the supposed safety of the trees. The first to reach them found no safety there. Shotgun mines cut them down and left those who had been lucky enough to escape that fate, as well, cowering in confusion in the middle of the road.

Another tank that moved forward shuddered under an impact against its turret rear, but boxes of retroactive armor neutralized the missile warhead's power and it kept going. It moved in alongside the first T84 and both began to pound the far bank of the river.

"Come on, you bastards, make a try for the bridge." Hyde had forgotten time. Finger poised over the activating switch, he waited for an attempt to force a passage past the mill. "They want that bridge." He held up his hand and made a small gap between thumb and finger. "I want them to be that close to thinking they've got it."

Revell knew that Hyde's section would not be back

on time. There was no mistaking the growing sounds of battle from the direction of the bridge. The sweep hand of his watch was brushing away the last moments to the expiration of the hour.

They were heard by Clarence also, and his thoughts as he listened were very different from the major's. It was two weeks since he'd had a live target in his sights. He wished he were with the section getting to grips with the enemy, actually fighting, not forever standing about waiting for something to happen. And then frequently being disappointed.

The last fractions of the hour ticked by, and still Revell did not close the firing circuit. It was Andrea who made him delay. He couldn't bring himself to be the one to cut her off from hope of survival.

All the men, pioneers and combat company, stood in the village street, turned to look at the castle. There was something else they were looking for as well, but it didn't appear. A man had been posted to watch, to signal with a flare if he spotted the ambush group on their way back.

Handing the detonator box to Voke, Revell knew it could not be his act that sealed Andrea's fate.

Voke lifted the safety cover. "It is a pleasure to do this for more than the reason you might think, Major. The castle was marked as an auxiliary storage facility for the main dump. Once it is destroyed I shall have no difficulty explaining what happened to a great deal of clothing and equipment. I shall write it off as lost in battle."

Five minutes past the hour, and still no flare, nor any diminution of the cannon- and automatic-weapon fire. If anything it appeared that the tempo of the exchange was increasing.

"It must be done, Major." Voke looked to the American for confirmation. He waited for an answer-

110

ing nod before crushing his thumb down hard.

There was a delay, a short one, as the impulse ran through the great length of wire. To Revell it was an eternity. A thousand times he'd wished he could be free of his obsession with Andrea, and now with this he was, and in his heart he knew it wasn't what he really wanted. With this he was not just cutting himself off from her, he was signing her death warrant.

A long plume of dust was driven violently from an upper window of the castle. It came out horizontally, its formation making no concession to the wind and rain until it had sprouted fifty meters from the wall. Then in rapid sequence it was joined by a dozen more. Feathers and bursts of the same leaden cloud gouted out from between tiles on the roofs.

The crack of the firing of the first charge was lost among the ripple of others that followed. With an almost absurd slowness a massive featureless slab of wall began to bulge as turrets began to collapse. It brust outward and a monstrous pall of dust rose to engulf the whole structure. As it rose it was stirred to wild turbulence by turrets and towers plunging to destruction inside it.

It did not rise far, beginning to spread in the wind and be beaten down by the rain before it was twice the height of the now-scattered walls. Lighter particles fanned out to merge with the stormclouds; most of the airborne debris began to roll down the vertical walls of rock, following the huge slabs of shaped stone and giant splintered roofbeams that were already settling at their foot. A dull rumbling was all that had accompanied the spectacular avalanche, and that died quickly, without echo.

Standing aside from the others of the audience, Boris pushed his balled fist against his mouth and bit hard on his knuckles until they bled. He felt as though his mind

111

were going to explode, it was in such a turmoil. Overriding everything though was fear. That was it: sheer, stark-naked terror. Always until now the communists had been in front of them in attack, or more often behind them in pursuit. With this action they had deliberately cut themselves off, locked themselves into a position that, no matter what delaying tactics were employed, would shortly be surrounded.

His hand went to his holster and unconsciously he unfastened it and felt the comforting bulk of the Browning automatic. He pulled it out and released the magazine. Ignoring the blood running down his fingers, he thumbed a round out, rolling it between his stained fingers. Deliberately he put the bullet into his breast pocket. He would save that one for himself.

CHAPTER THIRTEEN

From the scanty concealment of the litter on the road Sergeant Hyde watched the Soviet combat engineers working to clear the mines. Smoke from burning vehicles masked much of their activity, but twice he saw fountains of dirt that marked where two of them at least had not been using sufficient caution.

He could have slowed the process even more with a few well-directed bursts, but that would have drawn attention to him and his section. As it was, the T84s sometimes came uncomfortably close with the random suppressive shelling of their side of the river.

"I think they're doing that on a 'just in case' basis." Hyde spat soil that stank of raw explosive. "If they thought they were really facing an opposed crossing they'd have called down artillery support by now."

Coming forward in short rushes from cover to cover, a squad of assault engineers reached the bridge and, edging along hugging the low parapet, they reached the back of the bus. The last few meters they came on more confidently, walking on the bodies of the dead. They all froze, and then laughed when one of their number slipped on a blood-covered arm and landed abruptly on his backside, without triggering any mine or booby-trap.

"They're getting a bit cocky." Burke checked that he

had a round chambered in his rifle, then took out another magazine and laid it by his side.

Timing was everything. Hyde subdued the strong urge to trigger the fuel-air device immediately, and waited. It was then they heard the dull rolling rumble of the castle's destruction. There was quite literally no going back now.

A Russian engineer climbed into the bus and worked his way forward, threading between the stacks of mangled seats and bodies. Reaching the front, he scanned the rest of the bridge, then called on the others before jumping down and making for the mill.

His squad followed, passing gingerly between the jagged projections of metal and plastic that was all that remained of the passenger vehicle's front third.

By this time their attitude was casual, almost lighthearted with relief at another dangerous task completed, and they stopped and took out cigarettes.

They sat on the parapet, legs dangling above the broken remains of a bar mine. Split open by flying wreckage, its contents lay scattered and useless.

Grinding and rumbling its way past the battle tanks came the huge angled 'dozer blade of an armored engineer's vehicle. The turretless machine lurched through a turn, and as it reached the bridge, elevated a powerful-looking hydraulic arm. As it extended, it deployed a four-pronged grab that swayed wildly from side to side. A final, less violent, course correction and its tracks bit into and climbed onto the civilian corpses, tearing them and crushing them into the road surface.

The T84s moved up behind it, waiting to cross, and with the mines in the woods at last neutralized, more APCs threaded their way between the ruins of those that still blazed and were decorated with the burned remains of their crews.

"Looks like a lot of our stuff down there." Burke

noted the several captured NATO transports among those backed up at the rear of the tanks.

"So the major was right." In a row beside her, Andrea placed five 40mm grenades. She hesitated before returning one of them to her belt. Long before she had taught herself that overkill was wasteful, but it was a lesson that by self-discipline she had to keep drumming home. "If the Soviets are using captured equipment in the front line, they must be suffering shortages that would make the capture of the valley very tempting."

Casually, not out of suspicion or interest, a Russian strolled to the wall concealing the pressurized container. He looked around, then swung over the wall and, planting himself with feet apart, began to unfasten to relieve himself.

Hyde threw the switch and then dropped the box to grab the glasses from Burke, snapping the strap. A moment to refocus . . . and there it was.

A gushing cloud of sickly yellow vapor enveloped the Russian and he collapsed from sight. It expanded, doubling and redoubling in circumference. It grew to the height of the mill and to a breadth that encompassed the bridge and the leading tank.

"It ain't gonna work." Ripper watched the rapid expansion of the fuel-air mixture, saw it start to spill over the sides of the bridge.

For that instant Hyde thought he was right, the automatic ignition sequence had failed . . .

A monstrous concussion lifted the sergeant and jammed the binoculars savagely hard into his eyes. The force broke open scar tissue that squirted tears of blood down his cheeks.

Mill, bridge and tanks were hidden inside an orange fireball of colossal size. From it hurtled a blast that snapped trees and stripped the ground about them down to bare earth. As it reached its maximum extent it began to rise, sucking upward with it masses of forest debris.

It revealed the old mill, slates and window frames and doors gone, slowly twisting to the right and foldling in upon itself. Tons of brick broke away to reveal the skeleton of its machinery, and then the tall structure was collapsing faster into a pile that could not be contained within its narrow site.

Much of it deluged across the bridge, sweeping before it the flame-sprouting hull of the combat bulldozer. Every external fitting had been ripped from it, even its tracks. There was no longer any parapet to offer resistance, and with the wreckage of the bus it was tumbled over the edge and down into the raging water. Violent clouds of steam leaped after the ascending fireball as the furnace-heated hull of the 'dozer and the semi-molten shell of the bus made a temporary dam.

Such a weight of water was not to be resisted for long. Beating spray high above the bridge, first the passenger vehicle and then the military were swept away.

Save perhaps as calcinated fragments, the Soviet engineers had been blasted from existence. There was no sign of life from either of the T84s. Both had obviously had their turrets dislodged and they now sat at odd angles to the hulls. Dark smoke wreathed from every hatch and port. And in front of both lay their broken tracks, stretched out almost to their full length, illustrating how far they had been shoved back by the force.

The mountain of rubble and giant cast-iron and oak gears and wheels were settling on the bridge when that overburdened arch began to produce harsh grating sounds interspersed with sharp cracks as load-bearing blocks fractured and crumbled to powder. When it

116

failed it happened suddenly, the whole width of the span falling almost in one piece.

All of them dazed by the violence they had experienced, they stumbled back to the Scammel and clambered aboard.

"Where to?" Wiping dirt and grime from his face, Burke found he'd been cut by flying splinters.

"There's only the one road, back toward the castle."

"It's not there anymore, Sarge. You heard it go down, same as we all did."

"It's still the only road we've got. Maybe there'll still be a way back into the valley." Hyde dabbed at the cuts about his eyes with a wad of cotton torn from a field dressing. It came away saturated. "And if there's not we'll find some farm track that'll enable us to put a bit more distance between us and the Reds. Maybe that one." He pointed at a narrow dirt road that was almost hidden beneath the trees. "Remember where it is in case we have to double back to . . ."

Burke had to brake hard. A tree lay across the road. He was reaching for his M16 even as he noticed that its base was sawn through.

A burst of automatic fire slashed across the cab front and punched star-edged holes in the windshield. There was a cry of pain from the back seat and blood spattered the cab's interior.

Wheels locked, the Scammel screeched to a stop and its doors flew open. Another single shot rang out from the woods and a Dutchman framed in the doorway let go his hold and pitched onto the road.

Firing from the hip on full automatic, Andrea sent the contents of a magazine spraying across the trees. From the ring-mounted fifty-caliber above the cab, Ripper hosed armor-piercing incendiary rounds into the woods. His face was set in a grimace of pain and he kept his finger down hard, not ceasing until he had a

117

stoppage. He cleared it fast, finished that belt and quickly reached for another.

Hyde saw the powerful rounds chewing and slashing the standing timber, and added the weight of his own fire. They'd been caught by surprise, completely off guard, but had fallen instantly into the anti-ambush procedure that was drilled into them. "It's coming from over by that forked tree." He ducked into cover to reload and came out again to see the girl send a grenade toward the area he'd indicated.

The white phosphorus burst in a dazzling spray of white smoke and golden globules of chemical fire. A scream soared up the audible scale and off it.

More automatic fire came from beneath the trees, but it was ragged and passed overhead. Burke hosed the general area of the direction from which it came and as he fired his last shot, Ripper laced the spot with a whole belt fired without pause. There came a yelp of pain and the sound of a body thrashing on the ground.

From within the smoke generated by the grenade staggered a blackened travesty of what had once been a human. It clutched an AK-47 that fountained a sparkling ball of incandescence from its ignited magazine. Two steps were all it managed; then it toppled and lay still.

"Is that it?" About to bring down the dying man, Burke held back when he saw it wasn't necessary. It passed through his mind how weird it was that seconds before the man had been trying to kill him, yet when he'd appeared in that appalling condition he'd been prepared to put him out of his misery.

In answer to his question a burst of sub-machine-gun fire punched bark from the pines about them.

"Can anyone see him?" Hyde tried shifting to a better position and had to dive back when the move attracted another and more accurate short burst. "Come on, someone must have seen where that came from." Hell, they had a Russkie column behind them that by now was mad as could be, and they were being held up by one cunt behind a tree. He looked around. Andrea was close by, looking to him and toying with a grenade.

"Put two H.E. into that tangle over there, fast as you can."

She nodded, slipped the shell in, sighted and fired in one fluid motion. A second was on its way before the first struck.

The explosions, both tree bursts, blended together, and as their sound died away it was followed by the drawn-out creaking and splintering of falling timber.

"Don't shoot, don't shoot."

A scrap of cloth was waved from behind a toppled fir.

"Look, I'm unarmed. I'm coming out."

A Sterling sub-machine gun was tossed out, followed by a pistol and a long glittering hunter's knife.

Taking no chances, Hyde stayed behind cover. The figure that stepped cautiously from among the smoking fragment-scarred trees was heavily bearded and dressed in a style that betrayed its inspiration as the uniform of several nations, but the predominant effect was British.

Moving his weight nervously from one foot to another, the man held his hands high. His fingers clenched and unclenched spasmodically.

Seaching him quickly and expertly, Hyde emptied his belt of spare magazines and hurled them away. He was about to do the same with a well-made clasp knife, but changed his mind and put it in his pocket instead.

"Can I put me arms down now?"

The gesture from Andrea made him jerk them back up again.

"Look, I'm sorry if there's any harm done. We thought you were commies. Just doing our bit you might say."

"Who are you with?" Hyde more than suspected he knew the answer before he asked it. He wasn't surprised when the man became vague and evasive.

"Yeah, well, we're not sort of like with anybody, not as such, that is, if you see what I mean."

Walking behind their prisoner, Hyde let him worry for a moment and then barked an order. The man sprang to attention, though even as he did it he tried to stifle the reflex reaction. He looked furious with himself as he tried to assume a more relaxed stance, but it was too late.

"Give us a break, Sarge, you know what it's like; we aren't all fucking heroes."

"Put your hands behind your back." To emphasize the instruction, Hyde jabbed his rifle forward, making sharp contact with the base of the man's spine.

With strips of cloth his hands were tied tight, and as an added measure were fastened to his belt. Hyde jerked hard on them to make certain the bonds were secure. "There's no breaks for you, chum, but I'd like to give your neck one at the end of a rope."

Knowing that he was not about to be shot out of hand, the deserter gained confidence. "No chance of that, Sarge; only the Reds top their own."

"Who were the other two?"

"Just a couple of Turks I fell in with. The ambush was their idea. Honest, Sarge, they were the bosses. I told . . . I thought you were commies."

"Clever of you then, if they were running the show, to wrangle the safest position for yourself, wasn't it?" Turning away in disgust, Burke went over to where the second victim of their return fire had fallen.

The frantic initial thrashing had slowed, but he went forward cautiously and was parting some bushes when a single shot rang out. Burke ducked, hesitated, then

120

stepped behind the undergrowth.

An ugly splashing, gurgling noise was audible. He knew what it signified and relaxed his guard. Unable to withstand the agony of the stomachwound from which his punctured intestines protruded, the Turk had finally managed to get the barreltip of his AK into his mouth and pull the trigger.

In the fading light Burke couldn't see it, but he knew the pulsing blood would be coming from a massive wound in the back of the ambusher's skull. Turning back toward the others, Burke made a cutting motion with his finger across his throat.

"Let's get him out of here." Hyde pushed their captive back toward the truck, and as he started, he heard a shuffling noise coming from the near-impenetrable pine forest to their rear.

"Hold fire." His shout came just in time.

With Andrea and Burke he watched as the file of young girls hobbled into view. That was the fastest they could move with their ankles fettered, wrists tied and nooses of thick rope joining each to the one behind.

Their prisoner whined excuse and apology without being asked.

"They'd have died if we hadn't rounded them up. It was the Turks' idea; we were going to take them somewhere safe. We haven't touched them . . ."

"Just a humanitarian act, is that it?" Not waiting for an answer, Hyde reversed his rifle and crashed it into the back of the renegade's legs, sending him sprawling. "You bloody scum."

CHAPTER FOURTEEN

"No, no. It was the other two. I just went along with them." Curling himself into a fetal position as protection from further blows, the deserter pleaded and begged.

"How long would they have lasted on their own? Oh shit, we haven't hurt them. I told you, we haven't touched them." Getting no response he began to panic. "Well, the Turks did, not the girls. I wouldn't let them touch the girls. There was this boy, he wasn't right in the head, they took him off one night. They came back without him. Fuck it, you know what those animals are like."

He paused, uncurled to look up at the three rifle barrels directed at him. "We thought you were commies. One of those stupid Turks had bogged our transport, right over the tracks. All we wanted was your wheels, we'd have let you go . . ."

Burke could sense the man's fear. They made eye contact and the deserter must have seen his thoughts, because he immediately switched to Andrea, but he found no comfort, no hope there.

He hadn't realized one of his captors was a woman. He directed his appeal at her. "We were taking them somewhere safe, that's all. You've got to believe me."

"I do not believe you." Her finger eased back against

the trigger.

"No, no, no. Ask the girls; they'll tell you. We haven't touched them. Go on, ask them, ask them."

"You hear these things, but you don't believe them." It took an effort for Burke to resist the temptation to empty his weapon into their cringing prisoner. "There was a rumor last year that a few of the bandit gangs had started a slavery business, supplying girls for the Russians and houses in the bigger camps, but you never want to believe things like that." His attempts to keep his temper in check faltered and then failed. He brought his heel down hard on the man's thigh.

"No, come on, lads, queen's reg's." He squirmed, fighting off the blow. "I got to have a proper court-martial and all that . . ." He gagged as another kick took him in the chest.

"That's enough." Hyde grabbed the man and hauled him to his feet. "You'll get your court-martial, but I've half a mind to hand you over to them."

It was not as much a threat as it should have been. Huddled together, the girls looked too frightened and bewildered to be thinking of revenge.

"I suppose you just happened across a group who were all in their teens and early twenties, did you?" Hyde found he was breathing heavily, not out of exhaustion but through forcing down his natural instinct to unleash another blow.

"Look, I told you, it was the Turks who did all the dirty work." He searched their faces, almost indistinct in the gloom. "I just told them the kids didn't fetch decent money and the old ones would never make it . . ." It was too late to retract and he knew it, but tried out of sheer terror, and in that he made the mistake of appealing to Andrea.

"You tell them what it's like . . ." He froze, the rest of the sentence stillborn. There was a knife in her hand.

Hampered by his bonds his recoil was too slow and he took the slashing attack across the face. The razorlike blade opened his cheek from below the left eye to the center of his chin, splitting both lips. The flesh peeled aside, exposing white bone and muscle tissue before being hidden by a gush of dark blood.

"That's enough." Only Hyde's intervention prevented a second a more deadly lunge. Clamping down on Andrea's wrist, the struggle brought their faces close together.

The proximity of the sergeant's horror-mask of a face had no effect on Andrea. "Let me finish him."

"We're taking him back. If his time's up, then he'll buy it when the Reds catch up with us. You're not going to play judge, jury and executioner like you have before. Get those girls to the truck and try not to frighten them any more than they are already."

Bewildered and bedraggled, the captives let themselves be led by Burke while Andrea sawed at each of their halters in turn. Even when released from that restraint, they kept their place in line like horses long used to being tethered and not knowing how to behave with a free rein.

"I sure am glad you're back. I were thinking I was gonna bleed to death." Ripper lowered himself down onto the seat and slit the blood-stained material to expose the bullet hole in his leg. "For the first time ever, I wish Sampson was with us."

Burke examined the neat entry wound and made Ripper turn on his side while he looked for an exit hole. "It's still in there. You got lucky—no breaks, no arteries cut. I'm afraid you'll live." As he applied a dressing he looked into the back of the cab.

The Dutchman had been hit twice in the head, through the left eye and the center of the forehead. His blood saturated the bench seat.

Taking the body by its feet, Hyde hauled it out of the cab and it flopped on top of the body of its compatriot. "Get the girls up on the back. Throw those pallets off to make room."

Realization of the change in their situation was dawning among the young women, and when Burke came to help the last few climb up, several tried to throw their arms around him to demonstrate their relief and gratitude. He was embarrassed by the emotive display and pushed them from him, but not hard, muttering, "Bitte sehr, bitte sehr, don't mention it, don't mention it."

A short blond girl, chocolate-box pretty even under layers of dirt streaked by tears and with her long hair matted, stroked Burke's arm as she waited, last to board. Over and over she quietly repeated, "Danke schon, danke schon." As he went to lift her she kissed him on the cheek, lightly and quickly, and then averted her eyes as for an instant they caught his.

"Ah reckon I've seen near enough everything now," Ripper chortled. "Didn't reckon I'd ever see a good old boy like you brought out in a blush." He just couldn't resist the dig at their driver as he climbed back behind the wheel.

"One more word out of you,"—Burke crashed into first, then remembered his cargo and let the eight-wheeler crawl forward to mount the fallen timber slowly—"just one more, and you'll have a matching hole in the other leg."

In a series of almost slow-motion lurches that brought stifled screams from their frightened passengers, the Scammel wallowed over the obstruction.

"There's no choice now." Hyde shoved their prisoner along the back seat until he was seated in the still-solidifying blood, prodding him with the barrel of his Browning. "We can't go dragging those kids around

125

the battlefield like this crud was prepared to do. We've got to get them back to the others. At least in the castle there's food and water. Even if in the next few hours it could have a horde of Reds hammering on the door."

"How the hell are we supposed to do that?" Burke was using every facet of his driving skills to keep up the best pace he could while not subjecting the girls to more danger and discomfort than he could help. "There's supposed to be the granddaddy of all minefields right around the place."

"I don't know." Hyde cocked the pistol and held it to the deserter's head as the man tried to turn so as to bring his bound hands onto the door catch. "Please do. If the fall doesn't kill you, I will."

Moving from the door, the man changed his tactics. "You've got to do something about my face. I'm bleeding to death." His words came out distorted by the wound. With each word fresh blood welled from his split lips and dripped into his lap.

"You concentrate on staying still and quiet." Hyde set the safety on the pistol and lowered it, but didn't lower his guard. "And don't worry about that little cut. Facial wounds are rarely fatal." His scar tissue crinkled in mockery of a smile. "I speak from experience."

"Shit." Ripper stared in disbelief. "It looks like they nuked the place."

Through the trees they glimpsed the castle, or the stump of it that remained. Only where it joined the rock was there here and there a section of wall that was recognizable. Dust still hung thick in the air about it and huge slides of rubble had cut swaths through the trees on the lower slopes.

"So come on, tell me." Burke braked to a stop just short of where a torrent of broken stone had obliterated the road. Piled to three times the height of the cab, from it poked jagged lances of roofing timber.

126

"Come on, Sarge, I'm asking. How do we get back to the others through this lot?"

Andrea craned her neck to survey the cliff. "I think I may know a way."

Only the great gateway remained recognizable. Every other section of wall was shattered, and topped with many meters of broken stone. Abandoning their transport on the road, Revell and Voke split their men into parties to clear a way back into the cellars, and to erect firing positions atop the mountain of rubble, and in those ground floor rooms that had survived being crushed.

The dust lay knee-deep and was being turned into an adhering slurry that soon coated them from head to foot, transforming them into gray specters.

Revell led a group through the huge hall, now partially filled with rubble where its massive roof timbers had failed to withstand the vast weight of the collapse of the main tower.

They were lucky; the smaller rooms beyond had survived and the door to the cellar steps was clear. Voke caught up with them as Revell groped for the generator switch.

Flickering fitfully at first, the machinery made hard work of starting up in the dust-laden atmosphere. It hung so thick that it made pearly halos around the lights.

Voke held a cloth over his mouth and nose to filter the worst of the choking particles. "This is the only way that is clear. It would take much time and heavy lifting equipment to break through to the other entrances. The demolition charges may have been larger than was truly needed."

"I agree." Revell spat to clear his tongue of cloying

grit, and failed. "It was definitely rather overdone."

Together they toured the warren of cellars. There had been roof-falls in two of the smaller rooms, but most, and all those with the weapons and ammunition, had survived intact.

They found Sampson already at work in the improvised dispensary, checking supplies, laying out isntruments and dressings on a cloth-covered stool beside a rough pine table.

"All I need is a couple of well-starched nurses and I'm ready to start up my own practice." He opened a case of morphine ampules. "Looks like I shan't have to tie anybody down this time."

"Let us hope that none of this will be needed." Voke winced as a bone-saw was added to the other implements of the surgeon's trade.

"I get the impression he'll be disappointed if they're not." Revell continued the tour of inspection.

Several of the working parties were now removing stores to stock the positions topside. Frequently the officers had to flatten themselves against the cold damp walls as men staggered past loaded with cases of mortar bombs, grenades and rockets.

They had just passed a door decorated with an ornate lock when something made Revell pause and hold the lieutenant back.

"What's in there?"

Voke shrugged. "It is a room we did not need. I do not recall ever opening it."

"It's open now." Looking again at the lock, Revell noticed that the escutcheon plate was scratched and dented. As he went to push it, from the other side he heard the musical trill of birdsong.

"Don't shout at me, Major." Dooley threw his arms wide, an unopened bottle in either hand, in a gesture of supplication. "I must be dead and this is heaven, and no one gets shouted at in heaven."

The vault was as big as the largest they'd seen, but its contents were markedly different. Down the full length of both sides were tall wine racks. In the center of the floor, standing over a drain grating was a small deal table and on it a row of glasses.

"You're not dead, but if you don't pull your weight with the others you soon will be wishing you were." Revell turned to the lieutenant. "Are any of your men teetotal?"

For a moment Voke's command of English let him down. "Do you mean abstainers? Oh yes, twenty at least."

"Well, put your best fire-and-brimstone man on this door."

"Old William that is who you need. If you wish, he would enjoy smashing the bottles and letting all this . . . demon drink, run to that sump."

"No, Major. You can't, you mustn't." Dooley was panicking at the thought. "There's thousands of bottles of wine here, and there's champagne, cognac, sherry . . ."

"Out!"

"Then can I leave my birds here? If there's going to be some mad prohibitionist freak on the door they should be safe enough. No one's going to get past him."

Above the ruins the pioneers were working hard and fast. Amid the jumble of stone they had already fashioned several interconnected strongpoints, improvising top cover for every pit and trench. In every position was emplaced a TOW anti-tank missile launcher or a clutch of Starstreak and Stinger anti-aircraft launch tubes. In the small area of courtyard that remained clear had been set two mortars, and close by them an assortment of ready-use rounds, including smoke, high-explosive, illuminating and, in greatest numbers, Merlin top-attack armor-penetrating bombs.

"Your men know their job well." Revell watched as a Dutch pioneer improvised a roof, from splintered doors, over the vulnerable ammunition.

"I think they are enjoying themselves, Major." Voke was handed a bulky satchel by one of his men. He glanced into it, then handed it to Revell. "A little present for you. Something you asked for."

Puzzled, Revell accepted it, and from its depths extracted three large drum magazines. "I don't believe it. I've been eking out my last seven shells and you come up with these."

He substituted one for the half-empty box mag on his assault shotgun. "Perfect, flechette and explosive."

"It is my hope that the communists do not get close enough for you to make effective use of that weapon." Voke patted his British Endeavour rifle. Its bull-pup configuration made it look insignificant close to the chunky mass of the wooden-stocked combat shotgun. "I prefer a weapon that can engage them before they get that close."

Revell clipped the spare magazines to his belt. "I don't think the choice will be down to us."

CHAPTER FIFTEEN

"Hold your fire! Hold your fire!" Carrington yelled at the top of his voice, and heard the instruction passed on in Dutch and English.

He looked again through the image intensifier. It didn't reveal a perfect picture, but it clearly resolved into a view of a soft-skin eight-wheeler of NATO type.

"Is it Hyde?" Smothering himself in clinging gray mud in the process, Revell hurled himself into the machine-gun nest and grabbed the vision-enhancing night glasses.

"Ought to be, but there's too many of them."

Adjusting the focus, the major saw that their hardman was right. Six, including Andrea had gone out on the mine-laying detail. He could see at least twice that number moving about the vehicle.

"Starshell?"

The suggestion made sense, but for Revell there was more than simply the lives of the sergeant's squad to consider, with action so close. Yes, the truck had to be Hyde's, perhaps returning with prisoners from their skirmish, but it might be a Russian reconn team who'd taken it over and were employing it. It was a stunt the Warpac forces had used many times to approach NATO positions.

"If it's Reds we'll let them get close before we hit

them. I'll want prisoners." Oh yes, he'd want prisoners. If they'd captured or killed Andrea he was personally going to make the death of every communist who fell into his hands very painful and extremely protracted.

Rummaging through the truck's tool kit, Burke swore as he caught the back of his hand on the unguarded blade of a hacksaw.

"There's got to be one in here somewhere." He cursed again as a sharp object, unseen in the dark, pierced his thumb.

"What the hell are you looking for?" Hyde was impatient. "Let's put a torch to this rig and get moving."

"You can't risk those girls to climb up there still wearing those leg-irons. The fetters are made out of what looks like old tin cans. Their ankles are already red-raw. By the time they're halfway up, the fucking metal will have cut their feet off." His hand lit on a familiar shape and he drew his long-handled bolt-cutters from the bottom of the locker. "Got them."

"Be quick about it." Unfastening the gas tank filler cap, Hyde threaded a strip of cloth in until he felt it slacken when it floated on the fuel. As he worked he could hear the repetitive "snick" as their driver severed the girls' bonds.

"Why do you bother?" Andrea watched the sergeant's preparations. "When the Russians arrive it will be destroyed anyway."

"If we're going to scramble up that lot, then we need a light. This wagon should burn for the best part of an hour."

"It will also make us perfect targets if they arrive before we reach safety."

Hyde noticed there was no real concern in her voice;

132

she was simply making an observation. "That's a chance we'll have to take." He applied a match to the protruding material, then hauled several pallets off the back and propped them against the big tank.

The dangling length of cotton had flared at the first touch of the flame. It almost went out when it reached the lip, then, fed by the fuel that saturated it, became gradually stronger and lit the area in an ever-widening circle.

None of them looked back as they began the ascent. The Scammel was simply a machine that had served a purpose. Only by being destroyed was its usefulness being extended.

The girls needed no goading or encouragement at first to make the best possible speed; it was Ripper who more and more frequently needed assistance as his damaged leg stiffened.

Several times they had to make changes of direction when they struck a patch where the going was too precarious over loose material. In other places they were faced by extensive slabs of unbroken wall that had somehow tobogganed over several hundred meters to come to rest intact. Their thick coating of dust, turned to a gritty lubricant by the rain, made them unscalable and forced further detours.

It was exhausting, punishing work. The wild shadows thrown by the burning truck played constant tricks with their eyes. Sometimes it smoothed deceptively a series of jagged crags, then would threaten them with a bottomless black gulf where none existed.

The way grew steeper and at times Ripper had to be dragged or lifted. Two of the girls were also in difficulty, but their companions helped them, urging them on with earnest words of encouragement.

None of them dared look up. The point they aimed for seemed as far away as ever. And if they looked back all there was to see was the burning Scammel, now alight from end to end as its diesel fuel boiled and ignited the wooden load bed and the cab.

Andrea felt herself to be climbing like an automaton, handgrip following handgrip, instinct taking over from reasoned thought. Her arms and shoulders ached but she pushed from her mind the urge to stop and rest. She suppressed the thought that not all of the thickly sown mines might have been triggered or neutralized by the great mass of falling stone and tiles.

She slipped, and felt the hard rock pummeling her body before her kicking feet and scrabbling fingers found holds to check her slide. Gulping air, she steadied herself, then began cautiously to edge to the left in search of an alternative route.

Looking back, Andrea saw the others, more strung out than they had been at the start, and working in small groups for mutual support. It was not just to avoid unwanted advances that had prompted her to be a loner; it had always been her way to avoid dependence on others or responsibility for anyone. But as now, that could work against her, force her onto her own resources, to near breaking-point.

They were halfway, almost to the top of the fallen rubble. Beyond that was bare rock for nearly a hundred meters before they might find some footing among the broken remains of the outwork.

A stone her foot dislodged tumbled away to miss their prisoner narrowly. She saw his upturned face mouthing obscenities at her, and purposely dislodged another.

Hyde could taste the paste of mortar and ground granite. It clung to him in amounts sufficient to triple the weight of his combat fatigues and drag him down. He felt as though he had been climbing forever. Concentrating only on the next hold and not dwelling on how many more there were to go, he was surprised when he caught up to Andrea. She had stopped in a patch of deep shadow between two huge blocks.

"This is no time to be taking a breather. Keep moving."

"How?" The light from the burning truck was diminishing but it served to display what lay ahead. Andrea slumped against the debris. "I had thought the falling material, besides covering the mines, would have shattered the cliff face. It has not. Instead it has swept it bare of any ledge or hold."

It was the first time Hyde had ever heard her defeatist, and by that he knew she was too exhausted to go on. Her iron will and rigid self-discipline, her determination never to be bettered was finally evaporating, beaten from her by the grueling climb.

"Right. We'll rest here a while. Wait for the others to catch up." Scanning the rock wall, Hyde could see only confirmation of her words. "There's got to be an alternative route. We'll find it. We bloody well got to, we haven't a choice."

Ripper hauled himself into the small space, and put his hand to the dressing on his leg. It felt freshly damp. He was bleeding again.

"Sarge, what we've done so far was tough, but not even a mountain goat is going higher. I got to tell you, I'm not feeling at my best, but I sure as hell don't want to be left here. Come daybreak I'll be a sitting target for the first commie that wanders down that road."

"Listen."

Shepherding the girls to join the group, and dragging the deserter with him, Burke shushed them to silence. It was hardly necessary.

From the direction of the mill, growing louder every moment, came the rumble of tank tracks. They were traveling fast, as attested by the thrashing and squealing of linked cast-metal over sprockets and return rollers.

"You know,"—tampering with the field dressing made Ripper wince with pain as the soft absorbent wadding moved across the ragged edge of the wound— "I think we are well and truly in the shit."

They watched the lead tank of the Warpac column slew to a violent halt on the apex of the bend before the roadblock. Its long cannon barrel swept back and forth as its turret oscillated to cover each side of the road in turn.

"Please, just don't look up here, boys." Ripper felt mesmerized, like a deer in the beam of a hunter's flashlight. "I bet he's getting his ears chewed off for stopping."

"Maybe." Hyde examined the T72 through his glasses. Every hatch was dogged down tight. While they remained like that there wasn't much chance of their spotting a small group high above them and trying hard to make themselves inconspicuous. "But maybe that jamming is a two-edged weapon. It's being pumped out at such a power it could be screwing up their radio links as well." He turned to Andrea. "Did you say that Spetsnaz creep you hit had a microwave dish?"

"Yes, and from the look of it I would say it had seen considerable use."

"So." Hyde looked at the long whip-aerial above the turret. "If their communications are buggered we should have confirmation any second."

The tank recoiled on its suspension as its cannon spat a 125mm high-explosive shell into the obstructing avalanche of stone at point-blank range.

The blast of impact and the sharp crack of firing

136

blended in one, and when the smoke cleared the ragged stack of material appeared undisturbed.

Tentatively the gunner's hatch opened and a figure, grotesquely distorted by the erratic light, lifted itself out and slid warily onto the rear deck. There came the tinny "clang" of a track-guard-mounted locker being opened. Unrecognizable pieces of equipment were taken out, and then a shallow metal dish that was handled carefully.

"Take him out, Andrea, fast." It was a terrible gamble, might have the fatal consequence of drawing attention to them, but for Hyde that was one consideration among many.

There was a perceptible delay, not long, but sufficient to be proof of just how tired Andrea was, and then she fired. The grenade's accuracy, or lack of it, was further demonstration.

As the grenade impacted on the road under the rear of the T72, the hull protected the gunner from the fragmentation effect but it was close enough to send the Russian scuttling head-first back inside the turret.

Reloading quickly, Andrea took aim for a second attempt before the hatch was pulled shut.

"Forget him. Smash that gear on the rear deck."

Hyde's instruction came in time and the second 40mm round arced down to the road to detonate on the tank's engine deck close to the open locker. The litter of unassembled equipment was instantly mangled and swept away, along with bedding rolls on the back of the turret.

Even as that second grenade did its work of destruction, the T72 and other unseen armored vehicles on the road behind it opened up with their main and secondary armaments and fired a protective screen of smoke bombs.

Long bursts from co-axial machine guns were

dwarfed by the massive concussion of heavy cannon and the rapid crackle of lighter weapons aboard APCs.

Unaimed, unleashed as a wild, blind, suppressive fire, the gun flashes hit the scene in a stroboscopic nightmare effect through which only the flashing blurs of orange and green tracer could be discerned.

Ricochets soared from the lower slopes and flew past the huddling party, and then a single 30mm armor-piercing round found them, tumbling deformed after its first contact with a boulder.

A piercing scream, and blood showered over them all. The body of a girl fell forward and flopped from projection to projection until it was lost amid the jumble of stone. Two more of the girls whimpered in pain, struck by shards of bone from the shell's unwitting victim. They slowly collapsed and their heads lolled as they went into shock.

The rest of them crouched lower, those on the outside questing with their fingertips for anything that might be dragged across in front of them to form a barricade.

"I told you all." Ripper got no satisfaction from the mass of young warm female flesh pressing against him. "We are deep in the shit."

CHAPTER SIXTEEN

Step by labored step Revell had watched the painfully slow ascent of what he had become certain was Hyde's group. There were men, volunteers, who could be spared from other tasks to go out and assist them. It was the lack of suitable equipment that had delayed the attempt.

One of the few cellars to be completely caved in beneath the crushing weight of the falling walls had been that containing the pioneers' specialized stores. Among the items buried were all the coils of rope and wire cable, the hand winches and the blocks and pulleys.

It had taken an hour's hard work and a measure of luck to salvage sufficient rope for them to entertain the hope of reaching the stranded party.

Voke entered the MG pit and looked down into the darkness. "We have spliced the lengths together. I think with what we have we could reach them from the outwork."

"That means opening the postern door." The information posed Revell a dilemma. "What with the generator and all the activity down there, the moment we open up it'll stand out like a beacon on every Warpac IR-scope in range."

"We could erect a sandbag wall immediately inside.

With all power off while we bring them up, the risk would be much reduced."

It was the straw Revell had been searching for and he grabbed it. "Get to work. Put as many on the job as there's room for down there."

From the road far below came the faint but distinctive grind and rattle of tank tracks. A moment after came the short sharp crack of a rifle grenade, quickly followed by a second.

At only a few paces Voke could hardly see the major's face. He hesitated, waiting to see if the order would be countermanded.

"Carry on." As Revell made his way to the courtyard he heard the storm of wild retaliatory fire, and hurried to join Thorne and the waiting mortar crews.

They stood ready, the absurdly long Merlin rounds held poised above the gaping tubes. The barrels were almost vertical, in anticipation of engaging close-range targets.

"I want two rounds dropped right under the wall, then four more walked back along the road, fifty-meter intervals. Fast as you . . ."

His last words were drowned and his ears punished by the blast as the first armor-seeking round was sent on its way. The second blast came only a fraction of a second later.

Revell was tempted to grab the pocket-sized fire-control computer and calculate the time of flight, but knew that in his unpracticed hands it would take too long. He tried to read the pale green glow of the display ticking away the time on target in Thorne's hand.

". . . three . . . two . . . one." For an instant, doubt flashed through Thorne's mind, then he heard the vicious screech of the warhead's detonation on a hard target. It was followed by a more powerful explosion. "Set the bastards' ammo off. Must have impacted beside the driver's position to do that. Second was either a dud or couldn't find a tank of its own."

At short intervals more rounds were slipped down the dull-painted tubes and each time the blast seemed little attenuated by the bell-shaped muzzle-tops.

The transit times of those rounds was fractionally longer, but there were three more audible indicators of successful hits.

"Right, move, you lot. Time to get our heads down." Unfastening a barrel from its bipod, Thorne led his men and Revell in a dash for the cover of a doorway. A makeshift dogleg barricade had been erected in front of it.

"They're slow off the mark." Thorne checked his watch. "The commies have counter battery fire down to a fine art. I'm amazed we got that many away without getting one back in our lap, let alone had time to bolt."

"Maybe they weren't looking our way." Revell propped the hefty circular casting of a baseplate against an ammunition box. "I expect they will be the next time. There's some telephone gear down below. Rig up a line from here to a good observation post on top. Once the fight starts in earnest there'll be no point in trying to hide. Until then restrict yourself to anti-armor shots at identified targets."

Far above the ruins, its bursting lost among the rainclouds, a giant starshell crackled into spitting magnesium light. The immediate effect was an unearthly glow that increased in intensity as the parachute-suspended ball of iridescence dropped lower.

"That's 155mm." Thorne looked at the slim 81mm mortar barrel he held. "Hardly fighting fair, is it? They must have some heavy self-propelled artillery supporting the column."

As the illuminating round continued its slow,

141

gyrating descent, Revell headed for the cellar entrance. He took the stairs three at a time and quickly reached the spot where Voke was directing and assisting in the erection of the sandbag wall.

"No time for that now. Kill the generator. Get the door open."

A bolt stuck and Revell grabbed a hammer from a pioneer and smashed at the rusted metal, breaking it with his third blow.

The door was pulled open not to the jet emptiness of an overcast night, but a flood of silver light that made them throw up their arms to shield the eyes. Somewhere behind them the generator died. Had it not been for the cessation of its almost subliminal humming they would not have noticed. The few lights paled to total insignificance against the glare.

Burning vehicles on the road, their flames fed by hundreds of liters of fuel, the bodies of their crews and all their ammunition could not compete.

Making the most of it, a young Dutchman started down the steep ramp of the outwork. The path was narrower than previously, and lacked its protecting wall, all smashed and swept away. Twice he had to stop to clear through mounds of broken brick. He reached the second tower, paused to examine the way ahead, then turned to wave for others to follow.

Three more followed, carrying the untidy coil between them. They wedged a pickax into a crevice and secured the rope by several turns around it, then began to feed the loose end over the side. As they did the light from the starshell was suddenly lost.

Hyde felt the frayed end of rope brush against his shoulder. His first grab missed and almost sent him over the edge. Regaining his balance, he waited for it to swing back and this time caught it just before it would have hit him in the face.

He accepted the blond girl Burke thrust forward to be the first, and began to fasten it under her arms.

"I will stay behind with this one." Andrea indicated their prisoner. "And will come up last."

"The fuck you will."

The little blond girl began to shake as he fastened the rope, and Hyde began to expect trouble from her, but some quiet words from Burke in his appalling German and she was still and made no fuss as she was hauled up. Small pieces of rock rained down. Absently he noticed the sparkle of quartz inclusions as they reflected the light from the fires below.

"You are not staying here on your own with this crud, because we'd never see him again." Hyde knew Andrea's reputation and had seen in action what it was based on. "Eventually this bastard might get shot, or maybe hung, but sure as hell he's not going to be diced."

"You tell her, Sarge, prisoners' rights. You tell her."

Hyde's left hook to the deserter's face would have sent him to his death if the same fist had not grabbed a wad of his clothing and pulled him back from the brink. "Any more out of you and I might let her change my mind."

His facial wound reopened by the blow, and still dazed by it, the man squeezed himself back into a niche. Slowly he slid to a sitting position and tried to stanch the renewed bleeding by pressing his face against his drawn-up knees.

Twice more the sergeant had to employ the same punch, the last time because he'd instinctively "pulled" the first go at quieting a girl who'd not responded to gentler methods to quell her hysterics when her turn came.

143

It was Ripper's turn. He was cracking weak jokes as he started up, but then had to turn all his attention to preventing his wounded limb from making hard and frequent contact with the rock.

A steady cascade of chippings marked the progress of those already on the path, as they cautiously shuffled their way to the sanctuary of the castle cellars.

"You're next." Pushing the rope toward Andrea, Hyde waited for the inevitable argument, but there was none. His offer of assistance securing the lifeline was brusquely rejected.

"Me next?" Even craning his neck right back until it clicked, and squinting in the poor light, Burke couldn't see if all the girls were now safely within the shelter of the massive walls, but he knew the first of them would be.

"What is this place?"

Ignoring the deserter, Hyde watched their driver safely on his way, before turning and roughly hauling the man to his feet.

"Is it some kind of blockhouse, a command post? What is it? I've got a right to know what I'm getting into. I'm a prisoner, right? Well, prisoners have to be removed from the battle zone, don't they?"

Not responding, the NCO waited for the rope to reappear, then threaded it through the man's pinioned arms.

"Here, no. Come on, play fair, Sarge. You got at least to untie me. I'll get broken to pieces being dragged up there . . ."

"Much the same will happen to you down here if you keep on whining. Be grateful I haven't tied it round your ankles instead."

"Hang on. I'm only a bloody deserter. Hundreds of blokes do it every month."

"But not all of them team with the scum of the Zone

144

and start up in the slavery line."

His anger would have led him to say more but the men on the path, sensing the weight on the line, began to haul. Hyde had to content himself with giving the man a hard twist that was certain to make his ascent all the more uncomfortable.

The wait for his turn seemed to extend into forever. In the distance the Russian artillery fire was perceptibly slackening, with the last of it appearing to be going down about where the river would be. So they must have achieved most of their objectives. NATO forces had lost sixty miles of territory in a few days.

A brief concentration of shells went slamming into a far-distant hilltop. The Russian artillery always had plenty of ammunition. That had been one constant during more than two years of bloody fighting.

Once the company had overrun an East German battery of super heavies. The gunners had been in rags, many of them barefoot and all of them hungry, but the stockpiles of shells for the guns and for its air-defense detachment had been vast.

When destroyed, the enormous mushroom of smoke and flame had given rise to the usual local rumors about nukes. The East German artillerymen had surrendered without a fight, after hacking to death their sleek and well-fed Russian commanding officer.

It was hard for him to be sure, but Hyde thought he saw movement on the road. The flames that belched from the hatches and engine-covers of the T72 made bizarre shadows dance between the trunks, and his eyes were tired and sore.

The rope came down and he hurried to secure it, but even as he did he continued to keep watch, and this time he could be certain that it was no trick of the light or his eyes deceiving him. Files of men were moving along the edge of the trees.

As the first harsh jerking tug lifted him off his feet and the rope cut in painfully hard across his back, he heard the sounds of more tracked vehicles. Trees were splintering, motors revving hard to overcome the resistance of mature spruce and fir.

He saw the occasional shaft of light from imperfectly shrouded headlamps and then had to turn all his attention to saving himself from being repeatedly dashed against the cliff.

The men above, on whom his life depended were growing weary and his progress became agonizingly slow. That, despite his efforts to find every hold he could to assist.

"You are the final?"

Coming from just above his head in an accent so thick as to be almost unintelligible, Hyde was startled by the voice so close at hand. He got a grip on the crumbling edge of the path and experienced a surge of relief through his whole body. It would have brought tears if his face had been capable of producing them.

"Yes . . ." God, he was struggling, don't let him slip now. "Yes, I'm the final. I'm the last."

Strong hands gripped him and dragged him to safety. Panting from the exertion, aching in every joint, he weakly resisted attempts to make him stand. All he wanted was just to rest a while, for a few moments.

They were urging him to get moving. He knew he had to, and began to force himself to his hands and knees. Again the hands grabbed him, some lifting, some pulling him forward. Others plucked at the rope still tight about his chest.

As they neared the door Hyde tripped and went sprawling, cracking his head hard.

Overhead, white light seared the night away as another huge starshell burst above the ruins.

In a far, vague distance, Hyde heard a heavy

146

machine gun rapping out a long methodical burst. Something bumped clumsily against him and made a screaming cartwheel of hands and face and boots down, down toward the waiting mounds of sharp stone.

He saw it impact beside a lifeless rag doll, saw the puff of steam as it ruptured. Then the path, just inches from his face, made a slow-motion million-mile journey up toward him and brought oblivion.

CHAPTER SEVENTEEN

"One more word out of you, man, and I'm not just going to sew your lips up, I'm going to sew them together." Sampson flicked a tangle from the surgical thread as he pulled the curved needle through for the last time. He snipped it off carelessly, leaving a long strand dangling.

"You're not going to win any beauty prizes, but in a day or two you'll be able to sneeze without your head falling in half."

"Can't you give me something? It hurts."

"That's Andrea's fault, not mine." Sampson dropped an instrument into a sterilizing solution. "You want me to go and ask her for you? After all, it's her handiwork I'm repairing."

The deserter waved a hand to signal a negative and went to lean with his head against the wall, cupping his face in his hands and moaning softly.

Sampson flexed his fingers. "Always thought sewing was a sissy game; never knew it could be so much fun. He's all yours."

From the deep shadow at the far end of the long room, Burke came forward. A blond-framed pale rounded face watched him from the corner.

"Where you going to put him?" Pouring surgical spirit over his hands, the medic took a swig from the bottle before recapping it. "Oh, man, that is one hell of a mouthwash. Seems pretty crowded down here. Where can you stash him where he can't do any harm?" For a moment he was about to step forward, thinking their driver was about to unleash violence on his patient, but was relieved to see him halt his menacing approach and make an effort to calm himself.

"The major's put a guard on the wine cellar. This specimen is going in there, but he won't be enjoying himself." Very slowly and precisely Burke reached for, and between thumb and forefinger took a tight hold on the length of dangling surgical thread.

"You're coming with me, like a good little boy, aren't you?" Burke accompanied the last two words with jerks on the thread. "There, I knew you would."

When they'd gone out, Sampson shook his head. "I don't think the commies have got to bother with employing psychological warfare. Our boys are doing that sort of harm to themselves."

"It's happening to their men as well." Hyde got to his feet. His head ached and felt as if it had been worked over with a large steel-shod boot. But he felt a lot better than he had ten minutes before, when he'd regained consciousness. He'd been reluctant to take it at the time, but now he was grateful for the medic's advice to rest for a while. "So now will you tell me what's been happening in the last hour?"

"It's two, actually, Sarge; check your watch. Now don't get mad at me. Major's orders were to let you come 'round in your own good time, and I wasn't to tell you nothing about the great big outside world until you'd rested."

Hyde began to gather his equipment together. A new M16 and several pouches of magazines had been left for him. "So am I rested?"

"You're as fit as you're going to be, without being

pulled out of the line for a spell. I can tell you, though, it was as much your general physical state as the knock on the head that put you out cold. That was your body showing more common sense than your brain. You'll know when you're about to crash out the next time. When it's due, the major and Andrea will collapse a few minutes before you."

Without fuss or drama, Hyde gently pushed home the pin of a white phosphorus grenade that had become partially dislodged.

"Sarge, that knock on the head must have made you stupid." Sampson breathed deep, looked hard and rose to his full height, his marine beret almost brushing the ceiling. "You ever do something so fucking half-witted as that again, anywhere near my patients, and sergeant or no fucking sergeant, I'll ram that grenade up your ass and shove you out the door. And I'll keep the pin as a souvenir."

Hyde choked down his instinctive reaction to the tirade and threat. He knew the medic was right; it had been a stupid thing to do. A look around the cellar showed him the row of bruised and injured girls, some of them heavily sedated. The results of his action could have been horrific.

"I wasn't thinking. You get so used to . . . sorry."

Closing the door behind him, Hyde leaned his back against the wall and waited for the cold and damp to penetrate and ease the sudden prickling sweat that itched so much.

An ammunition detail passed, bowlegged under the loads of mortar bombs and belts of machine-gun ammunition. He followed them toward the surface. It would be good to breathe clean air. Down here it was foul, laden with dust, thick with imperfectly vented exhaust fumes and heavy with the smells of gun oil, raw explosives and stale bodies.

150

Reaching the steps he had to be patient for a while longer as a ghostly file of sludge-coated pioneers trooped down. The door at the top was open but when he stepped through it the atmosphere was no better. Not until he had climbed the well-worn path through the rubble to the top of the ruins was he able to gulp a reviving breath quite free from taint.

"Welcome back to the land of the living, Sarge." Garrett had jumped at the NCO's sudden appearance, and pushed his half-eaten chocolate bar into a crack between two blocks. Inwardly he cringed as he heard it slide smoothly far beyond hope of retrieval. It was his last.

"What's been happening?" Hyde experienced an unidentifiable type of shock. His first words had been barked; now he added, almost in a whisper, "What the fuck is happening?"

The quiet was unnerving, so totally unexpected. As he'd climbed up he'd been speculating with himself on what he'd find, but this he hadn't even considered. It had never entered his thoughts.

Without the distant glow of artillery fire to offer reference points, the stump of the castle seemed to be an ugly pale gray island in a matt-black sea that stretched to eternity. Save for the gentle patter of rain, and that further muted by the universal coating of soft mud, there was no sound at all.

"How long has it been like this?" As though in a church or library, Hyde felt he had to keep his voice lowered.

"Since about ten minutes after you were brought in." Fishing for the lost candy, Garrett gave up when his watch followed it. "Could be the war's over, couldn't it?"

"Wishful thinking."

As though reluctant to prove the sergeant's pessimism correct, there came a hesitant low rumble of sporadic rocket artillery in action. The missile flame-tails made brief shooting stars of white light as they zipped skyward. It petered out apologetically, the last round to be launched departed like an afterthought, barely visible, hardly audible.

Making a round of the defenses, Hyde came across Revell in a strongly roofed TOW position overlooking the road. The burning armor was almost extinguished, only occasionally giving off brief showers of silver sparks or a white smoke-ring from an open hatch. "Are they up to anything?" He slid into the small irregular-shaped pit between the officer and Dooley.

"Take a look for yourself. There's movement, but not enough to present a target worth our giving away our positions for."

Hyde could make out individual and small groups of Russians flitting between the trees. They represented too fleeting an opportunity for the missile weapon they possessed. If they'd been able to call down artillery fire . . . "I suppose they're still jamming?"

"Yes, but they're being rather more selective now." Revell stared out into the night. "I would imagine that our lot have managed to smear one or more of their big transmitters by this time. Those remaining are having to be a bit picky about what channels they choose to fuck up."

Dooley unclipped a handset from a radio and passed it to the sergeant. "Here, have a listen."

The frequency-hopping agility of the set was still being defeated by the colossal output of the enemy's electronic countermeasures, but just as Hyde was about to hand it back he heard the radio find a clear channel. Before he could mention it, the jamming resumed across the wavelength. In that brief moment he'd heard a score of voices break in, and then be swept away.

"If the interference stopped this minute,"—Revell clipped the handset back in place—"the backlog of radio traffic must be enormous. We aren't the only ones cut off. Everyone is going to be screaming for priority. It'll be like the Tower of Babel brought up to date by high technology."

"What happened to the barrage?" After days of being drenched with the sight, sound and smell of shellfire, Hyde was having difficulty adapting to a world without it.

"I don't know." It was a question that had been burrowing in Revell's brain, but he had as yet come up with no answer. "Perhaps the Reds' jamming really is working against them as well. You know what they're like for setting a timetable for an advance. If the barrage was prearranged and they got too far behind, they'd lose much of its advantage. And if they were steamrolling forward too fast, then it'd be landing on their own heads. In either case, without reliable communication they'd have problems. Might have been simpler to stop it for a while until they got themselves sorted."

"Or maybe they've cleared our guys out all the way to the river and are digging in on this bank and don't need it anymore." Spitting loudly, Dooley panned the launcher across the countryside below. "Not that I find that any sort of comfort, because if that's the case then we're a few kilometers and a wide river away from home. Not to mention the mass of Warpac troops we'd trip over on the way."

He jerked the mount back to examine an area more closely, but failed to identify a target. "It's just an idea, Major, but if I let them have one of these down their throats,"—Dooley patted the fat barrel of the tube containing the missile—"it's just going to make them

153

dig in. Chances are anyway that I'll more likely get one of them by having him run into the trailing wires afterward than by tearing him apart with a direct hit."

"Make your point."

"Well, I was thinking, one Red in exchange for a few thousand dollars' worth of equipment sems pretty poor value. I guess that Clarence could achieve the same at a fraction of the cost."

Revell could have kicked himself. Would have done if there'd been sufficient room. It made it worse that it was Dooley, of all people, who had brought the obvious to his notice. "Get him over here."

". . . six so far." Ripper kept working on the machine-gun belts, adding tracer to some, substituting armor-piercing incendiary rounds in others. "One he hit right through a couple of bandoleers he was wearing. Turned him into a miniature Fourth of July."

Frustrated at not being allowed up top to join the action, Ripper could at least enjoy the involvement of passing on stories he heard from the non-stop procession of ammunition haulers.

"Shit, what must that take his score to?" He began to strip tracer from a long belt of fifty-caliber bullets, replacing them with ball. "It's a good thing he don't carve notches in his stock; he'd be on his tenth by this time."

"More like his twenty-fifth." Burke had been only half listening. Sent out of the dispensary by the medic, he hung around in the corridor. "I lost count when his score passed three hundred, just after he turned down that medal."

"Is that for real?" The reverberations of Ripper's shrill whistle brought trickles of fine powder from between crumbling brickwork. "Pity we can't infiltrate

154

him into the Kremlin. War would be over in a day or two." He blew dust from a round and slid it home. "What the hell keeps him going?"

"Hatred, pure and simple." Hearing footsteps, Burke hoped Sampson was about to leave the nearby room, but was disappointed.

"That is a lot of hatred. Is that anything to do with the way he can't bear anybody touching him? I've seen him scraping himself with a dry cloth fit to draw blood after someone brushed against him."

"Possibly." Burke had his hopes dashed again by the sound of more movement that came to nothing. "He puts up with Andrea though, but she's the only one I know of. He's been a one-man army since a commie bomber came down on his married quarters in Cologne, right back at the start of things. It killed his wife and kids. After that he was a machine, good one though."

"Three hundred plus!" About to whistle again, Ripper remembered the consequences last time and thought better of it. "Hang on, though; I thought they were trying to weed out all the guys who'd got to like the killing, rotating them out of the line."

"He doesn't enjoy it." Giving up waiting, Burke determined to return later when perhaps Sampson wouldn't be so vigilant. "I've seen him retch after putting a commie down with a clean headshot."

"Then how does he keep going?" Finishing the last belt, Ripper flexed his blood-stained fingers and lounged back against the wall.

"That's a piece of information he's never volunteered, but I can make a guess." Not wanting to go, Burke knew he'd soon be missed and Hyde would be hunting for him. "I think he's set a price, in Russian lives, on his revenge. God only knows what it is, or if he'll ever achieve it."

155

"Then what—he goes on killing? Like it's become a habit?"

Reluctantly Burke began to move toward the stairs. "Could be, or perhaps when he decides he's finally done he'll stand up and make a target of himself, or put the barrel of that beautiful rifle in his mouth."

The sniper waited, patient, unmoving; the rifle sights were aligned on a space between two trees where he knew the Russian would reappear. It was three minutes now, but still he maintained his unwavering pose. He ignored the dirt in which he lay, the cold, the rain trickling down the back of his neck.

At six hundred meters the gusting wind made the shot, with its short engagement time, a difficult one. If he missed, it could mean a long wait before another target presented itself.

Long experience of observing battlefield behavioral patterns had developed in Private Clarence almost a sixth sense, and for no obvious reason his trigger finger gently took up a fraction more of the precisely set one-kilo pull-weight.

He anticipated the recoil and the flash-hider saved his night vision. Panning downward he saw an indistinct hummock of camouflage material lying between the trees. It moved, sluggishly, and Clarence unconsciously made a mental calculation to make a further slight allowance for the wind.

Setting up again, this time the wait was much shorter. A figure appeared over the fallen man and the sniper saw a white face turned toward him as he lightly squeezed the trigger.

The bullet must have met minimal resistance, perhaps entering an eye, or the open mouth. In any event it was a killing headshot. But the target, his victim, didn't fall.

Standing, and still appearing to stare up at the distant sniper, the soldier's body wavered slightly from side to side as if held upright by a supernatural force.

Knowing that so strange a scene was certain to attract other targets, the sniper's experience told him to wait, but he had three rounds remaining in the magazine and he emptied all of them into the standing corpse.

He didn't watch the result, sliding back into concealment to reload. His hand was shaking as he slipped the carefully selected rounds into the magazine.

Nineteen targets to go, only that many more and he'd be free. It was a minute after midnight. This could be his last day. Even as the thought formed, his hands stopped shaking and a feeling of relief and calm flooded through him. It was nearly over.

CHAPTER EIGHTEEN

The first of the explosions came a little after two in the morning. They continued at erratic intervals until an hour before dawn. Sometimes they came singly, at other times in ripples. A few were from close at hand, most from various distances away in the circle of high ground about the valley. Often there were other sounds as well, the wail of pressure-driven flame, the stutter of automatic fire, and most frequently of all came the screams.

As Revell toured their positions atop the broken walls, he thought that he knew how the ancient Crusaders would have felt, waiting for first light and the onslaught of the Saracens. The weapons were more modern, could strike farther and harder, but you were just as dead from a hit by a crossbow bolt as from the lashing shrapnel of a Russian 155mm airburst.

The wind had abated and finally died away completely, and the rain had eased until it was no more than a feeling of saturating dampness in the air. Together the changes signaled the chance of a better day, but they threatened a danger as well.

By imperceptible degrees, fingers of mist began to creep between the hills and ridges. Thickening rapidly, they merged to form a fog that filled every dip and hollow and began to climb the confining slopes.

*   *   *

"I don't feel nature is on our side." For the tenth time in as many minutes, Dooley wiped condensation from the lens of the TOW sighting unit.

Scully passed him a mug of coffee and sat down to drink his own. "Be bloody fair. If you were Mother Nature and you'd been mucked about like she has in the Zone, would you be on anybody's side?"

"That's not the point." Using his finger to draw the skin from the top of his drink, Dooley tried to flick it away, failed, and wiped it down his front. "We're the fucking goodies. We didn't go marching into commie territory; they came crashing in here yelling provocation. I'd love to know how that poor old granny they hung in Munzenberg had ever provoked them. They only had to kick her zimmer away to do it."

A sharp explosion, slightly muted by distance and the shroud of fog, was followed by a secondary detonation, and then another.

"How many tries is that they've had at getting through the minefields?" Scully listened intently. Faint shouts could be heard, shrill and panicky.

"Lost count." Dooley wrung out his cloth and wiped the launch barrel once more. "What I can't understand is why they haven't had a crack at us yet."

"They don't realize we're here yet, not in numbers." Hyde crawled in beside them and tilted the can to examine the dregs of coffee. "Far as the commies are concerned there's one sniper operating from here and that's it." He waited to be offered the residue and when he wasn't, took it anyway. That it was cold he didn't care; it sluiced the taste of ground stone from his throat.

"That's better. I can swallow now without sandpapering my tonsils. One bit of good news. The major's torn up standing orders and put Boris back on the radio. Garrett's a bloody clown, worse than useless."

159

"No luck yet though, I take it." Scully dropped the mugs into the can, and cringed at the noise they made. "Sorry, Sarge." He hastened to change the subject. "So we've not got through then, yet."

"Picked up a few snippets from a Russian field commander in the area. Reception is terrible, but according to Boris the commies are having a rough time in those minefields. They were expecting to virtually walk in unopposed through the main entrance; seems we rather screwed that up for them."

"Shame."

"That's not quite the word they're using." Hyde watched Dooley wring drops from a cloth he'd have considered bone-dry. "They've lost two companies of assault engineers and four mine plows so far. Had to call for the divisional reserve. Boris says there's a few threats flying about."

"So what they going to do next, bugger off and leave us in peace or start chucking nukes, like they usually do when they're narked about something?" He said it lightly, but Scully knew that when the Russians became upset and frustrated by unexpected reverses those were real options. The first was one rarely employed.

Dooley blew his nose, then swore when he realized he'd done it on his wiping cloth. "I know what they'll fucking do, same as always. The man on the spot has tried the sledge-hammer tactic; now his boss will apply typical Russian logic and finesse and try an even bigger hammer."

There was nothing further to be said, and they just sat there, each alone with his thoughts and his fears. Occasionally they would hear a voice from one of the other positions. It grew lighter, but the rising fog made the castle as isolated in the day as it had been during the night. There was nothing more they could do; their preparations were complete. Everything was as ready as it could be to withstand an attack from any quarter.

A powerful explosion lit the fog and sent it into twisting eddies. Six minor detonations followed so closely as to blend with the first.

"Fuel-air. Nothing else has that punch." Hyde looked over the rough rampart, but there was nothing to be seen, except a patch above the hill about a half a kilometer away where the natural obscurity was thickened by black smoke. "Too far off to have been meant for us; they're trying new tactics to crack the minefields . . . Shit."

Howling noise accompanied a Russian gunship that loomed from the fog, its whirling blades chewing the air hard as it sought lift.

Torrents of small-arms fire lashed toward it. Every detail of its construction was clearly visible as it slashed past the top of the ruins so close they could have reached out and touched the tips of its rotors.

Storms of debris and mud were whipped into their faces stingingly hard, and it was that hail that saved the helicopter. It banked steeply and offered only its armored underside to the streams of bullets as it clawed its way to safety.

Belatedly the sights of a Stinger were wiped and the missile launched, but by then the air was full of decoying strips of aluminum chaff, bright flares and every type of decoy device. There was no loud report from a successful interception.

"They know we're here now." Scraping his eyes clear, Dooley hurled a rock after the gunship. The futile act didn't make him feel any better, but he felt he had to do something.

Another of the vapor bombs was heard, but it didn't share the slight success of the first. Built to resist the shock of the massive over-pressures, most of the buried

161

mines remained sentient, waiting for their intended victim.

The trees, though, could not withstand the onslaught and fell outward in great swaths from the center of the ignition. For some seconds after the beat of the second, unseen, gunship had receded, the creaking, tearing and splintering of their collapse continued.

A Rapier missile skimmed past an angle of the wall and clipped a projection. It tumbled out of control and broke up under the tremendous G-forces exerted on its thin casing.

"Slow off the mark." Scully ducked as pieces of fin and motor components zipped over his head. "But I'm glad to see the guys at the farm are at least awake. But who the hell are they aiming at?"

The stump of a leg beneath his hand trembled as his patient went into a spasm, and Sampson lost his grip on the protruding rubbery length of artery. A pulse of dark blood was hosed at the wall, and then the man on the table went limp and the rapid flow became a sluggish ooze.

Stepping back, the medic swore. He'd known in his heart he had no chance of saving the man, but not to have the time to even try . . . The terribly punished body had given up its fight for life seemingly willingly, with hardly a struggle.

A rocket's warhead had stripped clothing, flesh and limbs from him indiscriminately and burned most of what it had left otherwise untouched. That was the first he'd lost who'd lived to reach him. Sampson closed the staring eyes and covered the blackened face. He put his hands palm-down into a bowl of tepid water heavy with the smell of disinfectant. It was soothing, until he looked down and saw that the solution had turned as red as the many drops and splashes on the walls and floor.

"Karen, will you find someone to take him out?"

The little blonde put down the mop with which she'd been attempting to swill away the worst of the blood and went out.

Sampson noticed that the mophead, contents of the pail and floor were all a muddy pink. He took hold of the long handle to finish the work and found that it too was sticky with blood.

Shells were hammering the ruins, and even deep below ground the concussion of the impacts could be felt. Sometimes a monstrous 182mm round would impact, and then the shock would travel down through the walls and be transmitted by the rock itself to the floor beneath his feet. The lights would dim and then flare once more to full strength, to highlight the dribbles of dust and floating cobwebs shaken from the ceiling.

He'd lost track of time; all he knew was that this was the first moment since the shelling had started that he'd not had a victim of it waiting for attention. Sampson did a round of those already treated. They were all quiet, making no complaint or fuss. It was something to be grateful for that the Russians had not as yet used chemical weapons. Working in respirator and full NBC suit with his patients at constant risk would have been a nightmare.

Most of the girls were still among the injured, but Karen and to a lesser extent a couple of the others had been a great help. Their presence, even that of those who were laid out in the far corner, had played a large part in controlling the situation when the trickle of wounded had suddenly become a flood.

Men with gaping cuts, broken limbs and extensive burns had been calmed by the sight of the girls going quietly about their work. Those who had been forced to wait for attention found new reserves of endurance while the girls moved among them, and their presence had not had merely a cosmetic effect.

As each man was brought forward in his turn, Sampson found them already prepared for him, clothing cut away, the wound cleansed.

But all their efforts could not rid the room of the smells that permeated it. There was no ventilation and the air was becoming foul.

Carrington entered, followed by a Dutchman who appeared reluctant to breathe the fetid atmosphere.

"Got a stiff you want carted?"

As they struggled out with their awkward burden, Sampson followed, holding doors open for them. Along the branch passageway, into the main corridor to the steps and up into a ground floor room that was unrecognizable since the last time he'd seen it so shortly before.

Sections of the ceiling had fallen in, bringing masses of plaster that had been crushed to a fine white powder beneath heavy army boots. Against a wall was a close-packed line of jacket- and blanket-shrouded bodies.

Lowering the latest addition to the growing tally, Carrington didn't flinch as a shell struck the outside wall and sent a fresh scattering of pulverized plaster over the corpses.

"Why doesn't the major bring you all down into the cellars?" Sampson hunched his head down between his shoulders as a big shell pounded another crater in the mercifully thick fabric of the castle.

"Can't."

Sampson found himself bobbing up and down while Carrington remained unmoved by the barrage. "All we're doing is taking stick and casualties, for nothing."

"The commies are pushing a road through the

164

minefield; we're trying to put them off. We let them have it every time the dust clears for a second."

A giant blow against the wall of the room marked the impact of a 182mm "concrete buster" shell. Cracks radiated from a point a meter above the row of dead. Shards of carved stonework skittered across the floor and a drop of molten lead splashed on the dusty tiles and solidified into a ragged star.

Clutching a face opened from brow to chin, a figure stumbled toward the medic. Dashing forward, Sampson caught him as he sagged, and started down the stair with him.

Reaching the bottom step he saw Karen runing forward to help. "It's okay. I've got him, I'll manage. You and the other girls start to get another room ready." He felt the man's blood soaking into the shoulder of his jacket, warm and sticky. "We're going to need it soon."

An airburst seeded the weapon pits with razor-sharp slivers of steel. One carved a long groove in the Kevlar material of Dooley's helmet; two more punched effortlessly through the launch tube of the TOW and crudely stapled it to the body of the missile itself, reducing them effectively to scrap.

Dragging a replacement forward, he noticed the lieutenant was pushing a wad of dressing inside the shoulder of his jacket.

"You hit?"

"I felt it pass right through." Withdrawing the pad, Voke showed that it had only a tiny spot of blood on it. "There was a burning sensation. Perhaps it has cauterized itself. That will save our overworked medic more work."

"Better get it checked."

"I shall, later, when there is time."

Dooley made no response to that. If an officer wanted to be a hero, then he was quite prepared to let him. But if he got a scratch himself, he'd be down those cellar steps before you could say "napalm." As yet he'd not been that lucky; all he wanted was a little nick, just a cut that looked worse than it was, anything that would get him down there among those girls.

There were several columns of smoke rising from various locations in the circle of hills. Working through the night to find or push a path through the minefields, the Russians must have taken fearful casualties. When the sun had broken through the midmorning it had revealed the main enemy effort. A freshly bulldozed track led from the road to the area flattened by the gunship's fuel-air bombs. The scar of turned earth had swarmed with Warpac assault engineers and their tracked and wheeled equipment, presenting a dream target.

Every weapon for which a space could be found on that side of the castle had fired until its barrel became too hot to touch.

Trapped by the mines ahead and to either side, the enemy's stampede back to the road had turned into a slaughter. The safe track became a killing ground as mortar bombs, anti-tank rockets and streams of fire from Brownings and mini-guns and grenade launchers saturated the area.

When Revell had finally called a halt there were no more targets to be seen. The armor and earth-moving machinery was wrecking and blazing and bodies were sprawled in literally a carpet of camouflage material across the bare soil.

Retaliation had come quickly, but by then most had made it to the comparative safety of the lower rooms and cellars before the first deluge, of artillery rockets, had plummeted down.

For half a minute they'd received the undivided attention of a battery of multiple launchers. Half a minute in which a pounding blasting, searing five tons of high-explosive drenched and pulverized the exterior walls and the layer of rubble overhead.

A single nineteen-kilo 122mm warhead had detonated against a lower floor window. The full force of the blast caught a group of pioneers on their way to the cellars. Those directly in line with the opening had stood no chance. Seven had died instantly, four more been so desperately injured that they lived only minutes, and another three were terribly wounded.

Mercifully for the first rescuers on the scene, the worst of the carnage had been hidden behind a swirling maelstrom of dust and smoke.

CHAPTER NINETEEN

Anticipating the Russian commander's next move, the instant Revell sensed the barrage was finished, he rushed a heavy machine gun to their best-protected position and had it range with tracer on the partially completed route.

He was only just in time. Smoke shells began to fall and rapidly masked its location. The near-silent eruptions of burning phosphorus fell so close to the truck that they must have caused casualties among the first of the combat engineers sent to restart the work, and the asphyxiating pall, forcing the men to wear respirators, must have made their dangerous work that much more difficult.

As the concealing cloud began to spread and thicken, the Browning began to fire short bursts on fixed lines.

Now death came upon the toiling Russians when they thought they were safe. Those hit by the blind-fire died without hearing or even realizing they were under attack.

They couldn't stop the work completely. Revell knew that, regardless of the cost in lives, but the MG fire, combined with such heavier concentrations as they could put down during lulls in the shelling, would reduce the pace of the work to a costly crawl.

As an added touch, he had the tracer rounds removed from the fast-consumed belts of fifty-caliber slugs, to enhance the demoralizing effect on the Russian troops. Now the powerful armor-piercing rounds would arrive and slice through men, trees and light armor without warning.

In answer to the harassing fire, the communists replied with their own, turning some of their biggest guns on the castle. Only the sheer scale of the target they were punishing enabled it to soak up the bombardment. The big artillery shells impacting on the enormous table of rubble could do little more than grind it into smaller and smaller pieces.

A near miss blasted the abandoned transport parked short of the gate and started fires that made an acrid cloud full of floating particles of lampblack from tires and synthetic cab fittings and upholstery. Gas tanks ruptured and sent showers of blazing fuel over the walls, but their great thickness made them impervious to the ferocious heat generated.

The hot black smoke hung about the site in the still air, and the first the garrison knew of the Russian attack was the distinctive sound of several Rapiers being fired and the crackling report of a Vulcan firing long bursts.

At the same moment the incoming artillery fire ceased, and to shouts from Hyde and the officers, men poured up to man every position along the walls.

Hugging the contours of the hills, about thirty blurred dots against the sky began to resolve themselves into the outlines of Hind gunships and larger troop-carrying helicopters.

The lead machine fell apart under a direct hit from a Rapier and another following closely fell out of control, its rotors reduced to splintered stumps by wreckage from the first.

A third Hind bucked and began a lurching turn out of formation as a Rapier passed through its cabin without detonating. The forty-kilo missile, traveling at Mach 2, wiped away both door gunners and sent the sliding doors and other sections of fuselage panel fluttering into the valley.

"Strikers engage as they come in range. The rest of you hold your fire." Revell saw the puffs of white smoke from the chin turrets of the gunships as their rotary cannons opened up, and then the flashes of flame beneath their stub wings as their missile racks emptied.

The range was too great and the few hits struck the base of the walls at their thickest point. Another Rapier scored a hit and a troop transport disintegrated and spilled its infantry cargo from a height of three hundred feet.

"They're bloody windy." Recognizing the ill-timed firing for the caution it was, Burke crouched over his mini-gun and began to wonder if they'd come close enough for him to have the chance to use it.

Spreading out as pilots jockeyed to put more distance and other machines between themselves and the Rapiers, the formation began to lose cohesion.

Viewed from the castle, the machines appeared to overlap, masking each other's fire, and presented a perfect target for the deadly Stingers.

"Look at them run." Finger still on the trigger, Burke raised his head from the sights to watch the helicopters break in all directions as a salvo of ten missiles lashed into them. "They've never seen fire like that."

If the approaching squadron was employing any sort of electronic countermeasures they proved no more successful than the showers of physical decoys they were scattering.

Six helicopters were hit, one of them twice, and they fell among the litter of flares and chaff they'd spawned. They filled the sky above the valley with tumbling burning wreckage.

A big-bodied troop carrier sideslipped through a series of jarring maneuvers and pancaked into the center of a field, bouncing viciously hard in an impact that drove its landing gear up through the fuselage and wrenched off the complete tail assembly.

Masses of flashing tracer from the distant Vulcan multibarreled cannon curled from the farm and enveloped the wreck in an inescapable wall of steel. It erupted in flame.

For the surviving machines that was too much, and they turned in every direction to take the shortest route away from the valley. For one it was a fatal mistake.

Keeping his finger down hard, Burke sent a full three hundred rounds across the side of the gunship's cockpit and cabin. Pieces of canopy flew off in a sparkling shower and the craft appeared to stop dead. His second burst passed low, glancing off the Hind's belly armor, but it wasn't needed anyway.

Rearing up, the helicopter virtually stood on its tail before stalling and tumbling into a seesawing motion that sent it smacking into the side of a hill.

The sound of cheering made Revell look around, and he saw all his and Voke's men yelling and dancing with glee and abandon. They'd got what they'd been waiting for, the chance to hit back hard, and they were celebrating.

"Sergeant Hyde." Revell knew the rejoicing would have to be short-lived. "I want five Stinger teams left up here under the best cover we've got. Everyone else down below." With a last quick satisfied glance at the pyres decorating the valley and surrounding slopes,

171

Revell made his way to the strongly sandbagged position on the ground floor shielding the MG ranged on the track.

He squeezed in between the walls of gritty jute and then almost fell as his foot slipped in a broad pool of congealing blood. By a terrible freak of chance, while the men above, virtually unprotected, had escaped the slightest injury this time, a single cannon shell had entered the small aperture left for the protruding machine-gun barrel and decapitated its gunner.

Unlocking the bloody fingers still clenched about the Browning, the major rolled the headless trunk aside. Ignoring the mess in which he knelt he gave the barrel a succession of taps to bring it to bear on the right coordiantes and fired. He kept firing until there were only three rounds left in the belt, and stopped then only because a round jammed.

Calmly, methodically, he cleared the blockage, fired the last two AP rounds, then threaded in another belt and blasted that also into the rolling smoke. Hands tingling from the vibration, he attached a third belt, but didn't fire.

Beside him the headless corpse broke wind and added that stench to the wreathing wisps of cordite. From a corner, in an untidy pile of empty ammunition boxes, a face looked at him, its glassy-eyed stare appearing locked in an expression of conflicting determination and surprise.

Overhead impacted the first of the restarted Soviet artillery fire. It seemed somehow remote, unreal. Revell ducked from the strongpoint, and after arranging a replacement for the dead man, headed for the cellars.

It was cool, almost cold, underground, but the tainted smoke from the burning transports had penetrated even to here, making his eyes water.

172

Wiping the tears away left clean stripes among the dirt coating the back of his hand. What looked like an old hobo leaned against a cellar door, and it was a moment before he recognized Old William.

The elderly Dutch pioneer looked as if he had dressed in the dark, making his selection of clothing from rummaging about at the bottom of a ragbag. His face and hands were deeply wrinkled, made more obviously so by the dirt that engrained them.

Revell wondered if even the lieutenant's upper estimate as to his age was near correct, but the man's grip on his over-oiled Colt Commando was firm enough and he passed him without comment, amused to receive a nod of recognition.

In a small alcove off the partially collapsed main hall, Scully had established an improvised cookhouse, on a small scale. Behind a thick blackout curtain made of tapestry he had set up two petrol stoves. A strong smell of coffee blended with the less recognizable aroma from a large pan of bubbling, glutinous soup.

Peering into the slowly churning brown sludge, Carrington took a deep breath and tried to guess its contents. He failed, but thought he detected a whiff of beef. "I give up. What's in it?"

Gesturing to a pile of empty ration boxes, Scully went on stirring the mixture, using both hands to keep the bayonet he used moving. "Everything except the Mars Bars. Don't worry, it's hot and there'll be plenty of it and it won't send you all tearing off for a shit at the same time."

An oatmeal block floated to the surface and he made several stabs at it, before it was churned back into the depths.

Not entirely convinced, Carrington took a taste from

the ladle. It was unusual, but not unpalatable. "I've had worse."

"One more word and you won't be getting any. Now sod off and let me get on with my work." Scully leaned across to look at the pan of coffee, considered for a moment, then added another half handful of powder. For good measure he added a bag of sugar.

A powerful explosion dropped a sprinkle of dust on the top of the soup. He went to skim it off with the ladle, then changed his mind and stirred it in.

Having improvised a crutch, Ripper was organizing the teams keeping the weapons supplied with ammunition, of the correct type at the right time.

Surprised at the Southerner's unexpected show of organizational ability, Revell saw no reason to interfere in what seemed to be a smoothly running operation.

"Just like when I was a boy." Ripper hopped about, talking loud and slow to his men, or waving his arms when that method of communication failed. "I used to work of an evening at our local supermarket, filling the shelves." He hobbled aside, bumping into the major as he dodged out of the way of a party carrying mortar bombs. "Got so good at it I could anticipate what was needed before it ran out. This is much the same, only I'm using my ears to figure what'll be wanted next, instead of keeping my eyes on a passel of old girls bumbling about the cookie section."

Sampson had matters under control at the aid post as well, but was fretting over the condition of one of the girls, and a man with a gaping chest wound.

"I can't do any more, Major, except to keep them comfortable as best I can." Rinsing his hands, he wafted them dry. "She needs surgery that's way out of

174

my league, even if I had the setup and instruments to try."

"And him?" Revell indicated the chest-wound case.

"Beyond any help, I reckon. Whatever it was that opened him up, it didn't penetrate, just cracked a couple of ribs pretty cleanly. Certainly don't seem to be any fragments floating about. Must have been the blast, damaged his lungs."

Gasping hard for breath, the man was beyond registering anything that was going on about him. The little blonde knelt beside him, constantly wiping away the blood that trickled from the corner of his mouth. Restlessly he tossed his head from side to side, frequently knocked her hand and daubed blood on his cheek. Each time she patiently cleaned him and began again.

"Is that the girl Burke's gone all broody over?"

"That's her; name's Karen Hirsh. My German's not so good, and she doesn't have a lot of English, but I gather she was some sort of a nurse, or was training to be."

"I'm surprised at Burke's good taste."

As they watched, a change came over the man she tended. For a brief moment, through his pain, comprehension returned, and it showed in his face.

With fingers crusted with dried blood he reached for his attendant's face. For an instant he looked puzzled, then he smiled. Perhaps he saw instead a wife or daughter or mother, but even as the smile formed he gave a long sighing exhalation and his arm fell back.

Very gently Karen brushed his hair back from his eyes and closed them. She pulled the blanket up over his face and slowly got to her feet. Pausing to make a mental adjustment to the situation, without a backward glance she went to sit beside the girl in the deep coma.

175

"That is one special little lady." With the officer, Sampson had watched in silence. He took in the swell of her hips and her narrow waist and back, but his next words held no sexual connotation. "I'd have her to Andrea any day."

Although he couldn't agree, Revell knew what the marine meant. There was no humanity in Andrea. Only a few years older than this girl, she seemed to have gone through so much that all feeling had been leeched from her by her experiences. But maybe, at the start, she'd been like Karen . . .

"Major!"

There was urgency in the shout and Revell was already dashing toward the stairs when a giant concussion shook the very fabric of the rock and jarred his ankles so hard that his next few steps were awkward, until the numbing effect began to wear off.

Visibility when he reached the ground floor was almost zero, and the air was roastingly hot. His arms were grabbed by Voke, and together, hobbling like cripples, they groped their way toward the open air. They were stopped by Clarence.

"There's nothing left up there. All the Striker teams have been wiped out."

"What did they hit us with?" The air was clearing with the draft from the broken windows, but Revell still found each breath scorching to his throat.

"A couple of Migs popped over a hill and dumped napalm and retarded bombs right across the top. The Strikers took out one, but that was too late."

"The Rapiers!" The new Russian tactic had worked on them; if the same blind-side approach was used against the farm it might succeed. Revell knew they daren't let that happen. If it did, then almost half of the valley would fall outside the protective umbrella of the shorter-range weapons they deployed from the ruins. A

176

proper defense of the complex would no longer be possible.

"Get every automatic weapon up on top." He turned to Voke. "I want everyone who knows how to point a rifle. No exceptions, walking wounded as well. Tell them to grab anything that will accept a mag or belt.

There were not even piles of cinders to mark where the Striker teams had perished. Blast and fire had obliterated them completely.

Small pools of jellied petrol still burned and the very stones were hot to the touch. All their careful work had been utterly destroyed. Every sandbagged position had been flattened, leaving only the smoldering shreds of jute among their scattered contents.

"You fire at anything that hasn't got its feet on the ground." Revell's shout carried. "You open fire when you see it, you stop when you can't." He swapped his combat shotgun for a well-worn M60, draping a spare belt over his shoulders and laying two more at his feet. He looked at the neat coils, and wondered if they would be enough. That's if he got the chance to fire off any of them.

CHAPTER TWENTY

The air was heavy with petrol fumes and shimmered with the heat rapidly being surrendered by the fabric of the castle. They found what cover they could, braced themselves and strained to hear the approach of the next attack.

A roaring blast of noise assaulted their ears as three Mig 27s screamed over a ridge and hurtled toward them. Streams of multicolored tracer hosed skyward and the massed clatter of the weapons drowned the rattle of the cascade of shell cases pouring onto and between the stones.

Firing its six-barrel gatling cannon, the lead aircraft flashed over the ruins, straight into and through the arcing lines of steel and phosphorus.

Five of the aircraft's external pylons were hung with ordnance, and as he poured a whole belt into the Mig's belly, Voke wondered almost absently what the chances were of their massed barrage detonating all or part of that lethal cargo.

Pieces fell from the plane but it didn't deviate from its course, and swooped down into the valley heading directly at the farm, trailing a thin filament of fuel vapor.

It ran head-first into a Rapier missile and dissolved in an incandescent ball of flame.

The following fighter bombers sheered away from the wall of flak, and only a couple of broken lines of tracer came close as they veered back on course and bore straight for the farm.

Twin stabs of flame marked the takeoff of more missiles, but even as they hurled themselves toward the Migs, the jets were using maximum thrust, afterburners glowing white hot, in a wild jinking series of sharp turns to lift out of the valley.

As they ran, their underwing stores of high-explosive and napalm tumbled toward the farm, some of the iron bombs falling in a different trajectory as their miniature parachutes slowed their headlong plunge.

Flame, smoke and tall showers of debris hid the distant cluster of buildings and smothered the fields about them. But the Rapier crews had a belated revenge.

Above a distant hill reappeared one of the Migs. A tongue of red and yellow flame licked from the root of a partially swept wing and it towed a growing trail of black smoke.

"He's trying to make height for a bailout." Watching, Carrington hoped the jet would complete its turn over them.

The damaged aircraft never made it that far. Immediately after its pilot had ejected, it was riven by a fuel tank explosion that tore away the burning wing and sent the fuselage into a flat spin toward the valley floor.

Snatched away from it by his deployed parachute, the pilot and his armored seat separated. Instead of popping open into a life-saving canopy, though, the chute remained a crumpled tangle of nylon.

There was a ragged cheer from the onlookers as the crewman impacted murderously hard not far from the remains of his fighter.

"We're on our own now." Thorne set down the thirty-caliber MG, and the unexpended portion of the belt swung to drape across his feet.

They reloaded, and waited, but there was no third raid. Revell stood most of them down and set those remaining to construct new air-defense positions.

Carrington found a hand, blackened, with the flesh hanging from it like the tatters of a thin glove. Casually he tossed it over the side. "Someone is going to get a telegram saying 'Regret to advise you, your beloved has been almost completely lost in action.'" He didn't bother to wipe off the adhering scraps of bloody tissue.

"You're bloody insane." Dooley had watched the act with an expression of extreme disgust.

"Did you expect me to keep it as a souvenir? Come off it. I've seen you chucking bits and pieces about without being too bothered."

"I don't care about that." Dooley resumed shoveling clear the floor of a weapon pit. Much of the debris had been fused together by a sticky black residue. "What's pissed me off is that it was wearing a ring, a gold signet ring."

Close by, Voke heard the exchange and flashed his metallic smile. "It is a comfort to me to know that when I am killed I shall not die alone. I am sure you will be close by, with pliers in your hand."

"Everybody's a fucking comedian." Changing the subject, Dooley called to the major. "How come they were content with just two passes? They didn't hang about to watch results; for all they know the Rapiers are still in one piece."

Revell had been thinking along the same lines himself. Using various vision aids one after another, he swept the valley and surveyed it thoroughly. From a window below, the Browning was again lacing the

Russian smokescreen with short punching bursts, now employing a high proportion of tracer. From the large number that ricocheted from unseen targets within the screen it now looked certain that the enemy were employing mostly armored clearing devices for the task.

It was tempting to send over a clutch of terminally guided Merlin mortar bombs, but to do so would be to invite an immediate and heavy retaliation. He would save that risk until he was sure the Russians had reached the narrowest part of the route they had chosen. If one of their huge tracked armored engineer vehicles was disabled in the defile between the hills it would block or at least seriously hamper their progress until it was towed out of the way.

His mind came back to the question of why there hadn't been a third air strike. And how had the other two been so precise; indeed, how had the Russian shelling been so accurate, with hardly a round wasted on the slopes below the castle mound?

Perhaps there was a second Spetsnaz operative, in the valley. But though he had no evidence one way or the other, Revell thought it highly unlikely. He had more than enough experience of the communists' special operations units to know that it was not usual for them to duplicate their efforts. That practice mostly came from their sheer arrogance. It was a failing frequently and successfully played upon by NATO interrogators.

He handed his field glasses to Andrea, who had appeared beside him. "Take your time. You're looking for an RPV."

It was a hell of a long-shot, Revell knew that, but if any of them was capable of locating one of the small remotely piloted aircraft, it was she.

With bad grace she shouldered her M16 and began a

181

systematic sweep of the sky above the valley.

Leaving her to it, the major checked the progress of work on the new Stinger positions. They were fewer this time, and positioned close to bolt holes that would give the operators a chance to make it to the lower levels in the face of an unexpected or overwhelming attack.

From inside the smokescreen came the blast of a large mine exploding, and then a fiercely driven column of gray smoke rose above the chemically created pall.

They wouldn't yet need to use the Merlins. No need to employ sophisticated top-attack homing warheads while the diversity of the conventional minefield was doing all right on its own. Revell returned to Andrea, in response to her call. Shit, even though it was "business," it was good to hear her wanting him. If only it was more than that . . .

Accepting the glasses from her, he let her guide his search until he found the object she had located. Her hands were cool and their grip light but firm.

"Got it." He'd been right, it was an RPV, apparently locked into a wide banking turn some fifteen hundred feet above the valley. It was closer than that to them in their elevated position. "The trouble with those little bastards is that they're damned near impossible to bring down."

It was galling. The small unpiloted aircraft, with a wingspan of not more than ten feet, represented a tiny target, and if it was the very latest type it offered virtually no emissions to home on, so that ruled out missiles. Carrying its own microwave link, it could receive its directions and beam out its gathered information in short bursts on tight channels that were virtually undetectable.

Back at some Russian HQ they could see real-time

transmissions of what was happening in the valley in perfect safety, and pass the information by unjammable land lines to their fighter bases and artillery positions.

"If we can take it out,"—Revell knew he was supposing what was virtually impossible—"then it would take them a long time to get another on station."

Andrea selected a grenade from her belt. "I have seen tens of thousands of rounds expended to that purpose. All without success."

"But it has been done." Not for a moment did Revell give consideration to employing the M60 for the task. Only a direct hit on the motor or a vital control wire—or even more freakishly, in the compact data link box—would disable the RPV.

"Yes, it has happened." Andrea loaded the 40mm round. "Usually by chance."

"Give it a try; we've nothing to lose." Without his field glasses there would have been little for Revell to see. Even with them he often missed the small puff of white smoke from the air-bursts.

With her seventh shot Andrea exploded a shell just in front of the aircraft, but frustratingly it flew unharmed through the rapidly dissipating cloud.

He was about to call a halt when her thirteenth attempt created a burst above and behind the target. It looked like yet another miss; then the RPV sideslipped and nosed down into a shallow dive. For a while he lost it, then when he found it again, saw that its outline was slightly changed. A piece of the tail was missing. Finally he lost it once more, for good, against the confusing clutter of the far hills. The descent appeared to have been due more to the RPV retaining a degree of aerodynamic stability than to any skillful control.

When he turned to congratulate Andrea she was already gone. It was easy to see why Sampson had made his remark about her, comparing her with Karen. There were times when, strong as his feelings were for her, Andrea could be unbearably independent and arrogant.

The smokescreen about the location of the Russian attempt to broach the minefield was thinning. It was no longer being reinforced by regular flurries of shells. As it dispersed, Revell saw it reveal a total of eight burning or burned-out mine-plow and roller-fitted tanks. An armored bulldozer wallowed in a large crater at an impossible angle, on the point of tipping over. Both its tracks were broken and an body hung from its open driver's hatch.

Though the RPV was eliminated, the enemy gunners already had the range of the castle to an inch, and Revell made every use of cover as he moved about. He'd have expected them to recommence firing as soon as it became obvious the first airstrike had failed to neutralize the strongpoint.

It was easy to imagine the report of the surviving pilot from the second wave, on his return to base. Sixty automatic weapons had been aimed at his flight leader and must have given the impression of a powerful defense. And that would have been reinforced by the beating off of the abortive helicopter assault on the valley, plus the continuing punishment of the ground troops trying to establish a land route to the prize offered by the huge dump of materials.

Their need was underlined by the fact that of the eight destroyed vehicles on the track, four were captured NATO tanks, Leopards and Challengers, modified for Soviet-style mine clearing.

"Here they come again." Carrington swung 'round a machine gun and sighted on the clutch of gunships hovering barely visible between the hills across the valley.

They were gone as suddenly as they'd appeared, and a pair of Stingers sent against them self-destructed when they reached the limit of their range, well short of their intended targets.

"What are they playing at?" Carrington waited patiently.

A single machine rose into distant view, unleashed a wire-guided rocket and hovered among the tops of firs only long enough to guide it to a direct hit on the gatehouse.

"Fuck knows." Keeping a missile tube shouldered, Burke waited for a realistic target to present itself before he fired.

Another Warpac gunship soared from behind a ridge and unleashed a ripple of unguided rockets toward the ruins, diving back into hiding before the projectiles had traversed half the distance. Of the twenty that were fired, none came close. Most fell a long way short, pulverizing a lower bend in the approach road.

"Maybe they're the same ships we scared away before." Hyde too was puzzled by the evasive tactics. "Could be they're still scared."

Again missiles were sent against the ruins, one to strike where the brickwork was keyed to the natural rock. The powerful impact left no mark but a black smudge and a slight pitting.

Cannon fire was added, from Hinds whose pilots were reluctant to make themselves visible for more than seconds at a time. From such a hopelessly long range only a handful of spent rounds flattened themselves against the unyielding ancient fabric.

"It's not like them to piss about this much." Reading off the range in his sight, Burke was aware there was no point in having a go at such elusive targets. "Could be that they're just decoys . . . Fucking shit . . ." He whirled about and fired wildly at a gunship only a hundred feet overhead.

The range was too short for the missile to arm itself in the time, but its sheer speed took it plunging in through the floor of the helicopter.

Disintegrating and scattering burning propellant as it penetrated, it turned the cabin into a roaring furnace. Out of control, the helicopter toppled from the sky to crash near the remains of the Scammel.

Torrents of mud and debris swept across the top of the ruins and three more camouflage-painted gunships closed in. From their open side doors came bright lines of tracer, and coils of rope were thrown out to whip about in the downwash.

Rolling onto his back, Clarence took aim and a door-gunner sagged limply, only restrained from falling by his safety harness.

The fight became wild, the choppers hovering and backing to give their gunners the best opportunities. Men who appeared at the cabin doors and made to slide down the ropes first hosed the ruins with their personal weapons.

Putting aside his sniper rifle, Clarence, hurling himself into an adjoining gunpit, pushed a body aside and wrenched a mini-gun hard back on its mount to gain the maximum elevation. Flicking the selector to the highest rate of fire he blasted several hundred rounds into the cabin top and rotor hub of a gunship banking in a tight turn to come in to drop its infantry.

There was a small flare of flame as a fuel line to one of the Isotov turboshaft powerplants was severed, and then as the blur of the mini-gun's rotating barrels slowed, the gunship stalled and fell onto a corner of the ruins.

Even as the cabin distorted and buckled with the impact, the still-rotating blades smashed themselves to

186

lethal slivers against a weapon pit. Blood fountained among the fragments of carbon fiber.

At point-blank range rifles and machine guns hosed armor-piercing incendiary rounds into the craft's shattered cockpit and gaping cabin.

He was so close, Revell could see the struggles of the pilot and gunner to free themselves, and the sprawl of infantry fighting to drag themselves clear.

Burning fuel dribbling onto the men spurred them to frantic effort, faces distorted by the effort of forcing broken limbs to respond. There came an ominous creak of metal grinding on stone and the machine appeared to sag and then shudder as it moved bodily sideways toward the edge. It teetered, a mound of rubble collapsed beneath it, and then it was gone, followed by a cascade of granite and sandstone chips.

As suddenly as they had appeared, the gunships departed, racing for the cover of the hills and woods. They trailed smoke and dropped a shower of external fittings and torn panels as they went. Unable in that condition to execute wild evasive maneuvers, they had to soak up more damage from the tracer that chased after them.

It had been a crazy tactic. Revell couldn't begin to understand what the Russians had hoped to achieve. They'd been trying to land troops in what had to be a suicide mission. Unless . . . unless Burke was correct and the whole episode was a diversion from some other piece of nastiness they were hatching.

A monstrous explosion rocked the whole fabric of the castle. Smoke and dust belched from every entrance to the lower levels in a raging blast that threw him over.

CHAPTER TWENTY-ONE

Pushing himself to his feet, he heard screams coming from below—girls' screams. Grabbing his shotgun and waving Hyde and Voke to stay, Revell raced for the cellars.

Burke was already ahead of him, Colt automatic in one hand, the other clenched tight about a grenade from which the split ring attached to the pin dangled brightly.

On the ground floor several men had been mowed down by the blast, mostly those who had been in direct line with the cellar entrance. Some lay still, heads shattered, but most still moved, hugging themselves against the agony of broken bones. Others stood dazed, stupefied by the powerful concussion. Andrea was among them, nursing her left wrist.

Pushing in front, Revell led down the steps. By a miracle the lights still functioned, but they served little purpose. He strapped on his respirator as some protection against the thick choking dust as he groped his way down.

At the bottom they stopped and listened. From roughly in the direction of the dispensary came the muted sobs of a terrified girl. Sensing rather than seeing what was happening, Revell held out his arm to check Burke's impulse to go straight toward the sound.

Revell was frightened at the prospect of the terrifying game of blindfold hide-and-seek that lay ahead. It would be as dangerous and deadly a fight as any he'd ever taken part in, as could ever be imagined.

Hugging the wall they stumbled forward, with Revell trying desperately to recall every turn, every doorway, every side passage.

He could see perhaps a matter of inches, six perhaps, not more. The air was hot and carried a strong scent of partially consumed explosive. His foot made contact with an object that rolled away. Still keeping the shotgun trained ahead, he stooped to feel about. His searching fingers found several of the items, grenades.

A few steps farther and another forced investigation brought about the discovery of the remains of the man who had been carrying them. Underfoot the floor was slippery with blood. From a helmet he touched, Revell determined that the bodies they were encountering were members of the Dutch ammunition detail. Groans came from a body he stepped on. Attempting to move it aside, he found it had no arms; both were off at the shoulder.

The clattering fire of a Kalshnikov punished their ears in the confined space, but Revell took no account of that when he replied with a three-round burst. There was no response to the hail of flechettes that filled every inch of the passageway with a quota of needle-sharp steel.

Wafting past, a current of cool air brought an improvement in visibility. Silhouetted against a circle of light haze dead ahead was a dark blur. It was slowly crumpling, and as he went down a second slumped from the shadows across it.

"Two down; how many more to go?" Burke felt the grenade warming in his hand, and knelt to roll it in the dust, to make sure it wouldn't stick to his damp palm.

Resolving itself gradually into the outline of the shattered postern door, the patch of light enabled Revell to orient himself. "They must have climbed up and put a charge on it, while we were occupied upstairs."

Before he could fire, Burke had snapped off a shot and a figure sidling through the opening was thrown back and screamed for a long time as he fell down the cliff face.

From the chunks of flesh and small splinters of wood to which the door and its surround had been reduced, Revell was sure that at the moment the demolition charge exploded the passageway must have resembled hell.

Men caught in the blast had been torn apart, and the loads they carried scattered. It was a miracle that none of the ordnance had gone off at the same time. With every other room packed with ammunition from floor to ceiling, a chain reaction of secondary detonation would have blasted the stump of the castle across the countryside and left nothing but the bare rock.

A small round dark object was tossed in through the doorway. They threw themselves down, but the Russian grenade burst between the bodies and, beyond bringing down more dust into the already heavily laden atmosphere, did no harm.

There was a tugging at Revell's foot, and he looked down. The Dutchman Old William was sprawled on the floor, his hair matted with blood and his face lined with cuts. Unable to talk, he gestured toward a door.

Burke cautiously pushed it open. It was the wine vault. The air was almost clear. There was a cage of songbirds on the table, but they were the only occupants.

"The fucker's skipped." Burke took a tighter grip of his pistol.

"He might not have got far." The smell of death and

the slimy mess beneath his feet offered the hope to Revell that the deserter, whether he had mistimed an escape or taken advantage of the confusion of the attack, was dead.

"That bloke is a survivor. I'll put money on his still being alive."

A heavy figure blundered into them from behind, and after the start it gave him, the major was glad to see Dooley. Even with his respirator on, his great bulk made him unmistakable.

Revell motioned toward the opening. "Dooley, stay here. Anything comes in through there you know what to do. Same goes if we flush someone out and he makes a bolt for it."

"What if he come this way instead? You want prisoners?" Straightening the belt of the M60, Dooley undraped another three from around his neck. He settled himself in the doorway of the wine cellar, after a quick glance inside to reassure himself that his feathered friends were all right.

"They were trying to kill your birds, weren't they?"

Nothing more was needed to settle Dooley's determination. He reached out and began to gather sandbags about himself. Noticing Old William, and after a cursory examination concluding from his shallow but steady breathing that he was still alive, he dragged him in behind the barricade as well.

The temptation to slip into the vault and extract a bottle was strong, almost overwhelming, but there was in his mind a more powerful reason, besides self-preservation, for not stirring from his position.

From within the cellar came a sad whistle of half-hearted song. He thought of the hard work it had been to gather the colorful birds in their aviary, with it almost encircled by burning sheds and garages. They'd been panicking, and he knew he must for certain have missed some that were hiding in nesting boxes.

"Miserable shits." Dooley talked aloud, but to himself. "Not bad enough they don't believe in God, they've got to go around trying to kill all his little creatures as well."

He was in that frame of mind when a grenade popped in through the opening. It bounced once, almost playfully, then detonated harmlessly among the tattered corpses. Holding his fire he let three of them enter, ducking low to avoid the long bursts they directed down the passageway. Only when they paused to reload did he open up.

Coming from what must have been to them an impenetrable dark, the Russians were caught by surprise. It must have been an agonizing shock when the heavy-caliber bullets smashed into their legs and brought them down hard.

Taking time to count how many belts he had, Dooley decided he could spare one. His victims were writhing and moaning, plucking at their ruined limbs, from which sharp white shards of bone projected.

Casually, standing so he could fire from the hip, he emptied the rest of the belt into the tangle of flesh and weapons.

Dooley listened. All sound and movement had ceased. "See, you commie shits. I'm a humanitarian as well as a nature-lover. Maybe I should join Green Peace."

Patting his pockets, he counted the number of spare magazines he had for his pistol, and checked that he still had his little hoard of jewelry and dental fragments. The simple action brought back memories of how he'd come by each item, the death he'd witnessed, and shared in. "Yeah, well, maybe not Green Peace."

*　　*　　*

Little of the draft clearing the main passageway was clearing the side corridor that led to the aid post.

Within a few steps Revell found visibility again down to nil. They were forced to inch forward, not daring to lose contact with the wall. There were two other rooms to pass before they reached their objective at the end of the passageway.

Revell tried hard to recall the distances involved, and and compare them with their present slow progress. In steps he could roughly calculate it, but how many shuffles were equivalent to one normal pace?

He tried using his thermal imager, but the invading Russians must have employed grenades whose smoke masked the wavebands on which it functioned, and he got virtually no picture at all.

His fingertips found the first doorway, and splintered wood where it had been forced open. It was tempting simply to hurl in a grenade, but some of the girls might have escaped or been herded into there. He had to be more discriminating in his tactics than he would have liked.

Making sure of the type of cartridge he had chambered, he hurled himself across the opening, blasting a shell at the cellar ceiling. There was no answering fire and he ducked inside, closely followed by Burke. They were hardly in before a hail of bullets ripped past the door.

The room was comparatively free of smoke. Lined with steel ammunition boxes, many of them displayed evidence of having been sprayed with automatic fire.

"You think they did the same all the way along?" Burke could picture the scene as a Russian had braced himself in the doorway and swept every corner with blasts of high-velocity rounds.

"Not if they saw what they'd hit in here. They must have shit themselves." Mentally Revell ticked off the shots he had fired. He didn't need to reload, yet. "What's in the next room?"

"Karen . . . that is, they were clearing it to take the overflow of wounded." Burke remembered something. "The stuff they'd hauled out they dumped in the passageway."

"Were they stacking it both sides, or just one, and which?"

Closing his eyes, Burke tried to recall a detail that had been too trivial to note at the time. "This side . . . yes, this side. Against the wall between the next door and the sick bay."

"Right. We'll make a dive for the next cellar. Same tactics as before. You still got that grenade?"

"If I lose it you'll know soon enough. The pin's out."

As he dashed for their next objective, Revell snapped off three fast shots that were rewarded with a muffled yelp of pain and the sound of a body falling.

Again there was no reply to the single flechette shot the major put into the ceiling, and when more bullets hosed along the passage they were already tumbling inside to a soft landing on rows of sleeping bags.

"How far now?" Pulling off his respirator, Revell gulped the tainted air. Before he had an answer to confirm his own estimate, they had to throw themselves to either side of the door as a grenade bounced past.

Fragments from it slashed through the opening, ripping apart the bedding and creating showers of down and lint.

"By my reckoning, three steps to the stack of boxes, then five, no, six to pass it and then an immediate sharp left will put you facing the door of the dispensary."

Revell drew a mental picture of what he expected to see when he got there. The trapped Russians would have herded their hostages to the far end of the room, to keep them out of the way and permit unobstructed action. Unless, that is, the troops were Spetsnaz.

There came the sound of a girl crying, and ugly grunted threats in Russian. The words might not have been understood, but their obvious menace was, and the crying ceased in a series of choking sobs.

"They're still alive." Burke said it to reassure himself, and then the hairs on the back of his neck prickled as there came a long wailing scream of sheer agony. The lunge he made for the door was blocked by the major.

"Not yet." Revell heard Sampson's distinctive voice raised in protest, more shouting in Russian, the thud of a heavy blow and then a silence that could be almost felt.

"What the fuck are they doing?" Again Burke attempted to push past. "All I want to do is get in there and sort them out . . ."

"Stay calm. Lose your temper and you'll make mistakes." It was taking an effort for Revell to keep himself under control, and was harder still when another scream, of shorter duration this time, came from someone in the last extreme of agony.

From that he knew they had to be facing the elite Russian Spetsnaz troops. Coming in with no knowledge of the underground layout, and quickly disoriented by the blinding smoke and dust, they must have blundered into this deadend, to be trapped by his and Burke's fast arrival on the scene.

Like the hate-indoctrinated automatons they were, even at the moment when they should have been scheming to survive, the Spetsnaz had turned on helpless victims, perhaps seeking confidence by falling back on the skills in which they were most practiced.

Another random burst from an AK flashed past the door. Revell knew the Russians were carrying on a reconnaissance by fire, probing to see what the

195

opposition would be like when they broke out. The moment they decided to do that, they would slaughter their hostages, except perhaps for one or two they might utilize as human shields, a standard Spetsnaz tactic.

At present, while they were sorting themselves out, they had most likely only one man on guard. He would probably be crouched low by the door, taking full advantage of any cover. Likely he'd built himself a rough barricade of boxes that were within his reach. He'd present a small enough target in perfect visibility; the chances of putting him down with a first-round disabling shot in these conditions was nil.

Carefully lobbed, a grenade might catch him, but fragments tearing through the open door would be indiscriminate killers. The enemy held all the cards. They daren't delay any longer.

Another screeching howl of suffering made up Revell's mind for him. For the sheath at his belt he withdrew his heavy-bladed fighting knife. In all the war so far it had done nothing more bloody than hack horsemeat steaks. Setting aside his shotgun, he replaced it with his Browning pistol. Weighing both, he settled for the knife in his right hand.

"Put that grenade, near as you can, just short of the next doorway. When it goes off we go in, fast."

Burke moved to the door. Sweat poured from him, but the dust-covered grenade stayed dry in his tight grasp. Just what the fuck was he doing here? He'd never pushed himself forward like this before. Shit, he was a combat driver; this wasn't his sort of work. But there hadn't been anyone special in his life before, not until a few hours ago.

There was the faint sound of a girl crying, and a harsh command in Russian was followed by the report of a stinging slap.

196

Without another thought he swung 'round the doorpost, tossed the grenade and ducked back into cover.

A shout of alarm was smothered, and his ears punished, by the explosion in the confines of the tunnel. Grabbing his bayonet from his side he charged blindly into the unknown.

CHAPTER TWENTY-TWO

The Russian in the doorway was sagging against the tumbled cases of his barricade. As Burke kicked out at his face he saw the bottom jaw was gone, but still didn't pull the blow.

A clatter of fire from the entrance gave him the direction he wanted and he fired three fast soft-nosed bullets toward the muzzle flash.

Searing pain in his side told him he'd been hit, but he ran on and thrust the bayonet to the hilt in a figure that was lunging at him.

The blade stuck, caught between the bottom ribs, and he fired with the pistol barrel touching his victim's stomach. His wrist jarred at the recoil, but the impact did the trick, throwing the impaled man back. The blade came free with a sucking sound.

Shouts, screams and the ear-splitting reports of gunfire blared through the dimly lit cellar. Revell snapped a single shot into the face of a Russian who swung a rifle butt at him, side-stepped the falling body and bumped into a blood-covered form lashed to a chair. Its head lolled, and then the whole body bucked as bullets intended for Revell struck it instead.

He fired twice at a slab-faced Slav wrestling to clear a blockage in his wire-stocked AK, and missed. There was a snarl of triumph from the Russian as he

198

succeeded and brought the weapon up, and then a look of blank incomprehension as a scalpel was skewered into the side of his neck.

On tiptoe to inflict the wound, Karen was thrown aside as the man lashed out, caught off balance. His rifle swiveled in her direction and then a blood-smeared bayonet sliced across his throat.

Reeling, bewildered, he turned to counter the new danger. The bayonet struck a second time, thrust at a sharp upward angle just below his ear.

Following the body down, Burke straddled it, took the hilt of the weapon in both hands and plunged it repeatedly into the Russian chest, each time lifting his hands as high as he could. He stopped only when he was exhausted, long after the man was dead.

Karen helped Burke to his feet and fussed over the blood that seeped through a tear in his jacket, making it cling to him as the material became soaked. He gently held her hands away and went to the figure in the chair.

Using a wad of dressing, he applied pressure to the hideous wound across the side of Boris's face. Accepting a roll of broad bandage from Karen, he wrapped it around their radioman's head, feeling the bulk of the dressing subside as it filled the empty eye socket.

Hauling himself to his feet, Sampson tentatively felt the large contusion at the base of the back of his neck. He knuckled his eyes to clear them of double vision. Gathering himself to take over from Burke, opening Boris's jacket and cutting away his undershirt to examine the tight cluster of exit wounds below his left shoulder. "They grabbed him on the way in. The stupid little guy was so scared he called out in his own language. Those animals started on him without warning. I tried to stop them and they must have swiped me a hard one from behind. They weren't even questioning him. It was like it was normal practice, just started cutting him."

There was a rattle of M60 fire from the corridor. Revell looked around the room. The smoke and dust were clearing. It looked like a charnel house. One of the attackers was still moving, and he crushed his boot down hard on a hand that was too near a discarded automatic for comfort. Looking up at him, the Russian tried to spit, but succeeded only in dribbling. It was an effort that proved fatal. Somewhere inside him a blood vessel ruptured and filled his throat to drown him.

The scene in the room was overwhelming. Several of the wounded had been trampled or hit by fragments or ricochets.

"I'll send you some help." Revell got no reply. "Old William and some other wounded are in the passageway."

"Okay." Sampson set upright a drip that had been knocked over, and hauled the corpse of a Spetsnaz off the girl with the headwound. "I'll be there in a moment. Hell and shit! I thought I'd seen everything in the Zone, but this is just plain horrible. Why the hell do we go on doing this?"

"To stay alive." Revell had seen enough; he started to leave.

"You call this living?" Sampson picked up the body of a girl. The side of her head had been blown away and white brain matter dripped from her shattered skull. "This is fucking butchery."

Revell had no reply. On his way out he checked Dooley. Old William sat beside him, cradling an M16 and grinning a toothless grin. He made his customary nod at the major.

"Added a few more to the collection." Dooley patted the M60. "Three more and I can send them off and get a set of storage jars."

There were at least eight bodies lying half inside the postern doorway. Wisps of smoke rose from tracer lodged in them.

Mounting the cellar steps, Revell crossed the ground floor, past the row of dead whose numbers would shortly be swollen. Already those killed by the blast were being hauled aside to join them. Andrea was helping, using one hand.

He would have sent her down to be attended to, but she studiously ignored him, and he passed on without comment.

There was sporadic incoming artillery fire, but it was arriving at predictable one-minute intervals, indicating that it was an East German battery employed. Though the air was full of the dust and smoke they pounded from the ruins, after the cellars it tasted clean and wholesome.

It was tempting to take advantage of the set intervals to take a shortcut across the rubble, but instinct made Revell choose the safety of the more difficult route under cover. That saved his life, when a twin-barreled 30mm flak tank blasted the top of the ruins with a thirty-round burst.

On the far side of the valley another smokescreen was forming. Out of range, another attempt was being made to breach the minefield. There were comforting reports of explosions to indicate that the work was going slowly or badly.

Voke was fussing with the sterile pad inside the shoulder of his jacket, but stopped when Revell came into the dugout. "You have noticed the timing of the shells?" He nodded knowingly to himself. "East Germans, always so precise. Their employment against us would explain why there have been no chemical rounds. The Russians do not trust them with them, since that time when a whole regiment tried to defect to the West, after hitting the Russian divisions to either side of them with sarin and VX."

"Not many of them made it though, did they?"

"True, the Reds bombed them to pieces as they crossed the Zone. But at least when we fight them it is one less factor to worry about." Voke grinned, glanced at his watch and held his helmet down hard as a 155mm shell crashed into the wall below their position. "Right on time."

"I think we're going to have to blow the dump. They'll be through into the valley by tomorrow morning." It was bitter for Revell to have to admit that defeat, but he had to be realistic. At least he would have the satisfaction of blowing apart the Russian's prize even as they reached for it.

"There is a problem, Major." Voke was apologetic. "I have tested the circuit, and there appears to be a slight fault."

"How slight is slight?"

Sweeping his arms wide and shrugging in a resigned gesture, Voke was no longer smiling. "The link was deeply buried, and was still working after the castle fell, but it is not now. I think it would be unlikely we could trace the fault; it could be anywhere between here and the complex."

"Shit." Gauging the distances involved, Revell estimated the nearest of the dumps would just be within range of their TOW missiles.

He was suddenly aware of Andrea by his side. Her wrist was bandaged and splinted. Reading his mind once again, she handed him a laser rangefinder.

The reading was three thousand six hundred meters. "There'll be a bit of wire to spare."

Voke shook his head. "The installation is hardened. With what we have I do not believe we could penetrate several meters of earth and then a meter of steel-reinforced concrete. And in any event, the munitions

202

and fuel are on the far side. A direct hit anywhere else would do no more than very localized damage."

Revell sat back and thought about it. His eyes met Andrea's. There was no expression in hers. For the first time he could recall, he felt no wave of sympathy for her, as he invariably had when she'd been injured in the past.

"Can it be done manually, from down there?"

"I was afraid you would ask that, Major." Despite his words, Voke's smile had returned. "The answer is yes. There is such an emergency system. When it was installed a joker hung on it a notice saying 'suicide switch.' There would be little chance of getting clear."

"We don't have a choice." For Revell now there was a lot of planning to be done. "It'll take the Reds the best part of the night to break through into the valley. By then we should be long gone, most of us. A small stay-behind group will have to blow the dumps at the last moment. Once they go up all hell will break loose. They'll know we've done a runner."

An airburst detonated overhead and chunks of shell-casing drummed against the roof of the strongpoint.

Brushing dust from his shoulder, Voke winced as the movement aggravated his wound. "If you are taking the wounded with you then you will need as long a headstart as possible."

Andrea looked up at the words. "It would be madness-to burden the escape group with wounded." She glanced at her wrist. "With the more serious cases, that is . . ."

"We are not leaving anyone behind; you know what they can expect at the hands of the Russians. This unit has never left wounded to fall into their murdering hands."

"I'm telling you, Major Revell, sir, that it don't

matter what you say—it can't be done."

Forcing down his instinctive response to the medic's insubordination, Revell waited for the explanation, drumming his forefinger against the stock of his shotgun.

"There's two down there with head wounds who'll die if we try to move them, three with open chest wounds who'll die when we move them, three real bad gut wounds who won't make it any distance at all, a double amputee who's hanging on by a thread and eight cases of multiple fractures of the hip and leg who are going to be hell to move. And that's not counting all the walking wounded who will either need help, like Ripper, or who are in no state to give a hand with the others, like the lieutenant here, or Andrea."

It was growing dark, and for Revell the gathering gloom was an accurate reflection of his mood. "How many have we got who are fit to fight or carry?"

"A lot of those still on their feet will need frequent kicks to keep them moving." Hyde had made the count himself. With the men dispersed about the various defense positions it had taken that to bring home how depleted their numbers were. "But if you want me to include everyone still with the strength to pull a trigger, seventeen." He looked at the lieutenant.

"Thirty-nine of my pioneers are still on their feet. Using the sergeant's methods I could persuade another eight to make the effort. We lost sixteen men when the door was blown."

"No luck with the radio yet?" Revell made no comment on the figures; they spoke for themselves. The radio was a forlorn hope, but he'd insisted Garrett keep trying.

"Nothing yet." Hyde had made the same report every ten minutes for the last couple of hours.

Dooley pushed his way into the group. He thrust a

bulky pack at the major. "You should see this."

Taking the bag, Revell noted it was Russian and sticky with blood. Inside was a signal gun and a selection of variously color-coded cartridges for it. There was also a large wooden case, strongly fastened with leather straps. Resting it on his knee, he undid it to reveal a compact microwave dish complete with all its related equipment, right down to spare batteries.

"I found it under the body of a Spetsnaz who didn't make it past the door." Dooley wriggled fingers through holes in the pack's carrying strap.

"Get Garrett over here on the double." Revell turned to Sampson. "And I want Boris up here. Before you say it I know he's in a bad way, but from now on your main task is to keep him alive for as long as you can—that's if you want to go on living yourself."

The sun set early, behind a bank of bluish-gray clouds that were growing on the western horizon. As the tops of the hills caught the last of the pale light a sharp breeze sprang up and added a distinct chill to the air.

From across the valley came the occasional report of a mine being triggered. No flash was ever visible inside the dense smokescreen but it gave notice that the Russians were making no faster progress over there, even without harassment.

At what would have been sunset, if the changing weather had not brought it forward, they heard a pair of gunships circling. For half an hour they maintained an erratic search pattern, but if the castle was their target, they never found it.

Gradually the beat of the rotors faded in the distance, and some kilometers off, an inoffensive, unoccupied hilltop received a deluge of fuel-air bombs, and as it burned was repeatedly strafed with cannons and rockets.

The Russians didn't dare take their loads back and admit failure. Revell could only hope their report of a brilliant pinpoint attack would allow them to be left in peace for a while.

It was shortly after that, as he wrestled with the problem of what to do with the wounded, that they established a radio link through a satellite relay.

Boris lay back, ignoring the discomfort of the broken surface. It was nothing compared to the throbbing in his head and the agony of drawing each breath. There was a curious bubbling sensation in his chest, and a growing numbness down his right side.

They had explained why he could not have more pain-killers and he had accepted their reasoning. Laid beside Garrett, he had directed the necessary modifications to the equipment to enable it to operate on NATO wavebands.

The clumsiness displayed by the young PFC, his impetuous rush into every task at the risk of doing irreparable damage, had driven Boris to the verge of distraction. Fortunately no serious damage had resulted from his frequent dropping, knocking and gouging of components.

He'd made every allowance for the work being done under difficult conditions, in the dark and cold and with only the fitful illumination from a small flashlight held by their shivering medic, but still the PFC's reckless ineptitude had made him despair at times.

"You lay down like that, you fool, and you're going to drown in your own blood." Sampson wadded a jacket and placed it under the Russian's head and shoulders. "You want that jab now?" Even as he asked,

206

he produced a hypodermic.

"Pozhalusta, da." Boris wrestled with his swirling memory, but the English words would not come. But he'd been understood, and as he felt the tip of the needle enter his arm he experienced an overwhelming sensation of relief, so strong that the comfort it brought merged imperceptibly with the effect of the drug.

He knew he was very likely one of hundreds who would breathe their last this night in the Zone. But he did not see it as a personal tragedy; he had been marked for death for too long, had come to accept the idea, and now the fact.

Lying at the bottom of the gunpit, he could see the crescent of the microwave dish resting on a plinth of broken stone. Vaguely he was aware of people gathered about the nearby radio. The only sound he could hear was his own blood rushing through his ears, in a hurry to find the holes in his body, to escape and take his life with it.

There was a face above him, and he was being gently shaken. They should leave him alone, he had done all he could . . .

"Can you hear me?" Garrett turned to Sampson. "How much have you pumped into him?"

"Enough to take away the pain. In his case that's quite a lot. The poor little creep is in shock. I'll lay money he can understand you, but he may not be able to answer."

"Boris, Boris, can you hear me?" Garrett felt like he was touching a corpse, the man was so pale and cold. "Boris, the signal is fading. The set is all right, but the signal is fading." He repeated it again, talking loudly and slowly. "What do I have to do?"

From a depth only a shade away from deep unconsciousness, Boris struggled to articulate. He could manage only a single word and it took forever to

207

form and virtually the last of his breath to utter.

"Batereyka." He was still being shaken and the question persisted, going on and on. By an effort of will he dragged his mind back from the plunge into blackness it had commenced and tried again. "Ak-kumulyator . . . batareyka . . . battery, the battery . . ."

The last word blended into a deep sigh. In the narrow segment of night sky that he could see, Boris watched the stars being snuffed one by one as the leading edge of a large cloud drifted in front of them.

He did not think it strange that he had no fear of death. How can a man who has known fear all his adult life be afraid of being released from that?

There would be no more KGB, no more GPU, no more foul prisons, no more brutish interrogators, no more thugs of the Commandants Service. And no more Andrea with her scarcely veiled threats and ever-present menace.

Pain was returning, but still as only a pulsing burning sensation so far. He was glad his last act had not been one to bring death to his fellow countrymen. Making the set function had been an act to save life, not destroy it. It no longer mattered that help would come too late for him.

"At last." Andrea bent over the blanket-wrapped form. "He is dead. Good."

Revell paused as he was about to replace the headset. "Andea." Her features were indistinct in the darkness, but he knew she had heard him. "Fuck off."

CHAPTER TWENTY-THREE

Scully had to steel himself for each journey down to the cellars to help with bringing up the wounded. Even the difficulties and sheer exertion of the task couldn't override entirely his abhorrence of the cramped passageways and low ceilings.

Manhandling the litters through the narrow doorways, around sharp corners and up steep staircases, and all the time trying to ensure that a drip needle wasn't dislodged, or that a fractured limb wasn't knocked against the wall. The work was exacting and exhausting for the patients, as well as the bearers, as they were tilted and jolted.

Several times Scully had seen Andrea stalk by, a look of savage determination on her face as she hunted for the missing deserter. A gruesome check of the remains scattered below ground had positively confirmed he was not among those killed. She had appointed herself to conduct the search among the warren of storerooms.

"Don't fancy his chances if she finds him." Dooley hefted his end of a litter higher and took the weight as two others supported its front end and started up the cellar steps.

"What the hell did the major say to her?" Scully staggered, but managed to maintain his grip.

"No idea." Arms aching, Dooley would have preferred to move faster but the pace had to be set by the men in the lead. He had to tap with his toecap to determine the exact height of each step before moving onto it. "Whatever it was it's broken the spell. I reckon she won't be twisting him 'round her little finger anymore."

They finally shuffled into the ground floor and under Sampson's supervision lifted the Dutchman off the litter and laid him on the bare stone floor.

The whole of the good-sized room was filled with wounded. Some were sitting but most were laid still, making no sound except for an occasonal low moan as pain broke through the heavy doses of painkillers.

"That the last?" Sampson made an adjustment to a drip, working with his nose almost touching it, by the light of a carefully shielded match.

"That's it." Dooley flexed his muscles to rid them of the cramp induced by the prolonged strain of the hard work. "Only thing still down there is Andrea and that deserter."

"They deserve each other. Maybe they'll run off together and we'll all be happier and safer." Looking about him, there was little Sampson could see, and less he could do.

Karen had the flashlight and was moving among the wounded quietly. The small circle of illumination flicked from drawn faces to dressing, to drips and then on to the next.

"Are we really ordered to stay put, and keep the dump in one piece?" Dooley couldn't make sense of the rumor that was flying about. "We can't hold this place now. We'll just be handing all those goodies to the commies on a plate."

"All I know is that I was told to get the wounded up to the first floor, ready for evacuation at first light or soon after. Won't take so long to get them into a chopper from here. Guess, as usual, the casevac boys don't want to be on the ground longer than they can help."

Checking the pulse of the last man brought up, Sampson felt it falter, pick up again, and the cease.

"Oh shit. I lost him, and I really thought he was in with a chance. You never can tell."

"That all you know?"

"Look, Dooley, you're so keen to find out, go ask the major. I'm busy, trying to stop people from dying."

Sampson disconnected the drip. He knelt beside the body and pulled the blanket up to cover the face. "Yeah, I'm trying, dear God I'm trying, but I'm not always succeeding."

There was no doubt he'd heard the orders clearly, but in the short transmission time he'd been allowed, Revell had been given no more than the barest facts. They were brutally brief and precise. Stay put, don't destroy the dump, casualty pick-up at first light. That was it.

It wasn't orders, it was a death sentence. They were a tiny NATO island in the middle of a surging communist sea. At best from now on they could be of no more than nuisance value to the Russian troops intent on capturing the valley and its contents.

By this time the communists would be confident that the handful of troops holed up in the ruins did not possess the means to destroy the dumps. Their mine-clearing effort had only to remain beyond the reach of the comparatively short-range weapons emplaced among the ruins and shortly all would be theirs.

It was only the fate of the wounded that deterred Revell from disobeying orders. Once they were away he would take matters into his own hands. It was more than likely that HQ did not understand the implications of the situation. Just because he'd had an acknowledgment of his signal did not mean that the staff officer dealing with it had fully understood precisely what was at stake. Shit, how could he? He wouldn't have seen the lives lost, the bodies broken and torn apart . . .

"The Reds have lost another bulldozer, by the look of it."

On the far side of the valley a bubble of flame rose through the piled smokescreen. Hyde watched it tuck in its tail as it climbed until it was a disembodied ball of dull fire, and then it was gone.

"Yes." Revell noted it absently. "But they haven't far to go."

"They'll have thrown away a lot of lives." Hyde beat his arms across his body to combat the cold. "Did the powers-that-be say if we'd be reinforced after the wounded are away?"

Flecks of sleet blew in the wind and Revell pulled his collar higher. "They didn't say anything. I don't know whether they don't know what they're doing or won't say what they're doing. We stay, that's all I got."

"You going to speak to the men? There's a lot of rumors flying about."

"They can't be any worse than the truth. Pass on what we know. I'll talk to them after the casualties are lifted out."

"There won't be a lot you can say, will there, except to tell them to check they've filled in their will forms."

Revell knew his sergeant was right, echoing his own thinking. Perhaps they were being left behind purely for their nuisance value. They could tie up quite a few Russian troops for some time. It was a tactic the Russians themselves had frequently used. Stay-behind parties could inflict damage out of all proportion to their numbers.

Hell, and he'd thought by defending this place they were making a real contribution to the NATO effort, giving the Russians a hard kick in the teeth. The truth was they were no more than pricking them with a pin, and would be brushed aside and destroyed as an afterthought of the main Warpac advance. Perhaps the NATO staff wanted the tempting stores in the valley to remain intact for the time being so as to act as a honeypot, drawing more and more troops onto them.

Another airburst cracked overhead. The flak tank that had been quiet for an hour joined in, hoping to catch anyone going to the assistance of wounded. Orange tracer flashed above the ruins to arc away in the distance and finally self-destruct at the limit of their range in tiny points of light.

"Sunrise in thirty minutes." Revell had to brush a snowflake from his watch to read it. "We've got about six-tenths cloud. Let's hope it stays that way."

"I'll get Scully to pass 'round hot drinks." Hyde wiped his face with the back of his glove. The leather was sodden.

"Good idea. Might be the last chance for a while. Then I want all weapons manned. When we hear that chopper coming in I want to hit every commie flak position with all we've got."

"What the fuck's going on?" Dooley scrambled up on top and hurled himself into the nearest weapon pit. He had to bellow at his loudest to make himself heard by Clarence.

"How should I know? I'm only fighting this war, not running it; that's if anybody is . . ."

"Shit." Dooley threw himself flat as a flight of

Harriers screamed past so low that they felt the blast of their slipstream and tasted the exhaust from their jet pipes. "The whole world has gone fucking mad . . ."

The rest of his words were lost as a pair of A10s followed the Harriers.

Tracer was coming up from among the trees, among them the 30mm from the flak tank.

"Hit it." Revell jumped up and yelled to the mortar crews. "Take it out now."

"Fire." Thorne and his men dropped bombs down the waiting tubes in a never-ending procession, pausing only to realign on fresh targets as they were called. Every location in turn was drenched by the deluge of explosives, and the anti-aircraft fire rapidly diminished.

Masses of tracer and whole swarms of anti-tank missiles plowed through the trees, and soon there were several fierce fires sprouting from unseen sources, and the crackle of exploding munitions.

More NATO ground-attack aircraft were visible in the distance, peeling out of formations to make diving attacks with rockets, bombs and cannons. Almost every time they were rewarded with dense pillars of black smoke denoting burning vehicles. The columns rose straight up in the still, pale dawn.

"This is fantastic. I thought we didn't have any aircraft left." Dooley sent yet another TOW missile on its way and gave it his full concentration until it blasted the camouflage from a self-propelled gun. He grabbed a reload.

"Some clever shit has been saving a few by the looks of things." Carrington had hefted his mini-gun onto the top of a broken wall and was expending ammunition at an incredible rate against a distant ridge. After a thousand rounds, showers of random tracer marked the destruction of his target.

From close at hand came the distinctive heavy double beat of a Chinook. The downdraft from his blades accelerated the sleet to stinging speed that hurt exposed hands and faces. As it reduced forward momentum and began to drop toward the ruins, its gunners were putting down a massive weight of fire from four mini-guns and as many grenade launchers. The machine was plastered with red-cross emblems.

The rear loading ramp was already half-lowered when it made an uneven touchdown. By the time it made contact with the broken stone the first of the wounded were lining up to board.

A loadmaster, linked to the flight deck by the umbilical of his intercom lead, did a double-take as he saw the girls. "Can't have been all that bad, Major. I wouldn't have minded . . ." His words tailed off as the line of wounded kept coming in a never-ending line from an opening among the piles of rubble.

"It's not been a party." Revell ducked as a cannot shell passed through the arc of the forward rotors and a shower of metal and carbon fiber fragments slashed past. "Have you got a combat air patrol? Can you get hold of them?"

"No problem. What do you want and where?"

"Everything they've got. Right under the castle walls and back along the road."

Less than a minute elapsed and then the air was filled again with the roar of jet engines as a line of A10s dipped from the clouds and swept low over the trees.

Firing rockets and letting rip with their cannons, the ground-attack aircraft tore the landscape apart, cutting great swaths through the trees. The last to make its pass released four tear-drop-shaped dull silver pods.

They tumbled end over end to burst in long broad avenues of violent flame. Pines became pillars of fire and burst explosively as water trapped behind their bark instantly expanded into super-heated steam.

Hyde clapped the loadmaster on his shoulder to get his attention. "That's it. They're all aboard."

"You better pull in the rest of your men, Major. We don't like to hang around."

At first Revell thought he'd misheard the loadmaster. "No, we're staying."

"Not according to the orders my captain was given. We're to lift out all troops in this location. Came direct from your C.O. A Colonel Lippincott?"

"Did you hear his words?"

"You bet. Nearly burned my ears off. Something to the effect that we were to haul out any fucking cunts wandering about on this heap of shit."

"That's Ol' Foulmouth all right." Revell had to shout to make himself heard. "But we can't pull out. There's a billion-dollar supply dump down there. The Reds are after it."

"You haven't heard what's happening, have you?"

CHAPTER TWENTY-FOUR

Bending his head closer to the loadmaster, Revell strove to catch his words.

"We've put down a couple of divisions of paratroops behind the Russian lines. So far they've taken a dozen of their command centers, complete with staff and generals. SAS and First Air cavalry have gone in and screwed up all their communications centers. They're running about like chickens with their heads off. Seems we suckered them into overextending themselves when we fell back across the river. We already slung ten bridges across and our armor is flooding this way."

"We're attacking?" After the last year of holding actions and retreats the concept was almost an alien one to Revell.

"You bet your life we are. No preliminary bombardment, just went straight for their throats. Our bombers are having a field day tearing apart roads blocked with their backed-up transport. It's Falaise all over again."

"This area is still stiff with commie troops." To illustrate Revell's point, a mortar bomb impacted against the wall of the gateway and its smoke was cut to ribbons by the helicopter blades.

"Not for long. We've seen them streaming back out of this sector. This lot can't have got the message yet; they soon will. Not that they've anywhere to go. We've got all the roads blocked. So come on, get them in here."

More mortar shells began to fall, most landing short, but now and again one would find a few extra meters of range and detonate on the walls to send hot shrapnel across the ruins.

A red-hot lump of tailfin smacked with its flat side against the back of Revell's hand and a large blister formed instantly.

Boarding in small groups, in short rushes from cover to cover, they made the comparative safety of the Chinook with only two more light casualties. Fragments wrapped on the fuselage armor.

They threw themselves down on the bare metal floor. There was no noise, no cheering, no celebration as they sat huddled together. This was always the worst time, when the helicopter was most vulnerable. A window cracked under a hard impact and several of them started at the loud report.

"Is that everyone? My captain's shouting at me fit to rival your colonel." The loadmaster paused to listen to his headphones. "He's calling in another strike to try and hit that mortar, but he wants to lift now, like right now."

"Andrea's missing."

It was Clarence who'd noticed, missing her among the crowd in which her face alone would have stood out.

"We can't wait . . ."

Revell leaped out, not giving the aircrewman time to finish. "One minute, just one minute."

"We could all be dead . . ."

Running without thought of danger from the incoming bombs, Revell raced for the cellars. He was shouting as he went, every swear word, every obscenity

218

he could lay tongue on, anything that would vent his fury.

She was coming out of the wine vault, an open bottle in her hand.

"I couldn't find him."

Her speech was slurred, and she retaliated to Revell's forcing her hand against the wall and smashing the bottle by jabbing at his face with the broken neck.

"You fuck off, Herr Major. I've had enough of all of you. Don't you like me anymore." Her dark eyes held his. "I killed your girlfriend in Hamburg; did you know that?"

"Come on, you stupid cow; you're putting everyone's life on the line." By a handful of the collar of her flak jacket he hauled her up the steps, past the line of bodies and out to the Chinook. He pushed her in hard to send her sprawling over a mini-gun, to the amazement of its baby-faced operator.

Still the chopper didn't lift, though the rotors were working up to full speed and the wheels were performing a series of bunny hops as it threatened to rise.

"Airstrike coming in." The loadmaster anticipated the officer's question. "The skipper doesn't want to get in their way.'

Through the gunport, over Andrea's still prostrate form, Revell saw two Phantoms boring in at high speed. It wasn't until they banked to begin their bombing run, so close that he could see the white-outlined black crosses of the Luftwaffe, that he realized the West German pilots were going for the wrong target.

There was no time to shout, to tell them to abort. He could only watch helplessly as they sped the length of the valley and unloaded their pylons immediately above the village.

The detonation of the thousand-pound bombs carpeted the floor of the valley in smoke and flame and overlapping white blast rings. A Bradley hull spun through the air; a house roof lifted, complete and intact, to twice the height of the instantly demolished building beneath it.

For a moment Revell could hope that no other damage had been done, that the underground storage areas had not been penetrated; then there came a long, low, powerful rumble and the whole valley and the surrounding hills appeared to shake.

The Chinook was pushed bodily sideways, puncturing a tire and buckling a landing leg. Thrown off balance, Revell regained the window to see that the site of the village was concealed inside a huge fireball that was beginning to rise. Only its seemingly deliberate slowness gave any measure of its awesome dimensions.

Countless secondary explosions raced through the ground at its base, the collapsing earth graphically marking the precise layout of the complex.

"Heck." The baby-faced gunner was wide-eyed with amazement at the spectacle. "Was that a nuke they dropped, was it? You can feel the heat from here."

Riding the turbulence of the strong upcurrents, the Chinook lifted and turned to head west. Revell beckoned Clarence to undrape the girl from the gun. He couldn't bring himself to have anything to do with her.

They were a hundred feet above the ruins, making the transition to forward flight, when she suddenly revived and shoved the sniper's hands away. Before he could get hold of her again she had thrown herself behind the machine gun and, ignoring the pain of her strapped wrist, was training it downward and

220

opening fire.

The stream of bullets struck a long way short of the lone figure that had climbed into the open. She tried to correct her aim, but fumbled as her target hurled himself aside, and missed again.

Clarence was less gentle the second time, and wrenched her away. The range was longer now, and he sent the tracer in a swirling cone of steel toward the deserter.

Almost into safe cover, he was struck across the back of the legs, below the knee. He collapsed with both calves reduced to a pulp of jelly-like tissue and small fragments of bone.

"You didn't kill him." Andrea hammered with her fists on Clarence's back, until she was pulled off.

Dooley had pushed his caged birds into a safe corner, and now gripped her in a bear hug from behind. "Keep still, you mad bitch."

"He didn't kill him, he didn't kill him."

Waiting until she was quiet, deprived of breath by the pressure of the hold, Clarence sat down, and taking a piece of biscuit from his pack, broke it up and began to poke it through the bars of the cage.

"No, I didn't kill him, but he'll be no more trouble to anyone. And in any event, he would not have counted." He pushed in the last crumbs, then picked up his rifle. "I still have five to go. Deserters don't count."

For as long as he could, Revell watched the series of explosions as the valley receded in the distance. There had been no open expression of the frustration most of them must have experienced. Except perhaps their medic. Sampson had muttered quietly and angrily to himself as he moved among the wounded.

221

They had all had a reprieve of sorts. A handful of them had come through with hardly a scratch, but all had picked up another layer of scar tissue inside.

With the NATO armies now on the offensive, the war in the Zone was going to be harder and nastier than ever before. He didn't doubt that the Special Combat Company was going to be right in the thick of it.

GREAT BOOKS

E-BOOKS

AUDIOBOOKS

& MORE

Visit us today

www.speakingvolumes.us

Printed in Great Britain
by Amazon.co.uk, Ltd.,
Marston Gate.

To: Val

T

Winter Wind

Memories of Spain 2020!

Hope you enjoy the journey with D.I. Murray ....

MICHAEL PATTERSON

Kindest Regards

Cover design and layout by

JAG Designs

ISBN: 9781973170754

This book is dedicated to all those fine individuals that have helped me thus far along the path.

The Mary Chapin Carpenter song - 'Why Walk When You Can Fly,' inspires each of us to take flight and be the best that we can be. And although we may all endure highs and lows, what a wonderful opportunity we have to make the very most of this amazing journey, on this beautiful, crazy adventure, called life!

May each of you take great pleasure and delight in creating the next thrilling, exciting chapter of your very own exquisite story.

"And in this world there's a whole lot of golden,
in this world there's a whole lot of pain
In this world you've a soul for a compass and a heart for a pair of
wings.
There's a star on the far horizon, rising bright in an azure sky
For the rest of the time that you're given -
Why walk when you can fly?"

The Winter Wind

Prologue

Monday 29th December 2014

Penelope Cooke was a bubbly, blonde, twenty-three year old second year art student. The 'Geordie lass' had been living in upmarket rented accommodation in the vicinity of Edinburgh's Royal Botanic Garden.

The scene currently depicted on this gloomy winter canvas, was a very accurate and vivid representation of 'still life!' A bare, delicate white arm lay outstretched on either side of her slender frame. No bowl of fruit, no vase of flowers, no collective group of fellow art students testing their talents with brush strokes, palette or shade.

Simply the motionless body of a young, promising, dedicated designer and artist in the making. An inspiring painter, a supportive sister and an attractive much loved daughter.

It's amazing what twenty minutes of police background checks can turn up!

ONE

*"The cliffs of old Tynemouth they're wild and they're sweet.
And dear are the waters that roll at their feet. Oh, give me
the cliffs and the wild roaring sea. The cliffs of old
Tynemouth for ever for me."*

- Traditional

Just as the historic Water of Leith twists and turns
throughout the vibrant streets, houses and multi
cultural townships within the heart of Edinburgh. So
too, the contours of this newly formed, animated river
of blood flow with energy and spirit.

Originating initially from the notable gash on young
Penelope's forehead, it was determined to forego any or
all impediments in its path. It's gathered momentum
slowed a little as it fused tenderly with her heavy,
mascara clad eyelids. Soon regaining its vitality and
speed it persisted. Provocatively winding itself down
her powder white cheek, until it zig zagged passionately
across the narrow, intimate hallway.

Unrelenting, it skated with grace over the recently
revarnished, one hundred year old oak wood flooring.

And like a gutsy miniature squall it continued with military precision down steps one and two, before pausing briefly for instruction at the third.

Finally, once more it slowed gently on approach, as if visualising a traffic light transition from green to amber. However, before the light sequence could change, it seemed to regain impetus. Seemingly on a final suicide mission it attempted one last surge and bravely stepped forward from the edge.

Unaided and without a parachute, it began an abrupt descent onto the deep, richly patterned, beige carpeted surface below.

As the nonexistent traffic signal altered for the final time, the lukewarm stream of death had arrived at its destination with a gradual, steady, definite stop. And as the crowning droplet was delivered into the newly formed man-made reservoir, it indicated clearly to all - No further road to travel.

On an artist's board this choice of blended deathly colour, could easily be described as - 'Bittersweet Crimson!'

There had been no sign of a struggle, prolonged or otherwise. And Penelope had always been regarded as healthy and fit. What caused the death of one so young? Fully clothed, make-up still on and her daily diary snuggled up by her side. This had been sudden, immediate and most certainly unexpected.

Outside, the congregation of trees hung limp and sorrowfully in the upmarket suburb of Inverleith. They were hurting. A combination of swirling wind and wafer thin rain gave the impression of fine, heartfelt teardrops descending painfully from their defeated branches onto the wet, deserted and shadowed streets below.

They had already heard the tragic news. The darkness of winter prevailed. Coupled with the aftermath and anti-climax of yet another season's greetings.

"And the bells were ringing out for....."

Suddenly, before the final two words - Christmas Day, could be bellowed from his lungs and distributed publicly out into the ether, the radio had been abruptly switched off and Detective Inspector Steven Murray had swivelled sharply on his legs and hoisted himself out of his vehicle in one swift movement.

He radiated an impressive aura. At six foot one in height, he strode confidently upon the leafy pavement with shoulders back and head held high. Fervently he approached the uniformed constable standing guard at the small, restricted driveway, of the cordoned off premises.

It's a fallacy and misconception often portrayed by the media that detective ranks are superior to those of uniformed officers. In the United Kingdom this is not the case and a Detective Sergeant had the same power and authority as a uniformed one.

"What's your name son?" the genial Murray quietly enquired in a sincere manner, of the tall, cherub faced PC.

"Hanlon, sir. Joe.... I mean Joseph, Joseph Hanlon!"

"Well, young Constable Hanlon, you appear rather tender, a tad emotional. Dare I say, sad or distant even." Murray then continued delicately. "Is this your first murder son? Your first dead body? It's alright to be a little shaken."

"No, no sir, it's not that." Hanlon swallowed and interrupted, "I'm sorry, it's personal, it's a family issue, I apologise sir."

The grizzly old Detective Inspector calmly reassured him. "That's alright young man. No need for an apology." Then as he went to walk away, he placed a steadying hand upon Hanlon's left shoulder and whispered gently. "In your own time son, all in your own time."

PC Joseph Hanlon was a doppelganger. He was the spitting image of Rodney Trotter, the dim witted, gormless character from the 'Only Fools and Horses' tv sitcom. Academically though, Joe was no dipstick, plonker or wally. Physically on the other hand, he was over six foot in height, with neat, short, dark brown hair. To complete the look - he had a body that Arnold Schwarzenegger would have been… ashamed off! If he had attended any intense weight training classes over the years, he most certainly was never overheard to utter, "I'll be back!"

That though was where the similarities stopped. Joseph Ian Hanlon was a single child, brought up in middle class surroundings and definitely with no 'Uncle Albert" in sight. He attended the prestigious University of Edinburgh, one of the UK's oldest, having been founded in 1583. He graduated with a first class Honours Degree in Business Management and then worked discouragingly for three years with a large established supermarket giant. Eventually, he realised the retail world could exist perfectly well without him and that there were plenty of others - 'Happy to Help.'

In late 2010 he found himself at a job and careers workshop hosted by the Edinburgh Chamber of Commerce. On his return home he began to assign the various leaflets, brochures and business cards that he had accumulated into two healthy piles.

Firstly, Interested In: Jobs and sectors that appealed to him, that he felt good about. They went to the left hand side of the recently acquired Swedish designed coffee table.

Secondly, Not Interested: Careers, positions, posts and locations that did not appeal they were assigned to the right hand side. However there soon became a great fear of the Ikea product tipping over with what seemed like a 'mini Everest' of NOT Interested literature. A call out to the Edinburgh division of 'Sherpas Anonymous,' could soon be required to help assist in making headway in this latest expedition!

Then Joe paused. "Mmmm," he mumbled excitedly under his breath. Before adding "sounds promising."

There in his hand he held a glossy A5 leaflet. It advertised most encouragingly the virtues of becoming a Special Constable. And as if then suddenly auditioning for his local amateur dramatic society, Lord 'Hanlon' Olivier commenced to read aloud:

"With a long and impressive history the Special Constabulary is a part-time, volunteer body consisting of officers with similar powers to that of police officers." His hands began to speak, in gentle whispers at first. "As a special constable, you'll work alongside our police officers – forging strong partnerships in the community, patrolling our streets, preventing crime and interacting with all kinds of people to help keep your local community safe." Forearms had now been raised, small deliberate steps taken and the gestures became more elaborate and bold.

"The role is diverse but demanding," the voice instructed as it increased in volume. "You could be doing anything from policing a football match to assisting at a road accident. Special constables also police major sporting and public events and provide an excellent bridge between the Police Service and the general public at large. They represent both the community within the police service and the police service within the local community."

His animated gestures were without doubt, helping Joe express his thoughts more personally and effectively.

He continued the performance, "Special Constables can act as a positive force for change - bringing with them an extensive pool of skills, talents, experience, local knowledge and diverse backgrounds - as well as enhancing the overall level of service provided by the police." Standing proud and about to narrate his final line, Hanlon's mind was already made up. He had found his calling and duly encouraged, concluded his literary monologue. "So whatever your walk of life, step forward now and find out how being a Special Constable could be the perfect fit to suit your lifestyle."

The silence lasted all tolled for about five long seconds. Then without warning, a mild applause broke out from the kitchen behind him. And there, stood in the doorway were his parents. The gentle applause had now grown into wild cheers, screaming support, whistling and high-fiving of each other. "We're not worthy" and shouts of "encore, encore," echoed down the hallway. Joe had thought mistakenly, that he was alone. But Mr and Mrs Hanlon senior, had been busy preparing a mid-evening snack when suddenly they had been treated to an impressive, impromptu Oscar winning delivery of - I am Spartacus. No I am Spartacus. Well I must be Rodney!

Likeable, loveable and not unlike that skinny Trotter kid in that he always wanted to do the right thing. Joseph Hanlon became a Special Constable in the Spring of 2011. In 2012 after 18 months as a special, he applied to join what was at that time the Lothian and Borders police force. Today, after the merger of the previous eight regional forces, it was known operationally as Police Scotland.

Having recently turned thirty one years of age, Constable Hanlon had never been happier. He had been a PC for two and a half years, loved the variety of his work and had adapted well to the flexible shift pattern. His recent marriage only six short months ago, was simply, the icing on the cake.

The EH3 postcode district of Edinburgh had more than its fair share of older, luxury properties. Murray explored and carefully analysed Penelope Cooke's lodgings. He spotted high quality fittings, carved mahogany dressers and antique standard lamps. There was a fusion of classic and modern styles. An opulent feel, sophisticated, yet timeless. Very impressive, Murray first thought. Then on further inspection he soon uncovered a large 'Georgian' style decorative mirror in her sitting room, further stunningly elegant furniture in her bedroom and completed with fine, rich, designer decor throughout. He had become slightly puzzled. Under his breath he questioned, "On a meagre student income?"

Just at that Cooke's landlady, who it turns out - was an actual 'Lady' appeared magically, as if upon request at DI Murray's side. The lady in question was Lady Dorothy Atkins and stood about 5ft 3in in height. She was well dressed in a pale blue twin set with matching skirt. The look was complemented with a small, rather alluring gemstone encrusted, cerulean choker. She could in fact have been a 'Queen Mother' waxwork in Madame Tussaud's, they were both so alike.

Letting out part of her home as a three room apartment, with its own private side door entrance, was not about the financial recompense. Her late husband, the politician Lord Mortimer Atkins had left her well catered for in that department. He had been a successful businessman in the pharmaceutical industry for many years, before turning to politics in the mid nineteen seventies. Until his death in 1998, he had served diligently for over two decades, as an elected Conservative Member of Parliament in his Edinburgh constituency.

Lady Atkins lacked company. It was as simple as that. She was lonely and most certainly welcomed the companionship. In an otherwise darkening world, Penny as Lady A would refer to her. "Was a bright light, a firefly in the intrepid marbled mists of life. She was gracious enough to spend one evening every week chatting with an old lady like me," she added. Then whilst dabbing a bona fide tear from her eye, she mentioned how, "Penny loved to learn about the exploits, the life and times of Dorothy Garrett," her voice tenderly quivered with emotion as she spoke. Sharing memories of her childhood and recollections of her past, no doubt kept Lady Dorothy Atkins young, her mind alert and most definitely lifted her spirit on an on-going weekly basis.

Detective Inspector Steven Murray hoped that this fine woman would soon find another confidante. That she would be able to unearth another gem of a resident like Miss Penelope Cooke. Her Ladyship also kindly later confirmed to him, that Penelope's rental agreement 'was not insignificant.'

Again Murray puzzled over the affordability of all this. An affluent area in Scotland's capital? A close companionship with an ageing wealthy widow. Did she even attend University?

Reports continued to be handed to him regarding background information. Dates, years here in Scotland, relevant family history, as well as financial and personal status. Including Twitter, Facebook and other social media apps. In fairness, it seemed they instantly answered several of Murray's initial queries.

Miss Cooke as well as being a brilliant student, had not inconsiderable creative talent, coupled with an enterprising mind and outlook. On a delightfully stylish coffee table in her 'studio,' lay her large, red leather bound order book. The Inspector opened it carefully at the page bookmarked by an old sweet wrapper. Running his finger carefully down through the names, he recognised a few prominent individuals and an occasional colleague or friend. Then he paused and time stood still for a second. He then began to knowingly nod his head. His eyebrows raised. He discovered the ledger also contained, the occasional foe!

Murray learned she had been using this room to develop, display and store a large portfolio of her work. It contained some weird, wonderful and exciting pieces of art. 'Would You Adam and Eve It?' sat in the corner of the room. It pictured on a grand scale, an enormous rosy red apple with an uneven bite taken from it. Ironically, it also contained the corpse of a dead female slumped on the floor. Art imitating life. He had often heard the expression, but never imagined experiencing it. The body in the picture was delicately surrounded by generous shreddings of the fruit's tempting peel.

Around the room, other strange, yet impressive pieces were entitled: 'Crabbit Auld Women,' 'Tickled by Tyneside,' 'If Only' and 'Dancing with Knopfler.' The latter an obvious tribute to Dire Straits frontman Mark Knopfler. The scene had a multi-coloured electric guitar serenading a young damsel high upon a balcony. Romeo and Juliet eat your heart out, Murray thought!

It soon became apparent that this highly gifted artist regularly sold many pieces online and had quarterly shows at various galleries all over the City. Through attending a busy schedule of networking events in the evening, Miss Cooke was able to distribute repeatedly, leaflets and cards for her mouth watering 'Chocolate Chip' art gallery business. Then, add into that mix the local community, include friends and colleagues in academia and 'Why Aye Man!' A real Tyneside 'recipe for success.'

Penelope had a healthy, wide ranging and ever growing list of clients. Murray was again, well impressed. So much so, that he felt encouraged to call DS 'Ally' Coulter immediately. He told him clearly and in no uncertain terms, "Tomorrow 'Ally,' once you've finished further investigations, I want you to drive over with Taylor and pay a polite, cordial visit to our Kenneth and his friends at DG Security."

As part of the legendary Nottingham Forest football squad, which rose from obscurity to win back-to-back European Cups in 1979 and 1980. The Glaswegian hard man defender Kenny Burns, would recall how only two people ever called him 'Kenneth.' His mother and the Forest manager, Brian Clough! As DI Steve Murray observed and inspected himself in Miss Cooke's full length 'Georgian' mirror, he thought out loud and smiled. "I'll bet you, a certain Kenny Dixon's mum doesn't even get to call him 'Kenneth!'

The Mr Dixon in question was 54 year old Kenny Dixon. He had been married to Sheila for 30 years and they'd been together for nearly 31. Ever since she was only 19 years of age. KD had learned his trade in the amateur ranks, progressing steadily through the junior lower leagues of dishonesty, deceit and desperately dodgy dealings.

As 2014 literally came to a dismal deathly close. Dixon sat arrogantly positioned in the comfort of the

Premiership when it came to skulduggery, mayhem and blatant murder. His sumptuous penthouse apartment, fleet of stunning cars and wide range of impressive investments throughout the city are testament to the 3 P's of his career success. In his case however, they don't represent Passion, Persistence and Patience. On a mighty scale they are replaced by: Protection, Prostitution and Pharmaceuticals. Night clubs, sports events and building sites galore, each help facilitate and ensure multi-million pound security contracts for DG Security on an annual basis. Modern, glamorous and well promoted adult sites on social media, enabled his working girls to stay clear of the streets and become 400% more profitable, than in days of old. As for the liquids, pills and vast assortment of tablets, only last year two of Dixon's men were given long term jail sentences. They had taken responsibility for a drug haul that had been discovered in a flat in the Wester Hailles district of the City. It had an estimated street value reckoned to be in the region of £300,000.

Mr 'Kenneth' Dixon had been promoted swiftly up the leagues. He now mixed within the 'Harrods' circle of crime bosses here in Scotland. However, he is still very much a 'Poundland' man when it comes to class and sophistication. Abercrombie and Fitch are more likely to be his legal team than his outfitters! Although, he was very retro in his clothing, tending to go with the 1980's understated American gangsta pimp image! If the B. A. Baracus/Mr T look is your thing, then Kenny D is most definitely your man. Quality leather boots and dark jeans took you to midway, where a black 'Harley' t-shirt covered his broad shoulders. Shoulders that could bear in weight and cost, several thousand pounds worth of bling! A dated medallion, an old St. Christopher and an 'I love mum' chain are among his treasured 'hanging' collection. Not to mention fingers adorned with an assortment of expensive, yet tasteless rings. Sheer class!

Originally a West Coast chap. His patch whilst growing up was North Ayrshire to be exact. At the so-called tender, innocent age of 12, he was the main lookout for a team of house burglars in and around the Three Towns area. The Three Towns was a district that consisted of Stevenson, Saltcoats and Dixon's own place of birth, Ardrossan. Two months after leaving school at age 16, he was 'inside' for the first time. As a young teenage boy you might think it was for shoplifting, assault or possibly car theft. Well think again! Petty crime wasn't him. Not for our dear 'darling Kenneth.' For him it had to be murder, pure and simple. Some poor sod looked at him the wrong way one evening and for that minor misdemeanour, he received several horrendous blows to the head with a paving slab that had been sitting upright in a nearby garden.

KD was on his way. He claimed self-defence. That he had been set upon and violently attacked first. Although he possessed no visible marks, bruises or injuries to his person to back this up. Coupled with several trusted 'reliable' witness statements to sustain Dixon's version of events, he plead guilty to manslaughter. He then served less than 5 years and was out in time to celebrate his 21st birthday bash! He's never been back in prison since.

Whilst 'banged up,' Dixon kept himself busy. It was rumoured he'd become an expert at solving puzzles. That he had developed the knack for completing crosswords and figuring out complicated anagrams, etc. In addition, he steadily gained a greater 'underworld' education. This was achieved by adding a multitude of important contacts, individuals that would and could benefit him as he aspired to move up the criminal ranks. The network consisted of fellow inmates, contracted staff and even included some exceptionally 'helpful' prison guards. Each of these characters all had their own particular area of expertise, a specific field that they excelled in. They ranged from 'personal healthcare,' 'medicinal distribution,' 'property realignment' and Dixon's own particular favourite - 'information geologist.' His simple role was to extract and unearth valuable inside knowledge, preparatory to upcoming opportunities! Indeed his education would soon be complete thanks to these specialist consultants available for hire, often at short notice and at an agreed price. Just for good measure, they were very, very discreet. After those few short years Kenny Dixon graduated from HMP Barlinnie with flying colours. He promptly moved to Scotland's capital city to establish 'His Empire,' multiply profits and fine tune his vision for entrepreneurial flair!

It was nearly two hours after having arrived before Murray was satisfied that, 'he had enough to be going on with.' Shaking his head in sheer disbelief that he'd even used that expression. He thought to himself and questioned - what does that even mean? Although he was in the room next to the dead body and fully aware that this was serious, he began briefly to laugh. Thinking, where do you hear statements like that these days? Apart from repeats of outdated TV cop shows he smirked to himself. On the other hand, Murray found laughter, nonsense and downright wacky antics kept him sane. They were his highly successful coping mechanism. His own personal window of sunlight, brightness and cheer. One, that when double glazed and closed tightly, helped keep at bay for a little while longer, those clouds of darkness and despair that he encountered far too frequently.

It was time to depart from the grand Inverleith Terrace home. It had been mildly opulent, obviously seen better days and was way past its peak. Murray noticed that according to a small unobtrusive white plaque positioned by the side of the slightly rusting garden gate, it was a property which had been built at the end of the 19th century. He was also aware that the architectural character in the area was dominated by rows of Georgian, Victorian and Edwardian villas and terraces. He then began to ponder on how the surrounding streets were complemented by a profusion of mature trees, extensive garden settings, stone boundary walls and spacious roads. A number of the large Victorian houses in nearby Inverleith Place had already been converted into flats he remembered. Many not unlike this current setup.

Intent on continuing with the next line of the song from his earlier arrival, Murray then began without warning...

"You're a bum, you're a punk, you're an old slut on junk. Lying there almost dead on a drip in that bed. You scumbag, you maggot, you cheap lousy faggot. Happy Christmas your arse, I pray God it's our last."

Recognising and understanding the finality of that lyric, Murray repeated the last few words slowly in his head: 'I .... pray .... God.... it's .... our .... last.' That day, it most certainly was for that gracious, kind hearted, 'Angel of the North.' At 11.00am on Monday December 29th, 2014, the beautiful Miss Penelope Cooke would never celebrate another festive season. Certainly not in this life!

TWO

"I know that things can never be the same, that's alright, that's alright with me. I've seen the truth, I've felt the pain and I'm heading for the sunshine once again."

- The Saw Doctors

As he stood guard shivering with pent up emotion, coupled with the numbing December chill, Police Constable Joseph Hanlon began to cast his mind back over the previous six days. A period of time in which his tender world had caved in and collapsed to rubble around him. Suffocating in the stour of distress and blackened broken dreams. His future seemingly shattered and gone in an instant.

Lauren, his adorable childhood sweetheart from Cramond Primary School and throughout their six years together at The Royal High School of Edinburgh, had been anxiously awaiting her results. These were not, 'to be celebrated' employment or University related exam tests that had been carried out. Rather, they were medical. And the Hanlon's had received confirmation after a further series of hospital visits and x-rays, that Lauren had as they suspected, pancreatic cancer.

Vibrant, bubbly, modest in both dress and nature, Lauren Hanlon was a beautiful individual that touched, blessed and influenced all around her 'for good.' Ironically as part of their short honeymoon celebrations only months earlier, they had toured the sights and sounds of London. Included were a few musical delights in the West End, 'Wicked' being one such performance. With poignant and touching lyrics such as - *"I've heard it said, that people come into our lives for a reason. Bringing something we must learn. And we are led to those who help us most to grow, if we let them."*

Doctors had informed them previously that the symptoms for pancreatic cancer were often hard to diagnose. So when they are finally diagnosed, it is often at such a late stage of progression it can be too late to treat. That sadly was now the case for Lauren Scott Hanlon.

Having noticed DI Murray go to exit the property, Joseph Hanlon tentatively walked toward him, leaned in and biting nervously on his bottom lip stated firmly: "It's my wife sir, she has pancreatic cancer. Only a matter of weeks I'm afraid." Explanation and statement made, the emotional constable then returned to resolutely take up his position at the entrance to the home.

As Murray tried to take on board the young officers chilling words. He was gently reminded and prompted of his 'tune of the day,' its musical creator Shane MacGowan, and of this socially hectic time of merriment, partying and seasonal good cheer toward all men. Simultaneously another lyric ran through his mind: *"Then pealed the bells more loud and deep, God is not dead, nor doth he sleep, the wrong shall fail, the right prevail, with peace on earth, goodwill to men."*

It was his job to help keep that 'peace on earth.' To ensure that the 'wrong' failed and that 'right' prevailed. No pressure then DI Murray, he thought.

He quickly reflected on the vast number of individuals who in and around this Yuletide season of Christmas and New Year, that sadly and regretfully throughout the world, in New York or wherever - that no fairy-tale awaits! He could hear the words in his head begin to resurface...*'I could have been someone, well so could anyone; You took my dreams from me, when I first found you."*

When Detective Inspector Steven Murray first came across the pale body of the Edinburgh art student, she had been pronounced dead for at least seven hours.

Her dreams had been taken from her and extinguished, at around 2.00am.

As he awoke next morning at just after six, Murray lay restlessly tossing and turning in his bed. This had become a fairly regular occurrence. Sweat dripped intensely from his brow. His own dreams and thoughts had 'found him' buzzing backwards and forwards, to and fro. Venturing from terminal cancer to Newcastle. The leather order book to The Pogues. Visions of sweeties, the Queen Mother and chocolate chip cookies, then fleetingly back again to the dreaded cancer. Perspiration ran for cover just as the phone rang.

Murray answered half asleep and half...... 'where am I?'

His only word sounding like a whole sentence - "H.......e.......l.......l.......o." He then bolted upright. "What? When?..........Where?.......... Give me twenty minutes." He managed it in fourteen!

He drove, nay intricately weaved through the early morning rush hour traffic. Reminiscent of Bullitt, the title named character in the 1968 movie starring Steve McQueen. It's enthralling car chase scenes throughout the bustling streets of San Francisco were regarded as one of the most influential in film-making history. Playing on the breakfast slot today were Joe Cocker and Jennifer Warnes. It was their turn to make an early morning appearance on the Murray in-car stereo. It was an uncomplicated system. One that consisted of his iPod classic being loaded with an eclectic mix covering many decades, delicately plugged into the auxiliary socket and hey presto - press shuffle!

"Who knows what tomorrow brings, in a world few hearts survive. All I know is the way I feel, when it's real, I keep it alive."

Whistling along DI Murray thought. How real, how true, how deeply saddening. He arrived unwashed, unshaved and unmistakably angry. Or, was it just a high measure of frustration that had him tapping both hands frantically against the outside of his thighs. His unbuttoned, jet black, long sleeved shirt with white t-shirt underneath made him appear like an impatient penguin from Edinburgh Zoo at feeding time! Quite the sight to behold. There was no further food on offer, although definitely something 'fishy' was going on. But what? Murray's experience told him that he'd just been thrown a fish, a smoked fish, one that turned red when cured. Indeed those traffic lights in the pit of his stomach had turned amber and were warning him......'red herring!'

He'd been reliably informed on his 'Grand Prix' drive in, that early indications suggested that Tyneside's Penelope Cooke had caught an infection or eaten something badly contaminated. Forensics at that moment were still desperately trying to narrow it down to a specific type of poison. It would appear that the bang on the head and the blood pool, were merely collateral damage from collapsing on the stairway.

However, two bodies in two days? No particularly obvious pattern shouting out at him. No blatant motive for either and no initial indication of a link between them. This is Edinburgh after all - drugs, prostitution and plenty of sleazy underworld crime abound. But not murder or murders plural on a regular basis. He then pondered to himself... 'This is something different and unusual. Something sinister and intriguing, yet rather surreal!'

He gave Detective Chief Inspector Brown a quick call. Part way through the conversation he casually mentioned - "Think it would be good for him sir. Remember we're operating one down with Sandy on maternity leave currently. Okay, look forward to hearing back from you."

Detective Chief Inspector Keith Brown was a good man, Murray liked him. Down to earth, respectful, old style - firm, but fair. He was a silver haired gent in his late fifties. In looks, he was not unlike the actor John Thaw from the Inspector Morse TV series. Morse though was an Oxford man. Keith Brown, a Cambridge Economics Graduate. Born in the Midlands. In the Leicester suburb of Belgrave to be exact. He was an avid fan of family history, loved gardening and all other things horticultural. He was also a very keen Scotch Whisky aficionado! His personal favourite was the Macallan Cask Strength Single Malt. Voted one of the top ten single malts in the world earlier in the year.

Murray had recognised replacing DC 'Sandy' Kerr whilst she was off on maternity leave, was always going to be difficult. The 28 year old redhead had been his partner and strongest ally for the past three years. They were kindred spirits in their love for all types of entertainment and willingness to take part in some regular banter. Kerr had gotten to know him well. His private, distinctive, idiosyncratic ways. Yet she still loved being paired with him nonetheless. When Murray encountered personal storms and choppy seas, Sandra Kerr was often the lone lifeguard. She was always willing to put, if not her life, most certainly her career on the line. She had rescued her friend in the past on numerous occasions.

Murray's star sign was Libra (the scales) and Sandy was most definitely his work/life balance. He would miss her, but was overjoyed for the Kerr's as a couple. He was fully confident that Richard and Sandra would make remarkable parents. After 4 years of marriage, this was to be their first child.

At Leith Walk with the forensics tent now fully functional, Murray popped his head in to see if the 'tinker' was present. The 'tinker' was Doctor Thomas Patterson, Head Forensic Pathologist for the Lothian and Borders area.

The 'tinker' was an affectionate nickname given to Tom for his inability, lack of desire or simple refusal to pronounce the 'th' in all words beginning with 'tat' prefix. So 'thanks, therapy and thumbs,' became 't'anks, t'erapy and t'umbs!'

Born in County Tyrone, one of the six counties of Northern Ireland. He fully embraced his county's motto to the full: Consilio et Prudentia (Latin), "By Wisdom and Prudence." In the Doc's own words, a good definition of 'prudence' would be -

"One: Quality or fact of being prudent, providing for the future. Two: Caution with regard to practical matters and discretion. Three: Regard for one's own interests and finally - Four: Provident care in the management of resources; economy; frugality."

And therein lay his wisdom. He had managed to offer several definitions without once using t'at prefix. Denying us all the opportunity to smile and be gently amused at his lovely, rich, sweet Irish brogue.

Patterson loved to regularly return across the Irish Sea, mainly to tour Southern Ireland. Travelling, he often took the *'twisting, turning, winding roads of Galway and Mayo.'* Which in itself was a reference to his favourite musical group The Saw Doctors, who originally hail from County Galway.

Tom had been a forensic scientist for over 30 years. He was a graduate of the Royal Society of Chemistry and began his career at the Northern Ireland Forensic Science Laboratory, where he developed a specialism in fire investigation. A widower, he moved across to Scotland in 1996 and resides in a beautiful two bedroomed cottage in the village of Athelstaneford, East Lothian. Over the years he has tried unsuccessfully to give up smoking. A black coffee man, with simple likes that include Scottish and Irish music, cheese on toast with brown sauce, and sitting comfortably with a grandchild on his lap whilst doodling his latest masterpiece. A work of art that will no doubt consist of eyes, eyes and more eyes!

Mindful, respectful and in reverence to those that 'Doc' Patterson 'worked with' on a daily basis. A Saw Doctors lyric was engraved on the back of his iPad: *"Life's too short for wastin', for if's and might have beens. Life's too short for wonderin', if you could have lived your dreams."*

With regard to the most recent deceased, the 'tinker' told Murray, "Early examinations would indicate she died late on Monday evening, or in the very early hours of Tuesday morning. I just t'ot you should know."

Murray smiled and said, "T'anks."

"Ah, be off wae ye. If yer goin' to be takin' the Michael, I t'ink I'll go slower."

"Indeed you will not Doc. We need all the help we can get on t'is." Murray felt special need to put the emphasis on t'is. Before winking and adding, "As quickly as possible."

The visually imposing ten foot high bronze statue of Queen Victoria, stood atop a solid stone base at the foot of Leith Walk. It was a celebrated local landmark, erected as a fitting tribute to the men of Leith who fought in the Boer War. The inauguration of the statue in 1907 was attended by a crowd of over 20,000 people. Today, going about their daily business, it had a rather more intimate, modest crowd of twenty or so plus. That gathering comprised of uniformed officers, C.I.D. and a forensics team of four highly capable individuals, including the 'tinker,' Doc Patterson.

The body lay covered. The tent had been erected over it, only yards from 'regal' gaze. No doubt with all the comings and goings and major upheaval, her Majesty 'was not amused.' Ironically the evidence to support the idea that Queen Victoria originated the expression 'we are not amused,' lies somewhere between thin and nonexistent. Exactly like the leads DI Murray and his team have to work with currently!

The deceased was Annabel Richmond. A mousey haired brunette, small in stature and all of thirty years of age. She worked flexible hours as a legal secretary in the Standard Life offices on Lothian Road, had never been in trouble with the law and was very sports oriented. She had completed several Edinburgh marathons over the years, played badminton at least once a week and was a regular at Pure Gym, the open all night - all day exercise centre. The officers were currently in possession of her handbag. It had lain open at her side, but interestingly, no mobile phone had been discovered amongst her effects. She'd grown up in the nearby coastal town of North Berwick and had been happily and blissfully married for just over.......... 72 hours!

Murray's mind was blown away by that. Three days! Who was the poor sod breaking that news to her husband? The current vision in his mind was of a large hot air balloon flying high across the Edinburgh skyline. 'Newly Wed' was the slogan it carried in various coloured artistic fonts along its outer circumference. A myriad of aspirations, goals, dreams and ambitions swirled excitedly in their heads and mixed contagiously with the warm draft circulating around them. Previously discussed aims, hopes and breath taking projects and adventures had quite literally been blown out of the sky, and were now to be found torn and tattered in tiny fragments at 'the foot o' the walk!' One of the longest streets in the capital.

The newlywed 'royal subject' had been discovered at the feet of her majesty Queen Victoria, less than two miles from South Leith Parish Church. The house of God where only four days previously the aisle and pews had been filled with radiant smiles of joy and gracious laughter. Celebration was the order of the day and the beautiful Annabel Richmond had arrived as is the norm - over twenty minutes late. Her dress was breathtaking. It was long, like something out of a Disney movie, and flowed luxuriously with small strings of satin petals intricately attached throughout. The ceremony was a creative mix of classically elegant - meets royally romantic. The scene was set, and all in the couple's garden seemed rosy.

The long standing tradition behind the groom being there first, seemingly stemmed from the idea that it was his duty to literally lead the bride into her new life of love and happiness. As a couple they had been due to fly out tomorrow morning for a ten day idyllic honeymoon in the Seychelles.

According to several guests in attendance, the service went well. The program included sincere prayers, encouraging humorous remarks and wonderfully uplifting hymns. To begin a union together all seemed perfect. Including the picture postcard weather. A light frost on the ground with a strong ray of sunshine in both heaven and heart. Over two hundred guests had been in attendance and witnessed precious, sacred vows be taken. Supposedly, 'for time and all eternity.' A memorable period, one that was meant to be measured and experienced in a multitude of exciting, adventurous decades..............never in hours and minutes.

That Boxing Day, as those gathered at South Leith Parish Church were looking for a host of angels, DI Murray was defending himself against his own army of demoralising demons!

His highs and lows are often so extreme that they interfere with everyday life. Four days previously on what should have been 'the feast of Stephen' was a perfect example. It was approaching noon and the sun was glinting in through the frosted bathroom window, as a world weary Murray looked in the mirror and contemplated shaving. Although crisp and bright outside on this sobering Winter's day, there was an imminent darkness clouding over in the world of Detective Inspector Steven Murray.

No songs, no music, no spring in his step. What step you may even ask? He had not moved from the comfort, the warmth and security offered from his King sized bed and duvet until that moment. His brain's schedule for at least the next 24 hours, would revolve around a state of mind that asked and pondered over -

What could have been? If only? And childhood recollections on a grand scale.

What had he done in this life?

Throughout those reoccurring bouts of feeling miserable and downcast, he often held the opinion that he had achieved very little, that he was surplus to requirements and would not be missed! He had childhood dreams, business ideas and a multitude of goals and ambitions that had not come to fruition.

The lives of others often seemed so perfect. Whereas his own seemed worthless, insignificant and of no value to anyone. His family would be fine, he thought to himself. They'd be better off without him. No more mood swings to put up with and no more treading on eggshells whilst in his company. Interestingly and importantly though, he had successfully learned to recognise the triggers and early indicators of an episode over the years. Most of his closest friends and work colleagues were still totally unaware. Yet the DVLA had been notified! It was a legal requirement to inform them. And as a so called, 'boy in blue,' he thought it in his best interest to do so.

Signs and symptoms included persistent feelings of sadness, anxiety, guilt, anger and hopelessness. Often it would manifest itself with disturbed sleep patterns and in his appetite. Fatigue and loss of interest in usually enjoyable activities were other side effects. The list continued with loneliness, self-loathing, apathy or indifference. And last but not least, especially in Steven Murray's case - morbid suicidal thoughts. Within the past turbulent decade, this police officer had all too frequently ticked the box in relation to many of the aforementioned symptoms.

Welcome to Detective Inspector Murray's world of melancholy, depression and the living hell that is...... Bipolar!

THREE

"Bonnie and Clyde were pretty lookin' people - But I can tell you people they were the devil's children."

- Georgie Fame

Six days previously, just before midnight on Christmas Eve, screeching and squealing could be heard. Lights performed wildly as if in 1970's discotheque mode. The vehicle with a couple of occupants careered around the tight bend on two wheels. They seemed to be offering an evening masterclass performance - It was an 'Outdoor Extreme Stunt Show' at it's best!

"Hello, Whiskey, Tango, Foxtrot; come in over. Calling: Whiskey, Tango, Foxtrot, over."

"Stop messing about," the 'officer' behind the wheel shouted in a timid, rather half-hearted manner.

"Excuse me! You're driving like a lunatic in the middle of the night. Sirens on, lights flashing and crazy, intense hand brake turns. Yet, I've to stop messin' around?" the other yelled. "Yer havin' a laugh, right?"

"Ha ha ha, ah suppose yer right. Carry on Constable!"

"Hello Juliet Bravo is that you? Charlie Delta wants to meet up in India for a wee bit of a Yankee Foxtrot!"

Roars of laughter from the two drunken Scotsmen inside the car went unheard outside, where burning rubber was still the order of the day. THEY, were not doing the chasing. THEY, were the ones being pursued. By whom you may ask? Absolutely no one! With imaginary foes they continued to play cops and robbers in their stoned heads. Heads that contained brains the size of 'Officer Dibble' and 'PC Murdoch.' Which in fact does a major disservice to those two fine animated characters. At least 'Top Cat' and 'Oor Wullie' possessed many qualities to be admired. Although like our 'Ferrari fetish friends,' they could be a tad troublesome as they constantly strived to earn a quick buck, usually through an illegal scam. Officer Dibble regularly attempted to evict Top Cat and his gang from the alley. While a bit closer to home Oor Wullie would be constantly on PC Murdoch's radar, mainly because his adventures consisted of unrealistic get-rich-quick schemes that led to mischief. They were however, both likeable, charming and cute - a pair of lovable fictional rogues.

It was approaching the early hours of Christmas morning. The streets in and around the Edinburgh docklands were deserted, except for the occasional lady of the night and two witless morons in a stolen patrol car! Presently we were watching the antics of a couple of nonfictional and often non-functioning buffoons. Currently, we caught them swerving past another concrete bollard, crashing over the pavement and straight onto the grass playing fields. Then, they managed to slide the vehicle unceremoniously up, down, around and sideways, as if signing an autograph of their latest artwork. Their encore consisted of smokin' tyres, dancing sirens, and their vehicle spinning around out of control before stopping with a severe jolt.

As they crashed headfirst into the base of the rugby posts, a forehead smashed violently against the dashboard. Blood filtered slowly from the wound and ran sluggishly down the rim of the radio's control panel. You never imagined that this particular 'special' constable would have thought to put on a seat belt for his Eastern travels that evening did you? His companion, the host driver was already out of the car celebrating his race victory. Grand Prix style, he sprayed champagne all across the roof, windscreen and bonnet of their triumphant machine. I'd maybe have to check with Lewis Hamilton, but I'm pretty certain that a bottle of vintage Bollinger does not normally come in a 5 litre plastic container, has substantially more fizz and sparkle to it and is most definitely not deep purple in colour!

The sky soon illuminated and the air became warm. It was the glorious, scorching, high impact red and orange flames that continued to define an outline of land and buildings. The Vauxhall Astra Estate was now fully ablaze. EM33 the Police Scotland roof identification was no longer visible. Tyres blew up and windows blew out. No advance warning, no waiting on death row and certainly no appeals system in place. SN60 CXM had been called for. He was obviously on St. Peter's official police roster for today. Like so many of us, never for one minute anticipating that when the day began, that this would be our last.

At the bottom of Leith Walk at 11.15am, on the morning of Tuesday the 30th December 2014, the name of Annabel Linda Richmond could be ticked off and accounted for also. Murray, his senses working overtime, had his suspicions that in the next week or two, St. Peter and his cohorts were about to become extra busy in and around Scotland's capital city!

"Oh, what do you know? That might be them now." Murray smirked, whilst answering his mobile phone.

At the end of May, thirty nine football fans, mostly Italians, died and over 600 hundred more were injured at the Heysel Stadium in Brussels, Belgium. The disaster was later described as, "the darkest hour in the history of the UEFA competitions." Meanwhile just over six weeks later, an event billed as the "global jukebox", was held simultaneously at Wembley Stadium in London, (attended by over 72,000 people) and the John F. Kennedy Stadium in Philadelphia, (attended by around 100,000 people).

Live Aid - held on the 13th of July, had an estimated global audience of 1.9 billion across 150 nations, and raised over £50 million for famine relief in Ethiopia.

...This was indeed the Summer of 1985.

That year having been together for two years and married for nearly nine months, KD and Sheila were still no closer to having children. It appeared to be a problem on her husband's part. Although, he certainly did not and would not accept any responsibility. He was a Scotsman after all, as well as a husband and rising gangland boss of influence. Machismo is the ultimate brand amongst the power brokers of organised crime. He could not be seen to display any outward sign of weakness, as he continued his ascent to the top. Sheila on the other hand, was desperate for children, at least one. She felt she had an abundance of love to offer. She recognised her childhood had been less than perfect to say the least and had a deep desire to make up for that. She longed to raise up a child in a loving home, to offer a boy or girl safety, security and protection from the perils of the world.

At that, her slim, willowy figure made its way quickly through the doorway of the small, rented, two roomed office in central Leith. His wife then duly informed Dixon, "Kenny, I've made an appointment with a specialist to help us with our problem."

"I'm a specialist in dealing wae any problems Kenny has," the 17 year old at KD's side said uncouthly, with a youthful, uneducated arrogance.

Dixon with a dismissive wave of his hand, instructed, "Shut up James and go and makes us some coffee,"

The teenager, James Baxter Reid had been at Kenny Dixon's side for the last three years. In fact it was he, who introduced Sheila to him. He'd always lived in a bit of a fantasy world, delusional even. An old fashioned braggart who simply loved to exaggerate. Continually filled with childhood fiction that never quite became fact. Like being a paratrooper, joining the Foreign Legion and playing football for Scotland. He had grown up in the nation's broken foster system. Continually shunted from pillar to post. He never knew or certainly remembered any of his parents, having been abandoned as a young three year old boy at a Salvation Army Home on Ferry Road in Edinburgh. Life had been a tough slog for our James.

As a fourteen year old, Reid's troubled past caught up with him and he came to the attention of one 'Kenneth' Dixon. Dixon by now had rapidly made a name for himself amongst Edinburgh's respected community of convicts, crooks and fugitives! He saw something of himself in Reid. A rawness, a thirst for action, for something more to life. It had to be said, he probably also liked the idea of having a young protege. With himself playing the role of mentor. His 'Manor,' was thriving, expanding at a steady rate and he was going to enjoy overseeing this growth, as its number one 'Lord'.

It was Kenny Dixon who initially christened Reid with the moniker, 'Bunny'. He had pronounced it on his young right hand man much like a father would pass on a favourite family heirloom, such as a beloved ring, watch or treasured possession. On the contrary though, nothing could be further from the truth. KD wanted rid of it, to totally disown it. Ultimately to strike it and the constant memories it conjured up from his mind forever. The reason for finding it a new home? Quite simple really -

Because it had been given to him whilst serving time in jail.

'Old Tommy' was a long term prisoner. A tall, slender gentleman with a high forehead and greying short hair. This look, complemented by his delicate, slim, silver rimmed spectacles gave him an academic air. Possibly you'd be fooled into thinking he was a friendly primary school headmaster. Which was exactly how he came to be inside in the first place.

He loved his music and was a knowledgeable man when it came to traditional folk songs. He could tell you the history, the legend and myth behind hundreds, if not thousands of nostalgic songs and tunes from days gone by. It was he, that had chosen and given the inexperienced inmate the nickname. One that he would come to despise and hate.

It was based on the old 19th century French/ Canadian tune, 'Alouette'. To many (of a certain age), schooldays would most certainly include hearing its familiar refrain: *'Alouette, gentille alouette. Alouette, je te plumerai'.*

However, those detained at 'Her Majesty's Pleasure' in the late 70's and early 80's, became better acquainted with the lyrics sung by the children's entertainers The Singing Kettle. In their version, they sang: *'Little Bunny Fou Fou I don't want to see you, scooping up the field mice and bopping them on the head!'* Given how Dixon had come to be incarcerated, Old Tommy thought it most apt! 'Bunny' it was from there on in.

The Ayrshire man had tried in various ways to get the ageing troubadour to change it. But he never did. He continued to laugh and dismiss Dixon at every turn. Just over a year into KD's sentence, 'Old Tommy' whilst on cleaning duty, was mysteriously, yet unsurprisingly found slumped unconscious in a pool of blood at the bottom of a prison stairwell. His head had been bashed in. His singing days were over. He never recovered and remained in a coma until his death nearly eighteen months later. No one was ever caught in connection with the incident, and it was finally recorded as an unfortunate accident. During his time maintaining the walkway he was thought to have slipped, thus fatally injuring himself as he fell down the metal staircase. Funny though, sat next to his body were two other items also recovered from the bottom of the stairs that day. Firstly, a bucket filled to the brim with fresh water, and also, standing upright - a clean, dry, unused mop!

'Little Bunny Fou Fou I don't want to see you, scooping up the field mice and bopping them on the head!'

As 'Bunny' Reid added the final spoonful of sugar to the coffee and began to stir. He could overhear from the kitchen area Sheila and Dixon continue their conversation regarding how best to proceed with treatment.

"I'll visit with him tomorrow morning," confirmed his wife, "and we'll see what he says and then we can move forward from there. It may cost us, but it's a price we are willing to pay, agreed?" Sheila asked.

Dixon listened, slowly nodded in agreement and stood up from behind his desk. He calmly walked over to Sheila and gave her a genuine, sincere and heartfelt hug. Then moving his head out from her body slightly, continued to plant the gentlest of kisses on her forehead, whispering, "It'll all work out, you'll see."

Touching and moving, and if you didn't know any better, just like a scene from the 1970 Hollywood movie Love Story starring Ali MacGraw and Ryan O'Neal. In spite of that, one still couldn't help but see a more striking comparison. That of a young, devious Faye Dunaway, in tow with the handsome Warren Beatty - Edinburgh's very own, Bonnie and Clyde!

Just then, 'Bunny' Reid arrived with the coffee and small talk once again became the order of the day.

As Sheila Dixon made her way through the intimidatingly heavy, dark green panelled door to visit with her 'specialist.' She remembered it had been over four years since she last encountered him. A member of his trained support staff walked with her the short distance to his ultra-modern, clinically clean office. He was noticeably startled, taken aback, amazed even to set eyes on Sheila again. Literally shaking, he was fraught with uncertainty and had no idea where to begin. They'd had previous challenging encounters and Sheila had never spoken to him in the last 48 months. She knew one thing for certain though, and that was that he was the man capable of ensuring success. That she would become a mother, and that he could give her a child.

After only three or four more visits to his office, over a two to three month period between July and September 1985. Mrs Sheila Dixon found to both the delight of herself and her husband, that she was expecting. Her faith in her 'specialist,' had paid off. But at what cost? The Dixon daughter would need round the clock protection. KD's lifestyle meant she would be vulnerable to attack, threat, possibly even kidnap? There had certainly been intimidating messages received regularly in the past. But for now, that all lay in the future.

The early years were wonderful. Sheila thrived with motherhood. You could tell she was making up for lost time. Music played constantly throughout the home, regular walks to the capital's parks and museums became a staple afternoon diet for mother and daughter, and baby books recorded all her 'firsts'. Throughout that period, KD's business empire was multiplying and diversifying at a speedy rate. Together though, up against whatever challenges came their way, they had made their young daughter's infant years safe. She would have felt that she had been deeply loved, sincerely cared for and genuinely spoiled!

Then, at six years of age and after a failed attempt to kidnap her from Primary School and several threats on her life, Kenny Dixon felt they had no option but to send their young daughter to Boarding School. They took immediate steps, told no one where it was, and enrolled her under an assumed name.

"It'll keep her safe for the majority of the time," Kenny told Sheila. "And that is the important thing."

As a mother though, Sheila was struggling to come to terms with the idea. Although she knew it made sense, she always dreaded that this day may actually come around and become a reality. She thought that she had let her daughter down. It churned her up inside and would continue to do so for years. Spending time with her only at weekends and holidays was tearing Sheila apart. She lived with it for a long while and made it work as best she could. A wedge however, had gradually crept in. At times manifesting itself as bitterness, a growing anger, a daily resentment. Never always clear who it was intended for. People she had yet to meet? Individuals that had no doubt hurt her in the past? Or those heavily involved in her life currently? It was corrupting her, polluting her mind and gnawing away daily at her very soul.

Constantly it reminded her of her own teenage years. Not a time she'd wish upon anyone. She had never fully confided in KD or others for that matter, with regard to her own upbringing. After being introduced by James Reid the day before, why was she all alone when they'd met up at Portobello Beach? How come she had nowhere to stay, no money and no family ties? An enchanting nineteen year old with no history for her past. Was she really to be believed? A scared, frightened and exceptionally cautious girl. One whose innocent view of the world had came crumbling down around her in recent times. In fairness to Kenny Dixon, he may be a so-called hard man, but even then he treated the fairer sex with respect. He made them feel special and was charming, charismatic and reassuring into the bargain. Often it had to be said, because they could earn him good money! Initially, that was exactly what KD thought about the forsaken adolescent, who went by the sorry name of Sheila.

Sheila who? She gave no surname, never mentioned her past and originally was very reluctant to become too close to him. Dixon though, with his mercurial ways, recognised something strangely different about her. Within days, any notion that he may have had, regarding having this pretty teenager work and walk the streets of Leith to pay her way, was quickly dismissed.

Mr Kenneth Dixon desperately wanted a Mrs Dixon. Someone he could trust and confide in. They very soon became an item. Sheila, quickly gained a believe in herself, a confidence that had either never been there, or, more likely an event or events in her recent past had shattered it all together. He had his suspicions. But that was all they were, suspicions! As much as she regained her vitality and zest for life. Kenny was always a little concerned that when asked 'how she was?' Her standard reply would be - 'good, great, fantastic, fine or wonderful.' However, it would always end, 'but I've still got a little score to settle!' He would never push for more, nor would she offer it.

Early in June 1986, one month after giving birth to a beautiful, dark haired baby girl. Sheila Dixon sent her 'specialist' an extravagantly wrapped box, which contained full payment for his services. Their baby girl continued to grow up safe and well. Over the coming years, only a handful of trusted individuals within their inner circle would ever become aware of their child's identity. Now, nearly three decades later and after earning an MSc in Business and Economics at a prestigious University, their daughter worked in corporate Finance.

FOUR

"Fee fi fo she smells his body. She smells his body it makes her sick to her mind. He has got so much to answer for - To answer for, to ruin a child's mind."

- The Cranberries

Fast forward nearly three decades, and throughout the April and May of 2014 there were plenty of adjustments taking place and appointments being made. Decisions: Guilty/Not Guilty. People being fired, others retained. Changes, repercussions, scores being settled. Spring was most definitely in the air.

Being a big football fan, Detective Inspector Steven Murray was not really surprised when earlier in the year on the 22nd of April, David Moyes was sacked as the manager of Manchester United Football Club. In life, football and business, we often face hurdles and obstacles throughout the course of the game. Relating back to his family roots in his 2013 autobiography, Sir Alex Ferguson reminded us that his clan motto is: 'Dulcius Ex Asperis,' - 'Sweeter after Difficulties.'

'Sweeter after difficulties?' Try telling that to former celebrity publicist Max Clifford. During his long and successful career as a publicist, he represented a mixed and varied range of clients. He himself was often considered a controversial figure. This was in large part due to his representation of unpopular individuals (such as those convicted or accused of crimes) and his work for people wishing to sell 'kiss-and-tell' stories to tabloid newspapers. Clifford was arrested in December 2012 by Metropolitan Police officers on suspicion of sexual offences; the arrest was part of Operation Yewtree.

Murray had kept up to speed and read with great interest at the time, how that particular case had developed. Operation Yewtree was a police investigation into sexual abuse allegations, predominantly the abuse of children, against the British media personality Jimmy Savile and others. "Yewtree" was chosen from a list of names which are intended to be neutral and unrelated to each particular case, in a system dating back to the 1980s for operations which are started to handle specific crimes, as opposed to more general, pro-active operations with names connected to their intent. Other prominent names convicted after being arrested in connection with Operation Yewtree, included singer Gary Glitter, DJ and Radio Presenter Dave Lee Travis and songwriter, composer, comedian, actor, painter, TV personality and all round 'good guy,' up until then, Rolf Harris. His 'Didgeridoo,' would now be behind bars for years. His 'kangaroo,' tied down and sportingly put out of its misery. The 'Two Little Boys' with their 'Two Little Toys' had reached retirement age and were never to be heard from again! Max Clifford underwent further investigation. He was subsequently tried and found guilty of eight indecent assaults on four girls and women aged fourteen to nineteen. At the start of May 2014 he was sentenced to eight years in prison.

That very same afternoon, May 2nd 2014, young Deborah Evans was adamant during her telephone conversation about her thoughts in relation to the sentence. "Totally deserved it, eight years is not long enough in my opinion. Still just wee lassies, fourteen and fifteen, it was disgusting."

"Justice normally comes around I find," offered the pleasant voice on the other end of the phone.

"You may be right," she paused. "But I still think where children, minors are involved - lock the door and throw away the key." Deborah was certainly unwavering, you had to give her that. Though her younger sister Yvette, had been wriggling continually in her seat at Debbie's side throughout the conversation. She had found it awkward, uncomfortable and judging by her body language, slightly distressing. Her older sibling having obviously forgotten that her youthful, adolescent and possibly rather inexperienced sister, was indeed currently over four months pregnant. This in and of itself is not overly significant. When factoring in though, that her 16th birthday is still over three months away. Then the topic of conversation takes on a very different dynamic indeed! The 'lucky' father? Nobody knows.

"So, sorry Miss Ingham, I digress" Debbie apologised. "Are you sure you don't want me to write down who he'll be meeting with?"

"No, it's fine. It will probably be myself. However, if you'd be kind enough just to mark down that it will be confirmed nearer the time, that would be lovely. Thank you."

"And he'll remember you okay?" Debbie checked hesitantly.

"Oh, absolutely," the female voice offered with an air of confidence, bordering on arrogance. "He'll remember me alright," she said quietly. "We go way back together. It will be a major shock for him to meet up with me again though. Especially on my birthday."

"That sounds terrific Jillian," Deborah Evans stated excitedly. "I'm sure Mr Taunton will be delighted to see you also." Finishing the conversation in a professional secretarial manner, she concluded. "So just to confirm, I've scheduled you in for a two o'clock afternoon appointment. That will be on Tuesday the 1st of July, and mum's the word. I'll keep the surprise on ice at this end, so no need to worry on that score. Nice chatting with you Miss Ingham. Have a lovely day and I look forward to meeting you in person in a couple of months."

"Me too," she replied, "Goodbye."

"Bye-ee," Debbie offered cheerily, hanging up the telephone.

Seven full months after that initial conversation had taken place, and starting their day together by eating breakfast in the canteen, Taylor asked Hanlon. "Joe, whatever happened with the patrol car that got nicked on Christmas Eve?"

Hanlon responded shaking his head, having just taken a sizable bite from his large red Braeburn apple. "Torched it," he managed to splutter, before swallowing, clearing his throat and trying once again. "They discovered it still smouldering on Christmas Day morning." He then took a drink to fully clear his airways. In the meantime, the impatient Taz Taylor continually rotated both her wrists. As if to indicate, go on, speak up, continue.

"It had been left abandoned on the north-eastern grass section of Leith Links," Hanlon stated. "Reckon it was joy riders. A couple of fresh faced juveniles determined this year to help Santa deliver all his gifts on time." Joe smiled tactfully, to indicate to DC Taylor that he was finished. Or so he thought.

"And Curry and Hayes are still looking into it?" Taz continued slowly with the interrogation.

Joseph Hanlon extended a courteous nod in her direction as confirmation.

"Alright you two, what's going on here?" 'Ally' Coulter asked politely as he slid out the bright blue formica chair from under the table and prepared to join them.

"What do you mean?" Taz said rather sheepishly.

Raising his voice in a bold jovial manner, Coulter continued. "What do I mean? What do I mean? - Those breakfasts, or so called breakfasts. They just shouldn't be allowed. They must be deemed politically incorrect these days. Offensive, aye that's it, truly offensive to," he paused for show, whilst patting a hand on his rather overweight belly. "How can I put this delicately? Wee fat guys like me!"

A chorus of laughter broke out amongst his colleagues. DS Coulter sat contentedly, screeched his chair back in below the table and gathered up his trusted knife and fork. He was now fully equipped to deal properly with the criminal scene in front of him. It consisted of a potato scone, 3 rashers of bacon, 2 fried eggs, a tomato, a lorne sausage, beans, mushrooms and a side portion of onion rings. Oh and obviously not forgetting, the extra-large glass of....... DIET COKE!!!!!

As the laughter subsided, the Detective Sergeant acknowledged his male colleague and in a more sombre tone offered. "Nice to see you laugh PC Hanlon. How are things? How is your good lady doing?"

"She's inspiring Ally," Joe Hanlon responded without missing a beat. "With all her medical issues and appointments, plus the fact that we lost the deposit on our new flat. She is still amazingly upbeat and cheerful. I have no idea how she copes." His voice became slightly more choked and emotional as he continued. "She's lost a bit of weight recently and has been visiting and phoning family and close friends. She wants to say her goodbyes. She's always been organised as an individual, so she finds it really satisfying to tie up all the loose ends." With a silent tear making a rapid appearance in the corner of his left eye, young Joe stood and in the manner in which he was brought up, excused himself. He wiped down his table and cleared away his 'offensive' tray. His breakfast had consisted of an Oat'n Nuts cereal bar, the Braeburn apple and a small pouched vitamin drink.

Tasmin Taylor and Robert Coulter glanced at each other knowingly, and nodded in understanding.

"Four bottles of Chivas Regal, please," Murray said whilst frantically searching his jacket pocket for his wallet. If spotted in the off-licence, someone may have gotten the wrong idea. Especially coupled with his occasional absence from work. Those interfering mathematicians putting two and two together, would have been so wide of the mark. The man's generosity knows no bounds. Many a so-called bad guy or 'alleged' offender had turned up for their day in court, wearing an outfit generously supplied by Murray Outfitters PLC!

Today was all about his regular routine commute. Driving regularly through the busy streets of northwest Edinburgh to his place of work at various times of day, DI Murray encountered several school crossing zones. Each was attended by a willing, diligent and friendly smiling 'lollipop man.' Though, in this politically correct and fancy job title aware age that we live in, one can assume they are no doubt referred to as: "Traffic vehicle management co-ordinating assistants!" Steve always gave them a wave and a nod of the head. This quartet of retired gents though, will never recognise, nor ever know, the massive support and major strength they are to Detective Inspector Steven Murray.

For on those days when the sunshine is brightest in the skies, but his heart and mind are darkened by other thoughts - these 'vehicle coordinators,' are life savers. In rain, hail or snow, there they are. Ever present, steadfast and dependable. Ensuring the safety of their young charges. Chatting and interacting generously with parents and grand-parents alike. Murray no longer had children that needed their help at a road junction, but nevertheless he always liked to express his gratitude to them. A 12 year old Single Malt over the Christmas period was normally much appreciated, and it literally, went down extraordinarily well!

Outward gestures of kindness and love such as these, are what helps to sustain and strengthen the Inspector. Enabling him to continue to wade through the dense, murky and dark pools of life. Pro-active, often anonymous good deeds enable him to remain sane. They conveniently shield and protect him from the rancour, bitterness and hurt that on many an occasion throughout the years, he himself has experienced. Often, in more recent times, he had allowed it to manifest itself and play a prominent, misguided role in the makeup, character and life of one devoted individual……. that of Steven Murray!

Hatred is a horrible thing. It ruins individuals. It churns continually, gnawing away and festering within the pit of your stomach. Slowly infecting and gradually rotting any remaining goodness you may have. Scowls are permanently on display. A darkness is then portrayed quite evidently in your body language, your words and even in what you don't say! It becomes a self-fulfilling prophecy. Over time your nature changes and friendships are lost. Were they ever really friends in the first place, you then question? Others play both sides. Time they say is a great healer. But so what? This is now! We live in a world of urgent schedules and instant gratification. Not a "it will all work out in the end," wishy washiness! Try as you may, key individuals have let you down, hurt you and personally attacked you. What makes it worse is, they probably do not even realise it! They most certainly don't lose any sleep over you, that's for sure.

Murray has to let the angst go. Park it elsewhere. Place it on a heavy duty shelf until he finds himself back in a position that would allow him to influence, persuade and redress the imbalance. Ever mindful of 'The Doc's' iPad message, he held an old black and white image of the Hollywood 'Great,' James Stewart in his mind. Then slowly thought to himself, 'Ah - What a wonderful life!'

Liquor now in hand, he made his way to eventually exit the store. The small trio of bells above the door chimed as he opened it. That would be his festive cue. Time to go belatedly and play Santa Claus. If not quite, a smiling Jolly Old Saint Nick.

FIVE

"When November brings the poppies on Remembrance Day. When the vicar comes to say, 'Lest we forget.' We will remember them - Remember them."

- Mark Knopfler

Tuesday 30th of December 2014

It's mid-morning when two of Edinburgh's finest find themselves meandering down a draughty, litter strewn corridor toward Unit 12a. Welcome to Dock Green Securities it states boldly in what was once, vibrant gold lettering on the office door. The small, rather run down and weary industrial premises are located at the edge of Portobello, just off the Seafield Road. And the aged, flaked fonts that remain on the door actually read - ' elco to ck reen cur es.'

Detective Sergeant Robert Coulter was born in Dysart. A former town and royal burgh located on the south-east coast of Fife. The town is now considered to be a suburb of Kirkcaldy. Known affectionately as 'Ally,' this is in reference to the classic Scottish folk song written by former Galashiels weaver, Robert

Coltart. Coltart died of a brain tumour in 1880, and was buried in an unmarked 'pauper's' grave in Eastlands Cemetery in Galashiels. His song was intended as an advertising jingle for the aniseed flavoured candy sweets that he manufactured in Melrose. Ironically, the recipe is no longer known, but the song lives on: *"Ally Bally, Ally Bally Bee, sittin' oan yer mammy's knee......"* Robert Coltart - the 'Coulter' of the song - made and sold his wares around all the country fairs and markets in the Border towns.

'Ally' considers himself to be a bit of a comedian. More on the Eddie Large side, rather than the Sid Little! At 54 years of age, he had served 32 of those in the force with no major career ambitions. He had been a Detective Sergeant now for over 15 years. Divorced, with two grown up children, he is also a huge sports fanatic, although mainly from a distance these days. A distance of about 8ft from his TV screen to the sofa. A big horse racing fan of both the flat and the jumps. He's been known to travel to race meets at Musselburgh, Kelso and Ayr. Even travelled as far afield as Aintree once for the Grand National.

It was the 136th renewal of the world-famous horse race that took place at Aintree Racecourse near Liverpool, on the 3rd of April 1982. The race was won by 9 year old, 7/1 favourite Grittar, ridden by amateur Dick Saunders. At the age of forty-eight, Saunders became and remains, the oldest jockey to have won it. Grittar never won another race after his National victory and died in 1998, aged 25. Dick Saunders passed away in January 2002, aged 68. DS Coulter could have informed you of all of the above. He loved his statistics, his facts and figures, and not just the horse racing variety! An invaluable resource was our 'Ally' in catching 'the bad guys.'

He's also mighty handy to have as the captain and leading light of the CID's pub quiz team!

The Sergeants equestrian highlight however, came about just four short years ago. It was Sunday, October 3rd 2010. He belatedly went abroad with a group of horse racing friends to celebrate his half century here on earth. The location? Paris, France, for the Group One horse race, the Prix de l'Arc de Triomphe. Over the years, the Arc de Triomphe has earned a reputation as the world's greatest horse race. Traditionally run at Longchamp, the Parisian course brings together the world's most talented thoroughbreds aged three years and over.

Whether they are breeders, trainers, jockeys or owners, all horse-racing professionals dream of seeing their horse first past the post to clinch the world's most coveted flat racing title. With good reason, because every four-hoofed victor and their entourage, earn a prestigious place in racing history. The 2010 winner was Workforce, a three-year-old colt trained in Great Britain by Sir Michael Stoute. Workforce had previously won the Epsom Derby. And the decision to run in the 'Arc' had not been confirmed until only three days before the race.

'Ally' was exceptionally glad he ran. He had backed him ante-post with a 'monkey' (£500) at odds of 12/1. With his winnings he was able to buy plenty of 'Coulter's Candy' that evening and it wasn't his 'mammy's' knee he was sitting on either. C'est la vie!

The office was completely locked up. Coulter having spotted two of Dixons men outside, nudged Taz softly with his elbow, made a slight head gesture and out into the yard they headed. As the CID officers appeared, the two 'gents' stood slightly stooped over, giving the impression that they were working under the bonnet of an old white Transit van.

Coulter gave a brief shout out to get their attention, "Hey, you two." They were only about 20 yards away and carried on regardless, making out they were so busy, and hadn't actually noticed the Police officers on the premises.

"Ye right," Taylor mouthed dismissively. They lifted their heads slowly in unison and looked over. Both men recognised Coulter straight away.

"Messrs Forrester and Allan," he laughed. "I'm just waiting for you two to break into song. You sound like an Irish folk duo." Coulter then lifted an imaginary microphone to his lips before continuing. "Ladies and gentlemen let me introduce, for your pleasure and delight this morning, live from Portobello Pier, Messrs Forrester and Allan." Taz Taylor graciously applauded, left hand over right in a polite, elegant manner. By contrast, 'Ally' Coulter bent over with unrestrained laughter.

Taylor then stared at him with a look that said, 'Seriously!'

The performers, well Francis Allan actually, the shorter of the pair, just gruffly asked, "What do you need Mr Coulter?"

"We're looking for your boss, Kenneth Dixon, or his Sergeant-at-Arms, 'Bunny' Reid. Any idea where we might find them?"

"No idea. Not seen either of them all day," Allan replied.

"This is a murder enquiry," DC Taylor chipped in. In her rather high-pitched voice, she failed miserably in trying to speak to them as someone in authority. "You boys might want to rethink that answer."

"And you might want to rethink that jacket!" Billy Forrester quipped. "Light brown, wae black troosers, a'

54

don't think so?" The pair looked at each. As if to say, 'good one!' And then laughed heartily and hard.

"When I need fashion advice from the likes of you, I'll ask for it thank you very much. Now your boss…….. his whereabouts?"

Allan, raising his voice repeated, "You're not listening dear, we've not seen any of them."

Looking to ease the tension and defuse the situation before it escalated, her Sergeant remarked - "It's okay Taz, I've an idea where one of them may well be. Let's go."

They proceeded to make their way past the large, ageing metal gates at the entrance. In the background, gesticulations and gestures were being offered by two blokes at a van! If you listened carefully, the tenor voice of 'Ally' Coulter could then be heard. 'Taz' Taylor was being gently serenaded to the strains of, *"I wandered today to the hills Maggie."*

To which she responded by shaking her head, pointing to her clothing and asking - "Really Ally, what do you think? Light brown with the black? Too much?" Coulter, now behind the wheel of their car, raised a hand and shook his head violently. He was far too wise to get involved in that discussion. Together they drove off in silence, in search of some medical assistance?

With easily a half hour drive through stop/start traffic, Coulter felt the need to update his partner with some juicy background to her 'fashion adviser' and his 'singing partner.'

"Billy Forrester was single and aged about thirty or so Taz. I'd be surprised if he has ever paid any National Insurance in his life. He was brought up nearby though, in the Granton area of town. He has served time for numerous minor offences over the years, but nothing serious." Taz nodded, as her partner continued with

Forrester's CV. "He got in tow with Kenny Dixon nearly a decade ago. Initially helping him with security, before progressing to learning all other aspects of the business. He's a big soccer fan and..." Coulter paused and pursed his lips, unsure about the merit of continuing that particular story.

"And," Taz screwed up her eyebrows, as if to say........go on, tell me more!

"He has a pretty distinct Celtic F.C. tattoo," Coulter concluded.

"The rest," she nodded impatiently. Knowing full well, he was holding something back.

"Well," 'Ally' continued. "He seemingly told the young tattoo studio apprentice, who obviously had no interest in football, that the team were formed in '88."

"And?" Taylor gently urged.

"And, he left him to start inking away," Coulter furnished. He then began to smile as he concluded the story. "So in conclusion Taz, he ended up with bold, colourful capital letters on his right forearm saying: CELTIC FC and underneath the date read, 1988! Considering they celebrated their centenary celebrations over a quarter of a century ago, that was quite some achievement."

Taz laughed satisfactorily, as if getting one up on her detractors. She glanced over at her stern-faced chauffeur and suggested, "That is quite funny Ally, you have to admit."

"Not for the poor tattoo artist Taz. He was never seen again!"

At that, they offered up a few moments silence. Belatedly paying their respects to the elusive, yet suspected dead tattooist. Coulter then interrupted the dead air by continuing his commentary on Taylor's recent adversaries.

"So, onto Francis Anthony Allan, aged 26, his resume is short, sharp and sweet, just like the man himself."

Taylor feigned the hint of a smile.

"As Meat Loaf would say, 'two out of three ain't bad!' He's an Ayrshire man Taz, Kilbirnie to be exact. His father was a school friend of KD. No academic qualifications, but a man of action. Just ask his wife Julie."

Taylor queried this with a simple drop of her head to the side.

"She has given birth to four children in the last few years," Coulter beamed. "The two oldest being girls aged 7 and 6. Then more recently, twin boys now aged 3. Frankie himself doesn't ask a lot of questions, normally just the one, and you heard it earlier - 'What do you need?' Usually that is followed up with: Give me the money and I'll start right away!"

"Wow," Taz exclaimed. "You do like your facts and figures right enough, don't you!" She knew she was getting a great education at the feet of a Master. She was so grateful to have a colleague like Robert Coulter. A professional, one willing to share his wisdom and expertise without ever feeling threatened.

In return, he had done well to be paired with a partner with a real desire to learn. In addition, she'd a keenness to develop her skills and continually strived to remain focused at all times - due in part to the personal commitment made to her late mother.

Tasmin Taylor, with her beautiful ebony skin, had just celebrated her 23rd birthday on the 11th of last month. She was named after her mother's favourite pop singer at that time. None other than Tasmin Archer. Sarah, her mother, gave birth as an unmarried mum. She always had high hopes for her beautiful daughter. The lyrics of Tasmin Archer's major hit 'Sleeping

Satellite,' reference the Apollo Space Missions of the 1960's. Characterizing them as "man's great adventure." They contained the lines: *"When we shoot for the stars, what a giant step. Have we got what it takes to carry the weight of this concept?"*

That No.1 hit single was on the album, 'Great Expectations.' And that was exactly what a proud mother had for her daughter, way back on Remembrance Day, 1991!

Sarah Turner had died suddenly in a road traffic accident eight years ago. Tasmin was only 15 years of age. Her death remains a continual spur. It has helped to motivate and drive her to succeed, to constantly improve (she had lost over 2 stone - to join the police in 2011) and has continually helped her to remain firmly focused ever since. Still in her early twenties, she can be impetuous, headstrong and bullish at times. However, that is in fact what most people normally admire in her. She loves to be active and that includes running, cycling and swimming. Plus, only recently she had taken up Tae Kwon Do. Physically she is tall and muscular and looks not unlike Sharron Davies, the former competitive swimmer who represented Great Britain in the Olympics and European championships in the late seventies and early eighties.

Like that 'sleeping satellite,' Taz Taylor continually shoots for the stars. She adores sport, she loves her job and she'll openly embrace the challenging adventures that await her in life.

As Coulter and Taylor pull up and park at their destination, two of their colleagues have other matters to deal with.

Over in East Lothian, DC's Hayes and Curry were currently following up with enquiries into the alleged arson at a local health food outlet. The fire on the town's High Street was the third Oat'n Nuts store to have been targeted over the past few months. The pair would also be working closely and correlating with their colleagues in the two other divisions, where the previous two attacks had taken place.

Located south of St Andrews, Anstruther is the largest in a string of pretty, old-fashioned fishing villages along the stretch of the Fife coast known as the East Neuk. December 24th was the date of their belated 'firework night' celebrations, within the community's Oat 'n Nuts store.

Then, you have to go even further back, to early July, when the health chains store in the Borders was the first to be singled out and torched!

DC Susan Hayes was in her early forties, unmarried with no children. She had hazel eyes, a bright pearly white smile, and glossy brown shoulder length hair, parted ever so slightly to the side. At 5' 8' in height, stocky and plump, she would be best described as 'matron like.' Firm but fair, she was experienced, knew the ropes and gave wise, sensible counsel. Although 'old school' - she loved her TV. Not surprisingly the cooking shows and period dramas, like 'Call the Midwife' and 'Downton Abbey.' After leaving college and spending a few years in the advertising world, Hayes joined the force when she was twenty-five. Because of her partnership with DC Curry, her current nickname was Hanna. After 'Hannibal' Hayes and 'Kid' Curry. 'The two most successful outlaws in the history of the West,' according to the 1970's popular American TV show 'Alias Smith and Jones.'

"One hundred per cent deliberate," the Chief Fire Officer confirmed to Hayes. "Real old school. Petrol poured through the letterbox and then a lit match or similar thrown on top. It's a dangerous way to carry it out. If you'd spilled some on your own body or clothing, you could have been asking for trouble."

"Not a professional job then," Hayes wanted confirmed.

"Absolutely not. Amateurs for sure. Brave amateurs though. No, no, that's not correct, let me rephrase that. Crazy, foolhardy, stupid and reckless amateurs!" He vehemently concluded.

The store had been extensively damaged throughout. And as police officers continued their investigations on the periphery, the structure was being monitored and carefully examined by specialists. Locals walked by opposite. Some pointed, others shook their heads. Several tutted and no doubt thought to themselves, 'this doesn't happen in our town.'

As he approached, "Just heard back from the other forces," Curry informed his colleague. Hayes was busy gleaning more information from a member of the forensics team on the site. "Exact copy," Curry had established. "Letterbox, petrol, then set alight. The same amateur or amateurs?" Was the question he posed.

Detective Andrew 'Kid' Curry had just celebrated his 21st birthday earlier in the year. He had been thrilled to learn the ropes these past 12 months partnered with 'Hanna' Hayes. With a good physical presence, he stood about 5' 10' in his bare feet. Drew Curry embraced a busy lifestyle, whilst living with his long term girlfriend Judy, in West Lothian. He enjoyed most sports, especially rugby - having been brought up in the shadow of Murrayfield Stadium, in the Balgreen area of the city.

SIX

"Welcome, Monsieur, sit yourself down and meet the best innkeeper in town. As for the rest, all of 'em crooks, rooking their guests and cooking the books."

- Les Miserables

Mid-afternoon and Edinburgh had its very own 'Sistine Chapel.' Over 50 shades of swirling grey frenetic cloud had arrived overhead, and it was about to descend swiftly upon the City Centre as 'Ally' and DC Taylor arrived at the Doctors. There was no serious injury or ailment, nothing wrong with either of them. The 'Doctors' was a rather run down, sawdust on the floor and a loan shark in every corner Public House. A hostelry that most normal law abiding members of the public would never be seen dead in. However, on second thoughts, that is possibly exactly the only reason they would be in there! Filled at any given time of day with the Capital's finest of the low. Ranging from petty theft, forgery and drug deals. To serious assault, rape and murder. You name it, BINGO, they'll have done it!

Taylor and Coulter strode confidently in unison through the unwelcoming graffiti scrawled door. Time travelling like Dr. Who and his latest female companion, back four decades to the early seventies. Floral wallpaper and formica tabletops. Growing up with Coronation Street, the only thing missing was Hilda Ogden's three geese taking flight on a nearby wall! Voice levels dropped by half as they entered. By the time they reached the dimly lit counter, and approached the shoulder of a wrangler jacket clad individual with a lengthy pony tail, conversations had all but ceased.

As young DC Taylor reached out to tap the gentleman's forearm, she winced slightly. She'd suddenly spotted a child's pink, soft toy rabbit (rather like the Duracell bunny from the adverts). It was leaning eerily against this man's pint of froth topped ale. Before she could make contact, the 'Hell's Angel' wannabe, turned sharply on his burgundy cowboy boots. He then began to snarl under his breath and look her menacingly up and down. As he turned wearily to his left, he heard a low dulcet tone ask:

"Alright Bunny, how ye' doin'?"
After an initial pause and brief deliberation, a response was offered up.

"DS Coulter, long time no see." The slow, deep, gravel tones continued. "I'm fair to middlin'. How about you? Must be due for retirin' soon, eh?"

"Not quite, not quite yet Bunny."

"Still got a liking for the gee gees Ally?"

"The occasional flutter Bunny, coupled with a visit or two here or there. Enough about me though. What are you up to? How's the security sector these days? Protecting, skiving, duckin' an' divin'? Keepin' yer head above water?"

"Can't complain Mr. Coulter. Can't complain!" He then began to turn his attention quickly to Taz Taylor. He nodded his head, giving her an approving glance. "So who's this you've brought with you Ally? She's a fine looking filly, must have a good pedigree." A nauseous look appeared immediately across Taylor's lightly made up face.

Continuing on proudly with his horse-racing terminology, he crossed the finishing line with, "Without doubt the most eye catching thoroughbred we've had in here for many awhile!" Admiring glances, wolf whistles and cheers went up at that remark.

Turning to face his female colleague, 'Ally' Coulter frowned rather reluctantly and with an arm outstretched in the direction of the 'livestock' agent' said: "Detective Constable Tasmin Taylor, may I introduce you to James Baxter Reid. 'Bunny' to his friends."

Reid took her by the hand and ever the true gent, proceeded to kiss the back of it. Suddenly, 'swoosh,' her recent martial arts training came to the fore and Taylor swiftly returned her wrist to her side within the millisecond.

"A normal 'hello' will suffice for now Mr Reid, thank you very much. Or may I call you Bunny?" she confidently asserted.

"You most certainly can call me Bunny, honey, and anytime you like. Day or night." he added with a leer.

"Two days ago Bunny," Coulter interjected. "Need to know your whereabouts. Any witnesses? And preferably ones that don't frequent here 24 hours a day!"

"Come on Ally, you serious? I've only got two words to say to you, and they're not what you're thinking love," he quipped to Taylor. "You've not thought this through too well have you DS Coulter? That would make it the 28th of December, correct? Need I continue?"

"Of course," Taylor piped up innocently. "Where were you?"

Slowly shaking his head in a disbelieving manner, as if to say - Really! "Leopardstown," he rasped.

"Leopardstown where's that?" she asked impatiently. "West Lothian, Fife, Berwick-upon-Tweed," Taylor randomly guessed. UK geography possibly not being her strong point!

Laughing in a gallus, self-satisfactory way, 'Bunny' Reid enlightened her. "Afraid not dear, bit further afield than that. Way outside your domain."

Coulter looked sheepishly and knowingly toward the ground. Taylor simply looked bemused.

"Three hundred miles outside it, to be precise. It's across the Irish Sea. It's in Dublin. Detective Sergeant Coulter is well aware that Kenny and a group of his 'business partners,' travel across annually for the Christmas race meet. It's normally held a couple of days after Boxing Day," he paused. "That would be your 28th of December covered then sweetheart?"

The thought of KD and a group of his cronies in attendance at that particular location, would bring a pleasing smile to DC Taylor's face if only she knew it's history. Leprosy was common in Dublin in medieval times and in the 14th Century a leper hospital was built near St Stephen's Green. It was later to move out to the foot of the Dublin mountains - the area where it was sited became known as Leopardstown. (Irish: Baile na Lobhar, meaning 'Town of the Lepers'). A more suitably named meeting ground for a bunch of Edinburgh's finest undesirables to gather at, you could not imagine.

"Okay, okay you've made your point Bunny. We'll check it out, but I believe you." Coulter was scolding himself for forgetting. He had bumped into the group several years ago in Dublin and became aware then, of their regular festive travel plans.

Suddenly, an unusual ring tone could be heard throughout the hushed bar. Who would personalise their mobile with The Fugees, 'Killing Me Softly With

His Song?' All eyes turned toward its owner. The ringtone was about to continue sounding, when a rough, course, worldly hand reached down to dramatically flip it open. A hand whose veins appeared so prominently, as if attempting to break through the very skin that encased them. Bold blue tracks that could easily be mistaken for a road map of the North-East of Scotland.

"Hello, 'Bunny' Reid here," the voice rasped. Whit? Aye. Gi'e me two minutes. I'll phone you back Marky."

"Let's go Taz," volunteered 'Ally' Coulter. "Let's leave the boys to enjoy their refreshments in peace."

As they made their way to depart, a gentle chorus of......*"Ally Bally, Ally Bally Bee, sittin' oan yer..."* began to echo in unison around the bar.

On reaching the door, Coulter turned, raised his voice and called back: "Just to remind you of a couple of things though 'Bunny.'

"Oh yes, and what would those be Sergeant?"

Silence fell over the bar again, as the verbal tennis match continued in an open forum.

"DC Taylor here is an expert in Tae Kwon Do, a black belt in fact." Secondly, 'Ally' added powerfully, assertively and with a touch of real bravado, "She is no longer an inexperienced filly sir. Detective Constable Taylor is a fully fledged mare. One with strength and character and a heck of a powerful kick. Remember you said it earlier. She has the pedigree and let me reassure you, she is an odds on favourite to succeed!" Then in a quieter, calmer and more reassured tone, he added as menacingly as any serving police officer could: "I would tread very carefully in future, if I were you 'Bunny.' Take care now Mr Reid, look after yourself."

Reid's face filled with fury and anger. He had just lost a short five furlong sprint on his home track. Until the next race meet, he thought privately to himself.

With a gentle nod and a wink at her promotion to 'expert martial artist.' Coulter then followed Tasmin Taylor out of the 'Tardis' and back into 21st century Edinburgh. Once outside she could hardly contain herself.

"The soft toy, what's that all about? What's the deal with the pink rabbit?"

Coulter responded knowledgeably. "That is why he's called Bunny! Or so he says. But there is much more to it than that. When we have time another day, I'll explain it fully. More importantly and always worth bearing in mind at future meetings is this." 'Ally' waited until Taz met his eyes.

"Go on, I'm listening," she nodded.

"It's also where he keeps his blade. Think 'Rambo, First Blood' and you've got the idea!"

As Taz Taylor visibly flinched, Coulter held his finger aloft.

It was his way of fully emphasizing, "You need to 'Be Prepared' Taz. 'Cause James 'Bunny' Reid is NO virtuous, squeaky clean Boy Scout!"

Sixty-seconds later 'Bunny' returned the call. The man's voice on the phone sounded in need of help and clarification.

"It's Maria, Bunny. He's gave her a right good hidin'."

The slow familiar, guttural growl responded with, "Aye, okay son, I hear you. Best send his wife a belated Christmas gift fae Santa. 'The Nuptials would be an appropriate response. That wid' be a guid idea."

"Okay Bunny, whatever you say. I'll send Rudolph and the boys round right away," he laughed nervously.

Mark Ziola was from Mid Calder in West Lothian. He got mixed up in drugs whilst still at High School.

Graduated to housebreaking at 19, and now at age 24, he had worked tirelessly for DG Security for the past three years. 'Marky' is like a young 'Robin Williams.' He never stops talking or walking about frantically - displaying the soothing, flowing arm gestures of a 'wild copulating octopus on methadone.' As opposed to those of a domesticated octopus! He also wore the most hideous, brightly coloured Hawaiian shirts on the planet. "Good Morning Gil----mer---ton!"

Today, this wily grandson of a Polish immigrant was standing in the doorway of a rather squalid and decaying two bedroomed flat. The premises were located just off Gilmerton Road, on the southeast side of Edinburgh. The property was one of several that belonged to DG Security. It currently 'hosted' two teenage Romanian girls. The European Union may have opened up marvellous trade opportunities for many successful small and medium sized companies. However, for individuals looking to prosper, it inevitably led to much seedier, darker and ultimately unhealthy choices being made.

Maria and Tanya were not retail fashion assistants in a Next store. You could not envision them, with their extensive lashes, grandiose hairstyles and their unnatural chests of plenty - scanning baked beans at the checkout in your local Tesco!

No, believe it or not. These girls were 'fully trained, professional massage therapists!' You spell therapists - E.S.C.O.R.T.S to be precise.

Upstairs, Maria was lying sideways on the settee in the small, dank sitting room. Wearing only a short grubby, supposedly white towelling dressing gown. She held an ice pack (a bag of frozen cod fillets), to her left eye and nose. Tanya continued to tenderly wipe the blood from Maria's waist and upper thigh. The poor girl had obviously been repeatedly beaten by a hand, a buckled belt or possibly both. Large welts, delicate sores and a copious amount of bruises were now becoming clearly evident.

The assailant had been restrained. Mark was the minder in charge that day. He remained in the apartment at all times and had heard the commotion. He was on the scene within seconds. The unfortunate client was now locked in the adjoining bedroom, awaiting his fate.

'Bunny' had recommended 'The Nuptials,' or 'Wedding Ring' treatment, as his boys often referred to it. Another trio of suitable P's would describe it aptly. It's most certainly not polite, pleasant or pleasurable. Then again, neither were the aggressors actions. Nobody gets the 'Marriage' sentence unless they are a previous offender. So this guy had been there before, done it and got the T-shirt. He knew the score. Raised voices could be heard in the corridor as the key turned slowly in the lock. Fearful and in a panic, the client jumped to his feet. Grabbing his jacket from the well-worn bed, he scurried to the far side of the room. Attempting in haste to get as far away as possible from whoever opened that door. On entering, Mark Ziola's normally talkative, chatty persona had distinctively changed. He stayed silent as he approached Maria's cowardly, weedy client.

The poor man swallowed hard. Sweat began to exude from his pores at an alarming rate. He began nervously muttering, stumbling over words. He was scared, panicking and afraid for his wellbeing, if not his life. Reputation was everything in this game and James Baxter Reid who ran the escort side of Kenny Dixon's business, had built up a rather impressive, imposing and intimidating one. One he was proud of. One he encouraged. One that he required to keep in place, come what may!

The deviant client's ramblings were gradually becoming clearer and ever more coherent. He pleaded incessantly, "I've got plenty more money in my wallet. Here take it. Help yourself. Keep it, it's yours." He paused for a whole two second respite. Before hysterically ranting, "Just let me go, it won't happen again. I'll never return, honest. Here, have the money." Unsure at what was about to .... Crack! Suddenly his left knee bone shattered as Ziola's powerful karate kick bent it sickeningly backwards. An unbearable searing pain shot through the man's body. Deafening screams of agony though were about to be muffled. As the 'by no means innocent party' lay doubled over on the deck, Marky's size eight boot was swinging forward like a professional golf club. It connected voraciously. Striking with full, maximum impact straight into the mouth. Shattering and registering with every tooth of Maria's attacker.

"I need something. One more thing from you," Ziola calmly remarked.

No one heard his utterance. The punter was fully unconscious. He had keeled over, slumped to the floor. His scrawny fingers briefly opened and relinquished their grip on the roll of banknotes that he'd been talking about just seconds previously.

Now however - life, activity, motion even, had become extinct, at least temporarily. They were deceased, defunct and had departed. Dead and gone for a brief afternoon siesta. Retrieving the scattered notes and depositing them in his jean pocket. The violent minder simply offered - "I'll be able to replace my scuffed boots now. Thanks."

Two tearful, Bucharest born female teenagers stood traumatised at the open door. Their gaze alternated between the twisted bones on the laminate flooring and the beautiful, peaceful palm trees of Marky's flamboyant cotton shirt. They were alarmed at the damage inflicted on the puny, feeble, non-descript businessman. They understood he needed to be taught a lesson. But neither of them had ever envisioned this. Ziola flicked his head sharply. The gesture was instantly acknowledged and received. Tanya and Maria hurriedly backed out of the room. Closing over the door as they exited, they looked anxiously at each other. As if to say - 'Did you just see, what I just saw?' A shimmering blade had just received a belated invite to the party!

Since 1991, 'Investors in People' had set the standard for better people management. Their internationally recognised accreditation is held by over 14,000 organisations across the world. The standard defines what it takes to lead, support and manage people well for sustainable results. In the head office back at Portobello, there it is. Proudly framed and displayed prominently on the back wall behind KD's desk. Having achieved all the levels of qualification required: DG Security were proud to say, that in 2013 they were accredited 'Investors in People.' Setting the standards in customer care and providing unrivalled service to the community. There was simply no arguing with that!

As a particular individual was being rushed to the intensive care unit at The Royal Infirmary of Edinburgh. An overdue Christmas gift was delivered to his loving, faithful and no doubt long suffering wife. The doorbell had been rung and the parcel left. Prying eyes watched carefully from across the street to ensure the delivery was received. A lady in her late fifties or maybe early sixties quickly opened the door. Seeing no one around, she curiously looked both ways. And then repeated the process, as if about to cautiously step out and cross the road. With no one present she shook her head in a rather bemused fashion. Then finally, she spotted the delicate box that had been placed on her doorstep. It had been decorated with a pretty red satin bow. Her face broke into a huge smile as she graciously knelt, picked it up and proceeded to open its lid.

Instantly, a high pitched scream was let out and the container dropped. Its contents landed partway inside the doorway of the house. The yell, cry and combined screeching increased. Neighbours appeared at windows, nearby dogs howled and people in the immediate street arrived on the scene. The wife had now collapsed.

Eyes unblinking, she stared disbelievingly at the severed, bloodied finger in her hallway. It was the fourth finger of her husband's left hand. She knew this how? Because the primary digit still had his 'wedding band' attached to it. The card inside, simply read.........Happy New Year!

SEVEN

"With all the will in the world, diving for dear life - When we could be diving for pearls"

- Elvis Costello

Less than eighteen hours previous, a successful City Centre property agent was anticipating a fruitful and rewarding business meeting. It was now mid-afternoon on Tuesday, December 30th.

In the heart of Edinburgh on the corner of George Street and Castle Street, you'll find a Starbucks. Ignore that and continue to head down Castle Street towards the fortress itself. Just before you get to Princes Street you'll find a Costa Coffee on the left. Go past that and a few steps later you'll find Castello Coffee. Possibly Edinburgh's best kept coffee secret and one of its more recent additions. It opened its doors to the capital's discerning public from as recently as summer 2012.

Betty Moore had walked past it twice before, without ever giving it a second thought. Everyone she'd talked to about Edinburgh coffee though, had said excellent things about it. So she thought it best to give it a go. It's a tiny place, with just enough room for a couple of tables and a bar opposite the counter. There are also a few covers outside and another tiny bar space by the window. Today, meeting up with a potential client, she had chosen the window area. The decorative hands on the wall clock signalled two forty-five. Her 2.30pm appointment seemed to be running late. She then checked her phone every other minute, just to make sure she has not missed a call or a text message explaining his absence.

Elizabeth 'Betty' Moore had worked around the corner in George Street for just over six years. She was one of an original trio of founder partners in The Re.Gal Property Group. Initially set up by three females, it's aim was to encourage and support more women to become involved in the property sector. For instance, to become landlords, owners, property developers, factors, maintenance contractors, etc. Suzy Gilmore and Karen Hillis are her co-partners. Karen, who stays in Cumbernauld now oversees their new Glasgow office. That branch only opened earlier in the year.

With the clock hands now perfectly aligned at a ninety degree angle. Betty decided that thirty minutes grace was long enough. Her phone call, once again went straight to voicemail. During her five minute walk back to the office she began planning her New Year festivity celebrations in her head.

Listed as one of the 'Top 100 things to do before you die.' Edinburgh's Hogmanay celebrations would certainly be the ultimate way to welcome in 2015. However, having been in attendance last year and having thoroughly enjoyed it. She and her boyfriend reckon they may face an anti-climax this year. Opting instead to go with a less stressful and slightly quieter option this New Year's Eve. Hence, she would deliberately work a little later tonight, so that she can forego work on the 31st. One of the perks of being the boss she reckoned!

Betty appreciated just how blessed she was to work in such a cultural and diverse city. She loved Edinburgh. Over 130,000 party goers from all over the world were expected to join the Hogmanay festivities, with three days of fantastic free and ticketed events. They included: The Shetland Viking torch-lit procession, a Lily Allen headline concert and various theatre productions. Then, you also had the spectacular fireworks and street party extravaganza. So it's not surprising that it's the only festival to appear in the 'Discovery Channel's Top 25 World Travel Experiences'.

Set beneath the beautiful backdrop of Edinburgh Castle. Party revellers would rock to the sound of bagpipes, DJs and some world class musicians and artists in Princes Street and Princes Street Gardens. With live stages vibrating to the sounds of favourite performers and countdown pyrotechnics at 9pm, 10pm and 11pm, the anticipation to 'The Bells' would become electric.

Tidied up and locking the office door just two minutes short of 8pm. Her trip home from Waverley Station will be on the east-coast bound train, with a scheduled departure time of 8.32pm. Then ultimately it would arrive at her destination, which is currently without a station building, approximately 80 minutes later.

Roughly a year had passed since the Dundee main station structure had been demolished. It had to make way for a new multimillion-pound building as part of the long term Waterfront Project. That is one major development program, that this 'Re.Gal' lass will now never witness.

Murray had amassed plenty of miles on the clock over the years, nearly matching the 106,000 on his seasoned, cobalt blue Volvo. He appeared to have accrued a 'greatest hits' vinyl album collection of experience.

On side one, some sterling work that included: Maturity, Skill Set, Judgement, Observation, Understanding, Patience and the final track, the admirable...... Wisdom.

On the reverse, we get to hear a few live recordings that included: Witnesses, Trials, Murders, Accused, Crimes, Robberies and Abuse.

Abuse, that's the one that continues to play loud and clear in Dolby Stereo surround sound on the classic turntable in Murray's head.

The stylus is stuck for sure, on side 2, track 7!

Parking two streets away from Sheila Dixon's home, he indicated and pulled up kerbside. His Bluetooth connection rang just before he made to take the keys from the car ignition. On seeing the caller I.D. he became excited. It was Sandra Kerr, his heavily pregnant police partner. She was currently on maternity leave.

"Hi, Sandy, nice to hear from you. How's things? Any news yet?"

"Absolutely, that's why I'm calling. Yesterday afternoon, 6lb 4oz."

"That's a good weight Sandy, 6lb 4oz," Murray stated with a smile.

"Yes, so is 6lb 2oz."

"Oh, 6lb 2oz, sorry, misheard you. I thought you'd said 6lb 4oz initially."

"I did say 6lb 4 firstly, then 6lb 2, she said exaggerating and fully pronouncing each word. Two weights sir. Two different weights," she emphasised.

Murray had pulled his mobile away from his ear and was facing it. He looked at it blankly. As if to say 'what on heaven is this woman on about.' Then the light switched on!

"Oh right," he exclaimed. Detective Inspector Steven Murray had finally grasped it! "Twins," he excitedly announced to all within the Edinburgh and Lothian boundaries. "Fantastic! How are they? What are they? Where are they? And who are they?"

"Ha ha ha," Sandy gently chuckled. "Slow down Steven. Calm down and relax. You're worse than my nervous wreck of a husband."

"Oh yes, and how is Richard doing? He'll be delighted, surprised! Did you know it was going to be twins? If so, you kept that a surprise." Murray just kept prattling on at a great speed of urgency.

"Sir, sir, deep breaths. Let's backtrack slightly and let us, moderate one's pace slightly."

"Moderate one's pace! What a rather lovely, polite turn of phrase DC Kerr," Murray responded, in an upmarket 'you'll have had your tea?' Morningside voice.

Sandra Kerr then took control. Beginning to speak slowly and deliberately. "Both children are doing well. They are identical girls. They are at the bottom of the bed sleeping right now and they are named Carly and Stephanie. As for Richie, he is 'thrilled to bits' and 'proud as Punch.' We are both 'over the moon' and 'on cloud nine' as all the familiar sayings go. They only told us last week that is was to be twins. So, surprised then? Yes we were. Absolutely!"

Murray listened intently, before adding, "I'll pop by at some point. As soon as I can make it, I'll be there. I'm so delighted for you both. Brilliant, fair chuffed, you've made my day. Nice to have a little bit of good news. Something to celebrate and smile about. Thanks Sandy, I need to go now, but I'll see you all real soon. I promise, real soon. Tell Rich I was asking for him and give each of those young ladies a kiss on the cheek from their friendly local 'Bobby.'"

On hearing a large aircraft overhead and still smiling like a Cheshire cat. The Detective Inspector looked up to acknowledge a combination of blue skies, assimilated with a range of dark scattered clouds. Inevitably, in Murray's world - Messrs Cirrus, Stratus, Cumulus and Nimbus are never too far away - even on the brightest of days in the middle of Summer!

The Willowbrae district is a respectable, middle class area. In recent years however, one or two more modern, exclusive properties had been established within its confines. Three storey townhouses with top floor penthouse views. They contained a host of luxurious, ultra modern fixtures and fittings. Not forgetting a built in garage below the spacious accommodation, with parking space at a premium all over the city, that is a wonderful added feature. The well liked and respected Dixon's had only lived in the neighbourhood for the past eighteen months.

After announcing himself at the gate, producing his I.D. and making his way to the front door. DI Steven Murray was greeted by a lady he would have guessed to be in her mid to late forties. Stylish, with a certain Michelle Pfeiffer quality, look and charm to her. Meaning, she can be either glamorous, sexy and seductive one minute, or cold, hard hearted and callous the next. That would just about sum up the character traits required to be a WAG of a 'undesirable villain' these days. Sorry! Murray immediately apologised to himself for his political incorrectness, even just in his mind. I meant to inwardly think 'respected local businessman!'

The star from 'The Witches of Eastwick' was wearing a top of the range, made to measure, dark brown trouser suit. With a designer price tag to match no doubt. An elegant beige blouse sat beneath the jacket, adorned with an attractive string of miniature chocolate Tahitian Pearls. Wow, the helpful knowledge one gleams from a diving trip in Hawaii. The beautiful necklace also distracted you from a small, but prominent two inch red birthmark on the lower throat of his hostess.

"Mrs Dixon," he said brightly. "Detective Inspector Murray."

She laughed. It had an edge of cheekiness to it. "Yes, I gathered you would be the same officer that introduced himself to me just seconds ago at the camera with his identification."

"Yes quite," Murray apologetically responded. "You'd be right, bad habit that." However, quickly trying to find favour, "Chocolate Tahitian Pearls" he confidently asserted.

Greeted now, with a large smile of astonishment and a nodding of the head. "Impressive," the lady of the house stated. "Inspector Murray you said. I'm amazed, not many people would have known that."

"Appreciate that. Part of a holiday in Oahu ma'am. Two days spent diving for pearls with a brief overview and history relating to a few current facts and figures thrown in. Thankfully, it looks like I've been able to retain some of the info. So maybe it was money well spent after all?"

Throwing her wispy, tousled hair to one side over her left shoulder, she replied back in business mode. "How can I help you Inspector? Is it my husband you're looking for? If so, he's not at home at present."

"Well," he paused thinking upon her words. "That's a pity, it would have been good to meet him. What made you think it was him I was after?" Anyway, I've every confidence that you can help me. You just seem that sort of woman!"

What sort of woman? Sheila Dixon thought. Wary of his slightly flirtatious manner, she led him to their main sitting room. A glorious space, resplendent with breath-taking panoramic views of the Edinburgh city skyline. That was thanks mainly to the spectacular fifteen foot high by twenty foot long sensational bespoke windows. Murray en-route stumbled over some sports racquets, a box of shuttlecocks and other equipment that had been left abandoned, piled up against one side of the wall in the hallway. The pyramid shape they created was directly below a rather sensual, sexy and seductive artwork that seemed to catch the Detective's eye. Possibly that, was the real cause of his clumsiness. Finding his composure for the second time in as many minutes, Murray sat in the, the .... wait, there was nowhere to sit!

"Sorry!" Sheila Dixon announced. "We gave our old suite to a charitable organisation yesterday and our new furniture has been delayed 24 hours. I just found that out earlier today. So we can make do the best we can until then," she stoically stated, before beginning to rearrange an overflowing vase full of beautiful flowers. The fragrance from which was enchanting.

What riches, what wealth and what a lifestyle Murray thought to himself. Then he quickly found himself singing under his breath. *"Bonnie and Clyde began their evil doin', one lazy afternoon down Savannah way."* DI Murray was gone. He was transfixed reading a small sticker on the edge of the window panels. It read: *'Dynamically Adapting Residential Glass - SolarSmart is a self-tinting, high performance glass that darkens in the presence of direct sunlight to block heat, glare and damaging ultraviolet light. It reduces the need for blinds and will significantly cut the cooling & lighting costs in your home, due to its Suntuitive interlayer. Even in its darkest state, sunlight responsive SolarSmart is still transparent, always preserving the view.'*

He stood mesmerized at the stunning windows and viewed with awe, the staggering landscape and spectacular setting. Murray observed the cold, crisp, frosty December day through melancholic eyes. Nostalgic for when as a 17 year old lad in the West of Scotland, he had a Saturday job at Arnotts, the largest department store in the mill town of Paisley. It was located directly across from the historic 13th century Abbey. Three or four floors packed with everything, including the kitchen sink! It was part of the giant 'House of Fraser' retail group at the time and reminiscent of the popular TV programme 'Are You Being Served.'

Mr Steven 'I'm Free!' Murray, worked in the furniture department at the back of the premises. It was the only major route through the store after shoppers had parked their vehicles in the private car park at the rear. 'Wee' Stevie had a well-rehearsed repertoire, and he could remember it clearly to this day:

"Morning madam, I've got a good one for you today."

Before they could respond in either way, shape or form, he'd ask, "What do you call a house without a sofa?" He'd then step toward them and before they could speak, respond with............ "A building!"

He continued, "We think that one of the many things that makes a house a home is a lovely, super comfy sofa. So we've dedicated ourselves to producing the best range of meticulously designed, brilliantly well-made and fantastic value sofas. Whatever your style and with over 100 fabrics to choose from, you can design your very own bespoke, made to order sofa. Whether you're the queen of contemporary cool, the master of mid-century style, or a slave to Scandinavian chic, we've got a sofa that's just right for you. What's more, all our sofas come with a lifetime guarantee. If you're not 100% delighted with your sofa, we'll come and collect it for free and hand you back your cash — with no grumps, groans or quibbles! It's our aim to make buying your sofa fun, easy and totally stress free!"

"Ha, ha, ha" Murray laughed out loud.

"You okay?" Sheila Dixon asked with a kind of, 'Are you nuts?' slant to it.

"Memories ma'am. Happy, happy memories."

By now Sheila Dixon had dragged in two red leather barstools from the nearby kitchen area for them to sit on. "So Mr Dixon is not at home you say? Do you mind if I ask what he does for a living? Whatever it is, he's obviously very good at it." Murray gestured with two hands in the air, to the exquisite surroundings he currently found himself in.

She dubiously questioned, "You don't know my husband Inspector? I find that hard to believe. He works closely with the police. Security and property though are his two main interests. He has a few flats he rents out and his Security business is DG Security."

"The one down Portobello way?" Murray questioned.

"I knew you must know him"

"Never met Mr Dixon ma'am, just aware of Dock Green Security. I drive by their yard on a regular basis. Now I get it though."

"Get what?"

"Its name. Why it's called DG Security."

"Need to be a TV fan of a certain age Inspector. Are you sure you want to own up?"

"Yep, and knowing the owner's surname certainly helps! Watched it regularly as a young lad growing up. It was on the BBC from the mid-fifties to the mid-seventies." Then with a smile, he declared slowly and sentimentally with a genuine 'those were the days' warmth.......... "Dixon of Dock Green."

"More memories Inspector?"

"Yes ma'am. Back to when common sense and human understanding, played a big part in successful policing. However, I digress."

Murray continued to ask a number of polite, seemingly unobtrusive questions. He was a canny man. Very much a Scottish version of 'Columbo.' Always knew full well what he was doing. Even when others around him, thought him bumbling, inarticulate and forgetful. Oh my, how wrong could one be!

He had Sheila Dixon show him around the premises based on her naivety, his humble background and the unlikeliness of him ever owning a property such as this on his basic policeman's salary. Not sure 'Kenneth' would have approved, but the 'classic' hand gesture from Mr. Clough? Absolutely! A masterclass in conducting a vital visual search without a warrant! Individuals love to talk about themselves and show you their wealth and what they've accumulated. Especially when they don't feel threatened by you, your income or your place in society!

A home is 'filled to the gills' with personal and private information just 'bursting' to get out into the public domain. His mind was now racing back to another popular TV show of the late 80's and early 90's. He could hear the distinctive, slow American drawl of Loyd Grossman asking, "So who would live in a house like this?" The Inspector then summoned up as much sincerity as he could before offering. "Such a pity you're husband wasn't home. Maybe next time, I'd love to meet him. He obviously has a great eye for modern art. Some of your pictures and portraits are stunning," Murray exclaimed.

"Really, Inspector?" Mrs Dixon questioned. "You really believe it was my husband that got to choose and decide on the assorted pieces we own?"

"Ha ha, caught you, thought not. Well done ma'am, let me congratulate you. Your collection is first class. Especially…" he paused, 'The Biker Girl,' the sultry blonde on the motorcycle."

"Anything else Inspector?" Sheila abruptly asked whilst opening the front door. "I have an appointment across town shortly. Sorry I couldn't have been more helpful."

Oh, you touched a nerve there Stevie boy, Murray thought.

"On the contrary Mrs Dixon, like I said at the start, I had every confidence you would be able to help. Thank you, I don't think you realise just how helpful you've been."

At that, Sheila Dixon stared at him intensely, looked him suspiciously up and down and bluntly proffered, "Good-bye Inspector!" She closed the door firmly behind him. Murray then waved, smiled and spoke out gently as he meandered casually down the immaculate, block paved driveway. Pronouncing slowly, with his best David Frost intonation - "Let's go through the keyhole - Evening All - Dixon of Dock Green - Jack Warner - The Biker Girl - and I say Lieutenant - Goodnight All."

EIGHT

"Now the first of December was covered with snow and so was the turnpike from Stockbridge to Boston. Deep green and blues are the colours I choose - Won't you let me go down in my dream - And rock-a-bye sweet baby James."

- James Taylor

Jillian, wearing a beautiful pair of luxury lambskin gloves, carefully removed a Ziploc sandwich bag from an inside pocket in her knee length, black leather jacket. Opening the seal, she cautiously removed the lengthy beige envelope contained inside.

Candidly she then informed William Taunton, "I need one more thing from you."

"And what would that be?" Taunton grudgingly replied. "Because you're pushing it you know. I recently delivered to you a colourful and stunningly beautiful 'duty free' gift. And I only have a few years left to enjoy mortality. So maybe a spell at Her Majesty's pleasure would be a satisfying way to round things off." He spoke as if deliberately goading his lady caller. "Fresh experience, original location, new people to get to know," he then continued in a rather sickening manner.

"I might interest a few of them in my 'special offers.' Here at Oat'n Nuts we cater for exotic and erotic tastes these days," he then added with an air of superiority, arrogance and showmanship.

She looked at him coldly. With a mixture of venom, disgust, hatred and pity. Her own mind now twisted and gone. Possibly forgetful that she was, and had been, no better over the years. Turning a blind eye to many of the shady deals and dodgy business ventures that her partner had been and continues to be, heavily involved in.

At this moment you can imagine Detective Inspector Murray making an appearance at the office doorway and serenading her with a couple of lines from Billy Joel's 'My Life' - *"I never said you had to offer me a second chance, I never said I was a victim of circumstance."*

You can't help but feel that abused individuals absolutely deserve that second chance. Like so many who have never known different. Young, impressionable minds brought up in a world of poverty, depravity and ignorance. A triumvirate of nouns that should make us hold our heads in shame. When love, knowledge and opportunity should surround us daily.

Bill Taunton stepped forward to receive the stamped addressed envelope. He grasped it firmly, scrunching it slightly between his right thumb and forefinger.

"No need, to look inside," he was reminded. "It doesn't concern you. Trust me." Jillian Ingham said with a rueful smile.

The old man peered curiously at the printed label beneath his fingers. Then with a slight 'whatever!' shake of the head, he placed it cannily on his out-tray. That had been his regular routine with all his correspondence over the years.

She raised her voice and stated emphatically, "I need you personally to close it and send it when I leave."

"I'll make sure it's sent, no need to worry on that score. Will we then be all over after that I presume? No more favours, recollections of the past to discuss? All our loose ends tied up once and for all?"

She made no movement and allowed all three questions to hang ominously in the air.

William Taunton gazed upon her intently as she went to leave. He no longer saw the young nubile girl he remembered fondly looking after and helping to raise. She was now a hardened, embittered woman. Female charm long since gone. Although it shone through if and when required. All part of the act, the facade, the barrier, the wall that had been built up over the years. Was it to keep others out, or to protect herself from further destruction? Who knows?

But given the circumstances, who's to say, you'd have reacted differently? The Piano Man's words of wisdom, continue to permeate the air: *"I don't need you to worry for me 'cause I'm alright, I don't want you to tell me it's time to come home. I don't care what you say anymore, this is my life. Go ahead with your own life and leave me alone!"*

What happened to allow his natural fatherly instincts to stray? For him to change and evolve into a cold predatory fiend? When did his harmless caressing, stroking and extension of love, become sinister, vile and that of pure evil?

"I'm sorry," he uttered slowly and in whispered tones. "So, so, sorry. I named the company after you, you know! Can you ever forgive me?" he questioned lamely.

His daughter, having lived in the shadows for so long, had forgotten what sunlight looked like. She had now set out to extinguish her demons and the places they began, were raised up and nurtured. Her fine, sweet, childlike spirit had departed that body many, many years previous. She now looked at him carefully before responding. She raised her right hand to her mouth and blew him a high-impact Ruby Woo kiss. A shade much loved amongst confident lipstick-wearers!

Closing the door behind her, she waved to the two girls in the office. Always careful to obscure her face as she did so. They were both in the far corner, busy making adjustments to a child's pram.

"Goodbye, Miss Ingham. Enjoy the rest of your day," the older of the two girls cried out.

As Jillian Ingham made her way through the swing door toward the unlined gravel car park outside, a voice from the owner's office could be heard shouting.

"Miss Evans, Deborah, Debbie, need a little bit of assistance in here please," Bill Taunton loftily cried. The Deborah in question, was Debbie Evans his personal secretary. The 24 year old that had just bade a polite farewell to a 'Miss Ingham.'

"Coming Mr Taunton," she cheerily responded. With a spring in her step, she literally breezed through into his darkened office.

"How can I help Mr T?" she said. Her helpful personality shining through.

In a sombre tone, he requested politely. "Take my out-tray Deborah please and ensure everything is stamped, sealed and ready for pick up in the next five minutes. Oh, and Debs - don't use 1st class postage! Thank you."

Bill had briefly pondered and reflected on Jill Ingham's stern words regarding personally dealing with this issue. And he had thought better of it. He reckoned, that if he was going to be dismissed and treated as second class, then so also, was her delivery service!

As Deborah Evans made her way back to her desk, her visiting sister Yvette was gently rocking her 3 month old child James in her arms. She was trying to settle him, before laying him back into the pram and heading off for home.

"Let me just deal with this first item and then give James a hug before you go," big sister said in her always exuberant, friendly manner.

"No probs," replied Yvette.

Just at that, young trainee Gregor Sykes looked in. He was on post duty that week. "Got anything for me," he enquired.

"Two ticks Greg," Deborah offered. Giving him a rather large flirtatious smile.

The blushing seventeen year old Master Sykes would have waited two months, never mind two ticks, for the lovely Debbie Evans!

Four or five items awaited her urgent attention to detail. Sitting patiently and suspiciously on top of the pile though, was the mysterious cream envelope that Jillian had specifically asked Bill Taunton to deal with. Deborah calmly reached down and picked up the package. It gave the impression that it contained photographs or small cards, something of that ilk. She weighed the envelope, then carefully licked and sealed it. It was then finished off triumphantly, by being stamped vigorously on the back with a rather edgy, bright green company slogan. One which ironically stated and encouraged: Oat'n Nuts: Live Longer - Become a Cereal Killer!

"Here, take this one Greg, the rest can go tomorrow and I'll see you then," she said in a low, teasing whisper. How hurtfully she played with the hormones and emotions of the besotted young teenager.

"Absolutely, you - then - see," he stuttered, tongue tied and panicked. He shuffled off, disappearing down the corridor red faced and embarrassed, but desperately excited to pop by again 24 hours later!

Straightaway Debbie stood up, a little shaky and weak-kneed. She reckoned she'd just gotten to her feet too quickly. Then, still feeling dizzy and rather unsteady. She leaned in calmly toward her baby nephew and gave him a delicate kiss on the lips. "Love you J," she said, whilst tugging gently downward at the peak of his hood. She offered a simple protective gesture in keeping out the cold. One that a loving, generous and considerate Aunt would normally make.

Suddenly, this attractive, larger than life, fun-filled assistant began wheezing. Clearly exhibiting signs of a respiratory problem. In an instant this elegant young lady seemed to lose the ability to move. She had become paralysed to the spot. Gasping, choking, desperately fighting for breath. Her cheeks had drained of their earlier rosy complexion. Her beautiful hazel eyes rolling in search of an emergency outlet from her doomed body. Fleetingly, they gazed toward her younger sibling. They indicated and hinted that Debs knew she was fighting a vain, hopeless and forlorn attempt to survive. Settling briefly, they managed to signal the ultimate message. 'I love you.'

Then, as if in conclusion, her head began to waver. A slight tremble at first, gradually building into a set of internal quivering motions. Then emerging with force into the public domain as an uncontrollable and aggressive shake. She wheezed one final time. A second later she slumped to the floor. Her head violently striking the corner edge of the sturdy, robust oak desk as she collapsed.

Twenty-four year old secretary Deborah Evans was gone. Her work had come to an abrupt, sudden and undignified cessation.

The audible crack to Debbie's tender skull would normally have made you shudder. But chaos ruled and there was a tumult of shouting and piercing cries emanating from the office. Strangely though, none of them came from a three month old child.

Panicking, Yvette screamed with alarm and terror. Young Gregor, having been on a recent first aid course, had charged back through the door desperately appealing for calm. Bill Taunton arrived having already dialled 999. His face was filled with fear. He was alarmed at the scene he was witnessing and was desperately trying to remain unruffled when he heard, "Bill, Bill," Yvette yelled. "It's James, he's not moving, what's wrong with him Bill? Bill help me."

William Taunton instantly looked across at the infant as he lay motionless in his pram. Still, static, unmoved by all the commotion going on around him. Sirens could be heard approaching in the distance. As they drove by, people in the street offered the normal 'first thought.' A four second condolence which consists of: "Oh, something's happened. I wonder what and where? Hope everything is alright. Watch my time, I need to be getting on." Then, they never give it a 'second thought!'

As the emergency services arrived at the scene, Gregor Sykes sat by the doorway with a traumatised Yvette sobbing uncontrollably in his arms. The amorous young staff member would have loved to cuddle in closely to either of the Evan's sisters normally. But most certainly not under these awful, painful circumstances. She was undoubtedly in shock. Dealing and coping with the sudden, unexpected, untimely death of a child to any cause, is devastating. When a baby dies - hopes and dreams are shattered - and lives are changed forever.

The Detective Inspector had been made aware of the dreadful, fatal events nearby. Firstly however, he had to locate something he felt could be significant, before making his way to Stockbridge and the scene of the double tragedy.

He checked out the side door panels of his car. Sure enough on the passenger side he was proved correct almost instantly. It was still there!

Two weeks previously, DI Murray had been dropping off some visiting dignitaries and police officers at Edinburgh Airport. They had flown up from London to deliver special training on 'Diversity within the Police Force.' The point being however, on returning to his vehicle after it had been parked briefly in the short stay car park. It had managed to accrue several pieces of advertising literature. A term DI Murray is more at home with using is ...BUMFF!

Included in these 'great reads of our time,' was a colourful flyer for Oat'n Nuts latest store at the Edinburgh International Airport. Importantly, Steven Murray remembered that on one side of the leaflet, it gave you a brief overview of the company since its inception. And on the other side, a straightforward advertisement selling its wide range of goods and products.

Murray began to read:

The Blurb:

At Oat'n Nuts we sell a large range of vitamins, minerals, homeopathic remedies, flower essences and herbal food supplements. Looking for advice on multivitamins or to treat mild depression the natural way? Call our staff now. They can help you find the right product quickly and easily.

We offer a wide variety of whole foods at Oat'n Nuts Health Food Store. Dried fruits, beans & pulses. Flour, oats, cereals and grain, in small or bulk sizes and all at competitive prices.

We buy and import an assortment of exotic fruits from all over the globe.

With over 80 stores throughout the UK, make Oat'n Nuts your first stop for a healthy lifestyle. Call us now, we deliver next day, nationwide.

Enjoy our latest store at the Edinburgh International Airport.

It then listed all of the store locations with phone numbers. Also included was a cut-out voucher worth 20% discount. Over the page, Murray read:

The History:

In 1970, aged thirty-eight Bill Taunton had a business idea whilst holidaying on the Inner Hebrides. The Inner Hebrides is an archipelago (an island group, chain, cluster or collection of islands) off the West coast of mainland Scotland.

Two years later, Oat'n Nuts, opened their first shop at Raeburn Place, Stockbridge, Edinburgh. Within another eighteen months they had further branches along the East coast at Musselburgh, Haddington and North Berwick. With an impressive range of over one hundred different recipes.Their speciality is original cereal bars made in Scotland. With dried fruits, seasoning and ingredients imported from all over the world. They are then baked, wrapped and delivered all over the country from their humble bakery premises in East Lothian.

From the classics like: Raisin & Yogurt, Assorted Berries and Oat'n Nuts Double Chocolate, to their current all-time favourite line - The Latin American Range: That line includes; the ever popular Citrus Sensation (lulo, mango & lime) and Carambola (citrus, grape & apple); to the recent best selling - Curuba bar (banana & passion fruit, with cashew nuts).

Stockbridge is an affluent area of Edinburgh. It is located toward the North of the city, bounded by the

New Town and by Comely Bank. The name in Scots is 'stock brig,' meaning a timber bridge.

Originally a small outlying village, it was incorporated into the City of Edinburgh in the nineteenth-century. The current 'Stock Bridge' built in 1801, is a stone structure spanning the Water of Leith.

With careful financial governance, perfectly pitched advertising and health and fitness continuing to be uppermost in most people's minds - Oat'n Nuts outlets now total more than eighty branches. They have opened on average 2 new stores per year, over the last four and a half decades. And are now firmly established as the No.1 health food outlet in the United Kingdom.

The outlets range in size from the stand alone Megastore on the outskirts of the historic county town of Guildford, England. To the relatively deceptive Dr. Who 'Tardis' of a store that sits in a large picturesque village on the Northumberland coast. It is located at the foot of the hill, in the shadow of the imposing and historic Bamburgh Castle, seat of the former Kings of Northumbria.

Businessman, buyer and enterprising entrepreneur Mr. William Taunton had overseen this steady, impressive growth from the very beginning back in the early nineteen seventies. The leaflet concluded, as if hand written: *'Best Wishes,' Bill.*

Murray, sat upright and pulled sharply on his seat belt. Clicking it in place, he then turned the ignition and made his way speedily across town. His destination was literally a five minute drive from Lady Atkins' residence. The home where only a few days earlier: Firstly - 'The Angel of the North' had been discovered. Secondly - He'd met Joseph Hanlon for the first time. And finally, thirdly - He was reminded of Nottingham Forest's euphoric European Cup triumphs. 'Kenneth!' he bellowed, holding his hand out in front of himself. The tip of the thumb and index finger touching, with the other three fingers held upright. Indicating: 'magnificent, excellent, a satisfactory job well done!'

He wanted to go prepared, well versed, armed and knowledgeable. Once again he held up his hand and used the same symbolic gesture, the small informative pamphlet had worked a treat!

In the quiet office of Managing Director William Taunton, yet just through the glass from the hectic forensics team and the air of sadness and disbelief, a gentle West coast accent filtered the air.

"Afternoon Mr Taunton, my name is Detective Inspector Steven Murray. I know it can't be easy for you at present. But I just need to ask you a few more questions and clarify a couple of issues."

"I understand," Taunton stated respectfully. Offered in true stiff upper lip fashion.

Lifting an Oat'n Nuts cereal bar, Murray specified. "I'll only be a few minutes."

The bar had been part of a rather splendid complimentary promotional display. It was set up on the coffee table as you entered the Managing Director's office. The arrangement was like the children's game 'Jenga.' Three bars laid vertically with about an inch between them. Then three further bars placed on top horizontally. A further three vertically, etc, etc. Creating a rather imposing, 'tasty,' yet low-calorie tower. Standing approximately two foot tall. It no doubt required to be rebuilt several times each day. It probably promoted about half their range of flavours. The one Murray had carefully manoeuvred delicately from the middle, without the remainder embarrassingly collapsing around his feet was the Borojo Bar. Brightly coloured yellow lettering on the distinct emerald green Oat'n Nuts branded wrapper, informed you that it was part of their award winning Latin American range. Coupled with their recent, rather fashionable, radically cool, ad campaign slogan: 'Live Longer - Become a Cereal Killer!' Murray simply raised his eyes at this.

"You know Inspector, among many popular foods in the world, Borojo stands out as one of the most amazing yet. With a unique set of health benefits," Bill Taunton offered.

Murray played along. "How so?"

"Well, if you want a food that according to natives can give you a little extra sexual boost, while at the same time bringing you a powerhouse of potent nutrients desperately needed by your body? Borojo is the one."

"Fascinating," Murray nodded. "Exceptionally popular with your male customers then I'd imagine?"

"One doctor said of this fruit Inspector. "That if it was to be grown on a large scale, it could address the problem of malnutrition in the world. It is so rich in minerals and vitamins that no other fruit on this planet could compete with it?"

Taunton then added, "In Colombia it is known as the Natural Viagra. People there have known about its natural aphrodisiac properties for centuries. On a worldwide scale, it has just barely begun to be exposed and is already gaining much popularity. It's our number one best seller."

Murray repeated, "Fascinating, simply fascinating." Before ensuring two more complimentary bars made their way into his coat pocket. With the slightest hint of a smile given the circumstances. He stated in a relaxed manner, "Trading standards you understand sir. Really have to put them to the test and check out those claims you made are valid!"

It was the Inspector's turn now to stare stony faced through the glass. He stood expressionless, momentarily examining the heart-breaking scene. His mind became dark. For the briefest of moments, 'Thelma and Louise' images flashed in front of him. Quickly regaining his composure, he glanced back toward the six foot tall, thin gentleman in the pinstripe suit. He appeared every inch the successful business tycoon that you witness regularly on the television. In recent times, he'd become Scotland's very own Richard Branson. Same height, not dissimilar in looks, sporting a neatly trimmed dark goatee beard. Mainly alike though, for being extremely media savvy. With publicity stunts launching products on a steady basis, combined with radio appearances and newspaper articles - He is certainly no shrinking violet!

Having introduced himself and gotten some product spiel, plus free medicinal advice on erectile dysfunction! The Inspector carefully considered his approach. With little hesitation Murray went for... 'direct and honest.'

"You've had your fair share of challenges recently I believe?"

"What do you mean Inspector?"

"Recent spell of fires. Arson, the Brigade reckon. And now this horrendous tragedy."

"We're insured against fire Inspector. But this, this is unbelievable. Who would do such a thing?"

"In many respects Mr Taunton, that would be my question to you!"

"What?"

"Who would do such a thing? Upset anyone recently? Your company policies divide opinion to such a degree. Maybe some of the radical element are fighting back."

"Woa, woa slow down my good man. We have been going for over forty years. We've built up a terrific reputation and we're known for being exceptionally eco-friendly. We've won awards for our innovation and our customer service. We strive to be part of the community, to sponsor a wide assortment of teams and events wherever we are located."

"Forget the diplomatic company line sir. I'm thinking on a more personal level. Any grudges, recent clashes with anyone? Court action, financial problems or the like?"

Bill Taunton sat shaking his head. "No, no, no, no, no, nothing like that. We are doing well, things are solvent, no legal nonsense, nothing. Anyway, why would someone want to target a young girl and a child? What is that all about Inspector?"

"Oh, I think we may be coming at this from different angles Mr.Taunton."

The businessman lowered his head and squinted defensively across the room at Murray before he spoke. "Different angles, how so?"

"Well," Murray responded. "Had it just been Debbie Evans, sir. Then we may have mistaken this for an undetected heart condition. Certainly a sudden death with a couple of question marks. However, the baby boy also? Now, I'm no forensics man Mr. Taunton. But I reckon when the Doc checks this out, you'll find that those two individuals have sadly been poisoned! And I'd even go further," Murray stated, raising his voice and staring intensely at Taunton. "Most probably, they were not even the target. That poison was plainly and most definitely aimed at you."

"Me, Inspector?" he questioned. Then repeating more slowly and reflectively. "Me, Inspector?" His eyelids fluttered. He had begun to take onboard his words. For an instant he looked heavenward. A sudden jolt to his memory.

"Yes, yes, you've remembered something sir?" Murray attentively responded.

"What, what's that?" He was badly shaken. With a look of disbelief, he began to tremble. 'A preposterous idea,' he thought to himself. A notion that cannot be considered. He tried to stand, but filled with shock his legs had no strength to support him. He collapsed back into his chair, beginning to whirl around and around in it. Like his own personal 'Waltzer' at the fairground.

"I'll speak with you later sir. Let you come to terms with everything. However, can I just ask you politely one more thing. I feel it could be most helpful to our enquiries?"

Bill Taunton, head shaking, proceeded with his circular carnival motions. He continued muttering, "Me, me. You really think that it was meant for me." Silence, before a final, "For me?"

"I'm sorry sir, I didn't mean to alarm you," Murray fibbed slightly. "However my question, well two questions actually, but both valuable and relevant. Firstly, do you know a man by the name of Kenneth Dixon? He's normally called Kenny or KD. Any Mr Dixon ring any bells sir?"

Taunton, shook his head robustly. Seemingly in a daze. He was still birling slowly around in his chair. He was most certainly alarmed and hiding something. Deliberately lying? Murray was uncertain.

"Thanks for your help Mr. Taunton. I'll make some further enquiries with regards to your store attacks. See if we can hurry things along a bit for you." he stated calmly.

As Murray began walking toward the door, Bill Taunton gestured with a slight wave. Raising his hand from his thigh with fingers apart. "That would be good, thanks," he added. "Oh, Inspector," he reminded Murray, "What was your other question?"

Murray having never forgotten at all, but wishing to ascertain just how 'with it' Bill Taunton was. Simply concluded, "Been away anywhere extra warm recently? Can't help but admire your tan."

No doubt fully expecting a different question, Bill Taunton regained a smiling demeanour and stated, "Afraid not Inspector. One of my guilty pleasures is the sun bed at the tanning salon. Don't tell the others though, I'll get a bad name."

Inspector Murray nodded, waved and exited gracefully through the doorway. He smiled appreciatively as he departed. 'Now I know you're lying,' he thought to himself.

NINE

"Mother is a gambler, the wager, the one card, to play. Birth has the burden, she says no children today. Midst all dishonour, she sees a heavenly noose. Since child is an angel - The mother, the one child, set loose."

- The Skids

On leaving the premises DI Murray instantly decided to get some of his team more heavily involved. He required them to interview members of staff away from the scene of the tragedy. Encouraging each of them to delve and explore a little bit further into each of their backgrounds.

PC Hanlon in particular found this a healthy and much needed distraction. It kept him fully occupied and he felt he would be able to make a valuable and not inconsiderable contribution to the investigation. He was thriving on it. Some of his initial legwork was quite basic. It involved confirming addresses, jobs and background checks. Important, fundamental information.

Take Deborah Evans for example. She had worked for Bill Taunton as his personal assistant for the past eighteen months, yet had only been with Oat'n Nuts for just over four years. She had started at age twenty as an assistant to his previous secretary Joan. Then Joan Alexander retired midway through 2013, allowing the charismatic Debbie to be promoted. Single and not in any noticeable relationship. She was well liked by everyone, had a good credit history, never been in trouble and stayed locally, nearby in Tranent. Overall, the ideal employee!

However by contrast, her sister Yvette the mother of young James, she intrigued Hanlon. Aroused a certain level of curiosity. One that revolved around honesty and truthfulness. The word that came to his mind was scruples. He typed it into his dictionary app on his phone and got: Noun - *'a moral or ethical consideration or standard that acts as a restraining force or inhibits certain actions.'* Joe Hanlon was about to become a 'mixed metaphor,' metaphorically speaking. He loved astrology, space travel and stars. Was fascinated by the rich opportunities astronauts had to discover new planets, minerals and other life forms. Yet, today, here he was preparing to put on his winter boots, a few extra layers of clothing and stockpile high on supplies. He was entering Roald Amundsen territory - his Antarctic expedition of 1910-12 discovered the South Pole. Joseph Hanlon's own East Lothian expedition here on terra firma, was hoping to be as equally successful. It was about to enter fully into the murky, dark waters of Yvette Evans' world. To become more fully aware of 'her story.' To understand her background, then identify and recover, her 'book of life.'

On discovery of said item, one then had to study discreetly, delicately and deliberately each and every 'chapter and verse.' PC Sandra Kerr could not have stated it more eloquently herself!

With only a brief flurry of snow falling, it wasn't quite Antarctic conditions. Hanlon smiled however, and with the energy and excitement of an astronaut and adventurer combined, he looked pleased and at ease. He then took that first brave, bold and momentous, 'Neil Armstrong' step.

Simultaneously on the other side of the City, DI Murray made his way out of a quaint letting agency in the Canonmills area. It was located, roughly midway up Saint Stephen Street. Pausing at the doorway, he turned. Slowly, he began shaking the hand of the small, balding gentleman on his left. This was presumably the manager or owner of the business. The folically challenged chap was dressed in a cream coloured Aran sweater and a pair of rustic brown corduroy trousers - a throwback to an earlier era! He would not have looked out of place on a stage in a smokey 1960's folk club. Possibly surrounded by the other 'Clancy Brothers' and in unison belting out - *'Fine girl you are!'*

Murray now clasped his left hand on top of the original handshake and as he looked directly into the eyes of the 'folk singer', spoke to him gently, but firmly.

"So we understand each other Mr Gemmill? You'll be happy to take care of that piece of business for me? Ideally in the next 24 hours."

A reluctant nod was all that he received in return.

"Appreciate that, most kind. That's a real weight off my mind," Murray responded with a broad grin. He then confidently made his way down the three granite steps and marched back to his car parked nearby.

As the month was drawing to a close, Tuesday the 30th of December was rapidly storming up the charts in true Top of the Pops fashion. It had arrived from outside the top forty with great gusto. Then with speed, haste and energy, burst excitedly into the top ten. Today, it had firmly established itself as the new No.1. Officially the busiest day of 2014........for murders!

Enquiries and investigations were ongoing into a multitude of areas. Mostly background checks, establishing alibis, timelines, etc. There was still no major lead, nothing jumping out, no concrete evidence. Hunches and gut feelings are one thing, but solid evidence, forensic proof and possibly even a suspect or two would be a more advantageous start.

With 'Hannibal' Hayes and 'Kid' Curry fanning the flames in East Lothian. Coulter and Taylor had recently set up a meeting with Alan Hikesend Accountants (Dixons representatives). Plus, with the young adventurer constantly sniffing around on the prowl, Detective Inspector Murray was optimistic that the New Year would bring exceptional results. But then, so too were football managers around the globe - especially those - six hours ahead of the game!

Located mid-way between The Royal Botanic Gardens to the North and Princes Street Gardens in the East. Circus Lane consisted of a line of beautiful, picture postcard Georgian tenement buildings. Businesses seemed to occupy the majority of the row. But several were still privately owned residential properties. Coulter and Taylor were meeting up with a Miss Melanie Rose. She operated her business - AH Accountants from there. But it was also her own private apartment. The detectives had been expecting a large, flash, corporate firm. Possibly one that was whilst reputable, renowned for flying a little close to the edge!

Miss Rose although noticeably pretty, was not someone that went in for the glamour model look. Of medium build, she was aged in her late twenties, maybe early thirties. She dressed in a dark navy business suit, with a white, crisp, wing collared blouse. She wore low heeled shoes, light make up and only one solitary item of jewellery. Curiously, it was a simple bronze coloured necklace in the shape of a mermaid.

Having just deposited a large beautiful bouquet of flowers into a crystal vase, the dark raven haired accountant with a bright radiant smile, proffered her hand to both Taylor and Coulter as they entered.

"Hello officers, come in," she said perkily, "take a seat."

"Thank you Miss," Taylor responded curtly, whilst giving Ally a questioning look that said - 'not expecting this, were we?'

Coulter, about to take a seat, desperately tried to hold in his infamous tummy. It seemed he was going all out to impress the gorgeous Miss Rose. Taz grinned, shook her head a little and let out a small audible laugh. Then quickly turned it into a deep clearance of her throat before speaking.

"Nice flowers Miss. Special acquaintance?" she asked cheekily.

Melanie blushed, "I should be so lucky. It's a regular weekly delivery. Helps to spruce the place up and to keep it freshly fragranced."

Ally Coulter's gaze, tilted head and fawning adoration, gave the impression that he was already sitting across from the most enchantingly fragranced rose in the room.

Taylor gave his knee a sudden jolt with her own and asked "Kenny Dixon, Mr Kenneth Dixon. A name you are acquainted with Miss?"

"Of course. He is," she hesitated. "One of my clients," she continued.

"DG Security?" Ally mentioned, by way of a question.

"Absolutely. Mr Dixon owns them also. Are you looking to know some of his further business interests?"

"Ye, ye we know," Taz Taylor sighed. "Come back with a warrant, same old, same old. We've heard it all before."

Melanie gave the officers a surprising smile. "Well, actually no. I was about to say I'm happy and authorised to give you an information sheet with all Mr. Dixon's current, up to date businesses on it."

"Oh," Taylor's jaw dropped, as her face slightly reddened.

Coulter admired the figure with the figures. She seemed upfront, honest and genuine. "We urgently need to track down Mr. Dixon though," Ally Coulter asked in a friendly positive manner. "Have you heard from him recently Miss Rose?"

"Not recently. We usually meet every Tuesday morning. But with the holidays over Christmas and New Year we left it." She then offered helpfully, "Not scheduled to resume until the second week of January."

Both Sergeant and Constable didn't feel the need for further questions. Walking confidently back toward the door, Coulter paused briefly at a few University photos he had spotted on a hallway cabinet. Obviously in awe of her beauty and charm, he again made to pull in his tummy. Then pointing at the pretty scholarly looking female in the front row of the group shot, he asked politely, "Yourself Miss Rose?"

With their sweet scent pervading the air, Tasmin Taylor sniffed at the adorable hand delivered flowers, just as Melanie Rose responded with, "It was Sergeant, several years ago now though. Alas time marches on."

They both courteously thanked the businesswoman and duly left. On the outside steps of the impressive property, they stood silent. No sound exchanged between them. Carefully they observed each other's face. Eyes focused, mouths pouting seriously and chins beginning to nod in agreement. Taylor held up a business card that she had clearly taken from the floral bouquet. With a quick slight of hand, she then delicately placed 'The Capital Florist' up her sleeve. A canny nod was then delivered to her Sergeant that silently stated 'you'll see, soon enough!'

Detective Sergeant Coulter however was not to be outdone. His eyes widened and as if to say - 'watch this,' was momentarily transported back to Paris for a silent horse racing bonanza. He embarked upon impersonating an 'On Course' bookmaker! He began to use what seemed to be professional traditional non-verbal, tic-tac signs. He was pointing at his chest, followed by a couple of swift two fingered taps to his left wrist and then a brief tug of the opposite ear. In reverse it went, ear tug, wrist tap and chest point. Wrist tap, chest point, two tugs.

Taylor could take no more. She doubled up in a fit of laughter. Coulter followed and they both lost the plot! Guffawing hysterically, tears streamed from their eyes. There was loud cackling and merriment for a further twenty seconds at least. Possibly they may reflect later and question, 'hey, we never lost the plot, in fact, maybe, just maybe, was that the day that the plot became just a little bit clearer and a lot less hazy?'

Call it what you may: A sixth sense, ESP or a dramatic display of mind blowing telepathy. As they drove off into the distance, both police officers knew without a shadow of a doubt, proof or evidence for that matter. That the eloquent and well educated Miss Melanie Rose was no normal accountant.

"Something felt off, wrong, out of sorts!" Taz said shaking her head.

Coulter agreed with a simple head movement and an knowledgeable smile.

"Go on, out with it. I know you have some wise thought to share."

"No," just a little bit of quiz trivia I've acquired over the years."

"I'm waiting," Taz said, rolling her hands in a 'get on with it motion.'

"It is the origin of - out of sorts." Ally told her. "Unusually, that expression was believed to have had its origin in the printing trade. Way before the days of computers and desktop printing. When all printing was done by hand and was a very laborious process."

"Is this going to be a laborious process?" Taz asked, pretending to be asleep.

In a Professorial voice Ally heeded, "All to broaden your mind WPC Taylor. Knowledge is a wonderful weapon."

"I know, I know, but get on with it.....it can also be a very, very laborious process."

"So," Coulter regained his train of thought. "Sorts were the small pieces of type Printers needed to make up a font. With a full supply of sorts, Printers could go about their duties and work steadily. But if they ran out of sorts they had to stop working. As many Printers were paid according to the number of pages they could produce per day, being out of sorts usually made them angry or bad-tempered."

"She wasn't bad tempered or abusive," Taz confirmed. "But I agree, there was definitely something - out of sorts. Agreed?"

"She was a fine looking woman," Ally said.

On receiving a scolding look from Taz. "Agreed," he quipped.

There would indeed be a return visit required to Circus Place in the future, they felt certain of that.

Presently, although the investigation was weighed heavily in favour of the poisoner. Singular or plural. Both Ally Coulter and Tasmin Taylor were convinced, just call it a gut feeling. That A.H. Accountants were in an extremely strong, knowledgeable and influential position to help re-balance the books!

A phone call informing you of two sudden and highly suspicious deaths, one of which includes a three month old child, will always get the adrenalin flowing! Earlier that morning he was up, washed, dressed and out in six minutes, not the ideal, no quality of life.

But, today, like many others, was just another - 'put on your public face and get through the next twenty four hours type of day.' Sad, but a reality for so many.

Murray always thought - 'It will be better tomorrow.....won't it?'

Given the difficulty of the day, it may not have been unreasonable to guess or speculate, that that very evening, along with the sharp drop in temperature and slippery conditions on the roads, Steven Murray was about to encounter another large blanket of dark emotional clouds.

"I hate my life!" he exclaimed. The house was empty, so was his soul. Yet again left lonely with only his thoughts for companionship. He was trying to reason and rationalise news from a few weeks earlier. It was a case he'd helped investigate. Yesterday's local paper told how a candlelit vigil had been held for a teenage girl who took her own life at her Pilton home.

Alison Thompson, aged 14 is understood to have died after taking an overdose of drugs. The Broughton High School pupil had dreamed of becoming a doctor. A police spokeswoman said: "Police in Edinburgh were called to an address in Royston Mains on Thursday,

November 20, following the death of a teenage girl. The death is not believed to be suspicious. A report had been sent to the procurator fiscal."

It went on to say how: The manager of Lowland League football team, Spartans F.C. had dedicated his team's Scottish Cup victory to the memory of a young girl who died in the days before the match.

Andy Ramage paid tribute to the club's entire community team following Saturday's impressive win over Greenock Morton and said: "the Lowland League outfit is mourning the death of a youth team member, 14-year-old Alison Thompson."

The teenager, who is understood to have died after taking an overdose of drugs, had been part of Spartans FooTea event. A program that gave kids a chance to play football and have a meal. Her funeral took place on Saturday, hours before the non-league side caused a cup shock with victory over the League One leaders.

He went on to say: "There is often a lot of negative news comes out of north Edinburgh and do you know what, there's a lot of amazing people in this area who do amazing things. It's been great that they can hang their hat on something as positive as this, because it's been a tough week. Sadly, we lost a young girl last week. It's been really hard for our youth workers and for the community as a whole. But it's funny how life can bring such a terrible low and such a huge high in the same day."

Thinking about that teenager with her whole life ahead of her, Murray gradually became tearful. The sunshine at this point was attempting to enter brightly through the upstairs bedroom window. Heavy, dark blinds repelled it at every opportunity.

Memories of a beautiful dark haired female came flooding into his mind. Youngsters growing up. A family heading for church. Summer picnics, swing parks, the riding of bikes and visiting with beloved Aunts and Uncles. A variety of recollections flickered incessantly.

The women's hand reached out to him and disappeared as he stretched to reach it. Roulette wheels, casinos, money squandered and tears shed. The sound of ambulances, police sirens and a covered body. Children could be heard screaming. A gracious smile, wedding bands and vows exchanged. More intense images of family followed. They depicted fun, laughter and death. His body jolted and sweating profusely he sat upright.

It was 11.30am. An immense tidal wave of pessimism overcame him. What was worth rising for? It's just another day, no real friends and never ending emotional turmoil. Questions. Questions dismissed. Additional questions, feeling miserable, no joy, why live? Sleep reassures, comforts and forgives he reckoned. Stretch your body and simply turnover. Slide back under the heavy quilt and watch all your troubles disappear! In reality your duvet is the glorious golden sand and no matter the amount of turning and tossing - keeping your head entrenched there will help no one, solve nothing and only prolong the acute agony. The weight of the world will always remain on your shoulders.

Murray could often give the appearance of being constantly agitated. The reality was - his mind raced nonstop. Grand Prix drivers beware! Lewis Hamilton, Nico Rosberg and Sebastian Vettel eat your heart out. At every pulsating chicane, Steven Murray, representing Scotland, will match you head to head.

In a multitude of diverse ways to become better, more productive, the marginal gains process. Thoughts, strategies, ideas, concepts. Introduce something new, think outside the box. Walt Disney would say, 'What box?' Reflections, pondering, too much chaos - organized or not. Grateful for so much and then within the same thought, no desire to remain alive. The mind is one heck of a scary place Murray often figured.

If in doubt, he knew, that for him - Edward Sharpe and the Magnetic Zeros did the trick and at least offered short term respite. Their lively anthemic song entitled 'Home,' got his feet tapping, pulse racing and voice prepped. He'd stand to attention in front of the mirror with shaving foam and razor primed. This was in full anticipation of wild body antics and primitive aboriginal dances in the shower! Before long he'd feel revitalised and energised by the music and 'the Lynx' effect. A fine rhythmic tune can certainly steady and reassure you. It installs in you the strength to face the world. At least for another prolonged period of time!

TEN

"From the mountain tops down to the sunny street, a different drum is playing a different kind of beat. It's like a mystery that never ends. I see you crying and I want to kill your friends."

- Aztec Camera

Later that evening around 10.25pm, Murray's mobile, which was switched to silent, lit up his kitchen worktop. Impersonating a Charlie Chaplin walk, it scurried at pace across the granite work surface and was about to leap to certain death. Only rescued in the nick of time by the Inspector's comedic goalkeeper like reactions with his left hand. Co-ordination though, was never one of his abundant strengths. As his phone appeared safe from harm in one hand, milk gently began seeping, then pouring, nay even cascading at regular intervals across the laminate floor from the opened bottle in his opposite. Eventually, he was able to swipe and answer - whilst standing in a cool pool of his favourite white stuff. He could see it was from Chief Inspector Keith Brown. Murray's face was a picture! He was about to answer, "Hello, Inspector Clouseau speaking," but he opted for -

"Sir, how can I help? What's up?" he dripped.

"Just wanted to let you know as soon as, sorry to phone you at home late on."

"No, no, don't be silly. Let me know what? New developments?"

"Well, yes, maybe. It's a bit unusual really, we've got another one. A fifth body. I need to meet with you first thing in the morning Steve, say 7am."

"I'll go now sir. I'll head over straight away," Murray said, keen to help. But knowing realistically he'd be half an hour just cleaning up his own mess! "Where do you need me? Let me note down the address."

"Well, that's just it Steven. She was on a train!"

"Okay, so I'm heading over to Waverley?"

"You most certainly are Detective Inspector Murray," Brown stated officially. He then paused for a second or two before finishing with, "But not until tomorrow morning after our meeting. You'll need to catch a ride over to Dundee!"

"Dundee?"

Brown had hung up.

Next morning, reading an old copy of the Edinburgh Evening News, Murray settled down for his healthy breakfast and blurted out aloud some back page headlines. "Jambo's tame the Hibees!" Randomly turning pages he then exclaimed, "New franchise creates jobs at Edinburgh Airport!" Finally his eyes settled on page 9 and "Edinburgh dad seeks book deal after appearing on Jeremy Kyle show."

"Holy moly! He slept with 15 girls, including two sisters, and four of them end up pregnant. What kind of world do we live in?"

No one answered. It was still dark outside. In fairness, it was 5.30am.

As often was the case, Murray got by on just 5 or 6 hours sleep. His mind never seemed to fully switch off. Relaxing was not on the agenda either. He was always playing match-up. Either with clues in a case, films and actors, or musicians and songs. How did they link up, connect, what was the common thread? It gave him an edge, but made him edgy - often transferring into what appeared as short temperedness. But in reality was more likely an energy and determination. He could, without doubt, wear his heart on his sleeve occasionally. Loyalty also, was important to him. He would fight your corner and defend you to the hilt, as long as you took responsibility, were honest and worked hard. He was most definitely a man to have in your corner.

Murray scrolled quickly through the wide variety of songs on his iPod. Clicking on a specific tune, he began gliding that winter morn to: *"It's beginning to look a lot like Christmas."* He then attempted to close the front door in true Fred Astaire fashion - drawing it behind him with his trailing foot, whilst his left arm conducted the music and his right hand's forefinger twirled the car keys around to the beat. *"everywhere we go-ooooo. Aaaaaaargh".* Losing his footing, down he went like a poor man's Torvill and Dean. Early morning workers passing by his driveway, could be seen reaching into their uniforms and hi-vis jackets for their respective scorecards, h o i s t i n g t h e m a l o f t a n d r e a d i n g: zero...zero...two...zero...and one respectively.

Dancing on Ice would need to be deferred for yet another year!

Brushing himself down, he was now more fully aware of the light covering of frost on the ground. He proceeded to make his way to his trusty five year old Swedish steed (actually Chinese owned), and no longer available Volvo S40!

Still smiling, he managed a *"Slip slidin' away, slip slidin' away. You know the nearer your destination the more you're slip slidin' away."* He thought to himself, Paul Simon eat your heart out!

It was exactly 6.58am as DI Murray prepared to knock the door in front of him and enter. He screwed up his face and briefly recognised how he really didn't fit in with the Police hierarchy. He knew now that he would never go farther than Detective Inspector. Deeply passionate in his approach, he was no good at keeping quiet. Thoughts that he had would ultimately be expressed vocally - thus becoming opinions. Opinions that then signalled him out as an agitator, a trouble maker. A perceived grief that his superiors could do without. He could hear them now - *'Don't be questioning those that know better. Remind us again, what rank are you? That may make more sense and be better thought out, but we've already decided! This is just to rubber stamp things. What do you mean, you disagree?'*

As he knocked firmly Murray thought: Just when you think we live in a democracy, think again!

Over the years from being an important player, a hub of productivity and a fairly innovative thinker. He would find himself cast aside, demonised and forgotten from time to time. Yet another round of new people in charge. Any wisdom, knowledge and experience that Steven Murray had acquired over the years, was now readily discounted. Often he would be deemed worthless and of no value by those in authority. However, to those at the coalface, his current and previous colleagues, they knew better. He was a man much loved, trusted and highly regarded within his profession and also by many of his counterparts within the criminal fraternity. He was still capable and highly effective in his duties. A team player and builder of others. When it came to the 'head heid yins' though, he should really look up the property market in Ireland. The most suitable destination for his particular individual skill set - would seem to be 'Lepers' town!

Entering the room briskly, Murray stated, "Morning sir." Maybe sounding just a little bit too bright and enthusiastic, given the circumstances. A strong scent of cologne wafted from the Chief Inspector as he stood respectfully to shake his colleague's hand. The two men had worked cordially and well alongside each other for a good number of years now.

"I know it's only been 72 hours Steve. But what do we have to go on?"

"Not a lot sir, I'm afraid. Although I am beginning to have a few interesting suspicions."

"Care to share?"

"Just a hunch at the minute sir. But our good buddy Kenny Dixon seemed to have some tenuous connection to the first victim, Penelope Cooke the art student. I'll hear back today regarding a couple of other lines of enquiry in relation to Anne Richmond. And there is definitely something more to our local celebrity Mr William Taunton and those two harrowing and heartbreaking deaths at his office."

Brown rubbed at his chin and nodded.

"Finally, with regards to last night's incident. I'll get working on that as soon as I tie up with DS Pollock in Tayside."

"He's a good man Pollock. You both seemed to work well together those few years back I recall."

"He is sir, and indeed we did." Murray coughed, "Maybe just a tad heavy with the after shave this morning sir." He continued, "Don't worry though, between us we'll figure this out. We'll get some ground work done and we'll make positive headway."

In the remaining ten minutes, they discussed some further updates and assignments. Then Murray rose to exit and make his way to the 'City of Discovery.' On opening the door to depart the Chief Inspector called Murray back into his office, obviously having remembered an important matter that he'd previously omitted to mention.

Quietly and in confidential hushed tones he offered, "Young Hanlon, I got that rushed through and approved for you." He then handed over an envelope. A moment, that had it been witnessed by a tabloid reporter, would have made a great, *'Policeman in secret bungs'* story!

Murray waved goodbye for a second time. Confidently stating before he left, "Appreciate that sir. I don't think he'll let any of us down, including himself!"

It had been a while since Murray last travelled by train. Normally always preferring to commute by car in and around his beloved Scottish homeland. This morning however, he felt inclined to retrace the latest victim's final journey. It would also give him the time and solitude to reflect on the events of the last week. It was still only Wednesday!

He did not remember the station as a rule being as busy as he experienced that morning. With Waverley being the second busiest railway station in Scotland after Glasgow Central, and the fifth busiest in the United Kingdom outside London, he really shouldn't have been so surprised. This year, Edinburgh had also been celebrating the 200th anniversary of Sir Walter Scott's 'Waverley' at the railway station named in the novel's honour. It had been decorated with quotes from Sir Walter's writings, marking the 1814 publication of what is commonly regarded as the western world's first historical novel. Adding to the footfall on this particular day were a team of Network Rail employees. They were offering promotional copies of the book that told the story of the author's life. All part of the year long, 'Great Scott' campaign.

Contributing also to the complexities of the day, were several dozen of Murray's colleagues. Uniformed and forensics officers were at the cordoned off platform that Ms Moore had left from the evening before. They would be on duty all day. Verifying, testing and measuring. Actively engaged in questioning, investigating and examining. As a collective unit they were exceptional at their job. He had every confidence that together they would solve this latest case.

Waverley was situated in a steep, narrow valley between the medieval Old Town and the 18th century New Town. Murray, like many a visiting tourist commuter in this wonderfully grand station, would come to a stop every now and then to read one of the aforementioned quotes. They had been beautifully etched across the floors and walkways. One particularly famous line made him pause carefully for thought. After a few seconds, the so called wise policeman, reflected on his earlier initial question. Why, was the only train station in the world named after a novel, so exceptionally busy on this day?

"Oh, you idiot Steven Murray," he spoke aloud. "It's New Year's Eve man!"

As his train gingerly pulled out from the 'Heart of Midlothian,' Murray pondered again on that last well known line he'd just read and it's illustrious history. He knew it was often mistakenly attributed to William Shakespeare. Yet to the surprise of many, *'O what a tangled web we weave, when first we practise to deceive,'* is in fact from Sir Walter Scott's 'Marmion,' published in 1808.

For a West of Scotland man, Murray had been surprisingly engulfed by Sir Walter Scott's work for the first two decades of his life! He was brought up in the 1960's, in a Paisley housing scheme that honoured the literary genius. Such illustrious addresses as: Tantallon Drive, Ivanhoe Road, Abbotsford Crescent, Durward Way and Bothwell Place. Built across from his local Primary School were a group of high rise flats, their names included: Marmion, Montrose, Waverley and Heriot Court. His own humble abode, the loving home in which he was raised for the first nineteen years of his life, was a three bedroomed, Renfrewshire District Council house. It's location?

The Sir Walter Scott inspired........................ Oliphant Oval!

Amazing, though never having read one of his legendary works at that time. Here he was, a young teenage Murray surrounded by Scott's presence, awe and influence. No matter how distinct or evident. He was totally oblivious growing up to the clues all around him. Those facts were there all along, staring him straight in the face.

Today, the adult Murray, the policeman, the Detective Inspector, is thinking along similar lines. Is he staring it straight in the face, yet unable to recognise it? The suspicious, the uncertain, the ambiguous and vague.

'O what a tangled web we weave, when first we practise to deceive.'

Murray questioned again. Have we been or are we being deceived? And if so, by whom? Was 'Bonnie Dundee' a separate case? Five deaths in three days, surely no coincidence? Who was lying? What trickery was involved? When was this all put in place? Was there a catalyst? Why now? Is New Year, the date, the season significant?

His mind continued to race on at Usain Bolt 100 metre sprint pace. Whereas his body, was quite content to linger and go with the slightly more relaxed long distance stride of Mo Farah. The starting pistol sounded again - What was the link, the reason, the purpose? Isn't there supposed to be a motive? A rationale? A cause? So far, he was drawing blanks. Currently it felt like trying to put together a 10,000 piece baked bean jigsaw puzzle. Experienced people would counsel you to simply take a step back, find the four corners and move forward from there. Murray smiled a futile smile. What four corners? he thought. There are none. At this moment in time, it was a circular puzzle!

As he journeyed onward across the Forth Rail Bridge and ventured into the beautiful Kingdom of Fife. It was then, whilst travelling beyond Dunfermline the birthplace of the victim Elizabeth Moore, that DI Murray's thoughts first turned to his final destination.

No matter whichever one of Dundee's three inward-bound rail lines deliver you to this dynamic city. A spectacular view across water is more or less guaranteed!

Arrive from Perth and for the final few minutes of the trip you'll hug the bank of the River Tay. Journey from the north and east and you'll follow that longest river in Scotland for even longer, having already skirted the North Sea coast from as far away as Arbroath. Most dramatic of all, the line Murray is presently on, sweeping straight across the river from Fife and the south. Crossing the slender elegance of the Tay Rail Bridge, with its distinctive flowing curve at the northern end.

Dundee station itself is situated in the waterfront area of the city, where history and modernity live side by side. A short stroll away lies The Discovery, Captain Scott's research ship on his ill-fated mission to the South Pole, now back in its home port. Also, don't miss another even older ship. HM Frigate Unicorn, one of the six oldest ships in the world. It is docked just a little further along the quayside.

Dundee's slogan, "One City - Many Discoveries" is apt though. For in the opposite direction to these grand old vessels, you'll find the Dundee Science Centre. It is a superb modern visitor attraction with entertaining and educational multimedia experiences as well as live shows. This impressive contrast of old and new is reflected throughout the city. Where a modern emphasis on science, technology and culture, rubs shoulders with an industrial past of textiles, marmalade production and newspaper publishing - more often summarised as 'jute, jam and journalism!'

Detective Inspector Murray sensed that he may just be at the very beginning of a very different and unusual 'Voyage of Discovery!'

On the the final stretch, as his train travelled over the Tay Rail bridge from Newport into Dundee, Murray heard the unexpected sound of a bubble bursting. In modern day life that would be, a text message! It read:

Re. Ann Raymond and Penelope Cooke. I can confirm that they were both poisoned! More later....Doc.

Even reading that text, Murray in his head could hear 'The T'inker' saying - 'I can confirm t'at t'ay were both poisoned. With an amused, happy expression now simpering across his face. He was ready for all that Scotland's fourth largest city could now t'row at him!

From the window of his carriage just three minutes later Murray spotted Detective Sergeant Brian Pollok. He and Pollok had worked together previously for a short time a few years ago. It was an intriguing, complex case involving credit card fraud. A ruthless, well organised group of Eastern European gangsters behind it. It began in Dundee and then took Pollok, a Detective Constable at the time, up to Aberdeen and across to Perthshire. Finally, the shady trail made its way hesitantly toward the 'Athens of the North,' that which is Edinburgh.

It was mid-March 2010, an easy date to remember. For Murray had helped celebrate the Yorkshireman's 40th birthday three days early at Murrayfield Stadium, home of Scottish rugby. The match day tickets had been sold out for months. But, as good fortune would have it, Chief Inspector Brown's youngest daughter Megan was due to give birth that weekend (their 5th grandchild, but her 1st). His wife Sandra duly packed their cases and they had headed off for Scarborough that Thursday morning. Not it has to be said, before an exchange of monies and tickets could take place between the two officers.

Murray had learned earlier in that week it would be Brian's 40th soon, and he'd been scrambling about trying to obtain some briefs for the match. 'God bless Megan', he thought and of course her imminent arrival!

Nearly 67,000 fans packed into the ground that evening. It was a 5pm start. Having lost 18 - 9 in their previous home match two weeks earlier, against the eventual Six Nations Champions France, the Scots fans were looking for a much improved performance against their 'Auld Enemy.'

Brian Pollok on the other hand would settle for a 0 - 3 victory. Saving him, the only Englishman in that 7,000 strong corner section of the ground, from jumping around and celebrating way too much! They drew fifteen all and both men seemed content.

Brian had played rugby for England schoolboys in his youth. His speed, physique and poise now though would probably have more in common with Dundee's other favourite son, the Dandy comic strip hero Desperate Dan! Similarities abound - The large overhanging belly, the unshaved chin or chins, due in part to their equal love of all types of food, especially pies. In Brian Pollock's case - the occasional one too many Scotch pies. Then of course for 'Our Dan,' his preferred culinary delight continues to be 'Cow Pie.' Legend has it, that it consists of an enormous meat pastry with all the horns still embedded!

Murray however, could graciously picture this strapping 6'2' man in his teenage years. Receiving the ball, grasping the opportunity and urgently sprinting down the wing. Twisting, turning, thundering at speed past opponents. Before determinedly, cutting inside and scoring. Diving low, torpedo-like toward the corner flag, just inches before the last ditch tackle arrived.

He had lived in Dundee for many years now. Settling there initially for University. Afterwards, he simply became overwhelmed and fell madly in love with the stunning beauty of a City by the water. As a self confessed bachelor, that seemed to be all that Brian Pollok had fallen in love with in recent years.

Now he was located on the outskirts. In the beautiful "Jewel in Dundee's crown". That which is, the awe inspiring Broughty Ferry. It's fine seafront esplanade and sweeping sands provide the perfect place for a relaxing stroll or a quiet picnic. The Ferry also offers visitors the perfect base from which to enjoy some of the finest golf courses, fishing or sightseeing to be found anywhere in Scotland. It's situated four miles east of the city centre on the north bank of the

Firth of Tay. On this particular visit, Murray unfortunately, hasn't packed his golf clubs and won't have time to take the open top bus tour!

As he stepped down from the train all DI Murray could hear in his head was the voice of a famous tank engine for 14 seasons. It was Liverpudlian actor Michael Angelis repeating those famous words: 'As Thomas pulled into the station.'

Very apt he thought, because there on the train platform, waiting to greet this Police Inspector from Edinburgh was the irascible 'Fat Controller'.

'Don't call him Dan, don't call him Dan, please just don't call him Dan,' Murray kept reminding himself. He didn't, he did very well. He greeted his old rugby buddy DS Pollock with a firm handshake, a rather cheeky grin and an important, yet highly relevant question. "Brian, nice to see you. How was your pie?"

ELEVEN

"Every day I sit and wonder how my life it used to be. Now I feel like going under, now my life is hard to see. So tell me people, am I going insane?"

- Black Sabbath

Wednesday 31st December 2014

Whilst Murray was busy over in Dundee and Angus, back on his own patch in the Willowbrae area of Edinburgh, a polite, friendly voice could be heard announcing brightly. "Hello Mrs Dickson, good afternoon." The voice then stated in a calm, yet authoritative manner. "It's Lynnette from the social work department here." Sheila Dixon had answered the intercom to her luxuriously opulent six bedroom villa, fully aware of the appointment she had scheduled for that particular day.

A few weeks previous this Edinburgh born, forty something, mother of four, had called at the Dixon family home in the exclusive part of town. She'd been a team leader - canvassing, knocking on doors and distributing leaflets as part of an Edinburgh City Council social work initiative. One of many that she had encountered in her twenty years of service.

Currently, her latest official title was 'Awareness Counsellor.' A fully qualified social worker, she was especially trained to offer guidance, support and advice in helping older teenagers and adults survive child abuse and trauma. Sheila Dixon had spoken to her briefly at the door last time. On discovering her name however (which had been printed on the flyer). She became more interested than ever, and gave her a call to arrange a suitable day and time to meet up.

Across the left hand corner of the leaflet in bright orange eye catching lettering, were the words: 'The Courage to Heal.' A smaller font in the centre of the page, then announced: 'Surviving Childhood Sexual Abuse.' As Kenny's wife continued to read, it became clear that it was the bottom paragraph that visibly and emotionally impacted on Sheila Dixon later that evening. It was a quote from trauma expert and psychiatrist Judith Herman, which read:

"As the survivor struggles with the tasks of adult life, the legacy of her childhood becomes increasingly burdensome. Eventually, often in the fourth or fifth decade of life, the defensive structure may begin to break down. Often the precipitant is a change in the equilibrium of close relationships: The failure of a marriage, the illness or death of a parent. The facade can hold no longer, and the underlying fragmentation becomes manifest. When and if a breakdown occurs, it can take symptomatic forms that mimic virtually every form of psychiatric disorder. Survivors fear that they are going insane or will have to die."

For one reason or another, Sheila Dixon seemingly felt compelled to contact Lynnette. As they sat together, spoke openly and shared experiences. You could witness a bonding, a close kinship. A warmth and simple, yet sincere trust seemed to be developing. Recollections - some uncomfortable, others tender, but almost all inevitably painful to recount. '

Lynn, as Lynnette liked to be called, listened intently. Comforting and supporting. She had a great ability to empathise. Sheila opened up to her. Sharing secrets that had never been revealed to anyone else before. She relaxed and smiled. She could feel an enormous weight lift from her shoulders. Sheila Dixon seemed to be genuinely uplifted and brightened by the whole experience.

"You have done wonderfully well for an initial meeting. How do you feel about it?" Lynn enquired delicately, with optimism in her voice.

Clearing her throat, Sheila Dixon's voice was mild and mellow in the first few words. Then it quickly modified itself, to become harsher and harder. "Loved it, very cathartic, liberating even. It still hurts, I continue to feel bitter and require some scores to be settled."

"We can work on not settling scores," Lynn calmly reassured her.

"Let's not!" Sheila said rather indignantly, then continued with - "Wow, I feel like I've just been on an emotional rollercoaster. Part of me loved the thrill and enjoyed the experience. Though I recognise it is now time to exit." She continued more enthused and animated than before. Knees bending, arms outstretched, indicating every twist and turn, every high and low throughout the high octane white knuckle ride. "The dark side of me never wanted it to end," she said animatedly. "I was prepared to stay on forever. Even when it seemed guaranteed to derail or have no brake applied and it was destined to head straight on fully at 120 miles per hour toward a reinforced concrete wall. Wow!" she gasped again frantically, arms falling by her side, seeking to regain her composure.

Surprised by Sheila's vivid and soberly thoughtful theme park ride experience, Lynn looked briefly uncomfortable. After a slight pause, she candidly added,

"I'll have to be going now Sheila. It's just after half past three and I've still got several reports to write up before I can finish and head home. It's my youngest daughter's birthday party tonight and there's no way I want to be late." The council employee was so excited at the prospect. They had been planning it for several weeks. Friends had been secretly invited from nursery, along with a few of the neighbouring children. The birthday girl's Gran and Grandpa were also driving up from Stranraer to stay for a short festive break. So plenty going on this evening in that family home.

Momentarily silenced, Sheila responded with, "Oh, right, excellent, that'll be fun," she offered rather insincerely. "How many children do you actually have Mrs Lithgow, I mean Lynn?"

"Four," Sheila replied. Beaming from ear to ear. "All girls! Married for twenty years and a quartet of kids to make any mother proud. I wouldn't swap them for the world," she enthused.

Sheila tried to muster a reluctant smile as she raised her head to offer a brief nod in acknowledgement. "Ages?" she summoned.

"Two in High School, one in Primary School and Laura, the birthday girl, who turns four. So, let me think, as of today - 15, 13, 7 and 4!" She continued bubbling with pride. "My husband Tony and I always talk about how they take us for wonderful journeys upon the high seas. The c's being - clever, cheeky, courageous and cute! Their individual character traits that currently match up to where they are in life. Sorry, I'm rambling on Mrs Dixon," the social worker acknowledged. "I get like that when I start talking about my own family. Apologies, but what about you and Mr Dixon, have you....?"

"Don't be asking about me," Sheila cleverly interrupted. "You need to be getting home and organised. We can catch up next week." Then slowly placing her hands one on top of the other in the centre of her chest, not unlike a church minister. Sheila Dixon paused and asked reverently, "Lynn could you maybe help me with one more thing before you go?"

Hastily looking at her watch, but mindful of the strong connection made, Lynn responded positively with, "Of course, what is it? What's on your mind?"

"I felt we bonded really well today. Women together, a united front, a trust."

Lynnette Lithgow countered with a slow, quizzical, "I would not disagree, Sheila, so how can I help?"

"You seem strong, confident, capable of taking on the world. I have an unusual evening routine that I would love to ask you to support me in tonight."

"Sounds intriguing. What do you have in mind?"

Sheila Dixon produced a large tub of wrapped chocolates from behind her back. Cadbury's Roses to be precise. There were only about seven or eight sweets remaining. As she held out the box, she smiled impishly at the 'Awareness Counsellor' and confidently stated, "Joint solidarity in our efforts. After studying or reading in the evening, I like to be able to reward myself for my diligence. Would you join me in that effort tonight? Again motioning towards 'The Magnificent Seven' on display. "I'll re-read the leaflet tonight about ten o'clock. Then, knowing that you'll be in receipt of a reward also, that will help galvanise me for the day ahead. I know it sounds rather corny Lynn, but it's a little like having a support group. Knowing we've all been through comparable experiences, working toward an end goal and being able to share in the spoils together also!"

With a relieved smile as big as the Forth Road Bridge, a certain Mrs Lithgow chirped up. "Now that's not a big ask at all Sheila. I'm watching my weight, but a secret choccy reward before bedtime, it's a deal! You have a wonderful New Year when it comes, and I'll look forward to hearing all about it at our next meeting."

Sheila Dixon nodded, looked Lynnette Lithgow straight in the eye and through a sincere smile offered up. "Lynn you are so busy running after family, helping clients and dealing with a multitude of work issues. I suspect by next week you'll be dead to the world!"

Laughing, the birthday girl's mum gathered up her bits and pieces, grabbed her coat and made her way to the door. In awe, she looked around Sheila Dixon's beautiful home 'one last time.' It was in stark contrast to her humble four bedroomed council house in Borrowstounness.

Bo'ness, as it is commonly known, is a coastal parish in the Central Lowlands of Scotland. It lies on a hillside on the South bank of the Firth of Forth within the Falkirk Council area. It had been home to Lynnette and Tony Lithgow for sixteen years.

Leaving Dundee at ten past seven on New Year's Eve, Murray guessed that the train may have been extra busy travelling into Edinburgh. He would have been irrefutably mistaken. The carriages were deserted. For those individuals that had made their way home earlier in the afternoon, they were either staying indoors or not joining the festivities until much later in the evening.

The day had been even more productive than Steve Murray could have hoped for. They ascertained, with Doc Patterson's help, that Elizabeth Moore was probably dead before she crossed the Forth Road Bridge.

In fact, 'The T'inker' said in his lunchtime phone call to the Inspector - "I t'ink you'll find t'at she was dead before t'at train left t'e station! I'm sending you over an update in the next t'irty minutes. I t'ink I should have her full information by about seven t'irty t'is evening."

As the two old friends caught up on the intervening years. It really was turning out to be a 'City of Discovery.' Earlier in the day Pollok uncovered some valuable CCTV footage from Waverley. You could just about make out the badge of a uniformed female police officer going on to the train. She boarded literally seconds behind the victim. Then she emerged from the next carriage up, just 60 seconds later. Worthy of following up on and waiting on Edinburgh getting back in touch with them in regards to who wore that badge number.

Murray also had plenty of other irons prodding and stoking fires delicately and discreetly from across the water. Hanlon still had his deerstalker on, working on the art of deduction. He was delving deeper than expected into the Oat'n Nuts murders and the previous possible arson attacks. He was also considering any potential links with any of the other recent poison victims.

'Kid Curry and Hannibal Hayes' were following up on any connection between the police vehicle theft and the Leith Walk murder of legal secretary Annabel Richmond. Finally, Coulter and Taylor were checking out the movements, whereabouts, times and dates of those qualified to offer fashion advice 'on light brown with black!' This thorough investigation was being carried out amongst the Dock Green hierarchy and their highly trained 'security' staff.

The return journey gave the Inspector an opportunity for some quiet introspection and to catch up with t'at rather lengthy email. He had received it earlier in the afternoon from The T'inker, at about 3pm. Murray though, had recognised it would require time to peruse over and take onboard several of his findings. It was fascinating, mind blowing stuff. He had to pinch himself and question aloud. "This is still Scotland, right?"

The Doc had already confirmed in the morning, that both Penelope Cooke and Annabel Richmond had been victims of poison. His team at the lab were making headway with the Elizabeth Moore situation. He had hoped to be in a better position to confirm or deny by later tonight. He could however, sign off and sadly clarify that the same poison was also responsible for the death of Deborah Evans and her infant nephew, James.

Murray pondered over that last comment. Because they were absolutely innocent of any wrongdoing! Each of those fine people for some reason had been caught up in a dark, odious web of murder, death and demise. It was highly personal, vengeful even. And it's currently moving forward with a relentless and unforgiving momentum and that was worrying!

The report continued. It stated:

Steve it would appear we are dealing with Batrachotoxin.
One of the most powerful naturally occurring neurotoxins.
With a dose equivalent to just 2 grains of table salt being enough to kill an adult human.
It works in two ways; both as a neurotoxin, causing paralysis and as a cardiotoxin, directly affecting the heart muscles.
This makes death almost inevitable and within a matter of minutes.
Although generally classified as a neurotoxin, batrachotoxin has marked effects on heart muscles. These effects are similar to the cardiotoxic effects of digitalis (digoxin), a poison found in the foxglove plant.
Batrachotoxin interferes with heart conduction, causing arrhythmias, extrasystoles, ventricular fibrillation and other changes which lead to cardiac arrest.

Batrachotoxin induces a massive release of acetylcholine in nerves and muscles and destruction of synaptic vesicles, as well. Batrachotoxin R is more toxic than related Batrachotoxin A.

Now highlighted in orange, was the part Murray liked best in any medical correspondence he received from the Doc.

IN LAYMAN'S TERMS:
Batrachotoxin binds to and irreversibly opens the sodium channels of nerve cells that they cannot reset.
The neuron is no longer capable of 'firing' (sending messages) and this results in paralysis.
Steve, currently no effective antidote exists for the treatment of batrachotoxin poisoning.
Speak later. Doc.

As the carriage continued rolling homeward bound from Tayside, physically Murray himself was now in a state of paralysis. Mentally he was in meltdown. "No antidote," he repeated to himself - "Seriously?" A frenzy of thoughts and a steady stream of relevant questions arose. How much poison was out there? Where did it come from? How can we possibly stop these fatal attacks?

Having processed the fact that the River Tay, was the largest river in Britain and internationally famous for its Atlantic salmon fishing. Murray quickly realised, that for his team to come out on top, to think outside the box, even to dare to ask - what box? They would be required to be at their 'collective' best. They would be the beautiful bold bind, the rich refined run, or the stunning shapely school of salmon! Overcoming the hurdles, obstacles and challenges along the way. Murray appreciated it was time to forget convention and the social norm. In his team, with its makeup and individual character, he knew he was surrounded by greatness and it was time for them to leap mightily against the raging torrent, and 'to swim against the stream!'

Based on that 'draft of salmon' collective noun logic. He concluded that maybe they were closer to securing answers than they thought. So far, the killer or killers had concentrated on individuals. It still seemed intimate, close up and in your face. A definite form of personal payback. Maybe, like the salmon, they were returning home to where it all began. But, where all what began? What reason? What purpose? What was the catalyst? Would they escalate to groups, larger communities, sports and music arenas? An endless list of possibilities ran through Murray's already often tortured mind.

Reflecting on the events of the day and trying to get an overall picture of things, the Inspector was diverted by a brief vibration in his jacket pocket. Caller display recognises the call. It was from 'Taz' Taylor. Now whether to answer it or not, that is another story. He feels deeply that people who speak on their mobile phones whilst travelling by public transport, then further feel the need to include the whole world and their Aunt in the conversation.... should be run over! (in an animated 'Wacky Races' kind of way. So he says)

He knew however, that the call would be important, relevant to their murder inquiries. He quickly swiped the screen and answered the call.

Taylor emotional, blurted out, "Inspector, it's about PC Hanlon."

"Yeah, it's exciting Taz. I'm looking forward to working with him. Is the secret out then, I take it?"

"What, no, what, working with him, no, no, sir, sir, let me stop you there. He.." Murray could hear Taylor audibly pause, hesitate and gulp. She strained to get the words out.

Conscious of using the right ones, she tried one final time. "It's Lauren sir, Lauren Hanlon, Joe's wife. He returned home earlier this evening to ...to...sir, she's dead."

TWELVE

"The child is a king, the carolers sing. The old has passed, there's a new beginning. Dreams of Santa, dreams of snow, fingers numb, faces aglow."

- Cliff Richard

"A-tish-oo, a-tish-oo, they all fall down." Ring-a-ring-a-roses was part way through and the children and adults were having a fabulous time. Young Laura Lithgow had been chasing her older siblings all afternoon. Her routine continued by resting on her Grandpa's lap for a few minutes. Then with batteries fully recharged, off again for musical chairs, pass the parcel, assorted dancing and endless helpings of crunchy crisps and chocolate cake! It was approaching 8pm, and that had been her regular circuit training for the last two and a half hours. The party festivities were in full swing and this young lady was having a ball. Once mum finally arrived home from work, the cake with a quartet of candles would be lit and the popular birthday song sung. Finally, they could all settle down as family and friends for Laura's special, celebratory birthday meal.

As the doorbell rang, it went unheeded at first. Shouts and cries were offered. "Is that mum? Finally mum's here. Get the cake somebody. Doesn't she have a key?" Eventually, Tony Lithgow, noticing the outline on the other side of the frosted glass panel, made his way toward the front door. Party songs, chattering and a multitude of boisterous youngsters singing at the top of their voice had drowned out all other forms of life. Today, for the previous hour or two, they had been young mischievous adventurers. Tiny, sweet laden pioneers. Mini astronauts, taking small steps and huge (as big as they can muster) leaps for mankind. They'd ventured into a world of their own. A world of joy and celebration. A world of innocent pleasure. A world, that was about to, *'a-tish-oo, a-tish-oo,'* come tumbling down!

A relatively young WPC stood nervously alongside her more seasoned male colleague. She spoke briefly in calm, hushed tones with the householder. One or two other guests had now spotted there was indeed ongoing 'life' outside. At that moment Tony Lithgow's knees buckled. He was about to collapse as a neighbour reached forward to grab his arm. The Police Constable then quickly lunged in to save his head connecting with the stone steps at the doorway. Adult voices came to a stop. The teenage Lithgow girls, Leanne and Lucy screamed. The adventurers, pioneers and astronauts carried on for a short spell before their journeys came to an abrupt end. Music ceased, voices stilled and everyone made their way back into, if not officially the Earth's atmosphere, certainly to a very distinct, different arena.

Laura Lithgow was finally out for the count on her grandfather's lap, and was being lifted and gently carried through to her bedroom to continue sleeping. This would be a memorable birthday for that gorgeous, 'CUTE' young lady. Unhappily now for all the wrong reasons. Both grandparents stood weeping. They desperately tried to console each other as well as comfort their second youngest grand-daughter Lynda. The distraught seven year old was enfolded in their arms. Collectively, they wept in the far corner of the humble family sitting room.

Nearby, in the damp, poorly built cramped conservatory to the rear of the house, Tony Lithgow now sat numb and motionless. His right hand intertwined and clasped tightly to that of his eldest, heartbroken daughter Leanne's. Nervously running the fingertips of his left hand backwards and forwards across his brow. Dropping it infrequently to the bridge of his nose to wipe, rub and clear away, what seemed like a continual stream of never ending tears.

Today's special occasion had been brought to you courtesy of the remaining Lithgow daughter. Thirteen year old CBO (Chief Birthday Organiser) Lucy. She was presently in an upstairs bedroom with Mrs Dawson, a neighbour from next door. Julie Dawson's own daughter Amy had been at the party. Although she was now safely back home, whilst Julie had volunteered to remain behind to help look after those children who were still awaiting parents picking them up.

Lucy loved planning and coordinating. Her ambition was to work in the hospitality and events sector when she was older. She'd helped put together the guest list, the invites, the games and had prepared all the music. She had even utilised a spare bedroom as the designated cloakroom. Disposable cups were lined up in rows and filled with juice. Plates of biscuits were displayed evenly and needed to be constantly replenished. Oh, and not forgetting her mum's personal favourite. An assortment and wide variety of milk and dark chocolates. Downstairs, a Little Mermaid themed birthday cake sat gathering dust. Nearby on the kitchen table lay four unused candles. Various, 'Death by Chocolate' themed events are often held. Today was never intended to be one of them. Nonetheless, it turned out it absolutely was!

At around 8.30pm the Inspector's train, in which he had ended up with a carriage all to himself, pulled slowly into the famous Waverley station. He then moved in a measured, languid manner. It was a walk of indifference. Slowly he made his way to the exit onto Princes Street, by-passing several more of Scott's famous quotes. He read them, but more often than not was somewhere else entirely. Twice though, he felt compelled to stop, to ponder and to re-read the beautiful literary line of passage. He simply wondered in awe at its relevance and application to his own life and current circumstances. He had taken time to pause at:

"In literature, as in love, courage is half the battle."
and then again at:

"The great art of life, so far as I have been able to observe, consists in fortitude and perseverance."

That 'Sir Walter,' had a fair way with words Murray thought. Hoping secretly that he would be blessed with a small percentage of that gift at his next port of call that evening.

Having caught a black cab, he arrived twenty minutes later at his intended destination. Genuinely filled with upset and compassion in equal measure, he stood to compose himself for all of two seconds. Steven Murray then tentatively removed his right hand from his jacket pocket and clenched his fist. With a deep, slow, undulating breath and over 30 years of experience. Two well-worn knuckles knocked tenderly, yet firmly, three times to the side of the nameplate. As the door began to open in a cautious and careful manner, one more quote spotted earlier on the station walkway flashed immediately to mind:

"When, musing on companions gone, we doubly feel ourselves alone."

The two men stood silent. Respectfully observing each other. A polite nod was offered and instantly mirrored by the other. One, with many of his best years possibly now behind him. He's had numerous experiences of heartache. The death of parents and two older siblings. Mistakes and decisions that time had gradually helped to heal.

The other man on the verge of greatness. With a career about to take off and still to reach his peak. Then, just when excitement, drive and opportunity beckoned, he found himself companionless. Left suddenly alone to embrace the magic of life and every beautiful thing it had to offer. Feeling, faintly forlorn and forsaken.

Murray being well versed and only too familiar with that emotion, was determined that no member of his team would have to endure feeling isolated, vulnerable and lacking in support. Still speechless, the Inspector naturally took a step forward and sincerely embraced the young man.

Death is like a magic conjuring trick, he thought, a sleight of hand. As a loved one leaves you, a departure, a longing, something is missing. Yet, like the row of handkerchiefs, the rabbit or the dove being produced from the magician's hat. There it is, there he or she is! A replacement, a substitute, someone you've known, but not known. They are there for you. You open up to them. You learn about each other - goals, ambitions, plans for the future and how to proceed. A new friendship is formed.

Understanding, empathy and pathos. In Detective Inspector Steve Murray's universe this would revolve deeply around a turntable and a stack load of classic vinyl albums. With Joe Hanlon that evening, it involved his iPhone, two speakers, the lovely Spotify and their, 'Music For Everyone!'

Tori Amos, the American singer/songwriter is attributed with the following quote: *"Healing takes courage and we all have courage, even if we have to dig a little to find it!"* Tonight Steven Murray was determined to spend time digging deep with his new friend. And 'courage' would be the treasure they'd seek.

Sittin' on the Dock of the Bay, Go West and More than a Woman resounded across the airwaves. Then, like a tropical storm in the night, up popped The Weather Girls and It's Raining Men. This was Lauren's latest playlist. She had created it only yesterday for her doting husband. It ranged from soulful classics, favourites from schooldays and party anthems, to love songs, instrumentals and sheer silliness.

Lauren and Joseph Hanlon were childhood sweethearts. A smile between them could convey and say so much. A little known Bruce Springsteen number entitled Terry's Song, was forever Lauren's favourite tribute to her husband's loving, kind and unique nature. It's splendid lyrics began to play and Joseph Ian Hanlon began to weep uncontrollably.

"Now the world is filled with many wonders under the passing sun, and sometimes something comes along and you know it's for sure the only one. The Mona Lisa, the David, the Sistine Chapel, Jesus, Mary, and JOE. And when they built you, brother, they broke the mould."

It was the final track, the music ceased to be. Cars could be heard muted in the distance, alongside those occasional noises of an evening that can never be identified. The two men sat on the floor like teenage school pals. Backs against adjacent walls, with legs close together and pulled up toward their chins. Joe's light grey shirt was adorned with what looked like a small Paisley Pattern print. On closer inspection, it was genuine 'to scale' teardrops that resembled the West of Scotland's world famous design.

It was going on 2.30am. Murray wanted to say so much. To apologise for outstaying his welcome. To offer his condolences. To say, 'everything will be alright.' Alas, none of those words echoed from his mouth. Like Lauren, his pursed lips, nod and small reassuring smile, hopefully said all that had to be said. Both men began to clamber up, haul themselves to their feet and get their bearings. The DI was due back in the office in just a few short hours.

Murray then handed Joe an official looking envelope with the Police Scotland stamp authoritatively displayed on the outside. Looking surprised, Del Boy's young sidekick, sheepishly began to tear open the seal and slip out the letter contained within.

"I'm so sorry Joe, now may not be the ideal moment. However, I thought it was important to let you know as soon as possible. In light of events though, you take as much time as you need to come to terms with everything."

By now, the inexperienced yet mature Joseph Hanlon, was again gently casting aside an emotional tear in his right eye with the well-rehearsed flick of his trusty thumb. On reading his hand delivered mail, he felt overwhelmed, humbled and filled with gratitude for the opportunity currently being presented to him.

It was clarification of a temporary secondment to CID. To partner up with Detective Inspector Steven Murray. He would be covering the maternity leave of Detective Constable Sandra Kerr until further notice. It did state however, that the starting date would be from January 1st 2015. That would now be flexible!

The young officer gave his superior another hug. It was an unspoken statement. Simply expressed it said - Thank you sir. Thank you for everything!

Opening the front door, Murray turned slowly and spoke softly. In a manner befitting a caring father. He offered, "Take care son, God speed."

This time, Hanlon did manage to vocalize his thoughts. "Thank you sir, thank you for tonight." Uncertain whether to continue, he stammered emotionally. "You know with all that has happened, I totally forgot to mention, and you'll never believe it. I got word this morning from the property company we had been dealing with. The owner said he was so sorry to hear about my circumstances and in light of such, had refunded our deposit in full with an enclosed cheque.

"Wow, now there is a turn up for the books," Murray declared, shaking his head.

"Oh, and sir," Hanlon added. "Happy New Year!"

With a wave, a thumbs up and a salute all merged into one. DI Steven Murray responded with his own jovial and bright retort. "Happy New Year Constable. Indeed, here's to a Happier New Year."

A satisfactory smile, tinged with the reality of the situation, beamed increasingly across the Inspector's face as he walked off into the distance. At that moment, he deliberately left behind him 2014 and stepped forward confidently into an optimistic year ahead. The upcoming twelve months would undoubtedly be filled with magnificent warm sunshine, and beautiful bright blue vistas.

Be that as may. On the flip side there will also be dark, depressing and debilitating clouds of gloom. Detective Inspector Steven Murray would be lost without those seasonal variances. Fluctuating periods that for most may supposedly come around every three or four months. Yet sinisterly, they'd enter and exit DI Murray's head every forty-eight hours!

THIRTEEN

*"Old dogs and worn out shoes, even children sing the blues.
How we must endure it all, to save God's creatures great
and small."*

- Barry Gibb

Murray was always singing to himself. With just four
hours sleep when he arrived in on January 1st at 7.40am
things were no different. Topical as ever and above the
sound of air conditioning or heating units whirring in
the background, you heard the karaoke strains of,
*"Though I want to be with you, be with you night and day.
Nothing changes on New Year's Day - on New Year's Day."*
Bono should not perhaps feel in any immediate danger
or threat of being replaced as U2's lead singer, just
quite yet!

It was an early start sure enough, but not early
enough to catch out an audacious and enterprising
Joseph Hanlon. The acting Detective Constable was
already at his desk re-reading some of his earlier notes
from James and Debbie Evans' deaths.

"Really Joe, it's not required," Murray said
sympathetically.

"Sir, sir, stop there." Hanlon straightened himself and looked directly at Murray as he spoke. "I really appreciate the opportunity. I really do and I don't want to let you down. I'd only be at home reflecting on a New Year without her," Joe insisted. Then with a touch of understandable melancholy in his voice, he added, "The first one, in a very, very, long time."

Offering a discerning nod of understanding and compassion. Coupled with an, "I suppose," Murray reluctantly agreed.

The DI had been curious about the road accident he'd heard about from the night before. He had telephoned ahead and requested a printed copy of the initial report and corresponding notes. Murray was still very much old school. Although he appreciated it was easy enough for him to view it on a computer screen. He seemed to process it much better in the written format. He would read it, mark it and highlight key words. He'd then add large question marks to particular statements, quotes or answers. The important thing was, it worked for him.

For others, with a keyboard at a monitor, they can do the same and that may well be their preferred option, but not for Steve Murray. The feel of the A4 sheets, placing them on the desk and running his fingertips across them. Valuing each and every one of them and the information they contain. Comparing and contrasting dialogue, surnames, nicknames, aliases and place names. Lifting them hastily to re-read specifics. Slamming them back down in frustration when a particular theory is finally shot out of the water. Then, just to be sure, you decide to turn them over one last time and ask, 'Did I miss something?' Finally, came the point where you open your drawer, throw them inside, close it over and now leave well alone. Time to ponder, reflect and hopefully wait for the 'Aha' moment and the light bulb to get switched on!

He opened the folder and began proof-reading it quickly. Mentally noting relevant key details. It appeared the M9 motorway connecting Bo'ness and Edinburgh was relatively free from traffic that night. Motorists had in the main returned home early for New Year. The gritters had been out regularly throughout the day and the road surface was wet, but fine. Visibility was clear. Without warning, the ten year old red Ford Mondeo had simply veered left from the outside lane. It had hit the tail of a small C1 travelling on its inside. It spun the beige Citroen and its occupants around at least twice before it careered off the motorway. It had slammed at great speed, side on into the cast iron entry gates of ironically the West Lothian Council Roads Department. Their base was located on a small slip road just off the motorway.

Lynnette Lithgow had been only seconds away from her turn-off for Bo'ness and literally two minutes from home. Murray did not realise that other vehicles had been involved. A third motor, a black Vauxhall Insignia had then hit the rear end of Lynn's Mondeo. Pushing it clear off the motorway and ending just short of the Czech Republic built French Citroen.

Murray remembered in 2010, Peugeot Citroën announced a recall of the C1. It was for a faulty, sticking accelerator pedal. Thinking briefly, Murray wondered, could this have contributed to the accident? He highlighted various sections and added a few giant question marks. They were noted in blue ink from his trusted Papermate pen. This in small part a tribute to another fictional TV character. Obsessive, compulsive San Francisco detective Adrian Monk. Thanks to him DI Murray carried a quality pen in every suit and jacket he owned!

Abruptly, Murray sat up. All of a sudden he became alarmed by something he had just read. The Inspector placed the reports directly on the desk in front of him. He sat perfectly still. Unaware up until that very moment, that there was more than one fatality in this tragic roadside collision. The startling fact that Lynnette Lithgow was a casualty, made Murray suspicious enough that this was no accident. He knew nevertheless that he would have to wait to hear from Doc Patterson to aid his enquiries further. In the interim however, he continued to peruse the documents in front of him.

The Insignia driver was a little shook up, but was fine. A forty five year old female, making her way back to Cumbernauld on the outskirts of Glasgow. She was looking forward to welcoming in the New Year with close family and friends.

George Kemp and his wife Janet, who had been the driver of the C1 were currently in hospital. The pair had both suffered broken bones, concussion and shock. Medical staff were confident that they would recover well physically. Murray guessed however, that mentally, they would find it perhaps slightly more challenging. He had then already anticipated what was coming next.

They were in their mid-seventies, though not alone in their car. Murray at this point did not want to read on. He had seen it all before and it never got any easier, felt better or became more bearable. Why could it just not have been George or Janet? They've both had over seven decades to experience and feel of the joys and pleasures the world had to offer. Could it not have been one of their friends? An ageing acquaintance, neighbour or old work colleague? Again, they'd have had near on three quarters of a century of ups and downs and memories. Led a roller coaster life of adventure, one jam packed and filled with a multitude of twists and turns.

Alas, it was not an individual who had lived three score and ten plus. The Kemps did not drive a Volvo. A vehicle that if you believed all its advertising hype would seemingly protect you from anything the world could throw at you. DI Murray could even testify to that!

Wistfully, as fate would have it, the Kemps were sat in a twin deck chair. It was held together with a few well positioned bolts. The minimalist wheels attached, were no bigger than those on Murray's yellow 1975 Raleigh Chopper bike!

He felt an angry tirade forming and about to be unleashed. Emotionally he was bitter, cynical and being sneeringly distrustful. He genuinely believed he could have built a safer car from one of his old toy Meccano sets! Filled with indignation his rant began: "How dare they build cars no bigger than Matchbox models and deem them safe to carry passengers. What kind of society do we live in these days? One that stupidly won't allow us to stack chairs more than four high. But hey, it's okay to sit in a Heinz baked bean can and travel alongside articulated trucks! Juggernauts that hurtle past you at seventy miles per hour and weigh up to 44 tonne............. geez!" Slowly, Murray tried to take that particular statistic on board. Forty-four tonnes. Never mind four tonnes, one ton or even half a ton - you were a goner!

Six year old Kirsty Fraser epitomised childhood. She was innocent, inquisitive and highly impetuous. The eldest of the Kemp's three great-grandchildren. She had just experienced a very special festive treat into Scotland's capital city with her loving Grandparents. Family visits to the historic Castle, the temporary ice rink in Princes Street Gardens and scaling the steps of the Scott monument would be among her final memories. The young 'astronaut,' a Windieknowes

Primary School pupil from Bathgate in West Lothian, was being called home. Her mission here on Earth complete. Steven Murray wept.

With it's amazing viewing figures between four o'clock and ten past five in the 1970's, ITV's World of Sport entertained a grateful public on Saturday afternoons. It was a national institution. Names such as Giant Haystacks, Mick McManus and Jackie Pallo, were all star participants. Not forgetting - Big Daddy, Les Kellett and the mysteriously named masked grappler - Kendo Nagasaki.

Counselling never seemed a serious option. In recent years Murray wept in isolation. Still extremely good at his job and getting the best out of others. But he recognised that daily life was becoming more and more problematic. He challenged, fought and actively wrestled with opponents every twenty-four hours of the day. Some irrefutably real and authentic. Many, many more, abstract and illusive! Wrestling continued to be a high profile sport for Steven Murray. He heard the bell and - 'Seconds away - Round Two!'

Joseph Hanlon had worked quietly and diligently for the previous thirty minutes. He was happy to give DI Murray personal time, to take stock and sit in solitude. Then allow him space to explode vociferously, to clear his airways and his mind. He had kept his eye on him and monitored him carefully. Just as new mum Sandra Kerr would have done.

Hanlon had read and re-read his scribbled notes with Oat'n Nuts employees, boss man William Taunton and Yvette Evans. He remembered when he was about to take that 'one small step for man,' striving to explore further into the background of this case. How he momentarily thought, 'What's the point? Will it do any good?' He recalled the night of Lauren's death. How himself and Murray had immersed themselves in music. A line from a David Bowie track now sprung immediately to mind. It had been on his childhood sweethearts playlist that evening! With a satisfactory smile of assuagement, ADC Joseph Hanlon began to quietly and gently sing *"There's a Starman waiting in the sky. He's told us not to blow it, 'cause he knows it's all worthwhile."* Simply and without straining, he repeated those last few words again clearly and with added vigour. Holding that last note just a little longer than necessary to fully believe it.

"Because he knows it's all wo-oorth...whh-hhiii-illll-lllleeee."

Joe needed that. He felt validated and reassured. His investigative endeavours were not only important. But valuable and personally rewarding, as he would later find out. In summary he confidently concluded: That although he and his fellow officers may take a multitude of small steps individually. Collectively and unitedly is when they truly matter. And within the complex legal system, that can often equate to 'one giant leap for mankind' and justice being served.

Hanlon had not only taken those small steps. He had made significantly great strides forward in the case also. He was continually puzzled and skeptical at why, when crying out for help, Yvette Evans constantly called Mr. Taunton by his first name? Not even William, but Bill. In his mind that was like a mix tape - it was way, way too personal and intimate. She was not even the employee. She was only visiting 'big sister.' Interviewing her, he found out much more interesting and hopefully relevant information. He followed up and made further enquiries. Much of which he had just had confirmed in the last twenty minutes. He then questioned, how many others all work over New Year?

Excitedly he scanned quickly over his handwritten notes on Yvette Evans: They read as follows - Deborah's baby sister had been seduced by someone? She had only just turned 16. But had a 3 month old child. She'd had under-age sex. Did she consent? She lived in a modern, one bedroom, rented flat in Musselburgh. A 16 year old, single mum, that had no job - really? Lived with a boyfriend - unemployed - only together last eight weeks. Though according to others - more accurate would be at least 18 months. They were in High School together. She showed me bank statements. I implied I was comparing her heating bills to mine!

His scribbled notes and thoughts became even more interesting. His black ink stated...She had a monthly allowance going into her account from, wait for it, Mr William Taunton. The flat is not rented after all. It is owned by, wait for it, Mr William Taunton. The child's father that she would not name? I'd guess is Bill! Not Mr Taunton, nor William, but Bill, Bill, Bill! he had underlined three times. His next page continued - Did she approach Taunton or other way around? I believe he thought he was the child's father. He had recently changed parts of his will. I reviewed news cuttings re. Mrs Taunton's death over three decades ago. Some interesting information and theories turned up. Anxious to report these findings to the boss!

DI Murray had chosen to sit at the back corner of the open plan, modern office. On his way there earlier in the morning the Inspector had grabbed a newspaper that had lain on someone's desk. It turned out to be two days old, yet just what he needed. It contained a full list of all those who were about to receive official recognition from Her Majesty the Queen in the New

Year's Honours List. Murray intentionally studied and deliberated over the various names included and the respective fields they represented. His eyes were drawn in particular to the section entitled:

Children and Young People Care.
It stated - *There is a particular focus in this list on honouring those who help vulnerable children and young people. As a result there are damehoods (DBEs) for:*

Esther Rantzen, founder of Childline.

Joyce Plotnikoff, who has revolutionised the way the courts treat child witnesses.

Oremi Evans, headteacher of the only special school to receive three consecutive 'outstanding' Ofsted judgements.

Professor Julian Le Grand, whose review of children's social care at Doncaster Council is now driving innovative practices elsewhere, also receives a knighthood.

Among the CBEs are:
Kate Lampard: Overseer of the NHS investigation into Jimmy Saville.

Professor Bill Whyte: Architect of the Scottish Government's whole system approach to youth justice.

Virginia Beardshaw: Chief Executive of the I CAN children's charity.

Eleanor Paterson's innovative work with young offenders engaged in community reparation projects has inspired many of them to continue volunteering after they have completed their sentences. She receives the MBE.'

Alongside those names Murray noticed that there were many long-serving volunteers who worked with scouts, guides, cadets and a range of other youth organisations on the list also. After half an hour of reading and reflection, he felt rejuvenated and inspired. A gentle acceptance of the important role he and his colleagues play and the difference that they make, had returned. It was time to get back in the saddle. The exact same conclusion his so-called 'rookie' partner had reached just minutes earlier!

Hanlon approached DI Murray, excited to share his findings. With hands in the air, in a gesture signalling his superior to come closer, he spurted, "Sir, sir, I think you'll be mighty interested in what I've uncovered."

"We're heading out 'Sherlock.' Grab your coat and tell me on the way."

It may still have been a bleak New Year's winter morning outside. But the sunlight was back, however briefly, in the world of Detective Inspector Steven Murray! As they exited the building, a young constable following on from the example of his older role model, could be heard singing merrily (if rather continually off key).

"There's a Starman waiting in the sky. He's told us not to blow it, 'cause he knows it's all worthwhile."

FOURTEEN

"Sherlock Holmes without a doubt is the greatest man on Earth. He's so much more than anyone else, that nobody knows his worth. A theft can only follow him, no matter where he goes ..... The one and only Sherlock Holmes!"

- Sherlock Holmes the Musical

12 noon on New Year's Day 2015

"Mrs Dixon, sorry to disturb you, it's DI Murray and..." The large security gate opened, although no words were forthcoming from within the impressive fortress. The door was already ajar when Steven Murray arrived at it with ADC Hanlon in tow. Tentatively, they crossed the threshold to a curtly delivered greeting:

"What brings you back detective? Oh, a partner as well eh! You're becoming a real Starsky and Hutch combination." Hanlon looked at Murray rather confused. He had obviously never heard of that particular crime solving duo before.

"I'll explain later," the Inspector whispered. He then lowered his head slightly and raised his eyes. As if looking above non-existent glasses. In a scholarly, head masterly manner. He could witness Sheila Dixon now at the far end of the lengthy, well decorated corridor. She was just beyond the portrait of the scantily clad young lady on the motorcycle, 'Biker Girl.' This time, Kenny's wife seemed more Sharon Stone, than Michelle Pfeiffer. Her voice clipped, brief and to the point. Unwilling to share social niceties. He suspected there would be no 'open top bus tour' around the premises a second time.

We'll see, he thought to himself. Murray was always game for a challenge!

Already he had identified the music playing throughout the upmarket home, on the top of the range Bose stereo surround sound system. It was Elvis! Not the so-called King of Rock 'n Roll though, but Declan Patrick MacManus. Better known to all and sundry as Elvis Costello to be exact.

"It's been a good year for the…" could be heard as the lady of the house swayed and gently sang along. Sheila was formidably attired in a jungle green, 1960's iconic 'jersey dress.' It was true Mary Quant style - sleeveless, mini in length and completed with a broad hoop of brown and yellow just above the waistband. Her body was adorned with colourful costume jewellery. Including a vast collection of jingling bracelets, an Aztec designed necklace and rather unusual, but fetching earrings. The same earrings she was wearing with the Tahitian pearls. Earrings that did not complement the look then and were becoming thought provoking for Murray now.

Were they significant in some way? Did they hold a special meaning to her? He was sure they must be relevant. Women of her stature and style, colour co-ordinate and match up outfits. Hats, scarves, jewellery and accessories are not just thrown together. Murray was led to believe hundreds of man hours are put into meticulously researching the latest styles, what's in, what's out. There is no way he thought, that a pair of earrings just get placed on those lobes without any forward planning!

Finally, her hair was tied back and neatly groomed. It was strikingly reminiscent of a successful Epsom Derby winner's luscious, flowing, skirted tail. DS Ally Coulter would have been mightily impressed!

"Ma'am," Murray proffered above the music.

"Sheila," she chastised him, whilst adjusting the volume.

He countered with "Mrs Dixon." Not forcefully, for he knew that would get him nowhere, but directly. Trying to get across to Sheila D. the urgency and importance the matter carried. He repeated, "Mrs Dixon, I missed your husband last time. Now it seems fairly imperative that I get the chance to speak with him. Sooner rather than later, given the circumstances."

"What circumstances Inspector? Why didn't you mention this before?" Sheila Dixon was getting rather worked up to say the least. Her voice becoming more concerned with each passing statement. "What's happened? I have a right to know! Is he okay? Is he in danger? It's New Year. Why would you be here, even working today if it was not something exceptional?"

"I take it, he's not at home then, ma'am?" Hanlon asked boldly. Murray though, already knew the answer as soon as the pair walked up the path. His marque car was missing from the driveway. A two month old, metallic black Range Rover Evoque, complete with a silver jubilee stripe and personalised number plate, KD1 X0N. The same vehicle that was spotted parked at the bottom of Leith Walk on the very night that Anne Richmond was murdered!

Sheila Dixon had become anxious, distraught and tearful as she poured herself a drink. Possibly not her first of the day Murray guessed. She was now shaking her head with the graceful precision movement of a pendulum on a clock face. Right to left.....left to right.....right to left. Desperate to confide, wanting to share, the need to conceal, the urge to speak, conflicted emotions!

"Mrs Dixon, Sheila, do you want to add anything? Help me out here," Murray suggested.

Grappling, clearly at war with her inner turmoil and raging thoughts. This seasoned, skilful, sporting (the badminton racquets were now gone) and semi-sophisticated lady was being cautious. Extra cautious in DI Murray's eyes. His professional opinion said, involvement! What that looks like, he is still working on. Covering something up? Masking her real feelings and suppressing important information? In Murray's world he would describe this as the 'deodorant' answer. Not so much the 'Lynx' effect, but the 'Sure' sequence.

Is she hiding something? Sitting on the truth? Concealing his whereabouts? At the very least being less than helpful?

Sure as hell. Sure as can be. Sure enough and Sure thing!

Sheila Dixon sat silent and still on the beautiful sumptuous, black leather settee. The expected furniture from last week had obviously arrived in the interim. She took a costly looking pen from her bag and began to write down some notes. Murray felt the need to persuade, pressure and intrude into Sheila's comfort zone of 'poor me.'

"Love the new suite and layout Mrs D. Your dress is rather retro, very impressive but I especially admire your earrings. They would appear pretty bespoke, a unique pair I'd guess." Sheila Dixon's head shot up smartly, an unloving glare seemed to make its way across the room toward Detective Inspector Steven

Murray. He continued, "I guess they're among your favourites. I noticed you were wearing them last time I visited. I'd love to hear their story and how you came to own them."

"What's your name?" Sheila asked sternly of the officer in Murray's shadow.

"Hanlon, ma'am. Police Constable Joseph Hanlon."

"Actually, he is Acting Detective Constable Hanlon," Murray reminded him. "Mrs Dixon," he went on. "I don't disbelieve you for a minute. However, if we can just take a quick look around to verify Kenny is not at home. Then we'll be out of your hair as soon as. What do you say? Or would you prefer to tell me about the earrings first?"

Flustered and in no way willing to talk about her jewellery. She quickly offered up: "Whatever! Check for yourselves. I'm going for a five minute shower and I fully expect to be showing you out after that!"

Murray smiled and nodded in her direction. "Thank you ma'am, Sheila," he quickly corrected himself. Inwardly his thoughts were - Well done my good man, hop back on the open top bus and enjoy tour number two! As they prepared to head off in opposite directions, Murray tapping his breast pocket, reminded Joe to take notes, plenty of notes.

Whilst the power shower was blasting Mrs Dixon and she washed away the worries of the world, silence came over the airwaves. Hanlon, curious, peered into the lounge. There was DI Murray holding a recently ejected CD in his hand. Looking at 'Starsky,' he quipped, "In this day and age, with such an ultra-modern set up. Why a CD?" It was a blank disc that had the letters MR marked upon it. Mr who? Or was it meant to be for a Mrs, but the 'S' had still to be added. Put together no doubt with favourite music and artistes. What tracks he thought? Briskly, it was placed back into the machine and through the wonders of the latest technology Murray began scrolling through the playlist. Jotting, nodding, humming and hawing. Offering a thumbs up to Hanlon. The same ADC Hanlon that had disappeared 30 seconds previously!

Murray left it on shuffle and as a bit of a folk fan, recognised the enchanting voice of Cara Dillon. Before leaving, they would hear a further selection from Bon Jovi, Bobby Vinton and the Irish ballad singer Christy Moore. An eclectic mix, taste and selection to say the least......But why?

Mix tapes have a purpose. To woo the boy or girl. To impress them, to share, to let others into your world, your mindset and your believes. They stand for something, they represent, send subliminal messages and pay tribute. Laura Hanlon's Spotify playlist stood for her and Joe's journey. Their adolescent adventure from childhood, mutual love and a selection of treasured memories gathered, garnished and experienced along the way.

As he made his way into the marital bedroom to take some photographs, Bobby Vinton began singing. Murray recalled from DS Coulter's pop quiz knowledge that Vinton was called 'the all-time most successful love singer of the Rock era.' From 1962 through to 1972, Vinton had more Billboard #1 hits than any other male vocalist, including Elvis Presley and Frank Sinatra. An impressive fact. One that had been retained in the mind of DI Steven Murray to this day.

Retention would again be key, as he continued scanning various locations, including the master bedroom in haste. Interesting range of literature Murray noted. He took some photos on his phone to view more patiently later. Including one of a strange portrait that hung above the shelf on the wall at the foot of her marital bed. It was a classroom setting. It included a large light bulb hanging from the roof and was entitled 'Idea Sir'. Surreal, yet powerfully endearing Murray thought. Possibly representing that light bulb moment, that eureka feeling we all get from time to time the Inspector guessed. Everybody will interpret it differently though he thought. That is the beauty of art!

Awaiting the imminent arrival of Mrs. D from her 'cleansing' shower. Hanlon had also checked out a range of rooms, taking notes with urgency as he went.

The bathroom door could then be heard to open and Sheila Dixon returned. She was resplendent in a lavish, arctic white luxury dressing gown. She could have delicately placed herself upon a 'Fox's Glacier Mint' and not have looked out of place. 'Huggy Bear' on the other hand... not so much! Ah, you have to love 1970's television.

Sheila's gaze met Murray's and she spoke confidently. "You'll be leaving now." It was a clear instruction, rather than a question.

"Just one point to clarify ma'am," Officer 'Starsky' mentioned mildly. Hanlon was in his element. "In the small study to the left of the bathroom."

"That room should have been and would have been locked," she said adamantly.

"Apologies, Mrs Dixon, but it was open. Why would it be locked?" He asked sympathetically.

"Yes, what about it?" Sheila Dixon asked. Ignoring, the why in his question.

"There's a tank, a glass unit," he mentioned hesitatingly. "It would appear to house what? I couldn't see anything in it, apart from the obvious logs, branches and foliage."

"A glass tank," she responded scoffingly. Then added in a much relieved manner. "It is called a vivarium and it's not surprising you thought you saw nothing. They will have been hiding at the back behind the larger of the two logs."

"I've heard of an aquarium and a terrarium, but a vivarium you say Mrs Dixon. What does that mean?" DI Murray asked.

Sheila looked crestfallen, her eyes widened. She obviously had no idea.

Happy to bail her out, Murray contributed by asking, "Exactly what, would have been hiding ma'am?"

"My pair of Panther geckos. A couple of exquisite small lizards and please, she reminded him, don't call me ma'am."

"I'm guessing given your admiration for beauty, the unusual and the exotic, that they didn't come from Pet's R Us or Salamander Street in Leith? Possibly slightly further afield Sheila?"

"Funnily enough, you'd be right for once Inspector."

Now that dig was a little personal Sheila, Murray thought. A bit of bravado showing. In Murray's book, bravado normally goes well with the occasional 'slip up' or 'touch of complacency.' Today appears to be looking more promising by the minute.

"Indeed, they are from Madagascar." She stated the fact with the educated air of a High School geography teacher. Continuing with her 'lesson' she informed her two captivated students further. "They hang out in fallen leaves and other hideouts on the ground, but do have the ability to climb small walls, therefore a secure lid is necessary. I hope it was closed securely when you were in Constable? Although, how you got in....." Sheila just held the young officer's gaze.

As they said their farewells, Acting Detective Constable Hanlon felt inclined to offer confidently: "In Latin, it is literally 'a place of life.' An area for raising animals or plants, for observation or research."

Puzzled, Sheila Dixon responded dismissively with, "Sorry, pardon, what are you going on about now?"

Like a naughty schoolboy, young Joe currently found himself being hurriedly led at pace by the collar down the driveway. Mischievous to the last, Hanlon then turned back toward the fluffy white mistress on the doorstep. He shook his head in a frustration of one upmanship. Then he raised his voice one final time with assured conviction and boldly clarified. "A vivarium ma'am, sorry Sheila. I thought you'd like to know that's what it means. A place of life!" He then paused for an instant before rounding off brazenly with, "Have a nice day............. Ma'am!"

Cheeky, impertinent devil, Murray thought. 'I like this boy, he'll go far!'

Steven Murray loved the energy, eagerness and boundless enthusiasm of Joseph Hanlon. His childlike nature and determination to complete a task impressed him.

Over the years he would often encourage young protégés by asking the following question. "In the game of golf," he would begin. "There is an interesting statistic when it comes to major championships - Old golfers generally don't win them. Why is that?"

He would then remind them of some valid points - "The older golfer can normally hit the ball equally as far as the young one. He chips and putts on the green in similar fashion. And you know what? With all his relevant experience he'll probably have a better knowledge of the course. So again I ask, why does he take the extra stroke that denies him victory?"

His Detective Constables, rookies or trainee cadets nearly always shook their heads, seem bewildered and generally offer up two words. And they were - "No idea!"

With a self-satisfactory smile as broad as the Amazon A to Z logo, Murray was then delighted to step forward and offer up the answer.

Calmly, yet succinctly he would state: "Experience! It is that simple. Good old fashioned experience. Experience is the so called X-Factor. The older you get, the more cautious you become. You question and ask what happens if it all goes wrong? You are aware of the downside, you recognise the pitfalls." He would then continue. "The young player, the rising star on the other hand is nonchalant, either ignorant or reckless to caution and that without question is what gives him the edge. It's the same with all of us. An understanding, awareness and knowledge can make us play safe. It allows us to be happy in our comfort zone and settle for non-challenging, yet steady mediocrity. The true secret is to have a winning mentality. One which would encourage you to continue to be fearless, strong and forever questioning. Put simply - remain childish!"

His students and underlings would then applaud generously!

He had witnessed that successful quality in ADC Hanlon. He may in looks remind you of Rodney Trotter. But without question, he was no 'dipstick' or 'wally' and was well worthy of his newly acquired 'Sherlock' nickname!

Murray though, remained puzzled by one of the day's earlier events. A thought that he would keep to himself for now. It concerned that study door. For he had tried it also, and like the aggrieved Sheila Dixon, he was positive, nay absolutely certain - it had been locked!

Later that evening the Detective Inspector would feel like a contestant on an Oriental version of the 1970's Generation Game. Alongside Joe Hanlon, who took Bruce Forsyth's role at his side, they sat in a dimly lit and fairly deserted Chinese Restaurant in the Haymarket district of town. They shared notes, observations and the obligatory 'prawn crackers!' Then, they collectively tried to recall all they'd witnessed on the 'conveyor belt' at the Willowbrae mansion. They combined it with a game of - Through The Keyhole and "Who lived in a house like this?"

The vivarium, complete with Gecko lizards. Several pieces of distinct art - obviously by the same artist. Stationery at bedside cabinet. Those bespoke earrings. Assorted leaflets from mail shots, including the Oat'n Nuts one with a list of their various outlets. Advice flyers from the District Council. DVD boxed sets of drama, crime and mystery. Those mix cd's, badminton racquets, toothpicks and chocolates. Not forgetting the various bouquets of flowers throughout the home, graduation pictures on the wall, teas-made and of course the standard 'cuddly toy.'

With the meal paid for and both men in receipt of a complimentary mint. They began to exit the premises when an, I Fought the Law and the Law Won ringtone sounded. Murray looked surprised and quizzically at Hanlon, before uttering his familiar often used special word, "Really?" By which point Joe had answered and was now handing his 'Clash' registered mobile to his Inspector. "It's for you. It's the Doc."

The one side of the conversation Hanlon could hear went as follows: "No, that's fine, don't worry about it. It's just good to hear from you now. Sorry, a species of frog. Right okay, you sure? Wow, on their darts, yeh I get it. So not in the U.K. then? Yes, thought not. Thanks Doc. South America, yep I understand. Seriously, up to a year. I feel we're actually getting somewhere now Tom. I think I even know where to start. Thanks again. No, that's been a great help. Just send the email through and I'll get it in the morning."

Hanlon shook his head when he heard DI Murray bid farewell to the Doc with his normal mickey-take. "T'anks, t'anks again, t'at's awful t'otful of ye, goodnight!"

He handed back the phone.

"Helpful?" Joe asked.

Nodding, slowly yet assuredly. "Absolutely, absolutely." Murray repeated. "I think our jigsaw might just have changed shape Joseph. The Doc is sending his written findings through to us first thing in the morning. However, I believe we may be able to put in place our corners now. Possibly all four corners and that gives us an important and significant swing in momentum."

Hanlon added encouragingly, "With a bit of luck sir, I suspect we'll get a few straight edge pieces also."

With a satisfied look that said - We're getting there. Murray wagged his finger in ADC Hanlon's direction. Then in real teacher/pupil mode, reminded Joe, "I hope you are right young man, but remember 'Sherlock,' luck will rarely have anything to do with it!"

FIFTEEN

"Now the face that I see in my mirror, more and more is a stranger to me. More and more I can see there's a danger in becoming what I never thought I'd be. Some days are diamonds, some days are stone."

- John Denver

When Detective Inspector Steven Murray arrived at his desk early on Friday 2nd of January (7.30am to be precise), an email from the Doc was waiting for him. He could tell from its time sent, that Tom Patterson had obviously stayed up late especially to have the report finished. This would enable Murray and his officers to make good use of it as soon as possible. On further reading it was no surprise that the Doc felt encouraged by his findings. As Murray duly went to print two copies, ADC Hanlon arrived right on cue. Joe was determined to help fill in the blanks and join up the dots, based upon the shortened one-sided version Patterson had given DI Murray verbally during their phone conversation the previous evening.

The Doc stated that they were dealing with an extremely dangerous toxin found in regions of South America, Colombia especially. It is a Batrachotoxin and primarily it's poisons are collected from the toxic secretions of frogs from the Dendrobatidae family. Mainly throughout the years they have been used by certain Amazonian Indians. Today, still the most common use of this toxin is by the Noanamá Chocó and Emberá Chocó Indians of western Colombia for poisoning blowgun darts for use in hunting.

The Doc went on to highlight how the Golden Poison Dart frog is the culprit. It is a frog around the size of the end of your thumb. However, these lethal creatures can afford to be outrageously brightly coloured as they contain enough venom to kill ten fully grown adults.

Poison darts are prepared by the Chocó Amerindians, by first impaling a frog on a piece of wood. By some accounts, the frog is then held over or roasted alive on a fire until it cries in pain. Bubbles of poison form as the frog's skin begins to blister. The dart tips are prepared by touching them to the toxin, or the toxin can be caught in a container and allowed to ferment. Poison darts made from either fresh or fermented batrachotoxin are enough to drop monkeys and birds in their tracks. Nerve paralysis is almost instantaneous.

Other accounts say that a stick siurukida (bamboo tooth) is put through the mouth of the frog and passed out through one of its hind legs. This causes the frog to perspire profusely on its back, which in turn becomes covered with a white froth. The darts are then dipped or rolled in the froth, preserving their lethal power for up to a year.

Given our nature, I imagine a few of these darts have ended up finding a human target with lethal effect. That would certainly seem to be the case currently. I can confirm that all of the following died directly or indirectly - poisoned by the Batrachotoxin: Penelope

Cooke, Annabel Richmond, Elizabeth Moore, Deborah Evans, James Evans & Lynnette Lithgow. It was signed, Doctor Thomas Patterson.

The Murray brain was now swirling with questions, thoughts, ideas and conjecture. Queries, proposals, recourse, demands and appeals. He was looking to debate, urge, argue, talk about and reason. Today Detective Inspector Steven Murray had decided was a day for mind games. Those frontal lobes were about to endure a marathon workout!

For the next twenty-four hours, he and his team had to peel back the veneer and explore a bit further. Give the third degree to some of the bland answers and written statements that they currently were in possession of. For Murray in particular, he had to challenge his colleagues, stretch them, ask that little bit more of them as they continued their learning curve under his impressive tutelage!

As it was still only the 2nd of the month and an official Bank Holiday in Scotland. A few more officers than normal were still off enjoying the festive season or described more accurately -Recuperating!

Nonetheless, Murray had plenty avenues to be checked. He must have given out easily over one hundred small facts and figures to be probed further. Statements that needed analyzed and scrutinized more thoroughly, with all the i's dotted and t's crossed. *"It's the simple things that make it all worthwhile,"* he exclaimed tunefully, ensuring a few heads turned in his direction.

"What? What? It's a song!" Murray argued, shrugging off their puzzled stares with a dismissive wave of his hand. He then quickly got dialling to hand out another round of imperative assignments. Everyone needing completed. Asap!

A fly on the wall would have been privy to:

"Elizabeth Moore, yes, all that was bagged at the scene, let me know as soon as, great, thanks."

"That's right, find out where he was staying on the Inner Hebrides."

"All the dates for the official store openings, correct."

"Full date and place of birth for ... Yes, full background details that's right, thank you."

An intriguingly interesting call Murray then made was to one of his 'Wild West' pairing, Curry and Hayes. He spoke only briefly with DC Susan Hayes, confirming that both herself and Drew Curry were back on duty next day.

"Susan, I need you to get young Tommy Wendel."

"Tom Wendel from the MLA?" she interrupted.

"Absolutely, the very one. Tell him Murray needs a favour returned. Have him on standby at a minutes notice. Although I suspect Tuesday, mid-afternoon, will be the likely strike time. Here is where I need him to be and this is what I require."

So Murray continued on from early evening until easily eight or eight-thirty that night with questions, questions and more questions! Taunton imports what? Dates? Pure Gym membership from when? Where are Capital florists located? What is the jewellery connection? MR CD? Estate agent details, etc, etc, etc.

"Get yourself home Steve," he heard himself say. It was now happily approaching the time for him to take on board that counsel. He was contented. It had been an extremely productive start to the New Year. Major strides had been taken that day.

Next day - Sat. Jan. 3rd
- *How does the weather impact your day?*

If you awake to lovely sunshine -

An early morning shower. Whistling, singing and dozens of small chores dealt with before lunch. A drive to enjoy the pleasure of motoring. A spring in your step for the rest of the day. Invitations to friends to pop over for a drink or a chat. Random decisions taken on a whim. The garden looks inviting, even weeding may appeal. Or to sit out and simply enjoy the warm rays as you rest, relax and reflect upon what you've been blessed with.

If you awaken to grey skies overhead however -

Stay in bed, no energy nor enthusiasm to achieve anything. Put on the clothes of yesterday, make your excuses and return to the comfort of the duvet. Knocks at the door go unheeded. Phone calls beep straight to the answering machine. This is your own private world. No one else is allowed in. Nothing is achieved. TV, computer, gadgets and tablets lie abandoned. You've no desire through social media to witness the wonderful holidays and events of others. Envy, jealousy, grudging ill will and malice are commonplace on these days. They need no help from the Facebook brigade. Retirement, old age, a life wasted, melancholia returns. Thelma and Louise are never far away as constant hitchhikers in your revolving thoughts. Always willing others to succeed, believing it is too late now for you.

But then you have to consider, what does success look like? You struggle to recognise it in your life. Contentment, a word you've not known for many, many years. Mail sits behind the doorway, dishes by the sink. Outside noise is all that gets into your fortress for the day. Birdsong, traffic, random shouts and aircraft overhead.

Maybe it lasts fractionally less than half the day. Would that be considered a success! Tears, memories, more tears, a tender heart, a shaking hand, nerves and even more tears. A hug, a cuddle, the reassuring touch of another. You are a natural romantic, but love and the feelings of love, left for pastures new a long, long time ago. Your heart is like an immigrant on a foreign shore searching for answers. Still seeking with a deep yearning to be understood and accepted.

It is late in the afternoon, having just turned 3.20pm. A toilet break is required. Pick up your 7 day a week personal assistant - your phone! It deals with your mail, answers your calls, takes photos, schedules your appointments, makes your tea, does the dishes, hoovers up, fills the car with fuel - No, wait the car is now charging in the living room, aahh modern technology!

A mobile phone, it's most important function for Murray? His music. So at 3.22pm arriving on cue are Edward Sharpe and his Magnetic Zeros!

"Alabama, Arkansas, I do love my Ma and Pa - Not the way that I do love you. Well, holy moly me oh my, you're the apple of my eye - Girl, I've never loved one like you. Home, let me come home - Home is wherever I'm with you. Home, let me come home - Home is wherever I'm with you."

It would appear this may be success after all. Only a half day, a pilot episode?
An episode that will remain private and go unaired to the majority of viewers.
A 'Groundhog Day' episode. One that will repeat and repeat and repeat!

It would appear this may be success after all. Only a half day, a pilot episode?

An episode that will remain private and go unaired to the majority of viewers.

A 'Groundhog Day' episode. One that will repeat and repeat and repeat!

It would appear this may be success after all. Only a half day, a pilot episode?

An episode that will remain private and go unaired to the majority of viewers.

A 'Groundhog Day' episode. One that will repeat and repeat and repeat!

The star of Groundhog Day was American actor Bill Murray (No relation).

The star of today - Detective Inspector Steven Murray.

Washed, dressed and reporting for duty, and it's only 3.57pm!

Murray realised that part of his Saturday morning endogenous depression and inability to rise and face the world, would have stemmed from the previous night's euphoria. He was now on a downer. His Friday evening fired up frenzy of phone call assignments, exploratory duties and mini missions had taken its toll. By the end of his eighteen hour shift he had left feeling quietly confident. That confidence he now questioned, but quickly reassured himself and divided it into 5 levels. Firstly, he was HOPEFUL that things were moving in a positive trajectory. Secondly he was SATISFIED that they were beginning to ask the right questions. Thirdly, he was POSITIVE that they had discovered a link or two. Added to all of those, he was now for the first time genuinely CONVINCED they were hot on the heels of the killer or killers. So much so, this reformed gambler would have willingly put a bet on conclusion of business coming about within the week. (The final

thought he decided to keep to himself a little bit longer)

Today though, it was to be the Inspector's New Year celebration. Timeout to ponder on his findings from last night. Listen to some of his favourite sounds and spend time with a little belated Christmas treat that he had gifted to himself.

First things first. He drove over to the office to pick up a few bits and pieces, gather up some notes and check if any other calls had been returned or new information gleaned. That was standard in a day off in the life of Detective Inspector Steven Murray. After a quick snack of toast with tuna, ketchup and onion all mixed together, he settled down and relaxed in his sitting room. DI Murray then exhaled gently, sat back slowly and smiled a smile of personal satisfaction at his most recent Festive purchase. A purchase he had earlier in the day managed to hang admirably from the wall above his fireplace. It was a good-sized portrait of a couple embracing. It was art. Art was subjective.

These images spoke of love to Steven Murray. Good old-fashioned love. An expression of caring and kindness. It spoke to him of generosity, of the fragility of life and the unexpected paths we may choose to travel.

The large canvas depicted an older, grandmotherly figure receiving a gentle, grateful hug from a young, tall, blonde female at her garden gate. Next to the gate you could just about make out a small, numbered plaque. Upon the plaque was a date - 1877. It had no official name when he purchased it, but he'd already entitled it: 'The Lady and the Angel.' It had been signed delicately in the corner by the artist, CCC.

SIXTEEN

"Let go of the little distractions - Hold close to the ones that you love. Cause we won't all be here this time next year, so while you can, take a picture of us."

- Frank Turner

Across town that Saturday morning, the local postman had made his way briskly across the yard. It was a typical winter sunrise in the east of Scotland, as in, it didn't bother. It remained dark, dull, overcast and without cloud. Scotland's local God of weather 'Noah Gain,' had managed with several extraordinary sweeping brush strokes to cover the City skyline in a definitive blanket of grey emulsion! The man was without doubt a hero in the annals of folk lore. An artistic genius, with the ability to make everyone in the Nation miserable with one magical wave of his mythical weather wand!

No visible rain permeated the air, but there was a highly effective downpour of drizzle. One that ensured by the end of this particular postie's route, he would be completely 'droochit!' In local terminology it would have been described as 'smirry, damp and dreicht.'

Repeatedly for the next twenty-four hours his name, those famed immortal words, would be revered and synonymous with describing the weather throughout the City - 'Noah Gain?'

Jocky Black had worked for Royal Mail for fifteen years and had been on the Portobello round for the last six. He breezed into the Dock Green offices and although drenched and soaking wet, gave Kenny Dixon a bright, cheery, "Good morning Mr Dixon."

"Morning Jocky," Dixon responded curtly without looking up. KD was anxious, he seemed cagey. Fingers tapping the desk, drawers opening and closing. Either looking for something specific or no idea what he was doing and simply try to occupy his body, as his mind tried to take stock and figure things out.

The postal worker handed him the usual bundle of mail. As per norm it would consist of an assortment of statements, invoices and official documentation. Paperwork that would need to be filed, collated and monitored. His accountant arrived weekly and efficiently kept all the books accurate and up to date. Elsewhere in the delivery would be the Dear Householder, special offers and advertising literature and leaflets. Today however, one particular item stood out. In this day and age of texting and email, it's not often you get private mail. The address on the cream envelope had been handwritten with a black fountain pen. As Dixon turned the package over, prominently stamped on the back was the very familiar and recognisable 'Oat'n Nuts' logo.

The brand had grown tenfold in recent years. It was everywhere, radio jingles, TV commercials and newspaper adverts. Throughout the land there was a major push to 'Become A Serial Killer,' and put away as many of those 'bad boys,' as you possibly could!

Kenny realised it felt heavier than a normal letter that size. Photographs he thought. The centre of the envelope had been damaged. A sharp object, possibly the edge of a postcard booklet had been looking for an escape route. Dixon ripped it open from that point in the middle and in hindsight that was to prove to be a very wise move.

As he tore, sure enough out they poured. About eight and then ten. Maybe even a collection of around a dozen or more. The tough gangland boss instantly threw his fingers up and open, dropping the item and its contents onto his desk. He sat back, alarmed and concerned at what lay before him. Staring at the mixture of mainly black and white Polaroid snaps. He began to feel nauseous, not fully able to understand the images. They included vintage concertina postcard booklets - one of the Inner Hebrides, another capturing beautiful images of the Borders. Catching his eye immediately was the only single high resolution coloured image. It was an enhanced digital photo of the portrait that hung above his marital bed!

Kenny Dixon with the caprice of a despotic king, alternated between kindness and cruelty in his normal daily life. Ordinarily he set the rules, knew the agreed plan and was fully in charge. So now, who dared mess with him? Or for that matter, would even make him part of their warped game without his consent?

Even street hardened toughened criminals become anxious, fearful and scared from time to time. This was one of those times! Someone had dared break into his home. And these were no ordinary premises. He lived in a modern day Fort Knox!

Who, he quickly questioned in his mind, had the capabilities to bypass all his security? Knew that he would be out? Where this particular piece of art was located? His mind was drowning. He found himself immersed in a multitude of questions, theories, and conjecture. He was struggling to come up for air. A new wave of revulsion and uneasiness was about to engulf him. Yet in reality he sat motionless, feet still, hands clasped fearfully to the desk and rooted to his seat.

Why send this collection to him? He had no idea who these people were or interest in what he initially thought was child pornography. Semi clad females, one younger than ten, the other in or around her late teens were cavorting around with a middle aged man. Dixon, even with his stream of massage parlours and escort girls, began to feel extremely uneasy simply by having these images in his possession!

He had to persevere though, this was a message. A sick, wayward and perverse message, but a point was being made. A cryptic communique, a veiled dispatch. Were they aware Dixon liked his puzzles? That he'd become renowned in prison for his ability to solve the most complex of teasers? He began to move his hands toward the assortment of memorabilia scattered upon his desk. Looking for clues he stirred the photographs, flicked at them as if each tender edge was burning hot. Again the man in the suit posed, this time with the younger girl sitting on his lap. She wore underwear and nothing else. He on the other hand, offered an insincere smile as he cuddled her underneath a sign that stated Manager's Special! There were only ever two people in a picture at any given time. The third person obviously the one taking the grainy Polaroid snap. Also in the envelope, Dixon came across photocopied journal entries filled with dates, times, years and ages. He glanced at them briefly, running his index finger along each line.

Revisiting the image that captured the portrait hung above his bed, he turned it over. Attached was a yellow post-it label. Written on it: *Near a tree by a river, there's a hole in the ground. Where an old man of Aran goes around and around. And his mind is a beacon, in the veil of the night. For a strange kind of fashion, there's a wrong and a right. But he'll never, never fight over you.'*

This had become personal, very personal. It was a deliberate puzzle - It required HIM to figure it out, why? They'd got past his ultra-modern security guarding his home - Someone close to him, in his core group. Who would it be?

The words on the post-it note were from a 1984 Nik Kershaw song entitled 'The Riddle.' Nik Kershaw was Dixon's favourite musician growing up in the eighties - Who would have known? This is no coincidence. It could only be a small elite few! However, James 'Bunny' Reid would be a common denominator.

Flipping it back over, he considered the glossy image carefully. It had a schoolteacher standing out at the front of his class. Unusually, it also had an old Grandfather clock in the corner of the classroom. Possibly set in the 1960's with about twenty pupils all sitting at their desks. We are looking at the back of their heads as they face the front and a speech bubble appears like a lightbulb, from the mouth of one young lad at the back of the class. The boy is raising his hand, as if to ask or answer a question and the words he offered were: 'Idea Sir.'

That's it - classroom - teacher - pupil - idea sir. That is what he had to go on!

Dixon peered again at the photo with the man in a suit. He pondered it, as if to question - do I know him? What age does he appear here? How would he look now? There is something vaguely familiar about him. The latest poor quality print he held had been enlarged. The older man no longer had on a suit. He wore a small pair of shorts and that same no-good, creepy arrogant smile. He appeared to be standing behind the young pubescent girl, softly massaging her shoulders. With his long narrow fingers he reached down east and west on the front of her soft, slender pale neck. He brought his eyes closer to the photograph, as if trying to magnify the image. He bit on his bottom lip as he strained to focus, concentrating his attention at the end of the man's fingers. KD let out a gasp! Then, suddenly, the light bulb switched on!

He saw it! He got it! 'Idea Sir!' He knew what it meant, who it was and what he had to do!

Wait, that also meant - He examined the ripped up envelope again - Oat'n Nuts logo - TV - their boss - newspaper adverts - the owner - glanced back at the photos - where were they taken? - concertina postcards - it was him - inside their stores - suggestive snaps - snuggling into both girls - "What the…" Dixon exclaimed. "No it couldn't be," he snorted. He looked at the enlarged image one final time to be absolutely certain. It was! "No! No! No!" he screamed, banging furiously on the desk. Displacing several items of the photographic puzzle to the floor.

His churning stomach soon moved to pangs of upset, bewilderment and loss. That quickly then made way for frustration and anger. An intense anger that was sliding sinisterly close into revenge territory.

Amongst the scattered debris, Dixon picked up a computer printed letter. It offered no initial clue with regards to the sender. But the need to settle the score was now paramount. Not about to hang off or think about things rationally, KD's emotional fire had been stoked. His flames were getting aggressively higher and higher. He now had one heck of an 'Idea Sir' and was set to action it - immediately!

Parking several streets away from his luxury home, Kenneth Dixon was extra careful to avoid any plainclothes police or unmarked patrol cars that had been assigned to his property. He entered via an electronic back gateway. A path not visible from the roadside and unless you knew of its existence, it would generally be overlooked.

Sheila Dixon was out on the town with friends. It was the final night of Roald Dahl's BFG at the Royal Lyceum Theatre in the City. The RLT sits in the shadow of the grand Usher Hall, which with a capacity of over 2,200 can hold three times that of its smaller neighbour!

With his anger subsiding only slightly, Dixon made straight for the main bedroom. He was careful not to switch on any lights. Entering his room, Kenny was glad to see that Sheila had already closed all the blinds and curtains and had left the small bedside cabinet light on. No need then for KD to fumble around awkwardly in the dark. He carefully moved up onto the bed and after taking two small steps on the floral quilt cover, he rested his knees gently against the padded headrest. Directly in front of him - 'Idea Sir.' He gripped a hand on either side of the framed picture and began to lift. With caution, he gently placed the medium sized canvas further back on the bed, revealing on the wall behind it - a standard sixteen litre Firestar Safe!

Many years ago, during his stint in Barlinnie, KD had learned yet another impressive craft, the art of safecracking. In three decades however modern technology had now taken over. Four numbers were still needed, but rather than listen to the turn of a wheel, digital selections were required.

It was all there, he knew that. Whoever had sent him the envelope knew of his abilities. They were relying on his strengths, skills and strong points. He had learned much over the years, mainly in the Edinburgh underworld. He'd had role models, mentors, teachers, guardians and ... wait. 'Whoa there,' he thought. Back up, take a step back, repeat, revise what you just said. Role models? - No! Mentors? - No! Teachers? Mmm, that was it, that was precisely it - A teacher!

A teacher in the classroom. A classroom with a Grandfather clock in it. Who had an antique clock in their Maths class? He now stared at the artwork signed by CCC, the same artist that had completed 'Biker Girl.' An artist that Kenny Dixon was now the prime suspect in murdering! He could just make out the time on the clock as eleven thirty. He began to enter the numbers. Beep, beep, beep and beep, the light stayed at red. An audible "Aaagh," shot from Kenny Dixon's mouth. Discouraged, yet possibly too straight forward he thought to himself. He then caught a glimpse of the digital alarm clock on the bedside cabinet at Sheila Dixon's side of the bed. It displayed 20:34. Nearly twenty five minutes to nine. He typed in 11.30 again. This time as 2 beep; 3 beep; 3 beep; the twenty four hour clock, he should have figured that out initially; and 0 beep. The red light then immediately.......stayed the same! "What, no, yer having a laugh," Dixon exclaimed. "It had to be…" He broke off, sighing. He shook his head, swore to himself. The combination of frustration, disgust and anger were not an ideal mix. He had to remain calm and somewhat focused. They, whoever they may be? They had faith and confidence in him. They had put their trust in him that he would solve this, that he'd figure out the combination given time. He lacked patience though. Again he racked his mind. He had served his time. Time was of the essence. Given time. It was all still at the forefront of his mind.........time, time, time, time, time!

He looked again at the photo. A clock on the wall, maybe? A grandfather clock in the class - Never! Time these days - Look at your phone or studying the picture even more intensely, he paused and then began to nod his head and laugh under his breath. It became a 'it was right in front of me all <u>this time</u>,' laugh. Lips together, shaking his head in knowing disbelief!

He quickly pressed in four digits. Beep, beep, beep, beep and then. - green, green, green, green. We have lift off!

The small door opened and there in front of him, alongside several video cassettes and another selection of no doubt seedy photographs lay three small, well used journals. Or as the CCC masterpiece had indicated all along with a blatant anagram, a range of 'Diaries.' The boy in the portrait, with the wristwatch set helpfully at 10.20 had continually questioned 'Idea sir?'

Dixon had always known that Sheila had kept a safe there. He'd respected her privacy though and had never tried to access it previously. He had guessed that she used it mainly for her keeping cash for her occasional lavish spending sprees!

Today though, someone wanted him to know exactly what was in it. To expressly know of her past, her secrets, her previous life. Everything that she had never spoken to KD about, was now there waiting for him to explore!

At the back of the safe was a small box with a jeweller's name on it. A short note sat under the classic black leather case, it stated briefly: 'I knew you'd work it out. Read, watch and return for safekeeping. Luv U.' xxx.'

"Wait, what, it was, no it can't be, it must have been, of course it was. Sheila, my Sheila, it was Sheila," Dixon said, baffled. Why?

Suddenly though, it all made sense. She had access to everything. Knew Kenny's capabilities and determined attitude and mindset. In that moment he now needed further answers though. What was all this in aid of? What did she require of him? Obviously something she could not ask him face to face?

As Kenny Dixon opened the box - the surprises continued. It did not hold a ring, as one would have thought. Instead, it contained a gold foil-wrapped sweet! Cool as you like, Sheila had left her partner of over thirty years, her last ROLO!

Dixon never expected that. He smiled, closed it over and placed it into his jacket pocket.

After he'd read through the bulk of the diaries, disgustedly forced himself to look at the pictures and endured brief snippets of video footage, he was on the move again. But not before returning everything back into the safe as he had been instructed. (Maybe Sheila Dixon had always been the one running the show, all these years. The real power behind the throne)

He now knew what was required to be deserving of that prized chocolate. His postal delivery from earlier in the day would be sufficient proof for his upcoming confrontation.

Close approaching ten o'clock in the evening, he headed at haste straight for Rose Lodge on the outskirts of Dalkeith. His ultimate destination, the home and dwelling place of the estate owner. A certain Mr William Taunton.

Within half an hour, a gleaming Black Land Rover Evoque with personalised number plates had pulled up at the edge of the forty-three acre Northcroft Estate. An impressive thirty foot stone turret sat either side of the gated entrance, connected majestically to the surrounding perimeter wall. The driver's window lowered smoothly. Then with accuracy and precision an arm reached out to press the intercom. Only a few seconds passed before Kenny Dixon felt the urgency to try again.

"Okay, okay, give a fellow a chance to get up from his seat," the agitated, but polite tones of William Taunton asserted. Followed by a slightly more forthright, "Who is it and what do you want at this time of evening?"

With a slight variation to his normal coarse Ardrossan accent, Dixon went for a rather more upmarket Ayrshire brogue. A mixture of Prestwick meets Morningside!

"It is Detective Sergeant Dixon here sir, I need to speak to you rather urgently."

"At this time of night Sergeant?"

"I have it on good authority that your life may well be in danger sir, can you let me in please."

"In danger! What? My life? Me! What? Are you sure? Oh, of course!"

The electronic gates between the twin towers began to open.

'My precious, my precious,' that was all Taunton was worried about. His own precious life. A self-serving, selfish coward he had always been throughout his adult years and would continue to be - for the short time he had left!

But 'Kenneth' Dixon, Edinburgh's underworld 'Kingpin' was about to discover so much more. More than he could have ever imagined!

Cruising gently up the large impressive stone driveway, Dixon noticed a small brick outhouse just about 100 metres from the main building. He had 'clocked it,' on the way in, taken a mental note and thought to himself 'that will do just fine I suspect.'

The newly qualified detective arrived with no colleague at the front door. As it opened a well-dressed

William Taunton frowned curiously and looked Dixon up and down with disdain. He was in his familiar boots, jeans, t-shirt and bling!

"You don't look anything like a policeman."

"What does a policeman look like, SIR?" He emphasised.

"Let me see your I.D." Taunton said abruptly.

"You want to see my credentials."

"Right now, show me your.....aaaghhh." Taunton coughed and spluttered, doubled over in agony. A swift kick to the groin will do that to you he discovered!

"That is by way of an introduction," Dixon spat out harshly. "And you know I think you may well be right. I don't look anything like a policeman. I am much more of a serial killer with an S. None of your poxy 'cereal' killer with a C advertising crap! However Taunton, you most certainly measure up to the description of one sick looking, perverted, warped paedophile."

Gasping for breath, but feeling grossly insulted, Bill Taunton began to muster a defence. "Let me tell y......"

It was short lived. KD lashed out with his sturdy leather cowboy boots once again. This time probably breaking the jaw of the Oat'n Nuts founder and most certainly rendering him unconscious.

SEVENTEEN

"Hello darkness, my old friend, I've come to talk with you again. Because a vision softly creeping, left its seeds while I was sleeping. And the vision that was planted in my brain, still remains - Within the sound of silence."

- Simon and Garfunkel

Often DI Murray would be seen in attendance at church on a Sunday morning. It was important that he be rejuvenated. He went to have his batteries recharged and to gain spiritual nourishment to face the week ahead. His smiling face and positive demeanour were both missing from his local congregation today however. The churchgoing congregation had become less and less as the months went on. The Inspector had his own thoughts and views on the reason why. Steven Murray no longer held a certain title or occupied a position within the church hierarchy. Like the police force in recent years, that seemed to make all his invaluable experience on the street, the wisdom accrued and any talent or ability to get things done...wholly redundant and irrelevant! It was crazy, he now counted for very little. If truth be told, not even that much!

These past seven days along with their demands had certainly taken their toll. His alarm clock had gone off over four hours ago. In less than twenty minutes it would be midday and the body of the tall west coaster was still to stir. In the words of The Small Faces classic, he was possibly about to enjoy a *'Lazy Sunday Afternoon.'* Not quite though. He'd been wide awake for easily an hour, but chose to lie still on his back reviewing the past week. He could picture it all on the dated artexed ceiling above his head. He'd already asked Mrs Jones *'how her Bert's lumbago was?'* He knew he'd *'no mind to worry,'* and thought about how easy it would be to *'just close his eyes and drift away.....'*

For the past 45 minutes he'd been busy watching the 3D version in his mind. Some of the edited highlights included - Chocolate Chip Cookies at the Botanic Gardens; Dixon of Dock Green with his motley crew - James 'Bunny' Reid and the folk duo Forrester and Allan. Also making fleeting appearances were Dixon's film star wife Sheila, who alternated her look between that of Michelle Pfeiffer, Sharon Stone and girl next door Helen Hunt. His private screening continued with the sad death of Lauren Hanlon; Health shop blazes; A Leith Walk murder; His own inner demons, plus the still, cold, lifeless body of young baby James. All of which were played in High Definition Technicolour, with Dolby Stereo Surround Sound upon the 1970's ceiling coating!

His mobile began to sound as it sat perched on his chest. At times like this, thank goodness for that ringtone Murray thought. Not very familiar, but most suitable for a police officer - it was S.O.S by Take That. It's lyrics include: *'Save our souls we're splitting atoms, go tell Eve and go tell Adam. Liberate your sons and daughters, some are gods and some are monsters!'*

Even when choosing between the police and the criminals, it can often be difficult to tell who is a God and who is a monster!

"Hello," Murray answered brusquely.

Slightly put off by his tone. DC 'Hanna' Hayes spoke nervously at first. As if she had just interrupted her boss during Sunday lunch. "Sor...sorry to bother you sir, I was…."

"Hayes, 'Hanna' is that you? No, no, don't be silly, I apologise, it was me that was out of line. I was…… anyway never mind that. What have you got that you deemed important enough to disturb my Sunday lunch?"

Hayes was now totally bemused and unsure!

"Just kidding 'Hanna.' What is it?"

Finally at ease, she mentioned, "Sir, you might want to join the Kid and I down at Dock Green Security right away. We may just have stumbled across something important." Instantly feeling that may have sounded slightly arrogant, Hayes added, "or not."

"I'll see you both in about twenty minutes or so." Murray slid out of bed and set about achieving one of his five minute wash, dry and dress sessions! He began on his way to the bathroom by belting out - "*Home, let me come home - Home is wherever I'm with you. Home, let me come home - Home is wherever I'm with you.*"

A strong vibrant noon day sun had begun to filter in through the curtains at the Rose Lodge cottage on the Northcroft Estate in Dalkeith.

The octogenarian's vision was blurry and bloodied as he attempted for a second time to open his eyes. Only one would respond. His left eye had swollen to make that side of his face unrecognisable. It looked like they'd placed Mount Kilimanjaro on the flat sands of the Sahara. He could still feel warm drops of his blood

188

move slowly across his brow. As he lay helpless on his right hand side, it flowed from its highest point at the top of his forehead, scaled the Tanzanian ridge, then began its steady descent across the bridge of his nose (which could well be broken) swept below his right eye socket and dropped with gentle aplomb onto the light beige linoleum flooring.

His once elegant cream chinos were now covered in a Burger King triple 'Whopper' combination of Blood - Grime and Dirt! He did notice surprisingly however, that his fifteen year old brown moccasin slippers had managed somehow to remain on his feet!

Linoleum flooring, lino, where was he? How long had he been unconscious? Why had this bogus policeman brought him here? What did he want and what was he prepared to do to get it? Finally, once again he wondered where he could be?

He found lying on his side awkward, painful and uncomfortable. Unsuccessfully he tried to turn his head. The pain was excruciating. If his jaw was not broken, it was at least fractured. Speaking up to plead his innocence was going to be nigh impossible, never mind wholly untrue!

From one good eye, he could see the side view of two impressive cowboy boots. Possibly they'd be even more impressive he thought, if they had not just previously tried to kick him into next week! Painful or not, he managed to get out: "Who ar'ye? What ye wan?" It was a little bit like listening to a Gaelic speaker attempting Chinese! "Whoye? Whayewan."

Dixon laughed arrogantly, with a deep, bitter resentment. He was filled with hostility and a currently restrained hatred! "You and I are going to take our time to get to know one another, don't worry about that Mr Taunton. By the time I'm finished with you, you'll never forget WHO I am, or WHAT I want! I wish I had never struck out at you though, sorry about that. Because it's going to make it just a tad more difficult to converse, or certainly at least it will for you!"

Taunton grunted, moaned or uttered some sort of verbal retort.

"I know, you're right," Kenneth Dixon said cracking his fingers slowly one at a time. "It is going to be another exceptionally long, long day!"

Dixon dragged Taunton up onto his feet and then manhandled him roughly into a nearby wooden chair. It was one of a quartet that sat around the frame of the tiny, circular kitchen table. An old, half full box of assorted Oat'n Nut cereal bars lay neglected on the table gathering stoor. Leftover perhaps from possibly a previous workman's visit? The multi-millionaire had just figured out where he was. It reassured him that he had not been unconscious for long. They were just over a two minute walk from his front door. This was the old disused outhouse that Dixon had driven past on his way up to the lodge. They had only stopped using it in the last six months. It was awaiting redevelopment. It was soon to become a guest apartment. At present the facilities were not up to William Taunton's normal acceptable standards!

"My anger may have gone Mr Taunton. But the malice and ill feelings I harbour toward you are still very much alive and will manifest themselves undoubtedly, as the night drags on. Manifest," he repeated. "There's a good word for you to mull over." His vocabulary had certainly benefitted from his time in prison all those years previous. He paused briefly before asking his guest, "Do you even have the slightest idea of who I am?"

Taunton tried to save himself pain. He slowly and cautiously shook his head.

"You've seriously no idea?"

It came out as "No iddy." But Dixon got the gist of it. Kenny then stood up and walked over to the old stove on the far side of the room. He lifted a carrier bag that had been placed at the side of the oven. Back at Taunton's side he emptied the contents of the bag across the surface of the small table. He then scattered the photographs, postcards and numerous pages of diary writings, that had been handed to him by Jocky Black early that previous morning.

Like a house of cards about to come tumbling down and possibly fearful of Dixon's temperament, several of the items made a bid for cover. Hurtling from the varnished table top to seek safety and refuge underneath.

At this junction, Bill Taunton may have been wishing he could have escaped Dixon's wrath also. However, he kept his nerve. He still had no definitive idea who this man was, what he wanted or ultimately what he was going to do to him! There was silence.

After only ten seconds, although it may have seemed liked a lifetime. The badly bruised face of the elderly gentleman made to comment - "I've no idea what all of this stuff is," he mumbled faintly.

"THIS STUFF," KD said, with his anger growing stronger by the minute, "Belongs to Sheila Dixon. It was delivered to my work and it had your company logo all over it!"

"What? Wait," Taunton's head ached, he couldn't figure this out. So this was the poisoned envelope? The one that he was supposed to seal and deal with personally?

Murray had told him in no uncertain terms that he was the target! Not his personal secretary and certainly not a baby child. He tried to recall who it had been addressed to. He couldn't remember. But he recalled it was a business, not a specified individual. Why would anyone want all this incriminating evidence to turn up at this man's company after he was supposedly dead?

Dixon had been continuing his verbal assault, "Become a Cereal Killer! I think I might just take you up on that old man."

Suddenly, the deep purple bruising that had flourished from Taunton's neck up, seemed to do a very good impersonation of pale lilac. The colour had drained at such an alarming rate from the remainder of his face that this could and should, absolutely be promoted by a paint company with the tagline: The latest bestselling shade from Dulux - new advanced, 'Scared to Death!' Available at all good stockists now!

"It's all here," Dixon stated with a look of disgust upon his face.

Taunton, barely able to speak, even if he had the desire to do so, sat wearily slumped against the chair with his eyes now both closed. Only one voluntarily.

Closing the car door, Murray waved at his colleagues as he approached the Portobello premises. "What brought you here?" the DI asked Curry curiously.

"We had been following up on those arson attacks at Oat'n Nut stores sure?"

"And you've figured out that Kenny Dixon was responsible I guess?" Murray said sarcastically.

"Not quite, but close sir," Kid Curry proffered.

"Forrester and Allan sir, his two sidekicks," 'Hanna' Hayes was delighted to chirp up.

Steve Murray confirmed slowly, "You're sure? Because that would tie in with a couple of theories I have," he added.

'Hanna' Hayes seemed to sum it up confidently. "All enquiries certainly seem to lead us to those two sir. Although we still had a few loose ends to tidy up."

"And that brought you here?"

"Exactly!" Detective Constable Curry confirmed.

Quietly, Detective Inspector Steven Murray politely asked, "And so what do you feel may be of interest or benefit to me?"

'Hanna' Hayes once again took up the story. "We came down here on the off chance that maybe one of Dixon's men might be working, hanging around or up to no good."

"The last one is no doubt correct, but just not here!" the Inspector joked.

"Quite," Hayes added. Annoyed that Murray had put her off her train of thought. She already got tongue tied enough when she was in his company. She always felt intimidated in his presence. It's something she is going to have to work extra hard to overcome.

As he saw her freeze, Curry quickly came to his partners rescue. He effortlessly took hold of the baton and continued. "When we arrived we flashed our warrant cards at our 'good pal' Charlie." Both Curry and Hayes as if well practised, waved simultaneously across the yard to the figure in the blue bonnet. Charles Wentworth was Dock Green's very own, resident silver moustached security guard! He sat resplendent in what looked like a twenty year old wooden booth. One hand nursed a hot cuppa, whilst his other attempted disastrously to return the gesture with a half rolled up cigarette between his nicotine stained fingers.

Hayes now back in full control of her words, simply went on to explain how they'd confided in Charlie that they were concerned for the safety of his boss, Mr Dixon. He then allowed them in and gave them access to his office.

"It was a mess sir," Hayes added.

"As if it had been broken into," Curry continued. "We found pieces of postcard and photographs that had been torn to shreds. Then possibly, attempts had been made to gather them all up."

"But not all successful," 'Hanna' added. "We managed to put one back together at least."

"Well done you two. You have been busy," their superior praised.

"A couple more things though sir, before we show you the blue-tacked photofit! Back over to you 'Hanna,'" Kid Curry nodded.

A sharp intake of breath to calm her down and Hayes smiled and rhetorically asked of Murray, "Where to begin?" He went to speak, but was silenced by 'Hanna' Hayes' gesture of putting her index finger instantly to her lips in a shoooooooo shh, don't you dare respond manner. Her confidence was growing. Murray grinned and gave her an encouraging wink that basically said, go on girl, you're doing great!

The female officer continued to offer up an adrenalin fuelled account of how they had found a cream coloured envelope in the bin addressed to DG Securities. They took a photo of it, front and back. It was then sent to Yvette Evans via phone, to clarify if this was the package that had been sent out the day on which her sister and baby son died.

Murray nodded his head several times, closed his eyes and simply asked, "And was it?"

"She got back to us barely five minutes before you arrived," Curry said. "So to put you out of your misery sir and in answer to your silent prayer, she confirmed it was definitely the same envelope."

"We never touched the seal Inspector. Thanks for asking," Hayes stated quite cheekily, before realising her error in tone. "Sorry sir, I meant it jokingly. Bad taste, apologies." All her good work up in smoke in one thoughtless remark she reckoned.

"What my senior colleague meant to say Inspector was, that we have bagged the envelope and got it ready to hand into forensics to check for poison. Added to which we located the postman who delivered the mail here yesterday morning. He confirmed it was KD himself that took delivery of it. He remembered it clearly though. Not only because of the bright Oat'n Nuts logo, but it was heavy. Felt as if it contained cards, small booklets or photographs even he said. Then, when he came back past the yard about ten minutes later, Dixon's vehicle screeched out through the gates at speed. No one has heard from him or seen him since."

"Wow," Murray said, shaking his head in positive disbelief. He reached out his hand and by his fingertips held onto the reconstructed image before him. His head seemed to noticeably and immediately retract back from the damaged snapshot.

"My oh my," Murray managed.

"Sir?" 'Hanna' Hayes enquired.

Detective Inspector Steven Murray studied and scrutinised for a few extra moments. Specifically concentrating on those long narrow fingers and especially the area they were massaging. The pretty blonde haired schoolgirl looked uncomfortable and nervous. Who wouldn't be at that age, wearing only two remnants of clothing and with a semi-naked, middle aged man hovering behind you? An early Depeche Mode song began to play in his mind, closely followed by its chilling lyrics, which on this occasion Murray poignantly articulated - *"What use is a souvenir of something we once had. When all it ever does is make me feel bad."*

His anxiety began to build. Shaking his head, he desperately tried to whitewash his senses, clear his mind, to think straight and remain focused. He knew he needed a blank canvas and clarity of thought. With a built up nervous energy, he revealed to the others, "I know this young lady. I know who she is," Murray exclaimed. "This is not good."

'Hanna' Hayes was then instructed to contact Joe Hanlon. "Get him over here straight away 'Hanna.' It's the man in the shorts we need to save."

'Hanna'bal Hayes and 'Kid' Curry just looked at each other mystified. Confused and baffled at what had just happened before their eyes.

Curry wanted to clearly establish, "It's the deviant masseur, we need to save?"

"I fear we may by now, be too late," Murray concluded.

Already dialling the number, Hayes responded in an urgent manner, "I'm on it sir."

"On second thoughts, give it here," her Inspector said, reaching out his hand.

"Hello, hello, Hanlon speaking. Is that you Hanna?" the voice asked as Murray lifted it to his ear.

"Joe, it's me," Murray began.

"How can I help sir," Hanlon asked, sensing the urgency in the voice of his gaffer.

"We need you to track down your favourite 'Bill.' Find William Taunton right away. I believe his life is in immediate danger. We may already be chasing our tails on this one Joe."

"Really sir?" Hanlon queried, "We are pretty stretched as it is."

"I know, but you'll have to take backup with you. It looks like KD may have chosen him first over Reid. Check out his home, office, factory, wherever you can think of. He may even do spot checks on a Sunday at some of his stores, who knows? Do the best you can and bring me up to speed soon. I'll work from this end trying to track down our beloved Kenny."

Back at Taunton's Northcroft Estate in Dalkeith, Dixon lifted a sealed water bottle from an opened pack of six. They had sat nearby gathering dust on the floor of the cold, grubby kitchen. Feeling an obvious need to vent further frustration and anger, he threw it violently toward some dishes and cups that rested on the draining board at one side of the sink. Smashing about six out of the ten items. He would have made a very average tenpin bowler! He then began rubbing his middle and index finger together with his thumb on both hands to indicate money, before breaking into a passionate rant, directed at someone he truly detested.

"William Taunton, successful businessman, impresario and newly knighted just a few short days ago in the New Year's Honours List. What a scoop this would be. I could make a fortune selling your real story to the tabloids. This would be a major earner for me if I were to turn over what I now know about you Sir!" he bellowed. "Rose Taunton was your wife and and she took her own life at age 33."

A flickering of a damaged eyelid was mustered by Taunton.

"Having given birth at age sixteen, was she your first? She was underage! Look at those photographs. It's you with your young bride and daughter! Many of them at your store locations obviously." As Taunton again attempted to open an eye, Dixon berated him. "Look at this!" he cried angrily, pointing out two particular snaps.

One of a naked Bill Taunton with his arm around the waist of his wife and in the other his arm around his child. It was perverse, disgusting and stomach churning in the extreme. Why? Because it had been deliberately taken underneath store advertising. The large sign at the end of the aisle which Taunton had them all position themselves under read: Buy One - Get One Free!

With that, Dixon then picked up the rather heavy claw hammer he had spotted lying on the kitchen windowsill when he entered the unused property. He swung it gracefully backward before delivering a fine forehand tennis stroke. Thus crashing the rusty aged head of the tool against the fragile tender left ankle of his house guest.

The almighty scream of blended agony and pain resounded far outwith the sheltered outpost these two opposing men found themselves in that Sunday afternoon.

Taunton continued to go in and out of consciousness. Dixon had to regularly throw water over him to revive him. This man may have been a depraved sexual predator over the years, but he was now in his early eighties. And although in good shape for his age, his body could not physically withstand much more of this sadistic treatment.

KD began to lash out, his voice level increased to a shout. In the isolated location he was more than comfortable to scream. "You ruined lives, deprived teenagers of their childhoods. Single-handedly you demolished their innocent dreams and gifted them a legacy of disheartening, fearsome nightmares." As Taunton cowered, Dixon became even more threatening and animated. Fierce, savage kicks and blows rained down at frequent intervals. "You're pure scum Taunton. You're a coward." The ironic yelling was coming from a man who made his vast fortune cowering behind the exploitation of the weak and vulnerable in our society. His outspoken angst continued. "You've left a trail of victims in your wake. Individuals who were instantly discarded. Your own family members were made to feel dirty, used and degraded. You're done Taunton! You and your grubby business empire. I'm going to finish you off well and truly, don't worry about that."

Drifting in and out, Taunton had only just figured out who his captor was. It was Sheila's partner or husband, whatever they called themselves. Bill Taunton knew this was only going to end one way. He was not going to see the next day's headlines. Although he may well be appearing in them!

Dixon continued to pontificate toward this man that he loathed. "Sheila had no idea that I knew you were helping us financially with the IVF treatment."

Bill Taunton was sitting semi-conscious. Oblivious to what Dixon was rambling on about. Helped financially? IVF? Child? What? He blacked out again as Dixon continued his narrative. "I had 'Bunny' Reid follow her on her appointment days. It must have taken a lot for her to even be in your company again. But now, nearly thirty years later, what caused all this to resurface?"

Sir William Taunton had just heard the last couple of sentences. He was trying to piece together how much or how little Kenny Dixon ACTUALLY knew. Sheila was the real sharp mind in that partnership. He had already figured that out. Was part of her problem, this all coming to a head, due to the fact that after all these years she still had gotten no credit or recognition. Kenneth Dixon's name was on the birth certificate after all. He needed and got that acknowledgment. Sheila Dixon was and still very much is, to those on the outside - KD's faithful, supportive and dutiful wife. Running the home, doing what was asked and then no doubt spending the ill-gotten gains as fast as her gangland boss of a husband could provide them!

Taunton was desirous to speak up. To better inform him and fill in the blanks. But he knew that Dixon intended to introduce him to someone later that evening. Kenny desperately wanted Taunton, to 'meet his maker.' Given the current circumstances, it certainly looked as if this introduction would be fairly imminent. Another swift and heavy kick to Taunton's gut, left the elderly man coughing up blood.

Kenny Dixon began to delve into his jacket, producing a little chocolate lampshade from his pocket. He unwrapped 'the last rolo' and flicked the scrunched up, golden foil wrapper in Taunton's direction.

Many people all around the capital that evening would sit with aged family, friends or loved ones. Caring for them, gently holding their hands, reading to them and simply being there to reassure them that they have nothing to worry about. Feeling relatively satisfied with his day's work, 'Kenneth' Dixon sat contentedly, yet inhumanely across the table from Sir William Taunton, businessman and philanthropist extraordinaire. His sole intention? To watch him suffer, bleed and die!

The Editors at the newspaper offices could begin to prepare their morning headlines!

A light frost had deposited itself in and around the streets of Edinburgh that evening. They had drawn a blank on locating William Taunton. Hanlon and a few others were still searching. In the meantime Murray had decided to head home. He found occupying his time with other distractions often helped him to centre his attention. So he added a few more lines to his latest sonnet-style poem. He always gotten a great deal of satisfaction from writing his amateur prose. As he arose and stood in his front room, reflecting on the exploits of the day. He quietly observed the fragile white crystals settle on the trees, illuminate the branches and sparkle like precious diamond dew drops on the ground below.

That brief, cherished moment of isolation was broken by the current vibration in his pocket. One that he hoped would bring good news. It had felt like a busy, industrious, yet unproductive twenty-four hours. Pop crooner Tony Christie came leaping into Murray's mind, not questioning, *'Is this the way to Amarillo?'* But because he reckoned they had been going around in circles all day. Searching the *'Avenues and Alleyways,'* facing dead ends, doubling back at roundabouts. He shook his head in frustration as he answered ADC Hanlon's late evening call.

"Tried three of his more local stores, no joy. The manager's all told us he never normally came round or popped in at the weekend. No answer at his Dalkeith Estate, although I got a number and spoke to his Estate manager. He and his family are making their way back from holiday. But he'll go in especially as soon as he returns. Which he thinks will be just before midnight tonight. He's going to check out his accommodation and let me know if there is anything unusual. How about you sir? Managed to cross swords with Dixon at all?"

"No," Murray said curtly. "Though it doesn't feel right Joe. Something has happened. I can feel it. I've tried Taunton myself three times, but no answer. Maybe things will surprise us and events will turn out differently." Wearily Steven Murray instructed young Sherlock, "Go home Joe and get some well earned rest. Catch up on your sleep and I'll see you first thing in the morning."

There was a brisk, invigorating Monday morning breeze blowing next day as Hanlon made his way into work. Murray, speaking on the telephone, signalled him over to his desk just as he replaced the landline receiver.

"There's still no sign of Dixon or Taunton. I've got people at the Dixon home. And Hayes and Curry are busy contacting all the Oat'n Nut outlets in Scotland."

"Airports?" Hanlon asked.

"Yep, we've had them covered since yesterday afternoon, as soon as those photos came to light. It's certainly not only Kenny Dixon that wants to get a hold of William Taunton, that's for sure.

Hanlon gave the impression of being at a loose end, although he knew there was plenty to be getting on with. He just wanted confirmation of what Murray saw as a priority.

"You know what Joe, let's leave the phone calls and contacting to some of the others today. You're an explorer, remember that! So get that hat back on this morning and go see what you can dig up. Speak with more people at Leith Walk; the staff at Re.Gal Property; if you can manage a catch up on my behalf with Brian Pollok in Dundee that would be great also."

"Yourself sir?"

" I suspect I'll be spending a bit of time with the dog this morning."

Joe nodded.

"After that I have an update scheduled with Chief Inspector Brown. I hope to be out by around three o'clock. We'll see what has developed by then. That sound okay?"

'Sherlock' gave a wave of his hand and muttered, "Just away to get my pick-axe!"

A busy, behind the scenes day took place. No urgent breaking news transpired throughout the day. And by four-thirty/five o'clock, shifts were finishing and surveillance teams had swopped over. The two 'outlaws' were busy driving back in rush hour traffic to the station. They had made dozens of private phone calls to the health stores local managers and to several key suppliers. They'd contacted anyone that they thought may help narrow the search, including personal visits to stores in Falkirk and West Lothian. Unsurprisingly no one had seen, heard or been in contact with their Chief Executive. Things did not look promising.

Within the hour Coulter and Hayes had returned from sitting outside KD's house all afternoon. As Ally made to sit down, his desk phone rang.

"Hello, Detective Sergeant Coulter speaking. How can I help you? Wait, wait, what? Hang on, slow down, calm yourself man. Take a breath 'Bunny.' I've no idea what you're saying. Start again, and I repeat, slowly."

After sixty-seconds or so the receiver was replaced delicately and cautiously back into its charging cradle. Coulter looked worryingly over to Taz. She just lowered her head, lifted her eyes and waited.

"That was 'Bunny' Reid," Coulter stated, with a concerned look on his face. "He's got information on those health store fires. Says there's a link to the burnt out vehicle they found at Leith Links."

"Well, send some uniforms around to visit and get the details. It doesn't require us."

"No, you don't understand Taz, he's terrified. He's in fear of his life. Believes Kenny Dixon is out to get him."

"When you say get him......"

"Silence him Taz. That's right, kill him! He wants to meet. Doctors surgery as it were, as soon as - 6 o'clock tonight.

Taylor looked at her watch. It had once belonged to her late mother. She wore it everyday as a gentle reminder and to keep her close. It was nearly a quarter after five. They had 45 minutes or so, to get a plan together, let the others know and travel through rush hour traffic to keep their scheduled 'Doctor's' appointment.

Not able to reach DI Murray, they left a voicemail. They informed another couple of officers of their vague plans. Where they were heading, rough schedule of times, etc. Although no names were mentioned, because they fully expected to be back within the next couple of hours. All going well by then, they'd have an informant in tow that would require protective custody.

As they approached the 'Doctors', it had just gone six o'clock.

DC Taylor stopped suddenly and looked up at the old hand painted sign above the door.

"What is it?" Ally Coulter asked. "We need to get a move on."

Taz, shaking her head incredulously stated slowly, "I can't believe I never clocked that last time."

She was referring to the tattoo style, animated image that immediately followed 'The DOCTOR'S' bold lettering on their overhead sign. It was that of a scantily clad nurse wrapping a leg waist high, around a cross armed bouncer. The nurse was casually preparing to inject his bare arm with a syringe!

"Wow," she exclaimed. "Talk about perfect advertising. There you have it. It does exactly what it says on the tin. Protection; Prostitution and Pharmaceuticals!"

As they headed inside, the 'Doctor's' evening surgery was buzzing. The place was heaving. Deals being done left, right and centre. For the second time as they made their way through the door, conversations paused. Heads were ducked and a few choice obscenities were proffered in their direction.

They caught Jojo the barman's eye. He nodded and gestured with his head toward the door near the back of the pub marked 'Storeroom.' Duly noted, the two detectives never altered their stride. They made their way quickly, like two 'Elmer Fudds' in search of Bugs Bunny. However, neither of this companionship had a blunderbuss with them. Unlike the pair, strategically positioned behind the door!

Whack! Thud! Down they both went. Neither a match for the butt of a shotgun.

Time passed - first one minute, then two, three, four.......it had nearly reached the five minute mark when Taz Taylor was first to stir. Gentle eye movements, slow head turns, everything seemed out of sorts. Blurred, hazy, confused and mixed up.

A voice from the shadows boomed. "So much for your Hong Kong Phooey and Bruce Lee malarkey DC Taylor."

Why he remained in the darkness, Taz couldn't understand. That voice was so distinct, clear and unmistakeable. It belonged to the so-called, 'terrified' Reid. He didn't sound very scared Taylor thought to herself. By now she was getting her bearings. Things didn't just seem mixed up......they were! Her hands and feet were bound with tape. She found herself hanging upside down. The tips of her fingers literally a few inches from the ground!

Until modern times, the slaughter of animals generally took place in a haphazard and unregulated manner in diverse places. Early maps of London show numerous stockyards in the periphery of the city, where slaughter occurred in the open air. A term used for such open-air slaughterhouses was shambles. There are streets named "The Shambles" in some English towns (e.g. Worcester, York) which got their name from having been the site on which butchers killed and prepared animals for consumption.

One would suggest that the two officers present predicament and investigation into the recent murder, could currently be described as: 'A right Shambles.'

Lord Robert Baden Powell would remind us all yet again to 'Be Prepared.' In Taylor and Coulter's case...........for what?

"Taz, Taz, you okay? I'm sorry," a voice began to mumble at her left hand side.

"Sorry! stop it," she said. "You've nothing to be sorry for. Don't you worry Sarge we'll figure this out.

Coulter though, thought differently. This was serious stuff. Determined, deliberate and dangerous actions that were being taken by James Baxter Reid. Coulters head ached. Coming around after being unconscious was never easy. This was the fourth such occasion throughout his career that he had experienced it. Awakening to view the shoes, knees and midriffs of his assailants though, that was a first!

"Never thought of you as dirty Ally." 'Bunny' Reid barked.

Coulter stayed silent, yet took on board the remark. He desperately tried to make sense of it.

"Are you nuts Reid?" Taz Taylor screamed. "What are you on about? You'll never get away with this, and what is THIS anyway?"

Reid began to tentatively approach the young female officer and came to a halt less than a foot away. He menacingly knelt down beside her. They came face to face with each other. Taylor hung like a piece of meat. Spinning slowly, identical to a small child's toy in an infant's cot. There was a definite cold chill in the air as 'Bunny' Reid opened his right palm. Large and claw like, it stretched forward and grabbed tightly on DC Taylor's loose hanging hair. Her circular motion abruptly ended.

"Guess who's invited to the party folks?" He quietly understated.

Then he suddenly stood up.

Coulter, still rotating, could just about make out that Reid was removing something substantial from his inside jacket pocket. Then, he merrily continued on his 360 degree turn, brief as it may be.

'Bunny' Reid delicately rubbed the said item, in a rather flirtatious, if not perverse way against the back of his female guest's bare calf. Lightly brushing her bare flesh with small erotic circular motions. Feeling very unladylike right now and on so many levels. The young officer was being held upside down by way of a robust, rugged and rusted meat hook. Her uniform trousers rested, creased on her muscular thighs, and layered just above her knee.

The 'Reidmeister' took a slight step back. Taz Taylor could now quite clearly and worryingly make out the pink material that had been tenderly and mildly massaging her leg. Her stomach turned and she immediately felt nauseous.

Reid spoke, "You guys set me up. The boss thinks it was me that framed him. He didn't do it you know. You're way off base on that score. Sadly though, for you two, he's out to get me now. Because in his book, someone always has to pay. I always tried to do things right by you Mr. Coulter. Thought that we knew each other. That we had a bit of an understanding you and I. Not exactly bosom buddies, but professional colleagues, as it were."

"Bunny, we've no idea what you are talking about. But you and I, an understanding? Absolutely," he agreed.

Coulter's phone sounded - Bunny looked at it and deliberated for a couple of rings. Eventually he answered it. With the liquid eloquence of a gravel voiced, Scottish 'Tom Jones,' Reid announced -

"Thought it might be you Detective Inspector. Sorry, they're both otherwise engaged at the moment. Aye that's right, they're literally hangin' out with myself for a while DI Murray. My sincere condolences on this one Steven." Reid then slowly dragged out his parting line, "But.... you.... are.... going.... to.... be.... way.... too.... late.... for.... this.... party!"

The mobile was then thrown with disdain to the ground. It was to be closely followed by Reid's thunderous and sturdy left heel. Creating yet another exciting Samsung jigsaw puzzle. One that saw pieces scatter far and wide throughout the room. Try finding those four corners!

Agitated, angry and nervous Reid continued, "All these years of doing his dirty work, protecting him, cleaning up after him, hiding the bodies! Thinking long term, that maybe, just maybe, I'd take over the reins. We can forget that, it's him or me now. It's schoolboy rules and I need to send out a clear, strong message. I can't afford any misunderstanding amongst my circle of friends as to where my allegiance lies! Co-operation and informal chit chat with the police, that just can't be happening Ally. Or more importantly, seen to be happening. No more. We're finished here. We are done my man."

DS Coulter hurriedly tried to engage, to reassure him. "Cut me down 'Bunny,' compose yourself, let's talk about it."

Like a discarded rag doll, the outside casing of the soft toy fell to the floor. No longer strengthened with its inner support. As if intended to signal the start of a fight, Reid roared, "Seconds away, round three!"

Upside down Coulter experienced the gleaming ragged edge flash past his eyelids. Like a chainsaw preparing to trim a hedgerow. Genuinely concerned for his immediate safety and deeply rattled, Coulter's words became louder and faster. "Bunny, Bunny, this would be a dreadful mistake, think about it man - I'm a police officer, it does no good harming me, I'm not involved, let me go and......."

"Shut up Coulter! Keep quiet and just listen for once," Reid bellowed furiously. He was seething, purple with rage. A destructive fury was building within him. A hostile merger of flight or fight had consumed him. He was convinced KD was coming after him. So he was on the run. Determined though, to make a stand and keep his reputation in tact with his peers. He was willing to scrap with the law and take the appropriate action. Pausing, he took a long, deep, calming breath. Still delusional, yet in a more measured tone, he stated. "I was a paratrooper once ye know. 'Utrinque Paratus' he whispered in broken Latin - 'Ready for Anything!' In the regiment, they say that when the throat is cut, the breath escapes it with a sound. A vibrant audible cadence - like the deep echoing sound of the winter wind. I've always wanted to listen out for that sound. But to hear it coming from my own neck would be ridiculous!"

Taylor became paralysed on hearing those words. She wanted to scream, to shout, to express her disgust, fury and anger. Her normal, assertive and authoritative voice muted. There was nothing, silence. He most certainly was no boy scout, and she was most certainly not prepared! Taz realized at that moment, for the first time in her life, as an individual that had taken part in numerous extreme and dangerous sports - that she was truly petrified. Fearful and afraid for the life of DS Coulter, her friend and colleague. Yet physically bound and frozen, unable to assist. Helpless tears of guilt and inevitability began to drop tenderly from her eyes.

Coulter was determined not to make it easy for his captors, but soon realised the futility in that. He was comparable to a small worm on the end of a fishing line. Wriggling frantically to survive, before being sent unceremoniously below, to certain death!

His pulse started racing alarmingly. Every tenth of a second, images of his children flashed before him. As babies, toddlers, youngsters, youth, teenagers and adults. Only two full seconds past and yet he had re-lived his time here on earth! Parents, school days, upbringing, marriage, mistakes, love and regrets. Nostrils flailing, eyes swollen, five seconds gone and emotionally drained. As his body froze, his heart pounded faster and louder than ever before. Resigned now to accepting his fate, he thought - I'm next, it ends tonight. For one final time he remembered and adjusted slightly his old familiar Scouting motto. Gone was the time for Detective Sergeant Robert 'Ally' Coulter to 'Be Prepared.' He was now at that moment, 'fully prepared' to meet his maker. To bring down the final curtain, to exit stage right and die with a degree of dignity and grace!

With a small intimate audience in attendance. The evening performance was about to begin. 'Bunny' Reid gave an emphatic cough, clearing his airways. He began once again to sing steadily yet with sinister overtones, the familiar kiddies street song. This time, with a deadly variation to the lyrics. *"Ally Bally, Ally Bally Bee, Now I bend down at the knee* (he squatted with ease between the detectives), *Greetin' scared, ye' ought tae be - Farewell tae Coulter's Candy!"*

As if switched to slow motion mode, his voice became a long drawn out drawl to the two officers. He repeated that last line one more time. Slowly elongated, it appeared as......."Fare - well.....to.....Coul - ters.....Can - dy."

He gradually turned, gently looked his victim straight in the eye and offered an evil, slow, sinister wink. Then, unflinchingly, he held the officer tightly by the hair and began to draw his razor-sharp serrated blade calmly, deliberately and callously, across the tender, delicate, pale throat - of Detective Constable Tasmin Taylor!

"Noooooo-ooo-oooooooaaaaaaggghhh!" Ally Coulter let out a mixture of anguished, uncontrollable screams. "Reeeeiiiddd, nooo, noo, no, aaaaaghhhhhhh." Painful, gut wrenching, heart breaking. Like the distant wailing of a female banshee!

The howl of the broken man reverberated throughout the room. He fell into an unconscious state. Like a mini red Bellagio fountain, blood continued to erupt and spray at regular intervals over his face. Cascading in all directions, as if in tune to the accompanying music. It rolled backward down into his nostrils, across his eyebrows and for an encore? It finished strongly and formed a modest, rustic red pool on the concrete floor between the two partners.

As if in unison, the frenzied eruptive spasm of Taylor's body began to relent and still. It synchronised perfectly with the previously persistent spurts of blood and began now to relax, slowing to a light trickle. With the room silenced, James Baxter Reid swept his flowing ponytail over his back and edged his ear up close and personal to her young female lips. "Aaahh," he rasped, whilst nodding satisfactorily. He looked contented and well pleased to hear her final acoustic echo. A constricted rhythm and strained muted sound.

Directly in front of DS Coulter, 'Bunny' Reid stood upright and bold in a final defiant vent. In his traditional, established and trademarked voice, he announced proudly and without any sign of remorse. "There she blows - The distant sound and the hallowed breeze of the deathly winter wind!

EIGHTEEN

"Heartbeat - Increasing heartbeat. You are a khaki-coloured bombardier, it's Hiroshima that you're nearing. This town ain't big enough for the both of us."

- Sparks

Having been alarmed speaking with Reid for that brief moment on the phone, Murray had immediately dispatched two groups of officers over to the 'Doctors' straight away. He and Hanlon were now also en route. By the time they'd arrived the premises had been securely sealed off. The Doctor's waiting room was now nearly empty. Familiar faces were spotted outside behind the cordon. Collars were pulled up and hands rubbed together frantically to keep warm. Many of them in T-shirts, with no apparent jacket or coat. No doubt because their outer layers will still be inside hanging over whatever seat or bench their owner was occupying before all the commotion began, and they commenced to scarper for the doorway!

"You know Joseph, half the crime committed in the past week would be solved instantly if we could huckle, (now there's a good word he thought to himself) all these short sleeved bystanders."

Hanlon, with his sheltered east coast upbringing, stared back at Murray and mouthed, "huckle?"

"Oh boy, I must be getting old. Or it is just a west coast thing."

"Both sir," Hanlon interjected.

"Aye, possibly," Murray grumped, before breaking into Glaswegian slang. "Huckled - grabbed by the fuzz, sent tae the pokey, busted by the pigs, nabbed by the filth, and arrested by the polis...... Huckled!"

The police colleagues laughed and smiled. Oblivious and unaware of how events had unfolded since the brief Murray-Reid telephone dialogue. Police were taking statements. Jojo, the barman nodded in Murray's direction. It appeared to be accompanied with a smirk or a self-satisfactory grin. That's when DI Murray began to brace himself. He then quickly considered the faces and body language of the other police in attendance. Those that had arrived ten minutes or so before himself and Hanlon, the early on scene officers that had discovered any unlawful activity. The signs were not good. Feeling heavy of heart and discouraged, he needed to find his trusted Detective Sergeant. Where was Ally?

"Sir," Hanlon yelled urgently. Murray looked up and across toward the storeroom at the back of the bar. He then caught a brief glimpse of DS Coulter, only before watching young Joseph Hanlon attempt to cover his mouth whilst throwing up.

The vomit came up looking like 'early morning porridge,' but smelling of 'Wotsits!' He resisted touching his face further with his fouled hands. As he continued to lean forward, he'd hoped that was the last of it dribbling from his lips. His inexperienced crime scene stomach however, decided to turn over - one more time.

The full story now quickly began to unfold and unravel at pace. Paramedics attended to Detective Sergeant Coulter, he was suffering badly from shock. Hayes and Curry had arrived on the scene and were soon up to speed. Three key suspects however, were gone. Forrester, Allan plus their immediate boss and Dixon's trusted, long time friend, James Baxter Reid.

Extra vigilant, careful not to contaminate the scene, the DI walked toward the pool of blood below the head of DC Taylor. With swollen eyes and continual sniffling, Murray struggled to contain himself. Though he knew he did not personally draw the knife that severed Tasmin Taylor's throat. She was in his care. She was part of his team. She was the apprentice, the novice, the trainee. She loved her job, she excelled in her role, she was a future Chief Constable in the making. That was how highly regarded this young lady was.

Murray admired her beautiful watch that dangled from her lifeless body. He reflected on it's marvellous story. It was her late mum's timepiece. The mother, like all mothers, who had only 'great expectations' for her child and what they could achieve in this life. Murray in a perverse sort of way, was so glad that Sarah Archer was no longer with us to experience this heartache. Something no parent should ever encounter. With no pun intended, but words linking and connecting within the brain process, he pondered. How did this happen on his watch? He, at present, felt ultimately responsible. However, try telling that to Detective Sergeant Robert 'Ally' Coulter.

Ally was now on a stretcher. He was in distress, suffering desperately from serious shock. It was quickly decided that he clearly needed to attend the hospital. He was incoherent, argumentative and becoming increasingly aggressive. From his lifetime on the force, Murray was aware that there were several different kinds of shock and to varying degrees. This was most definitely neurogenic shock. The one brought on by severe emotional disturbance. "Noooo, nooo, no," they would hear him scream. Then he'd physically lash out at the paramedics. His team were distraught even to witness this unnatural behaviour from their much loved, older and wiser colleague. He was in a bad way. Steven Murray could take no more. He could not be a bystander. He had no desire to observe his good friend struggling like this.

Silently he sought solitude outside. His team would follow up diligently with procedures. The forensic boys and girls had just arrived. He had given Dani Poll a solemn wave as he exited the premises. It was a quarter past eight, the night was chilled and 'last orders' had been served. This 'Doctors' surgery would be closed for the foreseeable future.

Back inside pathologist Danielle Poll could be seen holding up three fingers to constables Curry and Hayes. She was explaining in layman's terms how slitting someone's throat would accomplish 3 things.

She proceeded to inform them, "That firstly, severing the trachea (windpipe) generally below the larynx will prevent screaming or yelling. Secondly, it severs the carotid artery preventing new oxygenated blood from reaching the brain. And lastly, it severs the jugular vein allowing blood to easily flow from the brain. These things will bring unconsciousness quickly with death shortly to follow."

Hayes and Curry tried to remain professional, but their sharp breathing and flaring nostrils were tell tale signs that the emotion was getting to them.

Poll continued, "But it's not like it is in the movies. It is a gruesome thing to see. It takes thirty seconds to a minute till the blood loss and lack of oxygen eventually kill the person."

Hayes covered her mouth and wiped a delicate stream of tears from her eyes.

"Unconsciousness would have happened much sooner," Poll continued. "But the heart will continue to pump, squirting blood from the carotid, as you can see, until there is not enough to pump. The whole while the person will be taking giant gasping breaths through their severed windpipe, gargling blood and coughing. It is neither quiet nor quick like it's portrayed on the giant screen."

After briefly using it himself, Curry handed Hayes his handkerchief. Their hearts jointly aching and breaking for their friend and colleague, and the excruciatingly painful death she had suffered.

Wholly inappropriate, yet continually running through Detective Inspector Murray's thoughts - A line or two from 'Smiles.' A novel published nearly a whole century earlier in 1919, by Eliot H. Robinson.

"Eventide is softly casting - O'er the earth a magic spell. And a love-song, everlasting - On the night wind seems to swell."

This evening it was a poisonous and dangerous spell that had been cast. No everlasting love song, no voice, but a commentary simply edited and deleted. Dubbed, syndicated internationally and distributed around the globe as - The Deathly Sound of the Winter Wind.

As he reflected upon those words reverberating in his mind, Murray gazed heavenward. He was convinced that as he witnessed a much loved 'sleeping satellite' be removed and gently extinguished. That on the far side of the firmament, he could further attest to another brand new shimmering star optimistically appear. As if to delightfully illuminate the wild blue yonder. Not only did it shine and sparkle more brightly than the rest. But Steven Murray reckoned it winked specifically at him. Believing that it spoke personally to him. In a reserved, quiet, hushed female tone he heard: "Thank you sir - all is well ....God bless."

Having been duly satisfied with the deathly sound of the winter wind emanating from the throat of the sanguine Tasmin Taylor. 'Bunny' Reid and his two accomplices, the Dock Greeners - Forrester and Allan, had hastily made their exit via a rear door at the 'Doctors' surgery. Billy Forrester was behind the steering wheel. Just as he had been on Xmas Eve at Leith Links during the Grand Prix celebrations. A scar had formed nicely on the forehead of Francis Allan, where his bleeding wound from that evening had been left unattended. In the dark January skyline they drove westbound at speed out of the city and headed in the direction of the Forth Road Bridge, seeking sanctuary and safety across the water.

Within half an hour or so they'd arrived at their destination. An old counting house car park in Cardenden, in the Kingdom of Fife. Back in the day when the premises had been a Royal Bank of Scotland, the lads would meet there regularly to divide the spoils from their weekly endeavours. Now it was an ultra-modern beauty salon. Hairdressers and nail bar all rolled into one. Not the kind of trendy bar this particular trio of 'gentlemen' often frequented!

Francis Allan's own car had been parked there in a customer parking bay earlier in the day. Seated in the back he nervously looked to catch Forrester's attention in the rear view mirror. A knowing wink and nod of the head was offered. Frankie then made to exit the vehicle. As a parting shot, the young, burly Ayrshire lad leaned forward toward 'Bunny,' who was sitting comfortably in the passenger seat.

He began to hesitantly stutter. "Well thanks 'Bunny,' thanks for everything. An' Billy, I'll see you tomorrow then!"

"Aye, catch you the morn", Forrester responded, with a look and movement of the head that told Allan to get a move on and get out of here sharpish!

James Baxter Reid paused briefly in a considered manner, before eventually pressing the button to lower his blacked out electric window. In a deliberate, well-thought out line he asked in a dark and disturbing tone, perhaps one level up from a whisper. "Best wishes to the family Frankie. How are they doing? You'll miss them, eh?"

Francis Allan had no idea what the 'Reidmeister' meant by that remark. He had never enquired once about his wife or children over the years. It's not done in the circles they mix in. Family are separate, apart, have no connection to their everyday under the counter deals and way of life. These comments now preyed on Allan's mind. They worried him acutely. He had someone of importance he had to meet before returning to his family, but in an instant his Nokia was out of his pocket and dialling home.

In the still of the evening, the shrill scream of the telephone cut the silence like a runaway train heading for a broken bridge, wheels screeching on twisted metal rails. Wheels turn, wheels shriek - Wheels turn, wheels shriek - Wheels turn, wheels shriek.......no response, no pick up. It was late in the evening, his wife would normally have been home. The kids should have been safely tucked up in bed and sound asleep. The word 'safely' made him uneasy. He shook his head more anxious than ever. He quickly glanced at Reid. Then hurriedly at speed, threw himself into his car and turned on the ignition. Foot to the floor, he raced away out of the car park as he pleaded with Reid.

Shouting hysterically from the driver's window, "What, what on earth have you done 'Bunny'?"

Within a second of Francis Allan speeding away from view, Billy calmly placed his tattooed fingers at the base of the car gear stick. Then with an almighty force.....CRUNCH! The protruding object in Bunny's grip went searing straight through the back of Forrester's big-knuckled, blue-veined left hand. Reid's functional, tough and exceptionally rugged Rambo knife tore through bone and tissue and was now fully embedded into the gearbox. Perfect, simplicity at its finest and no amount of screaming and movement from Billy Forrester would enable it to budge. It was a modern day re-enactment of The Sword in the Stone, and 'Excalibur' would only be removed by the hand of King Arthur. In tonight's performance that role was to be played by none other than James Baxter Reid. Renowned voice coach, thespian and award winning villain!

As if a sizeable crowd in the outdoor Fife amphitheatre were waiting in anticipation for more. Reid could imagine and hear the shouts of encore! encore! encore! Filtering around the outdoor auditorium, just before he began to break into a brief but intense verbal attack. A diatribe of scolding questions and retribution. Delivered as always in his laid back, heavy duty rasping style. Sponsored by 'Lockets' the throat lozenge specialists!

"Do you think I'm a daft wee boy Billy? That I had no idea what the next part of the plan was? That I didnae know about the gun down the side o' yer seat?

The delicate nods, the sly winks. A've been there, got the t-shirt pal. You two are no so much Francis and Billy, mair like 'Francie an' Josie!' Yer just a couple o' comedians, but withoot the laughs. Thanks for everything the wee man says. As if he'll never see me again. He just couldn't resist the cheap shot, could he? It's his family he'll never see again! Gettin' rid o' me is no that easy son. Did ye think a wis past it like? Dixon no brave enough tae try it himself?"

Desperately trying to remain absolutely still to reduce the agonising pain shooting through his body, Billy Forrester could only muster - "What, what are you talking about 'Bunny'? It's not Kenny!"

Reid twisted the knife, "Aaaagggghhhh," then silence. A well delivered clenched fist, driven hard straight to the bridge of the nose equals - unconsciousness. Years of experience coming to the fore. He manhandled the motionless body into the boot of the car and set off once again. Destination........undetermined?

Forrester, may just have bought himself some extra time though. The final curtain cannot come down on this particular scene just yet. 'Bunny' Reid mulled over Billy's closing words. What did he mean 'It's not Kenny?' If not Kenneth Dixon that wanted him dead, then who?

NINETEEN

"I guess the winter makes you laugh a little slower, makes you talk a little lower about the things you could not show her. And it's been a long December and there's reason to believe - maybe this year will be better than the last."

- Counting Crows

It was now about to turn midnight on that fatal 5th of January. The two paramedics were no doubt thinking that it was yet another drunk driver. A reveller who's had one too many over the festive season. The car appeared to have careered through the traffic lights at the T junction. This was in preference to choosing the normal option called: Turning! Possibly the man in charge of the vehicle had a little 'angelic pal' on one shoulder, and his nemesis, a 'horny red devil' on the other. Maybe the competing forces were rather tipsy themselves and routinely squabbling as is normally the case. Right and wrong, good versus evil, turn left or turn right. Their yuletide counsel, poorly advised him 'to phone a friend.' Too late! Season's greetings at this point had been offered by a rather formidable red brick wall. Ho! Ho! Ho!

It was clearly obvious, that the front-impact airbags that had been designed to protect the head during a frontal crash, had been deployed. The eight foot high barrier was officially just over half that height now. The remaining fifty percent was set out like crazy paving across the mangled bonnet, through the shattered windscreen and upon the badly damaged and caved in roof of this Cobalt Blue, Volvo S40! There was no one occupying the passenger seat, but the driver's eyes were closed. His lips were blue and ashy. His inanimate frame lay covered in tiny fragments of shattered glass.

Brian Simpson was the older, more experienced paramedic. He spoke quietly in a clear tone to his colleague, twenty-two year old Derek Carruthers. "I recognise this man, I'm sure I know him. It'll come to me no doubt." Suddenly, his head thrust backwards like the recoil of a gun. "It's Murray," he exclaimed, shocked. He now clearly recognised the stilled figure in front of him. Becoming more certain than ever, his voice grew louder. He then reiterated, "It's Detective Inspector Steven Murray." Disbelievingly shaking his head, he finished with, "he's one of the good guys."

"That may well be," Carruthers said. "But is he going to be a good, dead guy or continue being a dead good guy?"

Above the sound of a seat belt being unclicked, came the reply - "Neither!"

"Mr Murray are you okay? What happened? You've been out cold for a good few minutes."

"It'll have been black ice," Murray offered slowly, wincing. Raising his bleeding head slightly, he sluggishly continued. "I was just approaching the lights. Next I remember is hearing voices and seeing your ugly mug. Timpson, isn't it?"

"Well done sir, it's Simpson actually. Brian Simpson, but close enough. It's been awhile since we last worked together. So this crash doesn't seem to have done much damage up top then. Me and my buddy Derek here will give you a quick check over though Inspector. Better safe than sorry and all that, you know."

Murray, with eyes closed as the blood was being wiped from his face, suggested, "It was at the Maybury Casino on the outskirts of town last Summer."

"What was?" Derek Carruthers asked.

"Oh, when we were last on a case together," Simpson answered. "Wow, that is some memory right enough."

"I'm glad something seems to be in good working order. The rest of me is feeling rather tender to say the least."

"You're going to be sore sir for the next few days. A week or so even. It's always after the event that's the worst."

"Well, it's unlikely to be before the event," Murray sarcastically whispered. It was not really the reassurance the officer was perhaps looking for. He began slowly rotating his neck muscles and rolling his aching shoulders for his two temporary nursemaids.

Then, without warning he heard a voice in the distance shouting. "Sir, sir, it's me Joe." DI Murray screwed up his eyes to focus. Sure enough, there jogging gently toward him, was the intrepid 'Sherlock' Hanlon.

"How did you get here so quick?" Murray asked. He was holding up his now unattached rear view mirror to his forehead and admiring favourably, the rather distinctive black eye that was beginning to take shape. The said mirror had appeared sitting on his lap, as if by magic, after the airbag had been deflated.

ADC Hanlon informed him that he'd been trying to reach him all evening on the phone. He was worried when he had just abandoned them all at the 'Doctors' earlier on. "Eventually, I got the station to track your car and was making my way here when I heard a call come out from the paramedics for assistance. There'll be a patrol car here soon."

"Aye, well, that's unfortunate," Murray offered at a rather leisurely pace. I'll be off before they arrive. No others injured Joe. And I'm okay, although the car's in a rather delicate condition mind."

"Don't you mean a write-off," Hanlon suggested.

Struggling to be too optimistic Murray replied, "Well, mmmm, sadly that may be the case. We'll see tomorrow in the cold light of day. Take me home son would you!"

Hanlon's look said ....'Sir?' But, he quickly realised Murray's utterance, was one of instruction, not question. "Sir, we should really wait for our colleagues, give them a statement, an account of what happened," Hanlon pleaded.

"Joe, it was bad enough getting these two paramedics to let me head off home. Never mind waiting an hour or two for a pair of politically correct PC's to dot their i's and cross their t's. Nobody else involved, I damaged a wall, no other witnesses. You can breathalyse me if you like? It was black ice, pure and simple. I hit the brakes and just kept going. He then emphatically stated, "We need to make sure we report this junction to the roads department as we travel back to my place. Remind me to do that Joe, will you?" Hanlon, the raw, inexperienced officer, nodded in the affirmative, before humbly opening his passenger door!

Cutting through the deserted, inside streets of Edinburgh towards Murray's home, ADC Hanlon had time for a quiet introspective moment. He made observations and asked and answered himself further questions.

Joe never spotted any black ice. The road surface had already been well gritted. Quite substantially from what he could see. The Inspector certainly hadn't been drinking and was fully aware of everything going on. He must have been travelling at good speed though, Hanlon figured. He was then puzzled at why there was no signs of slowing. Especially on an approach to traffic lights and a junction.

No matter, his trusty companion the faithful Volvo S40, would be getting 'put out of his misery' in the morning. There would be no recovery from that impact. The enquiring mind of the young constable continually ticked over, and he questioned again: Had that not been a Volvo with such high safety specifications, "Would Detective Inspector Steven Murray, even be alive to tell the tale?"

Throughout the night and into the early hours, Murray was restless. He sat up in his bed and added a few more lines to his latest sonnet. The light was then switched off.

Musings, possibilities and a fascinating list of theories rampaged through his clarity of thought.

He couldn't sleep -

He had just swilled downed some pills -

He had just experienced the murder of a colleague -

He had just tried to exit this world and take his own life!

Becoming drowsy within ten minutes, there would be no need to count sheep. The medication had kicked in and he could look forward to a peaceful night's rest. One filled with pleasant dreams of contentment, serenity and calm.

Of course, other dreams are available...... By 3am, ideas, arguments and hunches were swimming in his mind. Doors opened into a large smoke filled folk club. Latin music was pounding to the exotic beat. The property agent Mr Gemmill, complete with Aran sweater being swirled around his head was the host at the microphone. He warmly welcomed everyone to 'The Cereal Killer' Nightclub. A waitress offered complimentary drinks. An elaborate image of a salsa shuffling William Taunton haunted Murray, as he watched from the sideline chewing addictively on Borojo bars. An art student dead. Why?

Horses then galloped through leper colonies. Chief jockey was Kenny Dixon. In place of a whip, he held a miniature brick to encourage his rides. All the time singing, 'Alouette, gentille alouette - then bopping them on the head!' A vendor offered free celebratory cigars to winning punters! Doc Patterson strolled around, calmly reassuring everyone with a regular vocal chant of 'to be sure, to be sure, aaahh to be sure!' A legal secretary dead. Why?

ADC Hanlon stood looking over his dead wife. He then played the violin at her graveside dressed as Sherlock Holmes. As a birthday cake lay rotting in a corner, a sales assistant offered free samples of the latest Cadbury's chocolate bar. Two newly born female twins fleetingly brought in laughter, smiles and joy. Their mother then looked on in horror as 'Bunny' Reid began to sing them a goodnight lullaby....'Ally Bally, Ally Bally Bee!' A social worker dead. Why?

The delirious montage of hallucinatory images and thoughts continued apace. A train engine crashed violently against waves on the waterfront. Another exploded on impact with several carriages including Thomas the Tank Engine at Waverley station! Desperate Dan, aka Brian Pollok looked on as a mushroom cloud of bright amber, tiger orange and honeycomb illuminated the skyline. At that, the chilling lines and gentle words, coupled with the beautiful historic lettering of Sir Walter Scott were jettisoned high into the air. Only to gradually descend feather like and land soft as ash at the feet of a smiling Re.Gal lady. The charred remains read - 'Abuse, Abused, Abuser!' An estate agent dead. Why?

Mirroring an ice cold glass of water, a fever like sweat had broken out across his brow. Pillows had been dispatched to the floor, but Murray was not for waking. This was a fascinating experience. He knew he was dreaming and embraced the opportunity. In his trance like state he began creating impressions, imagining mental pictures and searching relentlessly for clues in this alternative gateway.

The Inspector smiled uncomfortably as he slept. Billy Joel would have been proud of him as he slowly immersed himself, further and further into his deep *'River of Dreams.'* Severed fingers floated on top and 'Markie' Ziola surfaced from the waves to shout....'Aloha!' He had been diving for pearls! Desperate Dan reappeared eating a cow pie, whilst 'Jojo' the barman cried out, "ONE HUNDRED AND EIGHTY," as Sheila Dixon stood at the oche playing darts! A loving Aunt and her baby nephew dead. Why?

Finally, Chief Inspector Brown was in his garden, surrounded by beautiful rose bushes shaped as rugby balls. Rolf Harris appeared with two vulnerable children sitting on his lap. As he looked up, he whispered menacingly, "Stylophone by Dubreq."

Steven Murray then began to weep in his sleep as he viewed images of a lollipop man. He was drinking whisky whilst on duty helping youngsters across the road. An obligatory yellow Raleigh Chopper bicycle then popped up and a less than sturdy metal Meccano car. Murray knew what they would represent and was now desperately trying to quickly awaken. Turning, tossing and about to sit upright, he was beaten by the lifelike portrait appearing in front of him of a small child sized figure dressed as an astronaut. The helmet was cut in half and removed. The image then changed immediately to that of a six year old girl lying lifeless on a slab in the City morgue. Kirsty Fraser was dead. Why?

"Why? Why? Why? Why? Why?" Murray awoke screaming. With sinuses blocked, sweat and tears merged. His hands ran through the combined greasy, slimy lather as he made to push back his hair, rub at his eyes and with forefinger and thumb wipe his nose. He sat shaking his head. His foot also shook anxiously. A key giveaway that Murray had adopted from his late mother. If things rile him, he disagrees with you or is becoming uptight - check out his feet in future.

He purposefully was trying gradually to slow his breathing, stop moving his foot and to calm down and feel at ease. He stretched across to his bedside table. His quilt cover was soaked throughout. As he picked up his leather bound 'carpe diem' notepad, he began to quickly write down a few of the most artistic, mind blowing visuals, graphics and imaginative representations he had experienced in a long while.

Could he interpret them? Possibly make sense, cobble together, guess what they stood for? Mysterious metaphors delivered as you sleep. Cryptic analogies wired to enlighten. It had been surreal, hallucinatory, but distinctly valuable. Murray felt refreshed that he'd been given a reprieve with no lingering dark clouds to write home about. He was already home he reminded himself and he was feeling great. Charged with renewed hope, bristling with energy and filled with a resounding desire and determination. He also now carried with him some definite New Year resolutions. They included checking out Keith Brown's gardening knowledge. Arranging new, more appropriate gifts for his friendly lollipop men and then ultimately of course, finding the answer to the ....Why?

IKEA bunk beds, Harry Corry interiors and a splattering of NEXT home furnishings completed the decor. It was a clean, tidy and well looked after home. Outside, the short garden path had been newly swept, curtains appeared bright and inviting. Lovely framed photographs had been strategically placed along one side of the hallway wall, no doubt in order of age. Firstly, you had Mum and Dad pictured outside a glitzy neon wedding chapel in Vegas. Possibly celebrating their nuptials one would assume. A blonde, curly haired girl was next, complete with beaming smile and mischievous grin. She deeply resembled her father, with her high forehead and rosy cheeks. After her, the curly haired female theme continued. Slightly more red looking this time with a few freckles thrown in for good measure. Next up - two for the price of one. Another set of twins, although unlike Sandra Kerr's recent arrivals, these two were clearly boys. Kitted out identically in their miniature matching football tops. Based on the replica shirt sponsor, this would be the most recent photo of the collection. One would have guessed the boys were about two or three years of age.

At 7am on Tuesday 6th of January, outside this small, modest semi-detached, three bedroom home in the Duddingston area of Edinburgh, events were heating up. Numerous marked and unmarked police cars sat parked alongside three ambulances and a Scottish Gas vehicle. CID, uniformed police and paramedics galore. All dealing and handling with their normal, routine everyday duties.

Although not quite.

It was a scene that would indelibly leave its mark on the emergency services personnel. Two WPC's and an experienced Sergeant had already either been sent home or relieved of duty and moved elsewhere. Chief Inspector Keith Brown was in attendance and was overseeing matters today. Murray and his team had just been through a gruelling ordeal the night before. Culminating in the sad loss of life and the abrupt end to a young female officers promising career. Not to mention the fact that her experienced partner had been hospitalised overnight and would be off work for the foreseeable future. Trauma and delayed shock can take their toll and CI Brown wanted to help ease the load over the next few days. Nothing though, could have fully prepared him for this!

Neighbours had braved the elements to gather just beyond the official perimeter barrier (tape, to be wholly accurate). Concerned citizens looking to form close bonds together. Able to unite, able to safeguard, able to GOSSIP, SPECULATE and cause much more HARM than good. At least that was always the Chief Inspector's impression and belief! "They would always increasingly damage or become detrimental to a case, far more than offer any helpful contribution," was his long term line. Today was no different, the rumour mill had begun and with it, plenty of speculation. It included, 'The mother had taken an overdose and had been found by her oldest child.' 'Someone had been killed and they are out searching for the dad. Given that he is already known to the police.' The latest one, given credence by the fact a Scottish Gas van is directly outside the home, is simply that 'a leak has had devastating effects for those in this home and that there are casualties.' Scottish Gas have since been inundated with calls from both worried users and a host of news and radio outlets looking for an official response or quote.

Keith Brown is not always at the coalface these days, and is well aware that his role has to be more politically tender and media savvy than ever before. He's genuinely glad to be supporting his colleagues and helping out on this distressing morning. As a parent himself he can also attest to being heartbroken and upset at the devastating consequences and the casualties found. Happily, he would also clarify that highly toxic fumes played no part in any of the deaths. In fact, the most dangerous leak was the one that came from the uninformed local forum of speculators, muckrakers and busybodies. If they were in the know at all, they would have been aware that last night the woman next door had her boyfriend stay over. His name was Simon, and Simon's a maintenance engineer with Scottish Gas!

Detective Inspector Steven Murray, although not present, would soon be made fully aware of all the events that had taken place at The Jewel in Edinburgh, and their undoubted relevance in his own investigation.

The mother's name was Julie. She had been well known to the police over the years for handling stolen goods, small petty crimes and the like. In the kitchen of the home, personalised named fridge magnets made from brightly coloured, durable plastic, held individual school photos, memos and other snaps onto the large American style two door appliance. In the first instance these helped quickly in identifying the remainder of the family.

Amy was 7 years of age and the eldest. 'Freckles' was Carol aged 6. Their twin brothers Sam and Adam had just turned 3. If they had been appearing on Family Fortunes your host would now be finishing with,

"Ladies and Gentleman, I give you.......The Allan Family!" A round of applause would soon follow, filling the quiet, sombre void that was acutely present today. An intensity prevailed. People were going about their jobs on autopilot. It seemed almost surreal. One adult and four youngsters. Each child under the age of criminal responsibility. For that part of the United Kingdom, it was eight!

All the dead were in one room, the lounge. Or as most people referred to it in Scotland, 'the living room.' That description today however was flawed, possibly misleading - actually, wholly inaccurate.

The small fingers on one hand of either Sam or Adam Allan could be seen gripped firmly, cold and blue around the side of his shared carrycot. His brother at the opposite end bereft of life. Their mother had probably been the first fatality. Sat calmly, nonchalantly unconcerned on her initially cream coloured leather sofa. No doubt chatting amicably, though possibly nervously to her house guest, as he paced arrogantly around the room. Julie was possibly exceptionally curious as to why he was there. Certainly she was not feeling threatened, until and without warning her head was pulled back and her throat cut instantly!

In two seconds it was over.

With Taz Taylor, it was different, that was prolonged for effect, both visual and audible.

With the lounge door locked, it would have been easy enough for him now to attend to the sisters. Amy was found slumped to the floor at the feet of her mother. She was probably victim number two, silenced within a second of her parent's demise. The younger, feisty sibling Carol, seemed to have put up a major fight. Blood trailed across the leather suite and beige carpeted floor, it suggested that she had escaped the clutches of her assailant on at least one occasion. Showing no fear, she had made for the window as a potential escape route. Smears down the inside of the glass and over large areas of the dismantled curtains would later confirm this. Despite her brave efforts, the ginger haired Carol lay like a defeated gymnast. Her slender, petite, inanimate body arched tenderly over the back of the now 'ruby red' sofa. Her youthful Primary School face stared heavenward, as the deep, apple red gash drawn across her throat, symbolically marked the starting point for the race.

The coverage and saturation of blood was overwhelming. Johnny Cash, the legendary Country and Western artist, had years earlier penned the words to 'Forty Shades of Green.' Today though, in that 'living room,' the variation, tints and shades of red witnessed were eerily chilling. It may have been the gentle wisps of 'the winter wind' that were creating advanced tones from standard scarlet, crimson and fire engine red, then incredibly turning them one by one into modern state-of-the-art descriptions of the colour. Headers that included candy, brick, berry and blush. Not forgetting cherry, garnet, wine and possibly Sheila Dixon's favourite, rose!

No matter. Amy and Carol were lost to the world. Extinct. Gone. No more. Their youthful energy departed. Their tight curls splattered and straightened, congealed with imperial red and majestic mahogany. Rust coloured freckles appeared on both of their smooth empty faces. Hope had been extinguished and even with a gas engineer nearby, the pilot light had ceased to be!

Chief Inspector Brown had been reliably informed that Francis Allan had never returned home last night. Was he ever a suspect? Brown had seen it all before over the years, but there was no way he reckoned this was the work of the father. In fairness, Brown didn't believe this individual was even trying to remain anonymous. Ironically, he was silently speaking up. He was making a point. And that point was, if he was going down, he was going down fighting. Like running any major corporation - running drug cartels and people trafficking can be a cut throat business. Today, that was literally what it had become. James Baxter Reid was on a spree. Many years ago he was notorious. Myth and legend did abound. 'Bunny' though, had never served time. He dealt in fear and reputation. In recent years no one could recall when they last saw 'the Reidmeister at work.' Today he was most ruthlessly 'back with a vengeance.'

Strictly speaking he had been true to his word, although in advance. He knew that he was about to be set up. That Forrester and Allan had been ordered to finish him off at an opportune moment when next it arose. Ahead of the game, as he had so often been these last twenty five years, 'Bunny' had visited the Allan family yesterday between the hours of two and three o'clock in the afternoon. No official witnesses to that, but very thorough forensics these days, coupled with Doctor Danielle Poll's valued assessment of the time of death, make it near certain.

The female pathologist, who had worked alongside 'The Tinker' for around three years now, had endured a busy, stressful 24 hours. First, Taz Taylor last night and then this horrendous scene this morning. However, the previous evening at around 10pm just as they were finishing up at the 'Doctors,' a body had been discovered slumped over the steering wheel of a car. She recognised now, that in some ways it was most probably a blessing in disguise. It was 'Doc' Patterson that took that one. And he was there until mid morning, which is why Danielle Poll found herself back on this job currently. Patterson had phoned her and Murray late last night, although Murray's went straight to voicemail. He had called to inform them that he had recognised the driver of the red BMW 3 series. It was Francis Allan. Dead! Probable poisoned cigar butt at his side. Smoking kills, there's no *'dout'* about it!

On their last meeting, 'Bunny' had put him through mental torture. Yet on reflection, there was nothing Frankie could have done. Earlier in the day, his whole family had been heartlessly slaughtered! The Allan family had lived at The Jewel in Duddingston. Sadly, on that fateful day, some semi-precious stones had fell into the hands of an expert gem cutter and invaluable young treasures were lost to the world forever!

According to the Chinese zodiac, the year just ended, 2014 had been the Year of the Horse. At Leopardstown in Ireland, Ruby Walsh had been crowned Champion jump jockey for the ninth time!

With his own special love and fondness for the equine community, James Baxter Reid had only been a few days late in displaying his silks for all the world to see. He had entered the stalls and was now fully involved in the race. Without question, he'd thrown down the gauntlet to his main rival.

Their competitive horse racing adventures were coming to the fore. These two Edinburgh gangsters were now rounding the bend and entering the final straight. However, Dixon may be about to come up on the inside with a late challenge. It would be close and bookmakers were reluctant to take any more bets.

Currently though it was 'Bunny' Reid, who, back in the saddle after a period of inactivity, was showing the elegant equestrian skills required to become Champion jockey.

Yesterday before callously butchering the thoroughbred Tasmin Taylor, Reid had already calmly dealt with a troublesome mare, two beautiful fillies and put to sleep a pair of anxious three year old colts!

TWENTY

"My world was shattered I was torn apart, like someone took a knife and drove it deep in my heart. If I could turn back time."

- Cher

Tuesday 6th January 2015

Having been informed of all the developments happening over at Duddingston, the Detective Inspector arranged to meet up with Joe at twelve noon in the office. Murray was met on his arrival by a rather efficient and well researched ADC Hanlon. Nodding furiously and in an excited tone he unleashed, "You were right sir, Bill Taunton has never been to a tanning studio in his life. I double checked with Joan Smithers who was his PA before poor Deborah Evans."

"Good work, 'Sherlock.' It would appear you are living up well to the nickname! All your own doing?"

"Eh, not quite, I had a 'Doctor Watson.' Their young trainee Sykes, he was most helpful. I asked him if he'd be kind enough to let me check Mr. Taunton's diary. Told him it was needed to confirm his hectic schedule on the run up to the dreadful day. Greg was more than happy to oblige. He desperately wants justice for Deborah."

"Good thinking Joe. Any joy?"

"Well, not really in regard to finding out more about the mysterious Jillian Ingham. The company name and contact details she gave, surprisingly don't exist. We reckon however that the poison was on the seal of the envelope that she had given Taunton to post. Yvette remembered that Bill (not Mr. Taunton), had specifically requested that envelope be closed and posted for collection that day. Sadly with ambulances, sirens and an extended group of police personnel in attendance, the post went off unhindered.

"Yes, that was not good," Murray shrugged. "Understandable, but not good."

"Don't dwell too much on that sir. You'll be more receptive to another couple of my findings. You know how much I love this job, right?"

"Is that one of the findings?" his Inspector asked smiling.

"Good one, sir! Anyway you were right a second time."

Murray continued to grin like a Cheshire cat and offered, "I was? Tell me more."

"Mr. Oat'n Nuts himself, entrepreneurial businessman William Taunton (or Bill, if you know him well enough). He had only just arrived back in the country sir. No more than twenty-four hours previously."

"Really?" Murray stated guardedly, but without surprise. "Someplace warm?"

"Oh yes, indeed. A country that is…"

Murray, with a raised voice concluded, ".......six hours behind the UK!"

"Well done, sir, bravo!" The junior apprentice was still at times in awe of his time-served gaffer! The voice of inexperience continued. "The other day, how did you figure that out?"

"Joe, seriously?" Master tradesman Murray was amazed at the numerous wonderful findings ADC Hanlon could turn up. But remained baffled, by the what he would consider, 'in your face' observations that continued to escape him. Holding up his left sleeve, he pointed at the cuff and reminded Joe Hanlon, "Taunton had an obvious tan line where his watch was." Murray, then held up his moderately priced, brown leather strapped Sekonda between his thumb and forefinger. "This old thing Joe, maybe not so much. But if I had popped into premises on the High Street, wearing a rather expensive TAG Heuer timepiece. It would most certainly be coming off before I jumped on to any 'cancer calling' sun bed!"

Hanlon lifted his head high to the side and held up both his hands, with fingers wide apart. An expression that body language experts would tell you signals - 'of course,' or a 'why did I not see that?'

"Regarding the other couple of items Joe. Firstly, take a closer look at that exquisite chronometer that Mr. Taunton wears on his wrist. He may well have adjusted it by now. But when we met, it was still 6 hours behind. Also, his passport had been placed carefully on top of his briefcase in the corner of the office. I figured it was just about to be put to good use, or had just recently served its purpose. So, I guess we are thinking America, Canada, or somewhere of that ilk?"

"Oh, WE are not thinking anywhere. WE know exactly where he has been. His diary was an exceptional help. Methodical, thorough, well done that diligent personal assistant. Unwittingly, she may have assisted enormously in bringing about the capture of those responsible for the repulsive and horrible death of both herself and 'sweet baby James.'"

"Well said son. But don't keep me hanging on, out with it, spill the beans as it were."

"Every 3 months sir. Once a quarter, regular as clockwork. His bestselling line: 'Samba Viagra,' 'Latin Lust,' or whatever he chooses to call it. Not the United States, not America."

'But South America!" Murray twigged, as they both now began to make their way out of the building.

"Columbia to be precise."

Walking across the car park Murray made a slight Samba style move and exclaimed, "Andale! Andale! Hurry up Joe this could be fascinating."

Watching Murray's attempted dance steps, whilst shaking his head and wincing. Joe promptly added, "No, not really sir, but what is fascinating though, is Yvette Evan's memory. As heartbroken for her as I am, the amount of helpful information in regard to herself that she has managed to omit is amazing. Especially given her recollection of the importance of the envelope. She was also able to accurately describe its colour and size. Now she tells me (Hanlon is speaking at pace, both excited and determined), she tells me that she recalls it was Jillian Ingham's birthday when she came in earlier in the year. To visit with in her words, you guessed it...........Bill! So I looked up that busy diary of 'our Bill.' Initially I would have surmised that with everything else surrounding her being false, so too the birthday story." He then paused.

"Joe, you are doing it again."

"Yes, that was deliberate that time," he smiled. Then rather unashamedly, in a brief moment of self-congratulatory smugness, he posed his boss the question. "With all of those involved or surrounding the case, you'll never guess whose birthday fell on that day sir?"

"Thank goodness you're not a betting man Joe." With the doffing of an imaginary cap and a renewed swagger in his step, the Inspector walked off into the distance toward his new temporary patrol car. Leaving acting DC Joseph Hanlon to witness little, short, modest white clouds of Murray's breathe take flight. As they rose gracefully in the cold, chilled air, his familiar voice could be faintly heard to utter, "I think I will you know. I think I will."

Two nights previous on that murderous Monday the 5th of January, Reid had left Cardenden on a 14 mile drive toward the old settlement village of Limekilns, on the Firth of Forth. For many centuries Limekilns was also the northern terminus for a ferry linking it to Bo'ness (the hometown of Lynnette Lithgow) on the southern side of the Forth. This found an echo in Robert Louis Stevenson's 'Kidnapped' and it was from Limekilns that 'David Balfour' and 'Alan Breck' were carried across the Forth in a rowing boat.

Late Monday evening, parked in a darkened lay-by next to the small harbour, Reid removed the cotton gag from his captive's mouth.

"It was Sheila," Forrester mumbled as he struggled for breath.

"What, what was that you said? You feel a, you feel what?"

With a couple of deep, precise gasps, Billy Forrester snapped, "Sheila, not feel a! Sheila! Sheila flamin' Dixon! It was her idea, no' Kenny's. Her scheme! Her money! Her plan! She's been in charge for a while now. You must have saw that?" he wheezed frantically.

Reid stayed silent. He had unknowingly witnessed the pendulum of power swing gradually away from Kenny Dixon, especially over the last twelve months. Sheila's initiatives had without doubt streamlined drug operations, improved working conditions for 'the escorts' and substantially increased market share and profit for everyone. So no one was complaining. It began to make sense... 'Pea and Ham, instead of Chicken!'

No one had spotted Kenny Dixon since the Saturday he picked up the disturbing mail from his yard. As well as the police, he would also surely be on Reid's trail by now. If nothing else, 'Bunny' Reid was a vindictive man. An eye for an eye was most definitely a mantra he lived by and believed in. One could then comfortably surmise, Sheila Dixon would very shortly find herself blinded! She would be made to pay, to pay greatly and with substantial interest!

He knew someone, although he reckoned it to be Kenny was out to get him. So he had struck early. Firstly paying a visit to Francis Allan's family. Then, when he had been convinced that Coulter had set him up, that Ally had turned on him and was throwing him to the wolves - he took away Taylor, the Sergeant's beloved precious colleague.

That niggled with him though, he had 'liked Taylor.' He'd been looking forward to perhaps getting 'entangled' with her from time to time! Suddenly he reflected upon Coulter's pleas and denials. The Detective Sergeant had actually been telling the truth after all. Reid grinned ruefully. Perhaps I'll give him a ring sometime he thought to himself. In a manner more keeping with that of a friendly, interactive local neighbour, as opposed to the smiling, sadistic and deranged imaginary cousin of........... Hannibal Lecter!

In his distinct voice that continually had to be dragged up from down deep in the trenches of his stomach, he was heard to utter dismissively, "Och well, them's the breaks I guess." Bunny Reid then turned away swiftly, snapping Billy Forrester's neck in the process!

TWENTY ONE

"Mama, put my guns in the ground, I can't shoot them anymore. That long black cloud is comin' down and I feel like I'm knockin' on heaven's door."

- Bob Dylan

On the Wednesday morning 8am news bulletin, Radio Scotland were reporting that detectives were trying to positively identify a dismembered body. A torso, an arm and a leg had been discovered washed up on the shoreline of the River Forth at South Queensferry. Police and HM Coastguard had been called after body parts in the water at Hawes Pier were reported sighted, at around 6.20 that morning. Officers said the man was white and that his hair had been recently cut off. A padded jacket remained fixed to the torso over a t-shirt. They'd found a ponytail in one jacket pocket and a pink soft toy rabbit in the other. A Police spokesperson stated: "Our investigation is continuing to establish this man's identity and we would ask anyone who can assist with our ongoing inquiries to contact police on 101."

Some of the clothes they mentioned, matched those that Reid was last seen wearing. Those that Ally Coulter had witnessed first-hand, upside down, during every

360 degree turn! The ponytail? The soft toy? As Coulter watched live TV footage of the discovery, it simply seemed too good to be true. He guessed someone had caught up with 'Bunny' before his colleagues had. Delighted as he was, he still felt it had been an easy opt-out for Reid. Although on reflection, to be dismembered, Ally reckoned he must have suffered and felt immense pain. At that, a faint glow of satisfaction spread across the face of the jaded Detective Sergeant ever so briefly. He blew a kiss high up into the air and mouthed, "For you Taz, for you!" Unwashed and dishevelled he returned to his music. His humble abode has been literally 'rocking' at Glastonbury noise levels since his return from his brief sojourn in the hospital. After a day's monitoring, a mere twenty-four hours later, he had been deemed fit and well? Or at least okay to return home and be left on his own!

As soon as they had apprehended their suspect at 9.15am. Murray instructed ADC Hanlon to take them direct to the station and await his arrival. He then allowed Tom Wendel access to their property to work his magic. When Hanlon duly returned with an individual in handcuffs, Hayes and Curry looked on bewildered. Murray then contacted 'Sherlock' to inform him of further developments. He would have to spend at least twenty minutes to an hour, having an intense review of this latest evidence.

"Keep our guest happy in the interim Joe, I'll get there as soon as I can."

Sure enough, just over one hour later Murray began to casually open the door to the interview room. Immediately he felt the need to take cover. He'd been hit by a barrage of bullets, each one disguised as a furious question. A merger of genuine desire for the truth, infiltrated with an assortment of dull, tedious, pre-requisite demands and petitions. A bombardment of concerns.

"What is this Inspector? How dare you treat me like this! Why am I here?" The high pitch voice offered up in a surprised manner. "Have you found Kenny? Is he okay? Does he know that I'm with you?" Concern at her precise location now came to the fore.

Murray took a deep breath on behalf of them both and responded. "Mrs Dixon, Sheila, have you heard the expression, 'ca' canny? Slow down ma'am, take a breath and by the way, it's wonderful to see you again also!" he joked.

Then in a more serious stern tone, he turned to the seated diva and asked: "Do you like music Sheila?" Surprised by the question, she opened her mouth. Murray though, continued uninterrupted, "I love music. In fact it's probably my biggest passion outside of work," he added with sincere excitement. She shook her head and shrugged dismissively.

Murray then continued. "Oh, I've just remembered, I know full well you love your music Sheila. I've heard plenty of it."

She looked up quizzically and offered, "What! When?"

"When you were having your five minute power shower, remember?" He gave her a cheeky wink to accompany his smug smile. "Now I love to sing too Mrs Dixon. But I can hold a bar of slippery soap better than I can hold a tune!" He allowed for a brief cessation before continuing. "However, the dialogue, the text and pronouncement of the script fascinate me. I have a hunch that words are important to you also Mrs D?"

In response to that being a question, rather than a statement. Ironically, no sound nor syllable came forth at that moment from the pursed lips of Sheila Dixon.

Her gaze was fixed intently on Detective Inspector Steven Murray. In equal measure it offered derision and indifference.

"This is a rather lengthy journey we're about to embark upon together," Murray informed his guest. "If you are settled? Ma'am," he added sarcastically. Sheila Dixon shook her head and tossed her currently tousled and unruly hair over her left shoulder.

Ignoring her theatrics, Murray continued. "I'd like to begin by sharing a trio of important and I believe highly relevant lyrics with you this morning."

Hanlon had no idea where this was going and his Western buddies 'Hanna' Hayes and 'Kid' Curry - 'Alias Smith and Jones,' looked on equally bemused from behind the one way mirror in the adjoining room.

Elegantly and politely Murray began. "A beautiful melody is extremely important. A catchy hook will entrance you and pull you in for more. But the formation of the words, those carefully chosen intricate lines, give a song it's heart and soul. Don't you think Sheila?" This was like conducting an orchestra for Murray, he was building up, increasing the tempo. He continued to raise his metaphorical baton. "They begin to play seductively with every emotion - joy and laughter, sadness and heartache, triumph and despair." He was reaching a crescendo, his pace quickened and his voice rose an octave - "They give the music depth and clarity. You begin to get a clearer understanding of what the author, writer or lyricist was trying to portray."

Silence! A sudden stop. He allowed his heartbeat to calm, before he offered up a soothing lament - "But not always."

Ever so slightly and even more deliberately, he slowed his delivery. "Sometimes Sheila, as you well know, it's a hidden message, it's subliminal, recognisable only to a selected few. Possibly the singer, the musician, the composer of the piece even. Then, and only then, there gradually becomes a method or meaning to their often chaotic, fragile assembly of letters and words."

Sheila Dixon appeared unperturbed, possibly as baffled as everyone else at this stage. Including Chief Inspector Keith Brown who'd now joined his junior officers behind the glass.

"I believe you and our 'Kenneth' had a small civil ceremony many years ago to celebrate your Union, would that be correct?"

Although wary and becoming alarmed at Murray's continuing revelations. She felt sufficiently unthreatened by that particular question, to simply nod in agreement.

"Your photographs for that event were taken where, may I ask?"

Still feeling on relatively safe territory, Sheila Dixon slowly and quietly offered, "St. Giles Cathedral."

"Thanks Sheila. I just wanted to confirm that. Or I would have looked extremely foolish with my very first point." Murray then paused slightly for breath before resuming. "I was raised mainly with a wide variety of Scottish and Irish tunes growing up Mrs D. One of the very few east coast songs I remember, included these lines - *In the capital of Scotland, by the great kirk of St. Giles. There lies a heart for all to see within the royal mile. Now many men have stood here from the humble to the grand, and it's known for all its greatness - the Heart of Midlothian.*"

Sheila Dixon allowed herself the faintest of smiles. She was becoming more confident. She thought to herself and not for the first time, he's just clutching at straws. He's going around in circles, hoping I'll say something out of place.

Murray though, had been operating on cruise control. It was now that he shifted up a gear. This time he began with: "Sheila, do you like Sir Walter Scott?" No riposte was offered. "He's a dab hand at the old writing game," Murray continued. "Likes his lyrics does our Watty."

Sheila Dixon then indignantly responded, "Are you mad? Watty, what? I think I've had enough now Inspector."

Murray, in true Beautiful South style, *'carried on regardless'* - "He wrote the novel 'The Heart of Midlothian' Sheila. And that brings me very nicely to my second set of lyrics. When I saw these recently, they were beautifully etched onto a glass panel at Waverley Station. I hope you're not superstitious Mrs Dixon? Because I feel strongly that these thirteen menacing words are most apt in regard to your recent actions."

Sheila swallowed hard. As if coming up for air, the tip of her tongue slipped briefly between her lips, before rapidly vanishing once again.

"What do you think?" Murray asked innocently. Before delivering mischievously: "Revenge, the sweetest morsel to the mouth that ever was cooked in hell." He allowed the silence to engulf the room. Leaving several seconds before permitting his conclusion. "Revenge Mrs Dixon, sorry Sheila. That simple age old motive - Revenge!"

At that, a realisation, a dawning, emerged over the perplexed features of Sheila Dixon. With an angry sneer of contempt on her face she lashed out vocally, although slowly and precisely at the Inspector. "My study WAS locked wasn't it?" She glared at Murray for confirmation. He hastily withdrew any remaining eye contact. She continued her verbal assault with, "Where is that mouthy, cheeky, pale-faced, big skinny constable?"

Gradually, he gathered his thoughts and delivered them calmly, in a very steady, deliberate manner. The man from the west coast uttered in a slightly patronising tone, "What about stories Sheila?

Everybody likes a good story. I for one, I'm especially glad that you could make it down here today. I think you'll find it very revealing. I know I did."

"Stories - glad I was handcuffed? - I'd no option - revealing - this is crazy - reveal what?" She now visibly demonstrated.

"Sheila, let me firstly reveal a song that was a chart topper back in 1964."
Sheila looked intentionally at every wall, but averted her eyes from Steven Murray.

"It hit the No. 1 slot on the 25th of June 1964 to be precise. Stayed there for only two weeks mind. It was a Roy Orbison song Sheila. Did you personally like the big O?"

"I don't care," protested Sheila Dixon. "I'm not interested in Roy Orbison, the big O or what was number one. And I've certainly no idea what is was called!"

"It's over, Sheila."

"What are you talking about. I haven't done anything. You have no right..."

"Let me stop you there Mrs Dixon. You misunderstand. The name of the song was '*It's Over.*' It was top of the pops during July 1st 1964. Co-incidentally, that was the very day that you were born."

Again Sheila found herself taken aback by his seemingly random meanderings. "Your maiden name was in fact..." Dixon shook her head. "Well, we'll come to that in a minute. Suffice to say you never actually married Mr Kenneth Dixon. However, you began to use his surname, giving the impression that you both were wed. 'From this day forward, for better for worse, for richer for poorer, in sickness and in health." And more interestingly Sheila - "Until death do us part."

Mrs D. I believe that from that day forward, for you personally, it was the beginning of the end. Today however, be aware, one hundred percent for sure .... It's definitely over!" Detective Inspector Steven Murray in true Clint Eastwood 'I talk to the trees' mode, began to recite: *All the rainbows in the sky start to even say goodbye - You won't be seeing rainbows any more. Setting suns before they fall, echo to you that's all, that's all. But you'll see lonely sunset after all. It's over, It's over, It's over, It's over.'*

Murray had used up his trilogy of lyrics: The Heart of Midlothian; Revenge and It's Over!

As the Inspector then began to pace around the small interrogation room, his body burst into life. He was alive, alert and animated once again as he spoke. With his arms chest high and hands opened, he posed as a question, "Mr and Mrs 'Kenneth' Dixon, a successful, wealthy couple? Certainly it would appear so," he continued. "Especially in the material sense. But, who do you have in your life......"

"I want to go now Inspector," she interrupted.

"To share that success with?" he concluded. Unabated, he persisted. "Hangers on, people on your payroll, an undesirable element of scroungers, wasters and petty two-faced villains! I ask again Mrs Dixon, who do you have in your life? In simpler terms, where do family factor in?"

Sheila sat nervously. Beginning to gently tap together the heels of her expensive, chocolate brown Valentino court shoes. She grew more noticeably agitated and began twitching. Filled with anxiety and appearing fearful. She had become gravely concerned at where Murray was going and ultimately the road he was travelling down.

In full flow, he paused slightly, gazed down at Sheila Dixon and offered a considered smile. He bent forward, put his arms either side of the desk and gently leaned into her face to ask quietly, "Is there family?"

Once again no response. Sheila stared coldly straight through him.

"To all and sundry it would appear on the surface that there are no children Mrs Dixon. So, we did a little bit of digging ourselves in regards to that Sheila. When I say we, I mean, and let me get this wholly accurate." Verbatim, Murray then recalled, "The mouthy, cheeky, pale-faced, big skinny constable! Did I get that right Sheila? The one that's a big fan of vivariums."

Hanlon grinned behind the glass.

In full 'Detective Columbo' style, Murray now stated. "Here's what I think happened, tell me how I do."

She once again swallowed hard and strenuously shook her head. The top half of her body tried to remain in control - calm, composed and collected. From her hips though, that was a different story altogether - they were off at a latin salsa class! Gyrating wildly at speed up the Royal Mile. Whilst her pulsating thighs moved to the rhythm of the personal ballet recital that her feet were now performing underneath the desk.

Half-heartedly and hesitantly, she offered, "You have no idea what you are talking about, or getting yourself into." It was tepid, tame and spiritless. You would not say, 'getting yourself into.' Unless you recognised the fact that there was a situation that existed. She was weakening and Murray could feel it.

He lifted up his iPad from the desk. He then opened it in a professional manner, as if about to read something. In actual fact a blank word document presented itself to him. However, in the tone of a genuine storyteller, he began the tale: "Once upon a time, a young, lonely and destitute fair maiden arrived in the East. Regretfully, she had the acute misfortune to meet up with an undisciplined adolescent by the name of James Baxter Reid. With hindsight, ANY other path chosen would and should, have been preferable."

Reminiscent of the suave Eamonn Andrews or the ultra debonair Michael Aspel, both with their large, leather-bound red books. Steven Murray at this point would have undoubtedly have made an outstanding host for 'This Is Your Life.' With the iPad in his left hand he continued gesticulating deliberately, confidently and powerfully with his right.

Saying, "He did however introduce you to his mentor and role model. An up and coming Ayrshire businessman. A young, yet battle hardened Scotsman. A hardy soul who was about to make Edinburgh his long term home. Step forward, twenty-three year old ex-con, Kenneth Dixon. Now remember to correct me at any time with parts of this Sheila." A second later he continued, "I'm excited to have you join up some of the dots as I go." He received a glare, a dramatic look. One that you would not automatically associate with love and affection that's for sure!

Dixon's wife was now breathing intensely. Her shoulder blades arched as Murray began every sentence. Desperately, she ensured she sat upright, no indication of defeat could be displayed. Another iPad page was swiped. Murray, characteristically smiled at the wordless grey screen in front of him and began to read aloud: "On meeting up with KD at age 19, moving in together and still never having conceived. I would assume then, at that particular point in your relationship, that there was obviously a problem somewhere in that department."

Sheila remained taut and vertical, her lips pursed ready to explode. Determined not to crack, she allowed DI Murray further time in the spotlight.

Penetrating her piercing eyes, he asked slowly and in a considered manner, "The gangster and his 'moll' were to be childless? Really? I don't think so."

Sheila turned, she hastily studied and scrutinised Steven Murray. From the tip of his unpolished black brogues to the edge of his lightly gelled, wavy grey hair. Hair that was cut short these days, in a style that often made him look distinguished and poised.

He was getting to her now, of that there was no doubt! 'But what did he actually know,' she thought. He's giving a very accurate account, yet generalised overview of her background. No real specifics, dates, times or even accusations in relation to anything.

'Oh my goodness,' she thought. 'He's after Kenny,' she figured. He's on a different path. 'We are good,' she reckoned. The ballet and salsa classes were over. No need for encores! Her posture relaxed. Hips, legs and thighs were stilled. 'Game on,' she thought.

A further screen swipe ensued. "Your options were restricted though. Kenny couldn't have children, and adoption would not have been a viable alternative given his 'responsible' background! Even with all his informers on the ground, corrupt officials in his pocket and virtual control of Edinburgh Castle, including all of those bent policemen within earshot of that famous 'one o'clock gun,' I believe confidently that your husband is possibly unaware of at least two key points I'm guessing? Sheila daren't look up, Murray would go from a sweeping generic thought, to a very specific revelation that breached the high security fence that 'Bonnie and Clyde' had managed to erect over the intervening years.

You know, many years ago Sheila when I was a teenager in High School. I missed more classes than I attended. During 5th year, I would make an appearance on a Thursday afternoon for two periods of football.

Then I'd find out from the P.E. teacher Mr. Millar, what the Saturday arrangements for the match were and return home! Sadly for you Mrs Dixon, things have changed. Back then I very seldom did my homework! These days, with the help, support and dogged determination of some wonderful 'classroom assistants,' I think you'll find, not only have we collectively submitted our findings. They have been thoroughly checked, marked and a nostalgic gold star firmly positioned on the page, just above the smiley face!" Simultaneously he raised his eyes, smiled and gave a cheeky broad grin.

"Sheila, I'm about to go out on a limb here. But firstly and rather significantly, I would be inclined to think that Billy Boy, our millionaire businessman and leading Scottish celebrity is ......how can one put this delicately? Oh, my apologies, I'm sorry, you just can't. However, I hope this terminology is agreeable, suitable and to your liking. Although in all truthfulness, as my original saying goes, I really couldn't care if the chicken went commando!"

Murray opened his hands at chest high, and circled his fingers, as if encouraging the audience to come closer and listen carefully. Behind the glass all the heads swayed and crowded noticeably inward.

Dixon on the other hand had no idea what he was on about. At this moment in time, she thought him mad!

Simply put, Murray now slowed to one word per second. "I - believe - Sheila - that - Mr - William - Taunton - is - your - Father!" Now speeding up he offered - "Yes, he is your Pop, El Presidente, The Patriarch of your Home. Bill 'Become a Serial Killer with an S' Taunton................is your Dad!"

The jaw of his solitary audience member dropped instantly. It became long, drawn and sharp. Similar in shape to those memorable, special, yet bizarre earrings that she had chosen to wear repeatedly, including today. By now, Murray was fairly certain that she wore them most days. And like his particular quirk for having a pen in each suit jacket. She doubtless had several identical pairs within her accessories wardrobe.

Sheila Dixon remained stoic. A slight tremble in her bare forearms worked its way down toward her weather hardened hands. The fingers on which were quickly retracted. Leaving two firmly clenched fists united in their solidarity against the prevailing truth!

In a reflective, understanding tone the Inspector expressed, "Back in the day, seeing a specialist would not have been cheap. What was then a revolutionary scientific advancement Sheila, has since become a routine medical treatment. My colleagues have informed me that more than five million IVF babies have been born. I know that you may have the financial clout now. But in the early eighties the Dixon 'brand' was only in it's infancy. I suspect a private donor was required. And that was where one William Taunton Esquire entered the fray."

Sheila watched as Murray continued to walk and talk. She was speechless. An occasional tear would now feature from time to time on her cheek.

The Inspector now back at full pace and volume continued. "Taunton's money would've helped enormously in getting you and KD's fertility treatments started. I'm not judging, or condemning, but I guess you got pregnant! You had not seen him for about four years. I know it couldn't have been easy for you to approach him."

Sheila's timid look toward Murray became more deliberate and more offensive. It became a fully-fledged scowl, a considered stare of deep loathing.

Murray stopped. He stood absolutely still for easily thirty seconds. It seemed like an eternity in the confines of that relatively limited enclosure. The merest hint at a bead of sweat, began to appear on the forehead of this middle aged woman. Who for the first time, was maybe beginning to look her age. "I can't empathise with you Mrs Dixon. But having read the accounts of what you went through." Sheila looked at him in sheer astonishment and disbelief. Her hands disappeared swiftly from the table and were now placed palm down under her thighs. She began to rock backwards and forwards, like a forlorn teenager. The Inspector continued, "Having watched the videos and having witnessed many of the photographs contained in your mother's collection. I can only express heartfelt sorrow and regret."

Sheila remained dumbstruck.

"No one should have experienced that. Let alone a daughter from her father," Steven Murray concluded! Joe Hanlon was awe struck, he had no idea at what had been found.

Whispering close up to his Inspector he asked, "Tom Wendel, MLA?"

"Absolutely Joe. Tom Wendel is the great, great grandson of Thomas Wendel. His family were the co-founders of the Master Locksmiths Association, originating here in Edinburgh and formed in 1904."

"A safe cracker!" Hanlon said, "Well played sir, I never saw that one coming."

Meanwhile Sheila's shoulders were rising and falling slowly. She was close to breaking, but was reluctant to let her emotions win out. She feared she would appear vulnerable. She had been taken advantage of all her life and she had vowed it would happen no more!

Trying genuinely to understand, to add a few more pieces of the jigsaw. The Inspector gently posed the question: "As you grew older, the abuse I take it, was that the catalyst for you leaving, running away or more aptly put, escaping from the clutches of your predatory father?"

With her eyes gazing downwards towards the bottom of the room door, a short nod was given. 'Oh,' Murray thought, slightly surprised and taken aback, an acknowledgement. The ebb and flow was for sure changing.

The DI continued at a slower unhurried pace. Sitting at Sheila Dixon's side now. "I'm guessing that all the documentation was to be the downfall of your poor mother also?" Sheila shrugged, as if in agreement. She went to speak, but licked her lips and simply sighed.

"Go on," Murray encouraged her. "It could help us." With a sadness and resignation, Sheila Dixon gently and nervously at first, began to break her silence. Murray's lips came together only for the briefest of moments to form a smile, as he thought to himself…….. 'seconds away, round four!'

In quiet melancholic tones Dixon softly declared, "I'm sure my mother reflected deeply upon certain actions that should not have taken place. Coupled with alternative actions that should have occurred, but did not. Yes, I believe all of those were contributing factors in her taking her own life Inspector." Sheila now stared at Murray with a look that implied - do you really need me to continue?

Sadly, it was the beginning of an all too familiar story. One of an abusive father with a penchant for young girls.

Murray informed her, "We've checked his appointment books and diary schedules from way back then. Amazingly, he also kept an accurate record. But mainly to do with his business concerns, rather than his social and leisure time pursuits. Around July/August of 1985 however, we discovered he met every Tuesday morning briefly with a Mrs Dixon. That would have been yourself."

Sheila wept. Never once looking in the Inspector's direction.

"After a couple of visits, it was then simply entered as S. After five or six more scheduled meetings, they finished. No more!" voiced Steven Murray.

Nodding his head in an understanding, yet, why did you do it manner? The Inspector continued to wax lyrical and elaborate on his speculative theory and conjecture. He thrust his right thumb and middle finger to his chin. His index finger ran up the side of his cheek (in real 'Thinker' mode) and he quickly announced -

"I have a hunch you handed over what was promised to keep your side of the bargain, the arrangement, or whatever terminology you used. Poor Mr. Taunton he probably kept it straightforward and called it blackmail. At that point I assume he would have had no idea that you had a plethora of other incriminating evidence, as well as a second diary!"

Sheila remained quiet again. Willing to let the tall, genial Scotsman dominate the room and the conversation, one-sided as it was more often than not. Now sat alongside, he turned toward her and looked longingly and hard into her eyes. Murray's years on the job had taken their toll. He never liked to admit it, but he could read people fairly well. Actually, exceptionally well according to various management test scores and courses he'd attended over the years. He could have even been a top profiler. He'd been approached once by a friend who now worked with the FBI. A job offer had been put forward. An attractive offer which Paisley Buddy, Steven Murray, politely declined.

Today in the eyes and nonverbal language of one Sheila Dixon, Murray was getting an overriding sense of solace and succour. An almighty wave and build-up of emotions had gathered and formed a huge mental dam over the years. Now, at breaking point, an enormous white squall was about to surge through. Tossing and turning the anguish, the guilt, the rage, the lost love and childhood memories in her unstable mind. Revenge, relief and recovery were all looking to find a port in this dangerous storm. Murray recognised fully that she had been deeply hurt, scarred and cast adrift emotionally for years. Setting course now though, Sheila had made some major errors in judgement. Actions of a confused, vulnerable and sadly dangerous lady. The devastating impact of many of those actions, had been most dramatically witnessed in recent days.

In Murray's mind though, a serious, pivotal unanswered question remained. He was about to go 'around the world in eighty days' with it and ask Passepartout. Had she been an innocent manipulator due to being regularly abused and constantly manipulated herself? Or had she grown to love it? To feel fulfilled and powerful, by continuing to be a devious, deranged and highly misguided Machiavellian Mademoiselle?

Murray's summation continued in an informative 'but keep me right manner.' "Nine months later you had a child. With Kenny Dixon as a parent however, you both recognised that an 'heir apparent' could be vulnerable. Possibly they had already been a target? So between you, you never told anyone outwith your inner circle. Having said that, no doubt Kenny was the one that insisted his name be put on the birth certificate." Sheila audibly sighed.

"He needed recognition as her father. There had to be no lingering doubts about his manhood," Murray figured. "You massaged his ego and duly obliged. However, your own private personal story Sheila. That has more twists, turns and somersaults than an Olympic gymnastic competition."

Dixon as well as clasping her hands and drumming her thumbs on the desk in front of her, now had her eyes firmly closed. It was as if this duet of actions rendered her deaf. Oblivious to all of the Inspector's intrusive words!

In a concerned tone, Steven Murray then hesitated to speak. "I believe there is, eh, there is however, a major problem. A considerable one Mrs Dixon. One that would lead me to the second item that 'Kenneth' would be completely unaware of. This is a classic. And to be honest, to have been able to have kept it secret for all these years, well, that is mightily impressive!"

Sheila swallowed, closed her eyes tighter and visibly shook as she waited for Murray to finish his remarks. The Inspector from being animated, brusque and making somewhat cocky, flippant assertions - seemed to stop in his tracks. He paused thoughtfully once again and his eyes showed a modicum of reflection ahead of speaking. He consciously steadied himself before stating and asking in a composed, serene and tranquil manner….. Suddenly there was movement at the door. A couple of distinct sounds were about to change the dynamic of the interview quite dramatically, and the outcome, most profoundly.

TWENTY TWO

"You're the ringmaster, directing attention away from the darkness to what you want them to see. You can't let anyone see that it's not at all as it appears to be, you've got an image to maintain."

\- Michele Barton Thomas

Two loud knocks and the hinges opened swiftly. Murray initially held up his open palm. Making a clear unequivocal: Stop - Do not come any further gesture!

He had left clear instruction not to interrupt him. However, based on the urgency written all over this callow, naive constable's face. A rather fiery and hostile, "What's up? was deemed a more suitable response. The fair haired youngster, PC George Smith moved to whisper in his Inspector's ear.

"Just tell me man," Murray snapped. "Mrs Dixon will get just as much pleasure from the surprise as I will."

"Another body sir."

Sheila, caught off-guard, looked across incredulously at the rookie officer. 'Good cop, bad cop,' she thought. I get it, they had already pre-planned this. It was being staged and very authentic it seemed too.

"Whereabouts?"

"Circus Place."

"What!" "What!" In near perfect unison, both Murray and Mrs Dixon responded. Sheila rising abruptly to her feet.

"It's the accountant sir."

"Melanie Rose?" He questioned.

"That's her."

"What about her?"

"It's her sir. She's the victim. She's dead!"

The chair overturned and the desk hurtled forward clattering at speed into Steven Murray. The Matriarch of one of Edinburgh's most successful business empires. An organisation that was sinister, sleazy and highly corrupt mind you, had collapsed to the floor.

These days in Scotland's capital, the rich and poor live increasingly separate lives. Face-to-face relationships are being gradually eroded by social exclusivity in the New Town and by the increasingly indoor life of most of the higher classes. The professional and gentrified families that dominate wealthy society now required few occasions for contact with the working class. Like all great cities, Edinburgh had become a place of contrasts - of good and bad, desirable and undesirable. This was the price that was inevitably paid for the rise and prosperity of the capital of Scotland. Built in several stages from the 1760s to the 1830s, the New Town of Edinburgh was the largest planned city development in the world at that time. And it proved an outstanding success in bringing commercial and cultural dynamism to the city.

Earlier that day a 'Ringmaster' had sounded the intercom at the upmarket Circus Place apartment of one Melanie Rose. In his mind he was determined to turn this poor, mediocre show into an outstanding, world class performance! Miss Rose had been kept fully occupied working at her desk throughout the morning. She had been making up for those extra few days she had taken off over the festive period.

Instantly recognising the voice at the other end, she proceeded to press the button to allow entry. Access to the stairway was like crossing over at passport control to one of the most idyllic holiday destinations on the planet. A passageway to a new country. Guests would experience a different culture, gain a flavour and enjoy a taste of life only a privileged few ever got to know. An enticing grand foyer with refined and elegant craftsmanship on display in every direction. From the magnificent marble flooring, to the ornate, delicate and most beautifully intricate finishing on the ceilings and surrounding stonework.

Her caller made short work in arriving outside her flat. A property that epitomised its owner. It was a delight to be around, full of charm and exceptionally graceful! The door had been left ajar for her visitor, enabling them to venture straight into her place of work. What happened next however, was unexpected. Rather than cross the threshold of the luxury dwelling, a hand reached up onto the door to where the A.H. Accountants nameplate was. Then, by easing their fingers steadily through the letterbox and gripping the edge ever so carefully, the individual began to edge the door, inch by inch toward themselves. Eventually, slamming it shut!

Melanie wondered where her guest was? Why the delay? What had become of them? Walking out into the hallway, she noticed that the door had shut. The accountant assumed it must have been a gentle draft, a small gust of wind or the like that had caused it to close over. As she looked through the viewer, she was reassured that it was who she thought it was. Then, still peering out and within nine-tenths of a second, she saw it being raised toward the spy hole and questioned instantly. Is that? What is he doing with a .... "Powww! Powww!"

The two explosive sounds could be heard echoing up and down the four storey building. The top half of the doorway was completely gone. The sublime artistic decor either side riddled with pellets. The sweet pleasant scent of the flowers now merged with spent shotgun shells and was redolent of manliness. It was the smell of danger.

The assailant fled the instant the weapon had been discharged. Neighbouring doors now opened in alarm. Screaming clients from the lawyer's office above, were streaming down the stairway. Many in a state of panic making their way to the exit. Others concerned and worried at what they had just heard. But ultimately, many had no idea what they had just heard or experienced.

The stilled, blood splattered body of Melanie Rose would soon allow those at Circus Place, to ascertain what they had heard were rounds from a shotgun being fired. And what they had experienced? A murder being committed, on their very doorstep!

In the 'Big Top' at Circus Place that day, the star attraction literally died on her feet. No safety net was evident, no witnesses complete with candy floss and popcorn. And as for The Ringmaster, he was no clown! In fact, he had departed swiftly and transformed into a fleet footed acrobat!

Murray travelled at speed over to Circus Place with Joseph Hanlon in tow. Dixon was resting, recuperating in the medical room at the station. The Inspector knowing what he knew, knew Sheila could wait a little longer. Given the latest murder, he recognised that the safest place for her would be there at headquarters, surrounded by a body of police officers. He was also well aware that when she awoke, given the circumstances, she would need the very best medical care in one form or other.

Arriving in the New Town, they made their way past a growing number of macabre onlookers in the street. In what is a very affluent, upmarket part of Edinburgh, Murray confided in Joe Hanlon. He was convinced he'd just at that moment, walked past a bearded lady, two pint sized jugglers and a female with a face that had been fired from one too many cannons!

Steven Murray at that precise moment, had just taken one almighty leap too many from a politically incorrect trapeze with no safety net. Joe calmly stated, "You maybe don't want to be repeating those specific remarks sir." Sensible advice Murray concluded, from a wise young man. A sensible, wise young man going places. 'Definitely going places,' the ageing detective thought.

Remnants of a slight mist, combined with a strange conglomerate of aromas. Wood, ceramic, glass and marble offered a mind-blowing tapestry upon the tiled floor. A veritable visual feast for the senses.

Ally Coulter had just lost his partner the day before. As colleagues, they had visited with this helpful woman only one week earlier. Both spoke very highly of her. Especially Coulter, who had been somewhat slightly under her charismatic spell. Together, they acknowledged that the accountancy firm were key. Key to what though? That, they still hadn't quite figured out yet. But they had both felt it. Alan Hikesend Accountants needed some very private TLC.

This was certainly no tender loving care. The body of the deceased lay beneath the amazing scattering of coloured shapes and pieces. Her death though, may hopefully bring new life to a secret once laid to rest, thought best forgotten and now reawakened. A dark secret of a past once gone. Undisclosed, private information that Murray had just been about to unveil and share with the world!

At that precise moment he caught young Hanlon vigorously shaking his head and asked, "What's up son?"

"It's gone sir, gone. It's incredible, dreadful." In disbelieve 'Sherlock' was shaking more than ever. Scratching, pulling at his hair, rubbing his brow and continually wiping his eyes. Murray, not making any sense of Hanlon's exasperated comments and strange body movements, looked pleadingly at a nearby paramedic who had witnessed their exchange.

Candidly, yet respectfully he informed Murray, "He's talking about her face Inspector."

"What! Her face?" the DI questioned, he seemed puzzled.

Murray then looked more thoroughly and diligently at the motionless frame in front of him. His hands instantly covered his mouth as the disfigurement to her attractive face became fully apparent. Her now inanimate body lay beneath havoc strewn shredded fragments of debris. Many of the materials, had been up until an hour ago visibly displayed, weaved and spread out across the once elegant and cultured hallway.

Wood from the doorway - Check.
Ceramics from vases and display china - Check.

Glass from mirrors and decanters - Check.
Marble from floor and tiled walls - Check.
Charred flesh, fragments of bone, human hair - Check, Check and Check.

The beautiful, educated, kind, courteous and refined Melanie Rose had been blasted point blank in the face. Separated from her assailant's gun by only three delicate inches of polished wood.

This was now highly personal. Murray was certain that the general public had no need to fear. Although try telling that to the immediate families of Debbie and James Evans. Two innocent parties already caught up in this heart-breaking crossfire of evil.

'Bunny' Reid was currently on the rampage. There was nothing complicated in his motives. He had felt betrayed. Let down by being set up! He was out for revenge, clear and simple. He was a bad man and he was doing exactly what bad men do. On reviewing the situation and with sincere apologies to the late Melanie Rose for the pun. Murray knew things were unquestionably, coming to a head.

After a few more routine checks and enquiries, the Detective Inspector stood tall and straight. He stared intensely toward Hanlon, as young Joe spoke with one of the forensics team. Feeling that strange sensation that you get, when you know someone is watching or hovering over you, ADC Hanlon turned gradually to have his suspicions confirmed. Murray stood with a semblance of a smile. Having said that, his look actually went straight past Joseph Hanlon and with a slight nod of his head and raised eye, his stare made 'Sherlock' look in the direction of the fancy name plate to the left of the partially destroyed doorway. Like everything else in the property is said class!

It was a beautiful piece of enamel grey slate. It was approximately one metre in length and less than half a metre wide. Elegantly etched upon it in a rich, deep burgundy shade, were the words: Alan Hikesend. No mention of 'Accountants,' 'Associates' or the like. Could that in itself be a subtle message? Hanlon turned back to Murray, whose smile had become even broader. Then, one final time back to the nameplate.

"You've lost me sir, I don't get it."

Astutely, Murray went for a Morgan Freeman *'wise old man drawl.'* "Remember, I told you about Dixon in jail. How he was the one that originally got 'Bunny' as a nickname. About 'Old Tommy,' etc, and how Kenneth Dixon was converted to puzzles, to a love of anagrams and the word search books we found at his bedside?"

Hanlon nodded. "Of course I remember. Of course, sure, all of that. Why, what is is? What are you thinking and what triggered it?"

"Maybe that was just a myth. Something that made him sound more capable, disciplined and mentally alert. Something that would help him inside if that were the perception, and certainly on the outside as he looked to further his business interests."

Joe continued to look perplexed.

"I believe he genuinely does possess those abilities these days. But I suspect he never got the desire to solve puzzles whilst inside! Think about it. Who would he learn from? Let's be honest Joe, prison mainly consists of: Wait, let me get this accurate and politically correct - Mildly dysfunctional reprobates, brain dead incompetents, perverted thieving ratbags, dossers, chookies and low-life nut jobs. How did I do?"

Hanlon raised his eyes!

"I started off well at least!" Murray snorted.

"Sir?" Hanlon said politely, looking rather confused.

"Joe," he paused. "Ally and Taz thought that this place held the key. That Melanie Rose knew more than she was saying. Well, I'm pleased to confirm that I think they were right. I suspect Sheila Dixon was actually the one that helped implant an inquisitive mind in her 'Kenny.' And that they have been way more of a partnership in recent years, than people ever realised."

Hanlon continued to nod supportively, with an intermittent shake of the head. In his best Sandra Kerr vocabulary, Murray stated, "It is a rather splendid sign, would one not say?"

"Aye!" was the best that Hanlon could muster, now partially losing the will to live.

Now going with a Doctor Watson tone, Murray began: "Oh, my dear Holmes, just like Sir Walter Scott was for me in my youth. Sometimes the answer is encircling you, it's all around you. This particular one is on the wall, staring us both straight in the face …'Alan Hikesend.' I repeat, there is no mention of accountants, associates or the like.

"Maybe it was a partnership?" Joe offered up.

"That was exactly what it was ADC Hanlon. You are one hundred percent correct. It was indeed the Alan Hikesend Partnership? That is because using the exact same letters, they could have called the company…….. Sheila and Ken!"

TWENTY THREE

"Every rose has its thorn, just like every night has its dawn. Just like every cowboy sings his sad, sad song. Every rose has its thorn."

- Poison

Murray and Hanlon arrived back at the station at around 4.45pm. Fully three hours after initially heading over to the latest crime scene. Sheila, who'd been comforted by a few sedatives earlier in the day, was currently being escorted back through the doorway of the interview room.

A soothing voice offered, "Mrs Dixon, welcome back, take a seat." Murray extended his hand and gestured toward the classic charcoal grey plastic and metal combo. A much favoured piece of furniture by libraries, community centres, schools and obviously police stations since the mid nineteen eighties. "I trust you are feeling better," Murray stated sympathetically. "Let me firstly, fully update you regarding the harrowing news that was broken in front of you earlier. Most people I guess on hearing the death of their accountant would certainly have been shocked."

"It's fine Inspector, I'm over it now."

Slowly, he began to ask in a puzzled manner. "You're over it?" He paused for effect, before adding more curtly, "I would somehow doubt that is the truth."

She shrugged and began to raise her voice in a lively, energetic and dismissive manner. "What... why would... when are... you don't know..."

"Oh, but I do know Sheila," Murray stopped her in her tracks and his voice intensified. "I'd suspected this past week, but your reaction today fully confirmed it for me. I apologise profusely though. I had no idea that Constable Smith when naming the murdered victim, was about to confirm it - as your daughter!"

That was it, the dam burst and the deluge began. The floodgates could not cope with the years of pent up emotion. Abuse, abused, abuser. She was mentally drained, damaged and deluded. A life taken, a new life that was never really her. A life taken - that of her daughter. Her childhood years spent apart. Their tender relationship kept hushed, quiet and way below the radar. No birthday celebrations, no Mother's Day cards and these past two weeks - No festive meals, catch ups or exchange of lovingly wrapped gifts with satin bows. Never had Santa Claus received a Christmas list from the young Melanie Rose. A woman named unsurprisingly after her grandmother. A desperately tortured soul that had committed suicide many, many years before Melanie was even born.

Murray then went on to explain enthusiastically and at speed. "Last week, during their journey back to the station, Ally Coulter explained his tic-tac signs to Constable Tasmin Taylor. The hand, the chest, the ear. These were not the latest odds being offered to Ally at a race meet. But significantly Sheila, he was referring to the various pieces of jewellery being worn on those parts of your accountant's body. DS Coulter is very much a ladies man and he recognised instantly the beautiful ballerina ring on her smooth manicured hand. Also, rather astutely how Melanie was wearing her mermaid pendant. Having wisely taken some snaps at her workplace on his phone. He had then sent them to me and pointed out the photo with an earlobe showing, with only the faintest section of earring visible."

Sheila made to quickly touch the side of her face before realising it.

"That's correct, Mrs Dixon. As you know, I've been up close and personal with that particular item of jewellery on several occasions. Intriguingly in fact, I find myself looking at it again right now!

Sheila Dixon swallowed hard. She had nothing left to offer up.

Hanlon was fascinated. He had sat engrossed. It was as if he was being given his very own private 'origami' lesson. He watched as a plain piece of paper was being carefully transformed. As facts and figures were stated, they appeared as delicate folds in the page. Every new piece of evidence added feathers, feet and wings. As clues unravelled and were placed in order, 'Sherlock' observed Murray's masterpiece take flight. His vision saw an impressive phoenix rising from the ashes to make sense of all this deadly, destructive mayhem. He blinked the image from his mind as Murray continued.

"Who attends University graduations? Why the importance of a flower? Sorry, bouquet of roses being delivered to both those homes every week? It was personal, right from the start we knew that. But we just couldn't figure out why?

"The Chief," Hanlon reminded DI Murray.

"Oh, yes, how could I forget Sheila. Our very own Chief Inspector, CI Brown actually usurped us with the jewellery and the flower delivery. It seemed like the start of a bad joke. It was too close to a Scotsman, an

Englishman and an Irishman for me. I had asked him if he knew of a connection between a mermaid, an iceberg and a ballerina?"

Dixon opened her mouth, shook her head and stared at Murray with incredulity! Worry was now transfixed across her furrowed brow.

"Surprisingly, astonishingly actually Sheila, he did! I wish I was still a betting man Mrs D. I could have won a packet on that little tri-cast coming up. Oh, and by the way, did I mention our boss was also an avid fan of horticulture? So it was no surprise to me, when he then went on to inform me of what he thought the possible link might be."

Sheila Dixon's chest swelled as she steadily breathed in. Her nostrils showed only the slightest movement. Tenderly she clasped her hands, placed them on her lap and gently closed her eyes. She may have tried visually to remove DI Murray from her mind, but there was no getting away from him audibly!

"The Chief was aware of a Ballerina rose," Murray said. "And an Iceberg rose," the Inspector teasingly smiled. "However, it required a little bit more green-fingered detective work from him, before he could firmly establish that in 1918 a Mermaid was added to the official list of named roses."

Dixon remained silent. Eyes closed, shoulders rising and lowering softly.

"It was your music collection at home Sheila that helped to tip me off. Your MR CD. Not MR for Mister someone as I had sadly mistaken. But now it had become clear. It stood for M.R. - Melanie Rose! She had graduated from University and was a financial whizz kid. As your bookkeeper, it was an opportunity to keep her close, to still have her as part of your life. Yet she was able to have her own identity without anyone knowing. It was intimate. It was a playlist for your daughter and no doubt in part tribute to your mother also. The songs: '*There Were Roses,*' '*A Bed of Roses,*' '*Rose of Tralee*' and '*Roses are Red*' all played whilst we were there. We would still have had no idea, if it wasn't for Sergeant Coulter stumbling across the graduation photograph. A small group of individuals obviously knew though Sheila. And they wanted to hit out hard at you, why? Why so personal? Who else knew of the existence of that particular rose?" Murray stopped suddenly. The lightbulb had switched on. Casting an intimidatingly long shadow across her body from the overhead fluorescent lighting. The eureka moment came to him as he stood directly over Sheila Dixon. "Tell me he didn't Sheila. Tell me he didn't know. Not Reid. You were not stupid enough…." He stopped to correct himself. "Of course you were. He was Kenny's right hand man. Of course, the only other one you would tell," Murray spat each word out with disgust… James - Baxter - Reid?"

Startled, her eyes resurfaced with a jolt. "Bunny? No, he wouldn't have." She paused briefly, then pleaded through what appeared to be a stream of genuine tears, "Would he?"

Murray shrugged and looked down at a poor impersonation of the Sheila Dixon he had gotten to know over the past week or so. The self-confidence gone. The hardened exterior, which was possibly always an act anyway, had evaporated. She was physically aging with each minute that past. Darkened eyes, sallow skin and blotchy, grey roots appearing, her zest for life rapidly diminishing.

"Who else knew Sheila?" Murray asked as he made to quickly exit the room. "I'll leave you to ponder over that for a minute." Hanlon stared at the door in disbelieve. Where had he gone? What was he doing? Joe nodded at Mrs Dixon. She bit her lip hard with worry.

A small trickle of blood appeared where she had obviously broken the skin. 'Sherlock' offered his white handkerchief. It seemed symbolic. Hanlon felt he'd extended a hand of friendship and provided the opportunity for a truce, for at least an unspecified duration. This time, she graciously returned the nod and accepted the finely woven square of cotton.

After fully ten minutes Steven Murray re-entered. He began by reminding Sheila, "Earlier I apologised for PC Smith breaking that news in front of you. He had no idea that it was your daughter."

The shadowed eyes of Sheila Dixon again began to look troubled. It seemed that every time this man addressed her, he undressed her! He had the uncanny ability to peel back layer after layer. To unveil, unravel and produce something new and alluring every time with frightening regularity. It made her feel naked and vulnerable. Stripped of any protection, her sordid past and equally sordid present laid bare for all to review, consider and judge. On one hand she quite openly detested him. Yet on the other, she could not help but secretly revere him. With dread, she wondered what the magician was about to produce from his hat this time? A 'Bunny' perhaps!

"When we were interrupted a few hours back, I was about to clarify a second issue that I'm pretty certain 'Our Kenneth' may have been kept in the dark about."

Nodding, Sheila Dixon intimated, 'well, what is it you want to say, or feel you know.' It's amazing that all that could be communicated from one simple nod of the head!

Murray then shrugged. "Actually, you know what Mrs Dixon? I'm going to keep that surprise on hold even longer."

Hanlon blinked numerous times. He'd been taken by surprise.

Sheila exclaimed defiantly, "What! No! Tell me, what issue?"

"Oh, and by the way, you'll be delighted to know that we've been given the okay to keep you in custody for the next four days. It doesn't sound too long when you say it like that. However," and the Inspector's voice noticeably slowed. "That is ninety six long, lingering hours to be precise." Putting on a fake American accent Murray then continued with, "You have a good day now, ye hear!"

Hanlon expected a struggle, a modicum of resistance or at the very least some verbal abuse as he escorted her back to her cell. Sheila Dixon offered none of the above. She politely handed him back his soiled handkerchief and remained silent. Now possibly forever stained and tainted. It was soaked in the tears and blood of regret, remorse and retribution. No one ever witnessed it being dropped into a nearby waste paper basket as they walked. But her disrobing had only been postponed. She knew inevitably what was still to come.

"The master safebreaker, I mean locksmith, Tom Wendel had been invaluable," Murray joked. Though in all seriousness he continued with, "We have uncovered an Aladdin's cave of depravity and perversion. Tom is on his way to check out another potential lead in this link of lechery." Hayes and Curry simply turned and looked at each other in bewilderment. This was certainly all new to 'Kid' Curry. And Joseph Hanlon had now found himself 'swimming with sharks,' having just learned to paddle for himself in the last ten days!

"I have a couple of visits to make tomorrow," said the Inspector. "We still have plenty to occupy us. Reid is the priority, but I feel we need to track down Kenny Dixon sooner rather than later. The fact that we have been unable to locate either KD or Taunton concerns me greatly. He'll know by now that we have Sheila in custody and try to address things in his own way. That's if he has not done so already. That would be a mistake though - he doesn't know all the facts."

"What is it you're holding back sir?" asked ADC Hanlon.

"Never mind Joe. Just get back in touch with that Estate manager of Taunton's again. It has been too long, far too long. And I don't think it's a coincidence that they are off the grid together. Go speak to him personally, get a read on him."

Before heading off, Hanlon tried one more time. "Remind us sir, what is Dixon unaware of? What information is he lacking?"

"Come on, you should have figured it out by now," he teased. "I'm sure 'Sherlock' would have. Like I said when we first met Joe - In your own time, all in your own time. Get home everyone," he instructed. "It's going to be a hectic journey for the next two days, but worthwhile. Get plenty of sleep, relax and come in prepared to get justice for Taz and Ally!"

The Thursday morning rush hour traffic had died down. It was only minutes after 9am when Murray took the relatively short drive over to Kirkliston on the outskirts of the Capital. As his mobile rang and appeared with Hanlon's name displayed, he had been pondering on his relationship with 'Ally' Coulter over the years.

"Morning Joe, what's up?" he asked

"You are not goin…"

"Just spit it out lad. The sooner you tell me, the sooner we can rectify it!" He said with a west coast 'gallusness!'

"It's Taunton's gardener sir."

"Yes."

"Remember how he said he had returned from holiday and checked the Estate?"

"I remember," Murray added hesitantly. "So what? Has he recalled something important or found something of significance?"

"No, to the first one sir. And yes, a definite yes to the second!"

"What are you telling me Joe? Spell it out man."

Now it was Joe's turn to hesitate. "Sir, he never came back from holiday."

"Wha-attt!" Murray yelled. Nearly putting his car into a ditch. "He what!"

"He just figured everything was alright and told us what we needed to hear, to reassure us. He didn't think his boss would want any police officers popping by. He was fully aware of his South American trips and thought it maybe had to do with that!"

Murray, having now cautiously pulled up at the roadside, encouraged Hanlon to get officers over to the Northcroft Estate immediately.

"Already done, sir."

"We have no time to spare on this, Joe. The Press will hang us out to dry. We'll get slaughtered. That is, if some poor soul has not already been? I'm on my way to see the Sarge. Let me know what you find. I'll get in touch as soon as I've finished."

Kirkliston was a quaint parish town. It was the location of the first recorded Parliament in Scotland. Today, Steven Murray had walked up the six slab garden path and stood in trepidation. The basic black nameplate with silver writing etched on it, read: R. Coulter. 'Ally' had only been monitored by medics for 24 hours. Murray had stood gathering his thoughts for what seemed like an eternity, before summoning the courage to ring the doorbell. He wondered how his long term 'buddy' would react? How he was coping at coming to terms with the loss of his partner, his colleague and his friend? And if truth be told, from Murray's observation's, his 'adopted' daughter.

Robert Coulter had two grown up children, both girls and around Tasmin Taylors age. They had all been on nights out together. She was very much part of their family. At that, Murray felt the urge to take the easy option. To turn and jump back in his car. Then make a return visit again in a few days' time. At that point DS Robert Coulter would have hopefully came to terms with everything, and been back on the road to becoming his old self!

"Yea, right!" Murray murmured aloud. Just then, he thought he could hear some music. Definitely a strong rhythm he thought. And it had been getting louder the closer he got to the door. Coulter had neighbours above him. They had a side entrance, slightly further along the path. The increasing sound though, most certainly did not seem to emanate from their premises. The Inspector peered through the small downstairs window of the two bedroomed flat. It looked directly into Coulters tiny kitchen area. Murray could make out his overweight Detective Sergeant stomping, swaying and supposedly dancing around. The small pocket sized umbrella was being expertly used with artistic license as a Freddie Mercury microphone! There were several whisky glasses on the table and an open bottle sat temptingly nearby. Murray's heart sank. Listening for a few more seconds, he heard Ally belt out, *"So I yell out for some kind of angel to come down and rescue me. Be as soft as you can, put a drink in my hand, I'm as scared as I ever could be."* Murray, even with Coulters accompaniment, recognised it as an Alice Cooper track. He then pressed the doorbell, just as his Detective Sergeant was going for it one more time with gusto. *"So I yell out for some kind of angel to come down and rescue me. Be as soft as you can, put a drink in my hand, I'm as scared as I ever could be...eeeeeee."* He opened the door, saw Murray and with a face full of sheer disappointment exclaimed, "You, you are my angel? Geeez!"

The music continued to blare. Not sure those are the *'Good Vibrations'* that the Beach Boys sing about Murray thought.

At that moment the upstairs door opened and his Kenyan neighbour of ten years, Brian Wontee, looked out in frustration. The Detective Inspector who knew Wontee from his frequent visits to Ally Coulter's flat over the years, gave Brian a look and a wave that said, 'It's in hand, don't worry, I'll sort it.'

"It's been like that on and off since he returned home Steve," Wontee stated in a clear, deep and rich accent. "I heard about his colleague on the news. How is he doing? I don't want to hassle him but…"

"I understand, no problem. I'll have a word with him inside privately. Oh and Brian, just one more thing. Any favourite tunes you'd like him to put on?" Wontee acknowledged Murray's help and had a wry smile to himself regarding a choice of music!

Steven Murray calmly reflected on Ally Coulter's plea for help through that song. 'An Angel - Rescue - Drink in hand - Scared as he ever could be.'

"Ally, you're safe now, pal. We are on the lookout for Reid, he'll not get far."

"But, I thought the body in the water.." he began.

"No, no, don't be misled Ally. I think you'll find that's Forrester."

"Forrester, one of the singing duo?"

"Ye, don't you remember, they were present at the 'Doctors.' It was probably him and his pal that knocked you and …….." He hesitated to use her name.

"Taz, it's Taz. Detective Constable Tasmin Taylor," Coulter irately repeated louder each time. "You can say her name you know."

Murray felt awkward. "I'm sorry Ally, it's just tender for everyone. Speaking of which, all the team are asking after you. That lead with Melanie Rose helped enormously you know. The earrings, the pendant and Dixons ring. We have her in custody by the way.

"Melanie Rose?" Coulter said in disbelief.

"No, Dixon, Sheila Dixon. She's the one that has been the mastermind behind all the deaths Ally. All the deaths by poison that is!"

"All the deaths by poison. what other deaths are we talking about? More than just Taz?"

Murray stayed silent and reflected: Four beautiful children. A hard working mother. A thug of a father and a lovely accountant his Sergeant had a soft spot for.

"For another day Ally. All will become clearer later this afternoon. Do you want to be at my side for the interview of Sheila? You helped identify her. I'm happy to have you sit in with me, if you are up for it? I would like you to be the one that officially charges her. What do you say?"

Coulter fell back, his legs had gave way. He sat himself at a chair next to the 'wee' circular kitchen table for two. He had probably been operating on shock and adrenalin for the past 48 hours and now it was seriously hitting home. The bottle of open Malt gazed longingly in his direction. He glanced at Murray who stood quiet and motionless at the doorway. His Inspector returned the look. Complete with an obligatory question mark on the end.

DS Coulter knew what question was contained within that stare.

"I haven't touched it Steve, honest. I bought it, I caressed it, I opened it and I even sang to it!" he said, attempting a smile. "But for some reason I couldn't quite pour myself one."

"Good for you Ally. How long has it been?"

"Well over two decades. I don't know exactly, but twenty something years."

"I'm proud of you. Your girls would be proud of you and Detective Constable Tasmin Taylor would be exceptionally proud of you. Let's put the lid on it and gift it upstairs to Wontee. It can be a fitting apology for all the poor music choices that you've made him listen to throughout the night!"

Steven Murray expected his pal Robert Coulter to be readily agreeable to that suggestion. It was just a little bit of light hearted banter. Instead though, Ally's shoulders slumped and tears began to emerge and trickle down his stubbled cheeks. He was broken: "I only played that one song Steve. All night long, Alice Cooper's Lace and Whiskey." He wept openly now. "I could see the angels. I saw my whole life pass me by in ten seconds. I was prepared Steve, I was fully prepared." He began to tremble and shake. The tears continued apace as he candidly questioned, "Then Taz, why Taz? Her whole life ahead of her."

"Help me catch him Ally. We'll review some…"

"We'll review nothing, I'm only good for nothing. I'm finished Steve. You are my good friend, but I'm through. I NEVER died that night, but I most certainly lost my life!"

"You can't think like that. You have two gorgeous daughters that need you Ally, you mean everything to them. Your friends at the station rely on you, we trust you, heck we all love you. We want you back. Possibly slimmer than before, more thoughtful than before and please it wouldn't be hard, but preferably funnier than before!"

Coulter offered a hopeful smile as a single tear ran smoothly from his top lip to bottom. Slightly choked he whispered, "You're a good man Steven Murray. Some may even deem you great, myself included. I hope you'll respect my decision. Actually I have 'every confidence' that you will."

Murray cried. Coulter nodded. Both men hugged. A pleasant, heartfelt hug. A clinch that encapsulated their long term friendship. An embrace of compassion, warmth and understanding!

Murray vividly recalled many years ago when Robert "Ally" Coulter had opened up to him about his alcoholism. How his wife had walked out on him with his two young children and Ally desperately hoped not to get kicked off the force. In the prevailing two decades he had done remarkably well turning his life around and rewriting many of its more recent chapters.

Alas, it looked likely that Murray would be requiring a fitting epilogue to Coulter's story this time. Capturing James 'Bunny' Reid, keeping Sheila Dixon and her aged father behind bars indefinitely and tying up any remaining loose ends would seem an ideal, 'happy ever after' ending. Both men shook on that deal!

On checking his voicemail, "Hell's Bells," the Inspector gasped. He appeared to turn and view the church just 200 metres from Coulter's home. Then on checking his watch, he had hoped for eleven o'clock to sound and offer a more advantageous and ecclesiastical start to the day. After a further thirty second wait, alas, silence!

Returning urgently to his car the Inspector purchased an imaginary fast-pass ticket for the full Oat'n Nuts tour en-route. To witness the scene for himself, he then headed off at speed in the direction of Edinburgh's latest 'Murder Mystery destination. The Northcroft Estate in Dalkeith. He knew he was about to encounter paramedics, pathologists and photographers, not forgetting Professor Plum, with the 'politically correct' lead-free piping in the kitchen!

TWENTY FOUR

"What have I become - My sweetest friend. Everyone I know……………...Goes away in the end."

- Johnny Cash

Two patrol cars sat at the entrance to the Estate grounds, flanked either side by the majestic thirty foot sandstone turrets. Fearless reporters and their cameramen had gotten wind of something and were audaciously out in force. In fairness to William Taunton, having just been named in the New Year's Honours list he had become a favoured celebrity with the media in recent times. Also as a major importer and provider of jobs in Scotland and the UK, he was a highly regarded and respected figure in the innovative business world.

It would have to be added to his CV however, that this morning was not going to go down as one of his more productive days. He lay dead!

As Murray stood gazing over Taunton's body, a voice calmly told him, "He's still alive!" Murray could feel the close unwanted presence of someone at his side invading his personal space. Looking warily to his right, he was greeted by the nodding, friendly, familiar face of 'Doc' Patterson.

"Alright, Steven" the Doc added jauntily. "He's still with us, but only just."

"Susan!" Murray cried out to DC Susan Hayes, waving her across toward both men.
As 'Hanna' Hayes made her way over to her colleagues, William Taunton lay inert. Paramedics worked frantically to offer him hope.

"Where is Hanlon? The Inspector asked, looking for an update on what had happened.

"He'll be back in a minute sir. He's just escorting someone to a patrol car to be taken in."

"What for? This?"

"He said you of all people would understand sir."

"Understand what?"

"His exact words sir. 'He was going to 'huckle' the Estate manager to set an example of him!'"
Murray had to work hard to suppress his laughter. It would have seemed rather inappropriate, even for him. All three individuals had now been joined by DC Andrew Curry, by far the youngest of the investigative quartet.

"I'm going to deputise you today Drew, his Inspector declared. He then pinned a make-believe badge on 'Kid' Curry's lapel.

"So what do we know Deputy?"

Curry, initially blushed awkwardly. Then he lifted up his notebook, surveyed the scene again, gazed back at his notes, and began. "It would appear Inspector that both men have been in the premises for between four to six days. It had been lying empty waiting to be renovated in the Spring. Fortunately for Mr, or should I say Sir William Taunton, a workman had been here just before Christmas measuring up for some bits and pieces."

"Fortunate," Murray quizzed. "Why?"

"Well sir, he was the one that seemingly brought in and mercifully by good fortune, left behind the box of cereal bars and pack of bottled water that may well be responsible for saving Taunton's life."

Murray nodded. Oat'n Nuts wrappers lay all around the local entrepreneur. Plastic water bottles that had been life prolonging reservoirs of sustenance and had been drained of every last droplet, were also bestrewn across the floor and table. Paramedics busily continued to apply strappings, connect tubes and tend to the lodge owner's life threatening wounds. The slightest of stifled sounds, gurgling, literally his every gasp to survive could now be heard. These professionals were working tirelessly to pull him through. With regard to Taunton's survival and knowing with a clear certainty many of the historical facts of the case, ashamedly Detective Inspector Steven Murray was indifferent!

A lift of his head (a number 31) indicated to Curry to continue. "He has three broken ribs, a fractured jaw and two broken ankles sir!" Murray winced on hearing those medical stats.

"Internal bleeding, severe bruising and a multitude of cuts, wounds and grazes. He is mighty lucky to be alive," Curry concluded.

"Why is he?" The Inspector asked. He turned to the experienced figure of Doctor Thomas Patterson and grinned.

"Well, Inspector," he graciously returned the smile. "It would appear Bill Taunton was being given a t'evere beating." Murray and his two constables nodded in unison. "A beating, t'at if sustained in a man his age would have meant t'ertain death. As it is medical staff are struggling to get him stable."

"But why is he not dead then, Doc?" 'Hanna' Hayes enquired.

"Because Kenny Dixon stopped beating him! It's as t'imple as t'at." Patterson offered in his beautiful native tongue.

"And t'ere we have it! T'imple as t'at." Murray mimicked with emphasis. He then shrugged, stared intensely at Curry and stated the obvious. "Have you asked him why he stopped?"

'Kid' returned the gaze, but found himself frozen to the spot by that question.

As Hayes gently punched Curry's left shoulder to bring him back to the land of the living, the Doc lucidly proffered, "Because Inspector, that particular individual is dead!"

Murray was stunned. He staggered backward a step before regaining his composure. "Dixon, dead! Where is he then?" the DI submitted. "I assumed you'd arrested him and he was in a car or on his way back to the station. How? When Taunton lies here at death's door like this. What happened?"

"No idea," Curry said. He then pointed opposite Taunton and added, "He was found slumped there. At the other side of the table."

Having only arrived back, ADC Hanlon made his way through the kitchen door just as Murray carefully examined the scene one more time. A few pleasantries were exchanged, hand gestures and head movements offered. Reacquaintance with everyone present had been established.

With the Inspector's head alone making a forward movement, as if peering at a distant object. A clearing of the throat then gave an early indication that communication was in the offing. "It was all about mining for gold," Murray excitedly expressed.

The others had no idea what he was on about, but remained fairly certain that all would become clear.........wouldn't it?

"I talk to the trees, but they don't listen to me," Murray warbled. He was in slightly better tune than the original version offered by Clint Eastwood.

"Paint Your Wagon," the TV fan Hayes chirped up.

Murray, on a roll, smirked then offered a short ten second medley of, *"I was born under a; hand me down that can o' beans, hand me down that can o' beans; they call the wind Maria!"* They all knew him well enough to know that he was most definitely onto something.

"Gold-mining," Patterson offered. "Tunnels under the city, coaches coming and going. What? What do you know? What are you up to?"

Inspector Murray gave a look of admiration towards the 'Doc.' "Go back to the first one Doc, look no further." He took a sharp intake of breath, there was another show tune on its way. *"Gold Fever - there were stars in the skies, not in my eyes. Then I got Gold Fever, Gold Fever!"* Some others may have continued to question his behaviour and tone. But his team all knew he was on to something. By this time Murray and his merriment had edged even closer to the kitchen table and the assortment of cereal bar wrappers. The very food product that had sustained the eighty two year old William Taunton these past few days.

Inspector Steven Murray, having placed a blue Nitrile examination glove on his right hand as he approached the messy surface was ready. It was reminiscent of an old-time favourite seaside amusement arcade game. His robotic blue claw motioned slowly upwards and set off, trying to manoeuvre delicately amongst the debris. The fingers were lowered delicately, before coming together at an angle to hoist up their intended prey. As was often the case in those misspent teenage years growing up, the large grip was unsteady, the treasure small and usually awkwardly shaped. The prize would fall desperately from your grasp and was lost forever! Or, at least until you foolishly inserted more cash and set off on another futile expedition!

Today, Murray was penniless. Who carried cash these days? His thumb and middle finger would have to be up to the job. As if rescuing a solitary climber from a perilous mountain crevasse, they edged down inch by inch, getting closer and closer before eventually carefully attaching themselves. A precise rescue operation was now required. They carefully strapped in their intended target before making their way back. Heading home, they narrowly eased up between a 'Fruit Festival' wrapper and one from the bestselling 'Borojo' bar. Then finally, there it was, recovery complete ...... Gold Fever! A tiny scrunched up piece of shiny, dark yellow foil. Spotted by Murray as it stood out from the cereal bar wrappers.

"This mini, compact gold nugget," he announced, "Is what saved our hosts life!" He then turned, looked at his watch and called out to Hanlon. "Forty minutes Joe, back at the station, ready to put this to bed."

As they reconvened later that day, Detective Sergeant Coulter was not present. Murray invited 'Sherlock' with a simple nod of the head. He didn't need to be asked a second time or even a first vocally it would seem!

"Bill Bryson, the travel writer, takes you on some fascinating adventures with him as he tours the world Mrs Dixon. He is a highly respected wordsmith and penman. However, he is so much more than that! On those trips, he is also an award winning helper!"

Looking less glamorous with every passing hour, Sheila simply turned her head away from Murray and offered a less than enthusiastic wave of her wrist. Her hand indicating… 'Not listening, don't care, heard it all before!'

"Mrs Dixon, he helps you experience the culture. Gives you a little of the background, then binds everything expertly together. Finally, he helps you understand the how, where and why, as you journey alongside one another."

Murray now had to tap into this woman's emotional psyche.

"I would be honoured to have you be my 'helper' today Sheila. To travel with me and assist me. Helping all of us to understand if we have got things right. To keep me correct!"

In a dark blue pinstripe suit, Detective Inspector Steven Murray had carefully decided against the blank iPad in hand routine for a second successive time. He was confident enough with the knowledge gleaned, that he knew most, but not all of what was going on.

In a rational tone he began: "Sheila, you must have been planning this for two years, eighteen months at least. During which time you've been playing location bingo! Desperately trying to track down unfortunate, innocent individuals that had never caused you any harm. I mean, they never even knew you. They had been oblivious to your very existence."

Sheila raised her eyes. She sat apprehensively next to her legal representation, waiting patiently for Murray to continue.

"This was a highly hazardous toxin Mrs Dixon. However, you knew someone you could blackmail again. Someone who visited South America often. How hard would it be for a man with his connections to smuggle back, I initially thought just the poison. But when young Joe discovered your vivarium in that 'unlocked' room, we knew then that something was keeping those gecko lizards of yours company."

Remaining absolutely still, Sheila Dixon was well rehearsed for this particular interview.

"We never met your colourful guest, the one without the proper visa entry qualifications. However, I guess he's well gone now. Unfortunately though, you forgot to remove the cocktail sticks, syringe and make-up brush from the room. One, the perfect instrument to pierce their skin, to have them ooze poison out of their pores. The others to then follow up and inject or coat surfaces with the quick acting, deadly toxin."

Hanlon coughed and added, "Remember vivarium ma'am, sorry Mrs Dixon. That in Latin it is literally, 'a place of life.' An area for raising animals or plants, for observation or research. Oh, did I already tell you that? Sorry," he smiled.

Dixon's current look of anger and outrage required a series of firm, reassuring pats on her thigh by her female lawyer before Joseph Hanlon dared move an inch. Beginning with a rather trepidatious gulp, just for a breath!

Murray swirled his hand in the direction of Sheila, simply to distract her gaze from Joe. "Taunton was now fully aware of you, your existence and the fact that more documented evidence against him was still around. He had no idea of the major connections that you had in Scotland's capital city these days though. Probably more clout, money and influence than the smooth talking business tycoon himself."

Her body language, although she remained silent, told Murray that Sheila Dixon cherished this inference. The Inspector then pointed toward the colourful Oat'n Nuts leaflet sitting in front of ADC Hanlon. Once again a simple nod in his junior officers direction, told him to metaphorically speaking - take the wheel!

Joe Hanlon, caught slightly unaware, cleared his throat and sat up straight in a simultaneous action. "This was the leaflet we found at your bedside ma'am," he stated rather nervously.

To which Sheila Dixon gave him the offensive 'you are stating the obvious, so what?' stare. This worked a treat as a booster shot to young Joseph, who then grew in self believe and the cheeky arrogance returned.

"Your bedside table to be precise ma'am. Just along from your unlocked study door where you kept the vivarium. Home to your lethal ……. frog!"

Bravo, Murray thought. Same as before, dismiss him at your pearl and he'll rebound stronger and sharper than ever!

Continuing, Joe Hanlon added, "This leaflet identifies many of the store locations. And from the riveting 'so what' look you are now giving me, I guess you'd appreciate me telling you what that actually has to do with anything."

Dixon glared.

Hanlon paused.

Dixon glared.

Hanlon offered.

"Only one had been circled in red pen!"

Murray piped up, "He knew you these days though, as Jillian. Or Miss Ingham as Yvette and Deborah Evans called you that day when you visited."

Joseph Hanlon spoke in measured tones. "Nice touch. Miss Ingham, Jillian. Jill Ingham. Yes, that's it, that was the store location that was marked off." Hanlon turned over the leaflet and pointed out the circled name. It was in Kent, Gillingham in Kent to be exact!"

Potential cracks and weaknesses were again beginning to appear in Sheila Dixon's imposing facade. Murray's bringing in of Hanlon at short notice, may well turn out to be a stroke of genius. The lady of the house was feeling the heat, and without doubt was under pressure on all fronts. The artillery continued to fire relentlessly.

It was Murray back up to bat. "By the way, did you think that was your half-brother you killed that day?"
Mrs Dixon focused on the painted walls. Decorated in magnolia a decade ago - they were now grubby, faded and flaking. A little like her own defensive shield.

"If it's any consolation, we did also for a brief period. But, as I keep encouraging everyone - Do your homework!"
Sheila Murray snorted and said nothing.

"Colleagues Mrs D," Murray mentioned quietly, whilst pointing toward Hanlon. "Colleagues who by the way are great at their jobs. Well they revealed that Yvette Evans was not as upright and honest as she could have been. In fact she too also went in for a little bit of blackmail."
Sheila this time, slowly glanced at him with uncertainty.

"As we speak, officers are presently picking up both her and her boyfriend from Taunton's little coastal love nest that he provided for her." As he strode around the room, he concluded by throwing both his hands into his trouser pockets, bending down toward her face and adding, "She may well be a devious little minx. However, she's a sheer novice compared to you....Ma'am!"

Hanlon took over, "Oat'n Nuts leaflet at your bed, complemented with word search and puzzle magazines at Kenny's side. The same stationary as the envelope we found at the Portobello offices, which we have no doubt the writing will match up with the ink from your lovely fountain pen. A beautifully crafted and valuable 'Montegrappa.' The same one that we've witnessed you use on several occasions now." With growing confidence he continued, "KD had opened the envelope side on. Otherwise he possibly might not be with us any more either, although we'll come back to that later!"

Sheila, was alerted by that comment, but still reluctant to engage.

Murray, gathering his thoughts considered, "Maybe not a bad option. Then again, maybe that was the plan? We'll run tests. Pretty sure we'll find traces of the poison though, eh, Sheila?"

As the Inspector pondered his next move, he gently reflected upon: 'Sheila's Story' - A sure-fire ratings winner for Channel 4. An award winning dramatisation. Possibly even, a star-studded Hollywood blockbuster. In recent years and especially in the last twelve months Sheila Dixon had become mentally unstable. Impacted firstly by a father whose evil and depraved actions damaged her beyond repair. An innocent child, whose recollections of what should have been charming holidays with parents, experiences of laughter, playful high jinks and a sweet tender middle class upbringing, were in reality - Dark dreaded days and nights away in strange locations, participating in actions that she believed to be the norm. Throughout her adolescent teenage years, wholesome, good natured affection passed her by. With a desperate vulnerability, she escaped that life. Her misfortune though, was to meet up with James Reid and be introduced to Kenny Dixon.

'Two roads diverged in the wood, and I, I took the one less travelled by, and that has made all the difference!' A Robert Frost quote that was to be her personal downfall.

Murray was about to begin his prolonged discourse. Hanlon could see he was preparing to dominate the conversation. To attempt further to penetrate this female's fortress. A Bastille built upon lies, deceit, murder and power. It was Detective Inspector Steve

Murray's role to attack, invade and breach that stronghold. Then, to deliberately dismantle it....... brick by callous brick.

"Mrs Dixon, Sheila," Murray began. "Lots of what we have gathered up is through good old fashioned police work, hard graft and educated guesses," he smiled. "Feel free once again to correct me of any glaring errors as we proceed," he encouraged Sheila. "We are told there is a knack to completing jigsaws. We are always encouraged to firstly discover all the edges, the straight lines and then seek out the four corners." Looking across to involve ADC Hanlon one further time before delivering his tirade. He raised his voice in a semi-playful manner, pointed once again at Joe and spoke. "Our four corners in this particular jigsaw were female, each had a name. Joe, enlighten us please."

"Certainly sir." Joe Hanlon stood quickly. "But, can I just add," he said looking directly at Sheila Dixon. "They were more than names. They were a spirited and forceful combination of mother's, daughter's and wives. They typified love, passion, excitement and family." Hanlon's current circumstances were making him emotional. Whilst Sheila Dixon deliberately stared coldly in the opposite direction.

Joe continued strongly. "Also, in so many ways they had represented the past, the present and indeed symbolised hope for the future. The mighty adventure of life and all it brings was for each of them, cut desperately short! Their names? Of course - let me remind you ma'am, Sheila," he quickly amended. Hanlon paused briefly to compose himself. With regulated breathing he rallied, offering quietly: "Penelope Cooke, Annabel Richmond, Betty Moore and Mrs Lynnette Lithgow." He then slowly and confidently rolled up the A4 notes positioned in front of him, placing them accurately in the right palm of DI Murray. To his surprise, it just dawned on him the implication of Hanlon's actions. The Inspector was now in full receipt of the baton. He was well positioned heading down the home straight and was about to press on at speed, toward the impending finishing line.

Murray motioned the paper baton nearer to his lips and instantly transformed it into a microphone. He then put forth the name of Penelope Cooke and began. "I would imagine it was through her strong networking ethos, that you originally came across her. As a means to get closer you then simply purchased some of her wonderful work. The Biker Girl portrait for one. That was why you shut me down when I became interested in it."

Sheila Dixon licked her lips. Although with no noticeable desire yet to add to the conversation. Neither to enhance, correct, deny or confirm.

"You even backed one or two of her events, or Dock Green did at least. Strange you never mentioned that previously Sheila. Although to be fair, it was your husband's name that all the artwork and corporate sponsorships deals were in. Nicely done starting to steer us down that road. CCTV even got his vehicle in the vicinity twice that night around the Botanic Gardens. I suspect somehow that he had no idea you were the one out driving his precious Evoque. You know the one with the KD1 X0N registration."

Mrs D's countenance, although non-committal, still seemed in an unsettling way to radiate an unseen admiration for the man with the black dog. Maybe she had her own? Maybe more than one? A hundred and one possibly? Mrs Sheila Dixon - aka Cruella de Vil!

"On the evening of the 29th December, I suspect you arranged to meet Penny to discuss another purchase or perhaps a further gallery promotion? Whatever it was, you would have played to her ego, her artistic talent. Enabling you to set up the meet at her own home at short notice. Unfortunately for you a piece of light brown plastic foil marked the page in Miss Cooke's order book. Initially I thought it was reserving a special place in the ledger for her. Of that I was wrong. It was a wrapper from a poisoned *Rose's* chocolate! Nice touch with the brand name by the way. However at least by investigating the order book more carefully, it brought to my attention the numerous works of art purchased by those world renowned art connoisseurs at The Tate Leith - Dock Green Security!"

"The Doc has since confirmed traces of the poison on the makeshift bookmark," Hanlon added.

This drew yet another contemptuous look from this duplicitous opponent.

Murray rolled his neck and cracked it at regular intervals to relieve the buildup of stress. He then thrust another photograph onto the basic formica tabletop in front of Sheila Dixon. The gangland matriarch, to give her an additional title, quickly averted her eyes from the image. It was a black and white of a young lady's contorted body. A body that lay cold and lifeless at the base of a century old, bronze memorial. A local Leith landmark that paid tribute to give her, her additional title also: The Empress of India!

"I don't know how you came across Annabel Richmond," Steven Murray exclaimed. "But you certainly endeared yourself to her. Your bank statements tell us that you have a monthly direct debit Pure Gym membership."

"My bank state…" Sheila had to stop herself.

"Oh," Hanlon smiled. "Didn't you know we had access to your bank details. Every account at that," he winked.

Murray turned to him. Joe, held up the palm of his hands to signal retreat.

"So we did some cross referencing," Murray continued. "Annabel was a member also. The shuttlecock and racquets made me think. I didn't peg you and Mr Dixon as natural badminton players Sheila. I'd guess that is a pastime that you'd both just recently took up. Would I be right?"

His adversarial foe simply swallowed, sniffed and remained steadfast and strong in her seat.

"With some more additional homework. We soon discovered that you both played regularly. In a small doubles league that the gym ran in a local sports centre. Imagine then my surprise, when I learned that the poor deceased also played weekly in that league alongside her fiance at the time. Sadly, her husband is now looking for a new doubles partner in life, as well as on the court."

Maybe it was the deliberately high temperature that the room radiator was set at, Hanlon thought. But as before, a bead or two of sweat was now beginning to surface on Sheila's brow. Interesting.

"I suspect you contacted her by text to hand over a wedding gift. That was why her phone was missing. You couldn't have us find it. Then as you chatted amicably, you possibly shared with her a celebratory chocolate."

Sheila began drumming her thumbs on the table. Groundhog Day seemed to play a regular part in her life also.

"Again it was a nice touch having a late night meal in the area. Because believe it or not your hubby's car again cropped up in our enquiries. He was never at home either. Wow! Poor Kenny, lots of little things all pointing in his direction. Coincidence? I think not!"

Retrieving the image from the desk to swop with another, the Inspector added, "Oh, by the way, I visited

Annabel's workplace the other day. I struggled to find her office. I wonder why that was?"

The next photograph that Murray displayed to Mrs Dixon was a glossy 6 x 4 colour print. Elizabeth Moore of Re. Gal Property. She had been pictured slumped in her seat on the train at Dundee Station. The land of Desperate Dan, Oor Wullie and the Village Green Preservation Society!

Murray's theory was that in Waverley Station that evening, a friendly, local WPC offering a tempting chocolate at the end of a hard day, entered her carriage. Her offer was a simple kind, generous gesture. One that could be expected at this time of year over the festive season. If only the businesswoman had been more Scrooge like and spluttered 'Bah, humbug!' She may still have been alive. Sadly and fatally for her, she accepted.

Hanlon rubbed both his eyes with the base of his hands. He then clasped those aforementioned hands behind his head and stretched his back. At that precise moment Sheila Dixon looked him squarely in the eye and smiled. Joe nearly fell off his seat, as he'd pushed it up onto its two back legs.

Steven Murray witnessed the exchange and knew then, that as things stood, she was never going to speak, own up or confess to anything!

"You know Sheila, she was known as Betty," Murray persisted. "Probably out of the quartet, I would put money on the fact that you did not even know her. Let's see now," Murray stated, matter of factly. "You had Forrester and Allan steal a patrol car. It went up in flames, but the uniforms and radios were gone before that. There was arson attacks you had them carry out on Oat'n Nuts stores. An estate agent already looked after several of his flats. So it made sense to arrange a meeting or two. You no doubt saw her 'Liz Moore sells more!' newspaper and tv ads. Her company are not far behind Oat'n Nuts when it comes to publicity and marketing ideas. Kenny, that 'Scarlet Pimpernel' of a husband of yours was in her appointment diary at least twice in the last couple of weeks."

He nearly had her there with the 'Scarlet Pimpernel' reference. A faint hint of an amused expression came to the surface for the briefest of moments.

The Detective Inspector persevered, "It was only when 'Sherlock' Holmes, I mean Hanlon here," he pointed in Joe's direction. "When he pursued it further for me, that we managed to confirm KD never actually turned up for either of his scheduled appointments. No doubt they were again scheduled by yourself Sheila. Kenneth Dixon may have been guilty of many things throughout his life, but here in relation to all these charges so far, no! Not a chance. No! No! No! No! He's being set up. I don't believe it for a minute." Pausing, the Inspector politely questioned. "Can I ask, what hair shade did you opt for today Sheila?" He proceeded, "Was it, warm amber? Bronze brown? Or my own personal police favourite from your amazing bathroom collection, copper red?"

Trying carefully to avoid Murray's gaze, she threw her head dramatically sideward. Instantly causing her flowing locks to cascade from one shoulder to the other. The perfect imagery for shooting that shampoo commercial!

The DI grinned and offered, "You made a wonderful WPC by the way."

Murray then instantly felt the need to substantially up the ante. He nodded, and ADC Hanlon passed him the folder. He really needed to patent, trademark and copyright that nod he thought to himself. The power within it was awesome! Inspector Steven Murray straightaway emptied the remaining photographs across the work surface.

"What do you…" again Sheila Dixon restrained herself.

In a growing tone of anger and frustration Murray exclaimed, "What's wrong Sheila? Does this upset you Mrs Dixon? Scene of crime and post-mortem shots not to your liking?"

Her lawyer made to interrupt. "And you, you can keep your mouth firmly shut. This has always been personal," he bellowed. "And so it continues. It's personal now between me and her." He pointed directly and undeviatingly through gritted teeth, straight into the face of the domineering matriarch.

With the slightest of facial expressions, she smirked gratifyingly.

"What is it Sheila?" Murray's voice continued to become more sinister and threatening. Slowly he explored, "What are those warped brain cells pondering over now? Are you thinking on how you can mentally seduce that no good husband of yours to do away with me? Get him to castrate, hang or drug me?" At a snail's pace he then asked menacingly, "Possibly, get him to leave me his last Rolo?"

That got her attention. This time Sheila went to speak, ignoring the last ditch tug on her forearm from her lawyer. "Why did you say that?"

It was Murray's turn now to remain silent.

"Go on tell me," she pleaded.

In a calmer, but more mocking tone, he disparagingly told her.

"Mrs Dixon we don't have many players left to star in our very own Edinburgh West End production of Chicago! Like you appear to be, it's all about the concept of the celebrity criminal." Bowing his head in respect, he added. "Sadly, we lost another couple of potential cast members tonight. And although they'll be too late for our auditions. I think it might be worth their while trying out for roles in the updated music video for 'Stairway to Heaven,' Murray beamed.

"What? Who? Where? When? Sheila gave each outburst equal measure.

"Aye, and the only one you never asked Mrs D. was... How? How come, how come you never asked? Because you know the answer to that, don't you?"

Sheila Dixon once again withdrew. But like before, she had came out to play. Willing to scrap and occasionally go toe to toe with her worthy opponent.
Joe Hanlon sat mesmerised by the whole proceedings and with a front row seat, relaxed and waited for the bell to sound. Seconds away round five!

Murray came out firing hard. Recognising that the quick fire jabs, with the obligatory uppercut every now and then would be his winning strategy. Aggressive, in her face, animated and slightly loopy! Murray pictured Mel Gibson playing Martin Riggs in all the Lethal Weapon movies and ran with it........

"Look at the wreckage," he said. Separating the photos for Dixon to view clearly. "It was pure carnage. Lynnette Lithgow could never have survived that crash."

"She could," a mumble emerged from Dixon's mouth. Overcoming yet again that regular tug on her sleeve by her expensive brief. Her lawyers were unsurprisingly less keen on having her open that pretty mouth of hers. It may well soon tarnish their impressive defence statistics, Murray thought to himself.

"Sorry, Sheila, I didn't quite catch that. Did you say, 'she could have.' How so?"
Silence.

"Oh, come on Sheila!" Martin Riggs was about to make an appearance. The tempo was increasing and

Hanlon sat forward in anticipation. "This silence rubbish is wearing thin. You are so much better than that. Help me here. I need a sparring partner and no one seems up to the task." He had begun to actually weave from side to side and throw a few fake punches. Hanlon tried to duck and fell from his chair as 'Rocky' Riggs caught him square on the jaw. Murray was in full flow and tried not to be distracted. Dixon's lawyer struggled to maintain a straight face, when Murray rocked back on his heels as if leaning against the ropes. 'Geez,' Hanlon thought, he's good at this like.

Sheila Dixon had no idea what was happening. 'Has this man lost it,' she thought. She became fearful. Not so much for her personal safety. No, not feeling physically threatened, but mentally. She was hesitant yet again of where he was going. The road he was taking, the intended destination and then, in any bout like this, the eventual outcome! This man, this mercurial opponent had invited her into the ring alongside him once again. The pull, the draw, the allure of taking a few hits and then catching him out with a beautifully timed delivery of her own. Well, that appealed to her no end.

She envisioned it now becoming a reality. Walking through the elegant parting of the massed crowds as she made her way ringside. Continual cheering, screaming fans on both sides chanting along to their respective anthems. Although dated, 'Eye of the Tiger' would suffice for Martin 'Rocky' Riggs.

For Sheila Dixon though, she had a much more visual entrance planned. Not for her, casually strutting toward the ropes. There would be no 'classic' walk from the back of the hall. This would be in the grand style of a Miley Cyrus 'over the top' sell-out tour. Her massive hit from 2013 'Wrecking Ball,' would play triumphantly as she came swooping down across the stadium. Swinging majestically from side to side on top of a sparkling, inflatable silver sphere. Then to the overwhelming crescendo of noise, she would be steadily lowered gracefully into the ring itself. Cheers would erupt and euphoric fans would celebrate wildly. It's most certainly all in the experience she thought. She briefly wondered what Murray's mindset would be right now, before further ringside images flashed into her mind. Her distinctive bright red cape with the impressive lettering SHEILA D embroidered in a beautiful assortment of golden threads. No cheap printed nonsense! She would take the applause, soak it up, wave to her fans. They treasured her. She had gone this far, she wouldn't falter now. What could possibly go wrong?

The referee called them both into the centre of the ring. 'Rocky' Riggs pushed his two gloves out to hit the bare hands of his second, Joe Hanlon. He then swaggered assuredly toward the ref, bouncing in anticipation as he did so. Sheila Dixon was still confident of knocking him out, as she waved her colourful elaborate gown one more time slowly above her head. Then with super-hero strength, she dispatched it proudly out into her sea of adoring fans. Abruptly, she then turned in the direction of the referee and her spaced out opponent. Straight away realising her mistake!

They could still both hear her song blasting out throughout the vast arena. How poignant she thought, as she listened to the echoing words. *'I came in like a wrecking ball. I never hit so hard in love. All I wanted was to break your walls, all you ever did was wreck me.'*

He had managed it before she thought. And this time, now standing in front of the gathered audience, referee, security and staff, he had emotionally beguiled her. He had enticed her into his lair and there she stood - Fully clothed, but naked! He had disrobed her just as she knew he would, and she was now at his mercy once again. Seconds away, round six!

Murray stood quietly and still before her. He gently smiled, offered a wink and threw his two arms victoriously high into the air!

TWENTY FIVE

"Aye, you never thought to question. You just went on with your lives. Cause all they taught you who to be - Was mothers, daughters, wives."

- The McCalmans

He jabbed with, "I believe Lynnette Lithgow was simply unfortunate to deliver you one of her district council flyers. I saw it initially at your home. Yet it seemed to manage to get into Kenny's sports bag when I next came to visit. Evidence on the surface, was certainly building up against your other half."

"Although worthless now," Hanlon quipped. Which quickly drew a displeasing look from his boss.

"You were happy to go for a shower that day ma'am, remember? Hopeful, nay I believe even confident that we would discover even more incriminating evidence. Not against you though. Surprisingly, the bulk of it would lead us toward your invisible husband. The one individual that never seemed to be around. That no one had seen for long enough!"

"What did he mean? Worthless now?" She questioned.

"Don't try and deflect the conversation Sheila. You knew that Lynnette Lithgow was also a fully trained counsellor. One that had tried to help you out. Yet you chose to end her life. Help me understand that."

Sheila shook her head in a rather tired and defeated manner. "It wasn't like that."

"Mrs Dixon, you not only took her life, but you're culpable for that of six year old Kirsty Fraser also. That particular trail of destruction..." Murray exasperated went on, "Left four beautiful, innocent daughters without a mother. A grieving husband without a wife. A young West Lothian couple without their child and a set of Grandparents with a broken heart, as well as several of their bones!"

Murray then moved aside several photographic pictures of Mrs Lithgow's automobile accident. Disclosing other equally graphic shots, he knew what might happen next. As Sheila Dixon took in the two new images revealed to her, ones that had been taken at the accountants on Circus Place. Murray witnessed almost immediately the strong contraction of her abdominal muscles. Her hands were placed over her mouth as a intense feeling of nausea struck. She retched violently, twice in quick succession. There was no vomit, just a dry heaving. This delicate portfolio would most definitely not be appearing on any Disney press releases in the near future!

"Help us put him away Sheila? Where would he go for cover?" Two more painful jabs connected. One more time for good luck Mrs Dixon made to retch over DI Murray's black patent brogues. This time she offered up the full contents of her stomach. She had returned with a careful left hook!

After five minutes cleaning up, floor mopped, face wiped, tissues and glass of water, they resumed!

Speaking more compassionately than ever to Sheila, "Melanie," he said sweetly. She looked up at him with genuine loss in her eyes.

"That was never meant to happen. The last three decades had mainly all been about her. Hadn't it? Safeguarding her wellbeing and ensuring her safety throughout the years? She enabled you to keep alive memories of Rose, your own mother. Nice touch with the graduation photos by the way. No faces, but we made out KD's ring. Sadly for you, as I mentioned earlier, I also caught the bottom of your distinctive earrings. The ones you were always most reluctant to talk about. With Kenny's arm around her in the photograph, it could have been easy for people in your circle of friends, if one can call them friends? Easy for them to misunderstand."

"You are on dangerous ground Inspector," her brief counseled.

"Yes, I might well be." His pace hastened. "But I'd most definitely prefer my underfoot conditions to your clients. She's on flamin' quicksand and sinking faster than the pound against the dollar!"

Slowing once again, his understanding and rational voice resurfaced. "It's just it could have been slightly misconstrued Sheila. You must have seen that? People thinking she was one of his working girls? Although I suspect she'd have to have assumed a Romanian or Polish accent. Latvian even, isn't that right?

Sheila just sat disillusioned. Vigorously shaking her head from side to side.

"I believe those nationalities are the prime movers and shakers here in Edinburgh. Each of them very popular as escorts. How do you   spell that word correctly these days? Would I be right in thinking it is T...H...E...R...A...P...I...S...T? Therapist!" he declared jauntily. Interesting Mrs Dixon, how visually on paper it translates quite clearly into .... The rapist!"

Sheila looked up at him with her arms crossed defiantly over her chest. Left arm to right shoulder and vice versa. As if covering her naked torso. She was in shock. Head still shaking and rising to stand before thinking better of it. A steady stream of sweat made a fleeting visit across her brow, before dispersing and depositing itself at various locations across the desk in front of her.

"Her face, her pretty face," she wept. As she lightly ran her fingertips across the fallen tears on the picture. Her lawyer handed her a stiff, white cotton handkerchief. Her trembling hands struggled to grasp it properly and allowed it to fall gently to the ground. Retrieving it, Joe Hanlon nodded at Murray and placed it firmly into Sheila Dixon's quivering fingers. At that moment and with no satisfaction, the Detective Inspector had guessed the distraught mother knew full well, what her action represented. She had let the material slip through her hands deliberately. Puzzling and cryptic right to the end. This undercover mother for three decades, had symbolically thrown in the towel!

In a reflective, tender voice, Steven Murray offered sincerely, "Sheila... Melanie Rose was your daughter - you were her mother. I am sorry for your loss, truly sorry." He went to continue, but paused.

Making use of the hankie, Sheila urged, "Go on, what were you going to say, finish it."

"It's just," he stopped again.

"Inspector, you've won, spit it out."

"It's just that 'Bunny' had brought the full force of the law down on KD and for all those at Dock Green after the brutal slaying of Detective Constable Taz Taylor. If you had excluded James Reid and not went after him, we would have tracked him down. I," he said slowly, "I believe one hundred percent, that your charming, clever and charismatic daughter would still be with us. She'd be alive........sorry!"

Blubbering wasn't really in the Sheila Dixon book of emotions. However, a much needed two minute sob was acceptable.

Joe Hanlon briefly submitted, "I reckon Mrs Dixon, ma'am, Sheila, I guess Reid saw no future for himself. He knew now that he was never going to take over as Lord of the Manor. He had watched you reign these past twelve months or so and ultimately was now having to protect himself from KD. Or at least, so he thought. It had become fight or flight."

The defeated opponent looked up at Murray. "My pal there," she gestured toward her favourite mouthy, cheeky, pale-faced, big skinny constable. "What he said earlier, worthless?"

Hanlon looked to the floor. Murray, looked her straight in the eye - "He's dead Sheila."

She examined Murray's face intensely and then slowly contemplated his words. It took a few brief seconds. She believed him. Another minute passed before the grieving silence was broken.

She offered dismissively, "He couldn't resist a quality chocolate!"

As Joseph Hanlon shook his head in disbelief. DI Murray nodded in understanding at her delicate, delightfully deranged phrasing. He'd be sure to write that thought down and pass it along to DC Sandra Kerr!

"Sheila, ADC Hanlon was right about Reid. But hey, you sent 'Bunny' poisoned photos too."

As she gave him yet another look of indifference. She serenely caressed one of her cherished earrings. It made for her, an ideal comfort blanket.

"Playing them against each other was always going to be a dangerous game Sheila. Innocent parties were inevitably going to get hurt. An thus, so it transpired."
Hanlon continued his education as he listened to Murray lay out some facts.

"You told Kenny that his Lieutenant was in close cahoots with the police. Even providing photographic proof of the said relationship. Which in actual fact, was just routine questioning involving Coulter and Taylor. You then paid off Forrester and Allan to silence him. That was when you realised he had not opened his envelope in the conventional manner. That was never guaranteed to work though. So, I suspect our singing duo would have always have been on standby with you. Especially with the opportunity of promotion to Kenny's side for one of them, and the impending vacancy required to oversee 'the escorts' for the other."
The forlorn figure, the Willowbrae widow, sat still and hushed.

Hanlon interjected, "Did you know about that poor man's family Mrs Dixon? Had you even considered how your actions would affect others? Woman, did you never play dominoes growing up?"

Murray, quickly retrieved the invisible baton. "The slaughter of Allan's family seemed to sum up the fact that James Reid was in today's politically correct 'don't upset anyone' society, suffering from an antisocial personality disorder.
Sheila looked perplexed!

"Yep, my thoughts exactly Mrs D. What utter tosh!" Off Murray went, volunteering with relish. "The man is a bonafide nut job. He's totally unhinged and dangerous. An out of control, fully blown psychopath!"

As the volume and velocity of his rant continued, his arms flailed and his facial expressions ventured into the extreme, as he articulated with venom. "He's a cross between a mental Oor Wullie, Willy Wonka and Wile E. Coyote! Pure, Dead, Brilliant. Made in Scotland from girders! And he just blew the face off of your beautiful daughter!"

It was another fleeting, left-field cameo appearance from Martin Riggs.

Sheila, colour drained from her face, glanced at Hanlon and he in turn, hurriedly observed the lawyer. Then, all three studied the decade old, grey, scuffed linoleum flooring. Avoiding contact as best they could with the currently disturbed DI.

Murray for his part, just smiled as he took Sheila Dixon's hand to escort her from the room. As he exited, he began singing, *'Abidy loves Oor Wullie, he's such a daft wee lad…'*

Throughout this time the remainder of his team had been gathered once again behind the glass. Detective Constables Hayes and Curry, with young PC George Smith all hoping to learn a thing or two. And there nestled behind all four, perusing all before him, was the imposing outline of Chief Inspector Keith Brown. Four figures, that's right. Because standing immediately in front of them all, viewing proceedings with great interest as he had done many times over the years, was Detective Sergeant Robert Coulter. 'Ally' had watched in awe, with admiration and respect for his kooky, unconventional friend. He liked his sport. Horses were his thing as we know. However, as boxing matches went, Coulter thought it was most definitely up there with the best.

Murray swallowed hard when he spotted 'Ally' outside in the corridor. A simple teardrop welled up in his eye as he walked the humbled, yet equally mixed-up Mrs Sheila Dixon over to Coulter. "All yours Sergeant I believe," he confirmed.

In an adjoining office they all met up for a brief review and update. In the main, because many of the team still had questions that needed answered. It felt like things had overtaken them at such pace in the last twenty four hours that they were still unsure and uncertain on many areas. Murray, although tired having gone flat out for six rounds, was happy to oblige!

".....So an accumulation of the material things in life then became important." Steve Murray had begun to share his recent observations of Sheila Dixon. "By now she had to have the best. Either by way of car, house, clothes or holidays. And although she believed KD had a love for her. There was no longer a love between them. Joe what did you notice?" he asked of Hanlon.

"Like you said sir, it was a cold relationship. They appeared to live separate lives. There was no natural warmth."

"Agreed."

"They were loaded sir. Was that not enough?" asked Andrew Curry.

Murray responded. "Where ultimately did the wealth stem from?" he asked his students. "Come on, join in the game," he advocated.

'Hanna' Hayes was up for this. "Drugs, prostitution, money laundering and lending. Counterfeit goods, dodgy property deals and numerous other illegal schemes that came and went from week to week."

"Exactly! But that is a harsh life. One that consisted daily of small time crooks, highly paid lawyers and an assortment of distasteful activities and transactions carrying on all around her. Think about it. It was her 50th year. A trigger event in itself! Growing resentment at her childhood or lack of one. Being molested as a young child, feeling abandoned, screwed up. She needed for someone to pay, to be held accountable. It became overwhelming. Sheila's perception now was that all other families led lives of sweetness and joy, unsullied and without challenge."

Throughout their various sparring matches, Sheila Dixon may have heard bits and pieces of Murray's occasional monologues. Although after being handed over into Coulter's care and custody, it was abundantly clear for all to see that this, once seriously sexy 'cereal' killer, was irrefutably damaged. She was broken and deemed way beyond repair. Which in reality she was. Now she'd be locked away for, as they would say - 'the rest of her natural.'

Would that be in a normal women's prison or a secure unit for the mentally insane? No doubt a lengthy trial with Judge, jury and lots of medical assistance, would decide!

TWENTY SIX

"So I'll cry with a limp, just get by on a limb, till these blue eyes of mine they are closed. So here's to an old fashioned peck on the cheek and farewell my sweet Northern Rose."

- The Beautiful South

Murray was getting close to the end of his summation.

"Now as you know, Chief Inspector Brown helped identify the name of the flowers at Melanie's flat. Same ones that were in the Dixon home. Flowers, that they had delivered on a regular weekly basis. It made me question several things. Why would a 'thug' like Kenny Dixon have a ballerina on his ring? It was the Inspector that informed me that it was also the name of a familiar rose. That is why I had Curry and Hayes check out the jewellery connection further. Well done you two."

"Iceberg, Ballerina and Mermaid. Those roses are getting pride of place in my garden this year," DC Hayes jubilantly announced. There was accepting laughter.

Murray though with hands outstretched and waving in a Professorial manner, enlightened his students further. "Let's briefly recap - Combined with the discovery of the diaries, unearthed pictures and assorted letters, we have been able to build up a pretty accurate personal profile analysis of our 'Billy Boy!' He started by abusing his future wife named Rose, when she was only 14 and he was 30. Then began the grooming and sexual abuse of his daughter when she was even younger, having only turned 13. It was at an Oat'n Nuts store opening. The one that had recently been targeted and torched in East Lothian to be precise."

Joe Hanlon, needing clarification, asked nervously, "All through her teenage years sir?"

"Pretty much Joe. We have no reason to question the diaries. She would have been continually assaulted on a regular basis. However, shop openings were made extra traumatic. At each of those he would 'dress her up,' then 'unveil his daughter,' and take 'instamatic' photographs. A treasured Kodak, 'making memories' moment right enough. There was no way his local Boots store was going to be developing those prints! In some photographs with mother and daughter, like I told some of you previously, he'd have them holding a sign - 'Buy one, get one free!' In another he cuddled his daughter under the banner - 'managers special.' Sick and perverse in a very special way to say the least."

"So, the victims were they just random individuals sir? Wrong place, wrong time?" DC Andrew Curry asked, biting curiously on his bottom lip.

Murray gave the Constable a surprised look. "I know you may not know why DC Curry. But I know you well enough to know that you are fully aware that they were not just selected at random."

"I guessed that sir, but I just can't figure it," 'Kid' Curry replied honestly.

With a renewed energy Steven Murray said, "Be mindful of the where Bill Taunton's business idea was conceived."

"On one of the islands," the 'Kid' responded confidently. "Outer, I mean Inner, the Inner Hebrides." Hanlon went to look through the paperwork.

"Don't bother 'Sherlock.' Fingers on the buzzers," Murray enthused. "For the connection think of the third victim."

Several hands lurched into the air. Heads racked their brains. Hayes, unable to restrain herself any longer shouted out.

"Betty Moore!"

"Betty Moore," Andrew Curry repeated, still shaking his head. "I'm lost sir."

"Have fun with her name," the Inspector urged. "They liked their puzzles, their wordplay. Remember Ken and Sheila and the accountants Alan Hikesend!"

Feeling brave, like the intrepid explorer they had come to value, Joe Hanlon jumped in excitedly with both feet. "Betty Moore, Elizabeth Moore," he stuttered firstly. Closely followed by "Lizzy Moore, Liz Moore, Bet Moore. Something sounded 'kinda' right there," he thought.

Murray raised his eyes and grinned, "Go on Joe…"

Hanlon again opted to express vocally, "Liza Moore, Liz Moore, Lis Moore….. Lismore, Lismore, that's it the Isle of …"

"Correct," Murray offered silent applause. "Lismore." His colleagues began frantically and feverishly in their minds to recall the other deceased. So, to give them plenty of thinking time, Detective Inspector Murray offered this thought. "I believe the original idea possibly began way back at the birth of their daughter. They had to choose a name that would not be recognised or connected to the tainted Dixon line. By way of a tribute to her late mother, like her playlists, flower deliveries and their individual items of jewellery that they wore in later years, Rose was chosen. Coupled with Melanie and there you had it. The beautiful Borders town, which played a significant role in the Oat'n Nuts story. Melrose!"

"Sir, sir!" Oh, they were fairly chomping at the bit now, he thought.

Murray held up his arm, he wanted to finish, "Melanie Rose though, as we all now know was never intended to be a targeted subject. That was all the work of one James Baxter Reid. Apart from the medical staff, he was probably the only other that knew in reality, exactly who she was. Sheila had made the mistake of trying to 'take out' Bunny through inexperienced third parties. In his quest for revenge, to cause maximum pain, loss and grief. He knew exactly what had to be done. As Billy Joel would remind us once again, *'she was the victim of circumstance.'*"

"Sir, you implied to Sheila Dixon that Bill Taunton was dead also. Did I miss something earlier?" A fired up Curry questioned.

"No, he is still with us," 'Hanna' Hayes told the room. "I contacted the hospital earlier. It was touch and go for a while, but it looks like he is over the worst. Once his ankle mends he'll be able to stand…"

"Yes, stand trial," ADC Hanlon added justifiably. "And serve out the remainder of his life behind bars."

Murray felt the end of the day draw even closer. Over the years, when the bitterness crept in, along with the feelings of malicious melancholy and time for retribution and payback, then out came the puzzles. In more recent times Alan Hikesend, set up for Melanie Rose to run. Again, the clues were all around. For

Sheila, locating the individual now became the challenge!

"Let's speed things up." Murray spoke briskly. "Further store openings began at a steady pace after Melrose. Approximately two to three every year."

Hanlon, feeling engaged with this train of thought, continued, "Lynnette Lithgow. Linlithgow," and as the momentum continued, he excitedly put forward, "and the Angel of the North - Penelope Cooke, was Penicuik."

"Oh, my goodness," 'Kid' Curry said in surprise.

Hanlon ended with, "Blatant clues right in front of us all this time." His voice having gone from jubilant celebration and the mighty euphoric 'aha moment.' To disappointment and despondency, knowing he 'should have done better.'

Curry one of the 'two most successful outlaws in the West,' then added, "So what went wrong with Annabel Richmond then? She doesn't fit. Was it mistaken identity, bad planning or an actual error?"

"Unfortunately, sadly not 'Kid.' Deborah Evans and her baby nephew James were the mistake, but we'll come back to that. No, in relation to Annabel young Drew, everything went according to plan," Murray replied. Feeling rather smug he began to rock back and forward on the balls of his feet with contentment. Then he threw it out there - "What if this tragedy had befallen her just a few days previous?" he asked.

"You cannot be serious?" Joe said. Doing a rather bad 1970's John McEnroe impersonation.

"Her maiden name? Really?" 'Hanna' added.

"I visited her workplace yesterday," DI Murray said shaking his head. Initially I walked right past it. None of her official documentation had been updated or changed at that point. It was far too soon after her wedding. I had been led directly into her office, did my

320

normal nosy around and departed. Only then," Murray paused. "As I went to close the door behind me, took a step back and reflected on those eight letters. Did another little piece of the jigsaw come together. The nameplate on her door read: Annabel." He then began to spell out each further letter. "S. T. R. U. T. H. E and finally R. Annabel Struther." He announced in a satisfied manner. "It may well be pronounced differently in the town itself, but there's no doubting where it represented. Where was the Fife store arson? Murray triumphantly questioned.

"Anstruther," Joe Hanlon muttered under his breath. He was still disappointed at not figuring things out sooner.

"You can feel like that to a degree, Joe," Murray advised. "Look at me, I grew up surrounded by Sir Walter Scott terminology for over twenty years. It just didn't twig! With our Sheila however, although blatant, they were never meant to be hidden. The individual was just playing with us. Making it a bit of fun. Knowing full well that they would get spotted and that they'd then get caught and be mighty relieved into the bargain. She was exhausted and simply tired of pretending. Her major psychological issues were getting worse. She had no real hold on reality any longer. She had become emotionless a long while ago. No matter who got caught up in her evil schemes, in her twisted, skewed mind, it was fully justified."

Joseph Hanlon had loved his experience working with CID. He accepted his DI's counsel humbly, but wanted to ask just one more thing. "Sir, throughout your interviews with Sheila Dixon you kept going to reveal something to her, but never did. I just wondered, you certainly got me curious. What was it?"

Murray with a rather resigned frown on his face countered. "It wasn't going to be news to Mrs Dixon,

Joe. I intended holding on to it, to announce it to her hubby for leverage. After Kenny was found dead, I just decided - best not to mention it at all."

"I get that sir and I've heard you be very tender and diplomatic with people recently." Hanlon then shook his head and screwed up his face. "However, you never answered my question."

"Sorry Joseph and apologies folks. Are you all listening?"

The room fell silent. Some may have guessed, but no one knew for sure.

Murray scanned the faces of his colleagues carefully before broadcasting live. "The elusive news that Sheila's kingpin underworld husband had no idea about, was the fact that the Oat'n Nuts founder had never actually helped finance any fertility treatment whatsoever."

Eyes narrowed and ears pricked up. 'Go on' was the overall facial expression offered.

Murray continued. "Sheila Dixon had never asked William Taunton for money in her life."

"Right," Joe said startled. Though still none the wiser.

"Anyone?" Murray asked.

He had no takers.

They all looked equally mystified.

Beaming with a huge smile, Steven Murray informed them in true animated 'Martin Riggs' fashion. "That was not what she required of him." He raised his voice, "Yes she blackmailed him to be the cure, the remedy, to rectify the problem that existed. Are you with me?" He nodded excitely. "Let's all get our heads around this." Murray paused for theatrical effect and simply took a step up onto one of the police issue standard chairs. He looked out at his team, mindful that they had lost a dear colleague. "So to be clear - Mel Rose was one hundred per cent Sheila's daughter. Mrs Dixon had absolutely given birth to her."

Murmurings from the floor began. "Sir, sir, no way, no, sir," various voices offered up.

"Nonetheless," Murray delivered strongly. "Kenny Dixon, Edinburgh's Commander - in - Chief of everything dodgy....... was not her dad!"

So to clarify, again he repeated. "Sheila Dixon was definitely her mother. Unfortunately, for the genealogists among us, she was also her half-sister!"

Gasps and hands on heads all round. Quizzical looks trying to figure it out. Personal disgust and disdain. Murray lowered his hands, followed by his voice and stepped down.

"Sir William Taunton was the true biological father to Melanie Rose!"

That felt like a fitting moment to end the day's proceedings. Murray, gracious to the end asked those gathered, "Any other points require clarification?" One hesitant hand was raised cautiously half way.

"Sir, in their last few meetings together and amongst others, Sir William Taunton was always reminding Sheila how she was at the forefront of his mind every day. Do you believe that?" Susan Hayes asked.

"Absolutely!" Murray confidently remarked as he made his way to exit the door.

With a generous wave of his hand to his diligent team-mates he responded. "Think carefully about where he'd concentrated his efforts, 24/7, for the past three or four decades?"

"Fully on his business empire, on Oat'n Nuts," his perceptive female colleague offered up hesitantly, still unsure if she was correct.

"Warped, but true." Murray agreed.

For the last time that day, a rather mouthy, cheeky, pale-faced, big skinny constable closed the meeting. ADC Joseph Hanlon gently nodded and shared profoundly, "Sheila Dixon sir. Amazing! For forty years he kept her by his side, for her though, there was no escaping from it."

Hayes shook her head, the others just shrugged.

Hanlon relished this moment. "It was her maiden name 'Hanna.' Taunton," Joe added. "Sheila Taunton - S. Taunton - Oat'n Nuts - One final anagram! Every single day, like it or not, she was close to him. An enduring, if not endearing legacy."

Murray smiled satisfactorily and thought of how it all began with Penelope Cooke.

He then closed the door and began walking down the long corridor - What next he wondered to himself?

The phone rang in the early hours of Sunday morning. Detective Sergeant Robert Coulter had been relaxing and was sat comfortably at his Kirkliston home. As he answered, he instinctively froze to the spot when he heard the distinctive voice chillingly say:

"Hello, 'Ally'........................ Did I ever tell you - I was a paratrooper once you know?"

EPILOGUE

"She went up the stairs, stood up on the vanity chair. Tied her lamé belt around the chandelier, and went out kicking at the perfumed air."

- The Boomtown Rats

Over the past twenty four months of his life, living with diagnosed depression, Murray was actually pretty proud that he was not on medication. He was learning coping skills, he was a high-functioning individual and (in his own mind) he didn't need to rely on anything or anyone.

Theoretically, he had nothing against medicating mental illness. He was just glad that he didn't need it. He enjoyed the independence of it and he had a lot of fears about it. What if he could never get off it again? What if it turned him into a character straight out of 'The Walking Dead?' What if he experienced things that weren't real? How would he know what was imaginary and what wasn't? Would he be able to fully function, to trust his own mind?

When someone very close to him chose to get medication for a mental illness, he was thrilled. He immediately saw and appreciated the effects. It felt to him that his friend was able to be his real self. He felt like he could see and appreciate life and reality better.

But even then, he was proud that he didn't need it. He was stable enough, he understood what was going on. He could look at his depression straight on and so he didn't need a crutch.

In reality, he was still in denial!
His notebook of poems and verse generally provided a fairly accurate guide to his mood swings. His latest piece, the one he'd been working on over the past couple of weeks, like this case was now complete.
He had entitled it - A Visit to the Vet!

It read:

I don't often catch sight of its reflection in the mirror - Though suddenly by my side it reappears.
As I strive to smile and seek the best in life; It growls, bares it teeth and reminds me of all my fears.
For days on end - a calm contentment. Life is pretty good, a walk in the park.
Then a gate to my mind is slowly unlocked and one hears again that menacing bark.
It has caught up with me in an instant - The sunlight's gone and there's no need now for that jog.
This hound of darkness is by my side: Companions forever - Me, myself and the black dog.
Joy, a smile and laughter. Straightaway it will turn to a frown - Me, myself or the black dog - I don't know which to have put down!

Man's best friend had once again been at his side for the past day, or possibly even thirty-six hours. Winter sun shining, busy people leading isolated, individual lives. 'What difference do we make?' Murray questioned.
Smaller than a grain of sand. What can we achieve and for what end? Having visited the United States regularly

over the years, he knew that the American television soap opera 'Days of Our Lives' displayed an hourglass in its opening credits. And since its first broadcast in 1965, its narration stated: "Like sands through the hourglass, so are the days of our lives."

Stomach churning, the bedside lamp offered a small chink of light during this dark period. Lost, lonely, worthless and scared. Steve Murray reflected, 'As I go, will I look back with regret?' People often say 'it's a coward's way out.' Leaving those you love to deal with the fallout and pick up the pieces. Is Cancer the way of a coward? Alcoholism? Gambling or Drugs? Are we just bad people making poor uninformed choices? Genuine illnesses treated with contempt, the 'I'm alright Jack' syndrome!

The Inspector needed time to 'Paws for thought.' Sitting at the side of his master was an invisible, yet highly disturbed and unstable guide dog. Present, but certainly not an aid for good, the DI thought. This mixed-up mutt will lead me directly out in front of oncoming traffic. Forget the green man, this powerful pooch wants me to play chicken on the dual carriageway of life! Then, upon my failure to successfully weave in and out of the vast volume of vehicles. As I'm hit, destroyed and dispatched. This 'canine' psychopath will move swiftly on to his next unwitting victim! To deceptively beguile and deceive them. To win them over with his incredibly convincing 'puppy love' audition. And so the cycle continues.
'Scooby Dooby Doooooo-oooooo!!!!!!!!
The mis-wired circuitry and multitude of thoughts continue to jar, jolt and impact Murray's ability to cope with life.

I had been fortunate, he told himself. I've met numerous inspiring people 'that I could not match.' And we are often encouraged not to compare ourselves to others. Okay, so how do we progress? Are they not role models to inspire us to change, better ourselves, make more of this life and achieve great things! Born in October, the Libran in me, the scales - encourage me to get the balance right. I know, I know, but getting the right blend, the mix, the combination just so, is exceptionally hard. Trial and error, yeh right...too many trials in life and no one likes to continually make errors. It becomes daunting, overwhelming and unbearable. Funny, if it were not so true - GoCompare.com is blasted all over the media as a highly successful advertising campaign when it comes to checking out prices, etc. Yet, it seriously damages your health if you do it with one another!

Trying slightly to defend himself, Murray profoundly thought - Possibly, hopefully this little speck of sand has been able to literally rub off on one or two others. Even tried too hard at times to do so. Inevitably though, this grain was lazy, not willing to put in the effort. He was happy for others to work hard, dedicate their time, deal with the grown up serious issues of life. Thus they received the recognition and rewards that their disciplined dedication and effort deserved.

As the middle aged detective made his way downstairs, he seemed broken. He gave out what seemed like one last sigh, thinking - 'I feel continually tired and exhausted with this life. Is there another? If so, maybe it's time to pack my bags and in the words of another Saw Doctors favourite, *Head Out for the Sunshine Once Again!*

Joseph Hanlon continued to be concerned over the mental health of his Detective Inspector. He had missed him that morning at Lauren's funeral. Certain that he would have made the effort to be in attendance. Two weeks ago he did not even know this man. A man he now admired and respected deeply. A man he now considered a close friend.

'For a Reason,' sometimes you just connect with certain people in life.

This afternoon though, his calls and texts went unanswered. 'Sherlock' had grown anxious. The station could not track Inspector Murray down. At his home, his phone sat switched off on his upstairs bedside cabinet. Downstairs, as Hanlon arrived and peered through the nearest window, a dining room chair lay overturned in the centre of the room.

Joseph Hanlon could hear music.
Sometimes, it's not the song that makes you emotional, it's the people and the memories that come to your mind when you hear it play.
Murray's ten year old cd player had been set to 'track repeat.'
The chosen tune played............

"They said she did it with grace. They said she did it with style. They said she did it all before she died, oh no no no no, I remember Diamond's smile."

THE END

R.I.P.
'Jimmy' Reid, my friend -
"He was a paratrooper, you know!"

Thank you for taking the time out of your busy schedule to read The Winter Wind, the first in a series of DI Murray novels. For some behind the scenes updates and information contact me direct at www.detectivestevemurray.co.uk

Michael

A small taster to book two…...

Departing Footprints:

Fighting intensely, akin to the busy bellows of a hearty overworked accordion. One heaving, gasping and straining painfully for every last precious ounce of air. Frantic breaths had become shorter and sharper. Lashing out had proved pointless. Futile shouts and screams had ceased as delicate, fragile airwaves filled rapidly. Hands that were set to auto pilot continued to fiercely block and stretch. Desperately they'd attempt but to no avail, to provide a barrier or barricade to keep it back.

The ferocious '*it*' in question, being the loose, fast moving, lightweight east coast sand. Sand, that naturally occurring granular material composed of finely divided rock and mineral particles. It continued at speed to cascade endlessly over her slender, virtuous body, like 'Pennies from Heaven.' As if, at that very moment, a lucky long-term Las Vegas gambler had successfully hit the jackpot on a crooked slot machine and was now being ceremoniously rewarded with endless streams of shining, shimmering gold!

Her ribs, head and internal organs were being relentlessly crushed and compressed from within. The precious gift of life itself, gradually and agonisingly withdrawn. Her personalised hourglass had been deliberately overturned and drained. Literally, grain by grain the sands of time were running out. She would be dead in the next twenty seconds........

24422964R00197

Printed in Poland
by Amazon Fulfillment
Poland Sp. z o.o., Wrocław